DEMON'S VENGEANCE

Also by Jocelynn Drake

DEMON'S VENGEANCE

The Complete Final Asylum Tales

JOCELYNN DRAKE

HARPER

VOYAGER

IMPULSE

An Imprint of HarperCollinsPublishers

Demon's Fury copyright © 2014 by Jocelynn Drake.

Demon's Vow copyright © 2014 by Jocelynn Drake.

Inner Demon copyright © 2014 by Jocelynn Drake.

EPub Edition APRIL 2015 ISBN: 9780062405968

Print Edition ISBN: 9780062405951

10 9 8 7 6 5 4 3 2 1

To All My Personal Demons
We've made some good books together.

DEMON'S VENGEANCE

Part 1

DEMON'S FURY

DEMON'S FURY

Part 1

CHAPTER 1

I looked like a fucking banker. The shirt and jacket were confining and the tie was threatening to choke me. I tugged at the French cuffs with the onyx cuff links for the fiftieth time as we walked down the empty sidewalk, fighting the urge to break something just to let off some steam. This had to be why the guardians slaughtered people on sight. Not to protect the sanctity of the Towers. They did it because the uniform sucked ass.

"Stop fidgeting," Gideon said as he walked beside me. The black-haired warlock had always dressed in these tailored suits, and he actually looked comfortable in them. Of course, it was rare for Gideon to show any kind of emotion beyond mild irritation. The bastard was polished black ice.

"You can't tell me you like wearing these monkey suits," I grumbled, feeling even more like an idiot as I walked beside him. Next to the warlock, I was a phony, a fraud, and it showed for all the world to see when we were together.

With my hands shoved into my pockets, I glared at the ground. I didn't want to see my surroundings as the setting sun cast everything in a rosy glow. I had no idea where we were, but that didn't matter. The handful of people who stuck their heads out knew who we were. You could tell by the terror twisting their faces seconds before they darted in the opposite direction. The Towers had come to town.

Not that I could blame them for their fear and hatred. The Ivory Towers had wiped Indianapolis off the map just a few short months ago with no warning and no known reason. Some small part of me died to be counted as a warlock.

"The suits are tailor-made to fit you perfectly and are embedded with charmed threads that help increase protection against glamour and various forms of attack," my companion recited, sounding like he was reading from a freaking manual.

"Yes, but do you like wearing them?"

"I don't see what that has to do with anything," Gideon snapped, coming to a stop in front of a three-story apartment building. "You're here to do a job—one that you agreed to do for the council. If you stop bitching, this might prove to be less painful for everyone involved."

I frowned, swallowing my next complaint. He was right. I made a deal with the Ivory Towers council to work as a guardian in an effort to help protect the

Towers as well as protect the rest of the world from the Towers. But becoming a guardian meant going back to the Towers, leaving the acidic taste of bile burning in the back of the throat. I had fought and nearly died to escape. Ten years later, I'm right back where I started, feeling as if I've lost everything.

Gideon would be the first to remind me that I was still alive and I had a better chance of secretly helping people than I had before. But standing in that damn suit while the rest of the world cowered and despised the sight of me made it hard to remember those little victories.

Shoving aside my disgust, I lifted my head to survey the region again. The sooner we got this task completed, the sooner I could return to Low Town. "What's the job?"

"Something . . . different."

I motioned for Gideon to continue as he stared up at the plain white apartment building. The narrow, worn street we stood on was lined with old buildings sagging in the fading light. A trickle of sweat ran down my spine while more gathered at my temple. It was way too hot for early December, but the palm trees that stirred in the faint breeze led me to believe we were likely in South Florida.

Several of the apartment windows were open to let in an evening breeze, causing curtains to flutter and dirty plastic blinds to flap. No one looked down at us. "I'm guessing that 'different' doesn't come up too often," I continued when he remained stubbornly silent.

"No, it doesn't." His thin lips were pressed into a hard line and his silver eyes were unfocused. He wasn't staring at the building any longer, but lost in some strange thought that sent a wave of dread through me.

Gideon blinked twice, snapping back from wherever his mind had wandered and glared at me. "Are there any protection spells? Any defensive wards?"

I directed my attention at the building and started to close my eyes so I could focus my attention on my other sense—the one that was tuned toward magic energy—but I caught myself. Since becoming a guardian, Gideon had been working as something of a mentor to keep me alive while quietly expanding my magical knowledge. Closing my eyes to focus on magic left me vulnerable to attack. Gideon had been kind enough to show me just that on more than one occasion. The bastard took too much pleasure in knocking me around.

"There's something here. Faint." I reached out my right hand to feel the air in front of me. A faint tingling pricked my fingertips as if I could actually feel each individually charged electron as it spun about, charging the air. "There's definitely a magical energy, more organized than just the usual latent energy, but it's not actually organized into a specific spell or a ward that I can identify. More like a heavy residue left from a massive spell."

"Good. Can you tell what the caster was?" Gideon's voice dipped low, as if he were afraid that someone would overhear his comments, not that there was another soul within a hundred yards of us.

"What do you mean?"

"Was the spell caster human? Elf? Pixie? Leprechaun?"

My eyebrows bunched together as I concentrated harder on the feeling hanging in the air. With each passing second, the energy grew a little fainter, making it harder to pick out details, leaving me more with just a vague feeling. "Not . . . fey," I slowly said.

The fey—elves, pixies, faeries, brownies, and all of that dangerous nature-based lot—had a distinct flavor to their magic. There was almost a sugar-sweet aftertaste in my brain from fey magic. For an incubus or succubus, it was sort of musky, while a phoenix was, unsurprisingly, like burning wood from a campfire. Warlocks and witches created a fresh, clean scent like a spring rain when they used magic.

Outside the apartment building, it was . . . different. Different from anything I had ever encountered before. "It's different."

"Which is why we're here." Gideon reached inside the black robe he wore over his dark charcoal-colored suit and pulled out his wand, adding to a buzz of energy in the air. "Two nights ago, the New York Tower detected an explosion of magical energy. It could be described only as something different, something we couldn't remember encountering before, but it was powerful. Despite its initial strength, it faded quickly and we had some trouble tracking it."

Reaching inside my jacket, I pulled out my wand

as well. It was new, after my first had been broken by Reave. The hawthorn wand gave me excellent control with a nice boost in power, but we were still becoming adjusted to each other. With every wand, there was a breaking-in period, and considering that I didn't go out with Gideon often, there weren't many opportunities to break in my wand.

"Could it have been a New One?" I asked.

Gideon shook his head. "This was too much power for a child, even for a late bloomer of twelve. And like you said, this is different."

Most humans revealed their natural talent for magic between the ages of seven and twelve. Referred to as New Ones by the Towers, they were quickly swept off for training upon discovery. It was the safest, though unhappy, thing for everyone.

"What about a hybrid or half-breed? Human mother and fey daddy?"

The dark-haired warlock motioned toward the building. "Does that in any way feel fey to you? Or even partially human?"

"No, but what else is there?"

Gideon's face was blank as he walked toward the building, but I saw his hand tighten on his wand. "Maybe it's something that we thought was dead."

For a moment, my feet were stuck to the cracked concrete sidewalk as I stared blindly after him. My heart thundered in my ears while my mind tried to sort through that comment. "Are you talking about someone from the Lost Peoples? Are you fucking kidding me?" I jogged after him, catching him as he pulled open the glass door to the small, grimy lobby.

"What else could it be?"

"Damn it, Gideon! Are you suicidal? I'm not going in there if we're walking into the lair of the last fucking dragon on the planet," I said in a harsh whisper, which was stupid, because if this was a dragon, the creature definitely knew we were there.

"It doesn't have to be a dragon," Gideon replied in a blasé voice, as if facing down dragons in their own home was an everyday occurrence for him. The warlock stood next to the metal railing that lined the stairs, looking around the first floor. After only a brief pause, he started to climb the stairs.

I growled, fighting the rising nausea in my stomach. "I'm definitely not going after a unicorn either."

During the Great War that pitted the Towers against the world, two races were slaughtered to extinction: dragons and unicorns. Two of the most magically powerful races outside of warlocks and witches, they had to be removed if the Towers were to ever be protected from them. The Great War had left several others barely clinging to life.

Gideon stopped on the landing and looked down at me. "You want me to report to the Towers that you refused to complete a task?"

"Fuck! I didn't agree to be a guardian to commit suicide now. The two of us can't handle a dragon and we definitely can't handle a unicorn if either is anything like what I studied."

"There's nothing to handle. This is an investigation. The council has not ordered an execution." Gideon could sound as rational and calm as he wanted but this was insane and he knew it.

Against my better judgment, I climbed the stairs after him, not feeling the least bit reassured. "Yeah, well, if we are faced with a unicorn or dragon, I really doubt either is going to be all that happy to see us."

"That is probably true," Gideon murmured as he reached the second floor. Again, he paused, looking down the hall at the four wooden doors that led to the second-floor apartments. The brown carpet was stained and looked sticky, but I wasn't willing to check to see if I was right. One of the overhead fluorescent lights was out, while the second was making an ominous noise as if it were a wheezing cancer patient on a ventilator. The shadows only helped this place.

Gideon continued on to the third floor after his quick inspection and I followed, holding my wand tightly in my right hand. The magic had grown thicker in the air as we crossed the landing and trudged up the last set of stairs. It crawled across my skin through my suit and prickled against my face. The closer we got, the more I could define the feel of the energy, but at the same time, the further it moved away from what I was familiar with.

The magic made me feel queasy and sick. It was getting in past the protective barriers created by my suit. My head swam as if I were developing vertigo. There was an odd taste on my tongue, like I had swished graveyard dirt around in my mouth.

"I think we should wait. Call in for reinforcement," I said, stopping one step before the third floor. "I know my way around a protection spell, but this feels nasty. You need better backup than me."

"While I appreciate your concern, we're going on," Gideon said with a wry smile before turning to walk down the dingy hallway.

Both of the overhead lights were out here, but there were windows at either end of the hall, letting in the faint glow from the nearby street lamps. There were no sounds of people moving around in their apartments. No sounds of cooking, conversation or the monotonous blare of a television. The apartment dwellers knew we were here and they were hiding, praying we didn't notice them.

Pushing that thought and so many others aside, I followed Gideon down the hall to the second apartment on the left. The warlock stood with his right hand hovering before the door while his left clutched his wand. A faint curl of magic swirled out from his right hand, dancing over the scarred wooden door before bouncing back toward him and me. There was no spell on the door, barring us or even threatening us if we dared to enter.

Quickly making a fist as if he were trying to capture the energy, Gideon rapped on the door. My entire body flinched and I jumped back a step at the loud noise. A crack of laughter leapt from Gideon, slamming into me so that I flinched again.

"Nervous?" Gideon chuckled.

"Me? Nervous? Why would I be nervous? You've only brought me to a crappy apartment oozing strange magic while talking about the Lost Peoples. I can't imagine why I might be nervous about having my head blown off," I said, ending with a snarl.

Gideon was still smiling, amused with my anxiety, as he knocked a second time. No one answered the door. There wasn't even a sound from the interior of the apartment. Either no one was home or they were hiding in hopes that the local Tower thugs would go away. Not likely.

Gideon stepped back, his smile gone. "Open it."

My mouth fell open with a bitter protest on the tip of my tongue, but I quickly closed it again. Arguing with him was a waste of time. It wasn't going to get me out of entering the apartment. The sooner we went in, the sooner we could get our answer and leave. I started to lift my wand to the lock on the door and stopped myself. The urge to break something still throbbed in my chest and I was potentially missing a great opportunity.

Taking a step back, I kicked the door as hard as I could right next to the doorknob and deadbolt. The door vibrated and rattled loudly in its jamb, but didn't budge. The jolt jumped up my leg and hammered my knee with pain. Frowning, I stepped back to regain my balance.

"Well, that's disappointing," I murmured. "They make that look much easier in the movies." Gideon rolled his eyes at me and let out a sigh. Grinning at him, I kicked the door again. This time, the doorjamb splintered as the deadbolt broke through the wood and the door swung open, slamming against the wall. The heavy scent of death surged out of the apartment, sending me reeling back several feet as I gagged.

"I guess the person didn't survive whatever spell they had cooked up," I said as soon as I could draw a breath of clean air.

Gideon cautiously stepped into the apartment. "We should be so lucky."

Pulling the handkerchief from my front breast pocket, I pressed it over my nose and mouth before stepping over the threshold. A glance in the tiny kitchen revealed bags of rotting takeout along with jars of bloody animal parts that looked as if they had been pulled from the creatures rather than cut.

I continued down the hall, stepping over nasty, charred globs of flesh that I didn't want to identify as I made my way to the living room. The only furniture was an occupied chair. The place had been run-down and grimy before the addition of the headless corpse. The body sagged, held in place by the limbs bound to the chair. The head looked as if it had been blown off the body, whether by small explosive or a giant gun at close range, I didn't know. The only positive was that it was likely a quick death.

My eyes were drawn to a backpack leaning against the wall. It was relatively clean and looked out of place among the carnage. The worn brown carpet crunched with dried blood as I crossed the room and picked up the bag. Unzipping one section, I found chemistry and pre-calculus books along with a couple spiral-bound notebooks.

"Fuck!" I dropped the bag with a heavy thud while shoving the useless handkerchief in my pocket. It was doing little to block the smell. "The killer grabbed some high-school kid either going to or leaving school."

"Interesting," Gideon murmured.

"Interesting?" I repeated, swinging around to see the warlock inspecting a pile of small dead animals rotting in the corner. "Some kid gets snatched and violently killed, and all you can say is 'interesting'!"

Gideon turned and glared at me. "Allowing emotions to cloud my mind would not help us to locate the killer faster. In fact, it would slow us down as we would likely miss important details." He pointed to the animal corpses spread about the room in various stages of decomposition. "Such as the fact that the killer practiced, working up to something as large as a human." When Gideon looked up at me again, there was a hard glint to his eyes, giving me a glimpse of the rage that he was fighting to hold in check.

I should never have doubted Gideon. Polished black ice. Cool. Smooth. Dangerous.

"Sounds like some psychotic serial killer who accidentally got a blast of unexpected energy. That's the realm of the police—not the Towers." I frowned, trying to look anywhere but at the dead body, but the death-strewn apartment wasn't giving me a lot of options. My only recurring sane thought was that I was a tattoo artist, not one of those hot-shot CSI detectives with their dark sunglasses and latex gloves. Next Gideon mission, I was stuffing some gloves in my pockets.

"This wasn't an accident." Gideon called from the next room.

Shaking my head, I tried to brace myself for whatever new horror he had found. I wasn't ready, but at least it wasn't another decapitated teenager. The tiny bedroom was empty of furniture, but the overhead light glared down on the four white walls completely covered in strange writing scrawled in black magic marker.

"What does it say?" I whispered. There was something ominous about the writing, as if the script itself could be evil.

"I can't read it." Gideon replied with some frustration. He walked over to a part that had been scratched out and rewritten slightly different. "But I think these are notes. Trial and error. Look here," he said pointing to a series of symbols that had been drawn, scratched out, and redrawn over and over again before the killer had decided on a final version. "Methodically experimenting."

"At what?"

"I don't know, but I think the person achieved the desired results because all personal items are gone. The killer is done with this location and this part of his experiment. He's moved on to his next target."

I shoved my hands in my pockets, my eyes locked on the symbols as my brain strained to put some order or definition to it all. "I'll give you this is bad, but does it involve the Towers?"

"I thought you'd jump at the chance to help your fellow man," Gideon smirked.

"Yeah, well my life isn't so great right now and I really don't need to add this kind of fun to it."

Gideon arched one eyebrow at me and I shook my head. I didn't want to talk about it since it was the usual shit, just more of it. We were busy at the shop, Low Town was getting dangerous as the local mafia thugs continued to fight it out after the death of their leader, Reave—not that any of them actually missed the dark elf. On top of that, Trixie was giving me the cold shoulder, hiding something from me. Of course, I hadn't told her about the whole Towers/guardian thing, so I wasn't feeling so hot about that as well. I needed to tell her, but it was a conversation I was dreading since it was something I was just getting a handle on myself.

"It involves magic so this is a Towers matter," Gideon said, drawing my thoughts back to the problem at hand. "We need to discover who the killer is and what they are attempting to do." He stepped up to one of the walls and ran his fingers over the surface. A frown creased his face as he drew his hand back and rubbed his fingers together.

I took a step closer, looking at his fingers. "What is it?"

"Soot."

"Huh? Phoenix magic is the only one that creates soot."

"This wasn't a phoenix. Different feel entirely."

I could almost hear the wheels turning in Gideon's head as he tried to puzzle out the writing, soot, and the dead.

"Take pictures of all the walls," he said with some frustration, and then marched out of the room.

Grabbing my cell phone, I quickly snapped pictures of each wall before heading back into the living room, but Gideon wasn't there. I poked my head into the main hall to find the warlock descending the stairs with a look of intense concentration. Stuffing the phone in my pocket, I followed.

"Should we call the police?" I asked as we reached the first-floor landing. The warlock halted sharply and looked at me over his shoulder like I had lost my mind. "Right. Towers. Who cares about the rest of the world?" I muttered.

"We have enough problems." Gideon continued down to the main floor and out the front door. "The killer is just getting started."

"How can you tell?"

"Because he's still experimenting, working toward his ultimate goal."

"Which is?" I demanded, getting more frustrated by the second.

"Nothing good." He stopped suddenly and turned to look at me. "I need to think. Send me the pictures. Show them to no one else." And then he disappeared.

I groaned, feeling tired and dirty. I had no idea where I was and there was a lunatic on the loose who was killing people for some magical purpose that I was tasked to uncover for the Towers. But what bothered me the most was that the longer I stood in that apartment, the more the magic started to feel familiar to me. I couldn't place it yet, but I would, and, as Gideon said, it was nothing good.

CHAPTER 2

"**G**age, this is embarrassing," Trixie complained as she stepped out of the tiny bathroom at Asylum and walked down the short hall toward me. I twisted in the tattooing chair I had been lounging in to look at her as she glared at me with her hands on her slender hips.

Dressed in green tights and a green-and-red tunic, she was the classic image of Santa's elf, right down to her green shoes with bells on the curled toes. She'd dropped her usual glamour disguise in favor of her true appearance of blonde hair, green eyes, and pointed ears. The outfit might have looked silly, but she was as sexy as hell.

"You look great!" I shouted, clapping my hands together.

"I look ridiculous! What idiot got the idea an elf would dress like this? And I'm supposed to live at the North Pole wearing an outfit like this?" She stomped over to where I was sitting, the sound of little bells ringing with her every movement. "I'd freeze my ass off."

"And it's such a cute ass," I teased, but she didn't crack a smile. I was seriously pushing my luck. Clearing my throat, I ducked my head, dropping my gaze to the cracked linoleum floor. "It's an old folktale. Maybe someone from the Winter Court got drunk and was sneaking through a village with a fat man in a red suit."

"Doubtful," she said as the back door opened and shut, announcing that Bronx had finished getting changed in the apartment above the tattoo parlor. The troll appeared a couple seconds later in the tattooing room wearing a bright red suit with furry white trim.

"Whoa," I said, sitting back to take in his appearance. He was the biggest Santa Claus I had ever seen.

"Damn, Santa," Trixie murmured. "You got big."

"Ha. Ha. Ha," Bronx blandly said, looking about as thrilled in his costume as Trixie.

"Actually, it's Ho! Ho! Ho!" I corrected.

The troll turned his narrowed gaze on me. "I can understand how Trixie and I ended up in these outfits, but why aren't you dressed up, when this was your idea?"

"Don't worry, Santa. I've got your sack to carry," I said.

Bronx hooked his thumbs on the wide black belt wrapped around his pillow-padded stomach. "I don't think you're man enough to handle my sack," he drawled, his wide grin partially hidden behind a large white beard.

"Oh, funny," I said.

"Ho! Ho! Ho!" Bronx said in his best Santa imitation, which was pretty damn impressive.

Trixie gave an unexpected snort of laughter and I flipped them both off, which got Bronx truly laughing as well.

"Now that everyone is in the Christmas spirit, let's get going. The kids should already be arriving." Pushing out of the chair, I handed Trixie her coat before we followed Bronx down the hall and out the back door to where I had parked my SUV. Earlier in the afternoon, I had packed it full of toys, food, and clothing donations I had collected from the other shops near Asylum.

Shortly after All Hallows' Eve, the Christmas spirit kicked me hard in the gut. It was most likely a need for something positive after I had sold my soul to the Towers in September. I organized a massive collection of food, winter clothes, and toys with all the shops and restaurants near Asylum. Tonight was the Feast of St. Nicholas when Santa Claus would appear at a special dinner to give away the toys.

"Do you think Bronx's size will scare the kids?" Trixie asked from behind me once we were in the road.

I glanced over at the troll beside me dressed in red. He'd initially balked at taking the passenger seat but it was more comfortable for him over the backseat because of his size. My battered SUV just wasn't made to accommodate trolls. "Maybe some of the really young ones, but most will just see him as a gateway to toys."

The drive to James Garfield High School was relatively short and the parking lot was nearly full when we arrived, but we managed to find an open spot behind the school, near the loading docks for the cafeteria. As I walked around to open the trunk, a door to the school opened, throwing down a bright square of light that outlined a thin little man in black.

"Gage?" the man asked.

"It's me, Father Barnes. I've got Santa Claus and his helper with me," I called, stepping into a nearby pool of light from a parking lamp. "I've also got another load of donations for you."

The little man scurried over to the car, though he paused for a moment at the sight of Bronx. He peered into the trunk and then smiled up at me. "God bless you, son. You've been a saint! You've nearly doubled our annual haul."

"Just trying to spread some good cheer, Father."

"Let's grab the toys and hurry in. I'll send some volunteers out for the rest. Everyone is nearly done eating and is anxious to see Santa Claus."

Bronx shifted a heavy sack of toys over his shoulder and adjusted his beard before heading inside, followed by Trixie. The priest and I grabbed armfuls of donations and went in as well to see all the amused and stunned faces that greeted the troll as he passed through the kitchen to the main dining hall.

I had barely managed to set my items down on an empty table when Bronx's loud "Ho! Ho! Ho!" was met with an explosion of cheering. Rushing out of the kitchen, I laughed to see Trixie and Bronx swarmed with kids of every race and species, all vying for just a second of Santa's time. While Trixie was looking somewhat overwhelmed, Bronx's eyes shined with joy. He may have looked like a scary troll on the outside, but Bronx was pure marshmallow on the inside.

After helping them get a line organized to the large throne they had set up for Santa, I dropped off my coat where Trixie had left hers in the kitchen.

"I thought that was you I saw with Santa Claus," Gideon said to my back.

My stomach jerked into a hard knot and I felt my soul shrivel up. He'd found me again—sought me out for another Towers job. I needed this night of peace and good cheer. Not more blood, death, and violence.

I was slow to turn around, but the sight of Gideon stopped all thought for a second. Instead of his usual dark suit and black cloak, the warlock was in a pair of faded jeans, a cream-colored cable-knit sweater, and loafers. His black hair was in a short ponytail and he wore a pair of trendy, black-rimmed glasses.

"What are you doing here?" he asked in a friendly tone for anyone who might have been listening, but there was a cold warning in his eyes.

"Helping," I replied dully, my brain still trying to understand what I was seeing.

"I see that." Gideon smirked. "Come. I'll introduce you to my wife."

I walked with the warlock out of the kitchen and along the back wall where the crowds were the thinnest.

"What's with the glasses, Clark Kent?" I asked as we hit an empty space.

Gideon shook his head, appearing as if he were trying not to smile. "Ellen says they make me look harmless."

"Oh yeah. Like a wet kitten."

A soft chuckle escaped him but his mood turned grim when we stopped halfway across the cafeteria and he began to search the crowd in earnest. After several seconds, a pretty blonde's hand shot up and she waved to us. She steadily made her way through the crowd of parents until she was standing beside Gideon, smiling broadly up at me.

"Ellen, this is an old friend, Gage Powell. Gage, this is my wife, Ellen," Gideon said.

"It's an honor," I said and I meant it. No one from the dark side of Gideon's life had met his wife. It was a gesture of trust and it humbled me after Gideon and I had spent so many years at each other's throats.

Ellen switched the large camera she was holding from her right hand to her left before shaking mine. "It's wonderful to finally meet you. After all the stories he's told me, I feel like we're old friends."

Smiling, I shot a look over at Gideon, who was frowning at his wife. "He's been telling tales about me?"

"Only because you're a walking natural disaster," Gideon grumbled.

Ellen hit him in the center of his chest. "Be nice!" she admonished and then smiled. "Better yet, go take pictures of the girls." She held up the digital SLR in front of his face until he took it. "I'm too tired to wade back through that crowd and the girls are getting close to the front of the line."

"Are you okay?" Gideon's stern expression immediately became a mask of intense concern as he laid a gentle hand on his wife's shoulder.

She waved her hand at him while keeping her eyes locked on me. "Fine. Fine. Now go. I want pictures of them with Santa."

Gideon hesitated, staring at me as if he was uncertain about leaving his wife alone with a walking natural disaster. "Watch over her," he said and then started to the long line of kids waiting for their turn to speak with Santa.

"And don't glare at those boys anymore! Paola is handling them just fine!" Ellen called after her husband, who raised one hand in a halfhearted wave to acknowledge he had heard her. "He's not listening to me," she muttered, voicing the very thought running through my head. Her scowl instantly dissolved when she looked up at me again. "Gideon didn't tell me you were going to be here."

"Probably because he didn't know. I offered to help with the donation drive and then talked some friends into being Santa and his helper."

She laughed a loud, joyous sound and I instantly understood why Gideon loved this woman so much. She didn't take any crap from the warlock and was filled with happiness.

"I'm guessing you were just as surprised to see Gideon here."

"That's putting it mildly."

She giggled softly. "I'm a nurse. I help out here and there with the Shining Hope Foundation when they give some parenting or first-aid classes. I come to this every year because they like to have a nurse or doctor on hand just in case. I've never been needed, but it doesn't hurt to be safe."

I could understand the Foundation's preference for having a nurse on hand. A werewolf or troll child plays too rough with a human child, and someone is bound for the emergency room.

"How's Paola? Is she adjusting?" I asked when my eyes finally tripped over the young woman standing in line next to Gideon's daughter Bridgette. She was smiling down at the girl, a look of affection on her face. Paola was one of the runaways. She along with four others had escaped from the Ivory Towers, where they were training to be witches and warlocks. It had taken a little bit of arranging, but Gideon and his wife had agreed to take in Paola, while three others were settled in other homes. Alice, one of the five, had been killed before she and her younger brother James could reach a new safe haven.

"Wonderful. Despite the ten years between her and Bridgette, they've really taken to each other. She's a little quiet at times, but I think she's homesick and missing Étienne."

"Really?" I arched a brow at her in surprise. Étienne

was the oldest and had been the leader of the little band. The young Frenchman was now staying with my parents along with Tony.

Ellen gave a little snort as she looked back toward Paola and her daughter. "You men don't notice anything."

"That's true. How's Bridgette? Gideon hasn't . . . mentioned . . . anything recently," I said haltingly, trying to be somewhat vague since I was sure this was a potentially sore topic. In September, Gideon admitted that he was concerned that his daughter was going to show a similar magical talent, which would draw the immediate attention of the Ivory Towers.

The pretty blonde gave a sigh, dropping her voice closer to a whisper. "She's good. Nothing has happened yet, but we're all keeping a close watch. Gideon has put some protection over the house so that she can't be detected, but the concern is if it happens outside of the house."

"I'm sorry," I murmured, feeling bad for her. "If something should happen and you can't reach Gideon, do you know how to reach me? I can give you my cell—"

Ellen laughed and looked up at me with shining eyes. "Oh, Gage. I've got your number and address already. Gideon gave it to me years ago, just after we married. He gave me a list of people to contact if there was ever trouble and your name has always been at the top of the list."

Shock coursed through my veins, tensing all my

muscles. Gideon trusted me with his family? Hell, Gideon trusted me? The man had put on a good show of hating me for close to ten years. It was mind numbing to hear that I was the person he trusted to protect his wife and daughter.

She gently patted me on the arm. "That man has said nothing to you, has he?" I shook my head and Ellen gave a little roll of her eyes. "Stubborn. Gage, he worries about you and he trusts you."

"Thank you."

Sliding her arm through mine, Ellen stepped close but her eyes were on her husband as he snapped pictures of both Bridgette and Paola sitting on Bronx's lap. "He told me what happened this past fall. I'm very sorry. I know he doesn't show it, but Gideon has been torn up about it. He feels guilty that he wasn't able to do more."

"There was nothing else he could have done. We just have to make the best of a bad situation. I'm adjusting." As I spoke, I could feel some of the weight on my shoulders lift. Just the idea that Gideon had wanted to do something to help made me feel better. Working for the Towers was far from an ideal situation, but it gave me access to their plans as well as better enabled me to help people who could be threatened by the witches and warlocks. I just had to remember to be careful.

"How's your girlfriend adjusting?"

I flinched at her question, though I tried to hide it. It didn't matter. She had felt it.

"Have you told her?" Ellen pressed.

I closed my eyes, frowning. "I haven't been able to talk about it. Things were too . . . raw for too long."

"I understand, but you have to be fair to her." I opened my eyes to see Ellen smiling at me, but there was a look of sadness in her wide brown eyes. "This is a difficult relationship to be in and the only reason Gideon and I have made it is because he talks to me. When things go bad, he tells me because he shouldn't have to go through it alone. Neither should you. But it's a burden for the other person and they have to make the choice to wade through the darkness with you. Right now, your girlfriend is trying to wade through the darkness but she doesn't know why it's dark."

"Don't you worry about the danger to you and your daughter because of Gideon?"

"Of course I do," she said sharply, glaring at me. "But I won't let that worry ruin our life. We take precautions and I trust in Gideon to keep us safe. In the end, life happens. I love Gideon and he loves me. We love our daughter. We are all happy together. I think it's selfish to demand more than that."

A bark of laughter escaped me. There was something so wonderfully practical about Ellen, and maybe that's how she managed to thrive in a forbidden relationship with a warlock. It gave me a little shred of hope for Trixie and me.

"Thank you. I'll talk to her."

"Soon?"

"I promise."

"Good." The smile had returned to Ellen's face and

she relaxed again. Turning her attention back to the crowd before her, she let a contented little sigh escape her. I followed her gaze and found Gideon kneeling before his daughter as he talked to her and looked at the board game she had gotten from Santa Claus. The camera hung around his neck and he had one arm across the girl's slim shoulders. At the same time, his other hand was holding Paola's hand as she clutched what looked to be a box with a chess set. Even from this distance, I could tell the young woman was fighting back tears, but they looked to be happy tears.

Something inside my chest ached for her and the other runaways. How long had it been since any of them had received a gift or celebrated a holiday in a warm, loving atmosphere? For some, it was close to ten years. Paola was safe and loved in Ellen's home.

As I looked up at Bronx and Trixie surrounded by kids, the sexy elf caught my eye and winked, putting the smile back on my lips before she turned her attention back to the task of soothing a frightened child. The last of the darkness that had a hold on me faded. The good will and cheer I had been desperately trying to find with this holiday party had soaked into my parched soul. I knew it wouldn't last, but it would get me moving forward again. It would help me get my relationship with Trixie back on track again.

I just needed to tell her what had happened that night in the Towers.

CHAPTER 3

Checking the time on my cell phone, I stuffed it into my back pocket and turned the heat down on the spaghetti sauce. Trixie would be arriving any minute and I was proud to say that everything was ready. The bread was out of the oven and the salad was chilling in a bowl in the fridge. Stepping out of the kitchen, I surveyed the apartment one last time. The place was mostly clean and anything that wasn't had been shoved in a closet or under the bed. Candles flickered on the card table covered with a new heavy linen tablecloth.

I frowned as I looked at the setup. The whole thing screamed "forgive me." It was what I was going for, but it didn't need to be this damn obvious. For other couples, it might have passed for romantic, but I wasn't known for grand romantic gestures. Romance was usually offering to pick up the pizza while she chose the movie we'd watch.

Two days had passed since my talk with Ellen and I needed to live up to my promise to her and myself. I couldn't put if off any longer. Trixie had to know, but I wasn't looking forward to the conversation.

A sharp knock at the door sounded through the apartment and I nearly jumped. This was not a good sign. I needed to relax, reassure her that everything was okay, but some part deep down knew it wasn't. There had been no fights, no shouting match where words bounced off our thick skulls. But the silence was getting deeper and I could feel a distance between us that hadn't been there months ago.

Smoothing the worry from my face, I forced a broad smile and opened the door. Trixie smiled weakly back, looking tired but lovely. She still wore her glamour cloak, making her appear as a brown-haired human rather than the blonde elf that I loved so much. She didn't need the disguise any longer now that the king of the Summer Court was bound to his wife, but the people of Low Town had come to know her as the brunette, so the disguise stayed for the sake of time and ease.

"Mmmmm. Something smells good," she said as she kissed me. I stepped back to let her enter. "Did you order from—" Her words broke off sharply and I found her staring openmouthed at the table. "You cooked," she finished in wonder.

I snorted, shutting the door. "Don't get your hopes up too high. It's spaghetti. You know, boil water. Don't burn the bread."

Trixie dropped her purse on the coffee table and tossed her heavy wool coat on the couch. "What did you do?"

"What do you mean?" I quickly replied. A little too quickly.

"You don't cook. I honestly thought your oven was broken. You never clean. And is that an air freshener I smell? You're either breaking up with me or you did something you need to apologize for."

For a couple of seconds, I thought about teasing her and batting her questions away but I'd only prove her right in the end. Why insult her intelligence?

I sighed. "There is something we need to discuss, but I think any potential breaking up will be in your hands."

Trixie took an involuntary step backward, fear flooding her wide eyes. "You're going to tell me what happened in the Towers that night." Her vibrant voice had become dull and flat, as if she had already started to steel herself against the horror of my words. I couldn't tell if she was asking or making a statement so I just nodded. She had never asked about that night beyond checking on my physical well-being and I never volunteered any information. Of course, it had taken about a month for me to get past the impotent rage and hopelessness that consumed me.

"How bad is it?" She had wrapped her arms around her stomach and pulled in as if to protect herself against what I was going to tell her. I felt like shit and I had yet to open my mouth. This was going to be a bad night.

"It depends on a lot of things. Why don't we eat and relax for a little while? Then we can talk."

She shook her head. "I'm not hungry."

I had a feeling this would happen. "Sit. I'll be right back." As she moved to the sofa, I jumped into the kitchen to turn off the spaghetti sauce, cover the bread, and grab two beers out of the fridge. Trixie frowned as she saw me approach.

"Can I just have water?"

Spinning on my left heel, I put one beer back and grabbed a bottle of water instead. When I sat on the couch, I was on the far end from her despite the fact that I'd have rather pulled her into my lap and held her tight, but I figured that she could use a little space. With my elbows on my knees, I leaned forward, staring at the coffee table without actually seeing it.

"You know I went for Reave," I started slowly as I dredged up memories of that night in September. The dark elf was threatening the safety of the world. He had gotten the exact locations of seven of the Ivory Towers, the homes of the witches and warlocks, and he was threatening to sell the information. The warlocks and witches were in a panic, killing people off left and right, as they searched for the culprit. Every living creature in Indianapolis had been destroyed because of Reave's plot. I had gotten dragged into the mess because Reave decided to use my older brother Robert as a courier, and because the Towers had begun to fear that I would reveal the locations of the hidden Towers. It became a fucking mess.

"I remember," Trixie said evenly.

"I took Reave to the Towers in hopes of striking a deal with them. They were determined to kill me because I was seen as a threat."

"A threat? Why?"

I looked up at her and smiled at the anger in her voice. "I stood against their ideology. They also realized that I could tell others of the Tower locations. I was a potential security leak. The best way to plug that leak was to kill me."

Trixie sat back against the sofa, relaxing a little bit more. "Obviously you managed to strike a deal with them since you're sitting here alive and well."

Alive? Yes. Well? That was a matter of opinion. There were nights I woke up screaming from nightmares that were old memories from my years in the Towers that had been dragged to the foreground of my mind. When I walked down the street, there was a little voice whispering in my head, warning me that if the people of Low Town discovered that I was a warlock from the Towers, I was dead. Before, I had been a former warlock-in-training who had escaped. Now I was a spy.

"What was the deal?" She gasped suddenly, clapping her hands over her mouth in horror. "They didn't make you kill your brother, did they?"

"No," I said with a relieved sigh. At least there was a scenario that was worse than the reality. Robert had been given the coordinates of the seven locations by Reave, but with a bit of magic and several potions, I wiped his memory, gave him a new identity, and sent him far from me.

"Then what? What was the deal?"

"I had to go back to the Towers," I said softly. The words became acid burning away the back of my throat. At sixteen, I escaped the Towers and got my freedom back after nearly losing my life. I had refused to be a cold, heartless killer like them. The world was not something for me to stand on so I could achieve my own goal of gaining more power.

Trixie leapt to her feet and backpedaled away from me as if I had lunged at her with a knife. I didn't move. "What are you talking about? What do you mean you had to go back?"

"I convinced the Towers that they were out of touch with the people of the world. I convinced them that there were going to be more Reaves if they didn't act. I . . . offered to be a spy for the Towers." Trixie's gasp was a lash tearing across my back, but I pressed on. "The position gives me value so they won't kill me. It allows me to stay here rather than returning to live in the Towers."

"You would turn the people of this world over to the Towers? Your friends and neighbors?" she demanded in horrified tones.

"Of course not!" I shouted, leaping to my feet as my temper snapped. "I'd rather die than turn an innocent person over to those bastards. But if I'm standing between these people and the Towers, I can act as a buffer. As one of their guardians, I know what's going on in the Towers. I can better protect people. Before, I was operating blind and couldn't do shit. Now I know what's happening, what they're thinking."

Trixie shrank back into herself at my burst of anger. "What about Reave?"

"What about him?" I asked warily, my voice dropping close to a whisper.

"You handed him over to the Towers."

"Reave wasn't innocent," I growled. "Not by a long shot. He was going to get everyone killed by auctioning off that information. We both know a war with the Towers can't be won. Handing in Reave was the only way to save us all."

"Then where does that leave you now? What do you have to do?"

The anger left me in a rush and I flopped back down on the couch. Leaning back, I propped one foot up on the edge of the scarred table. "That's still a little vague." I mumbled. "I'm regarded as a guardian, though I don't have all the rights and privileges that go with such a title."

Trixie edged back over to the sofa and sat on the corner. "What does a guardian do?"

The urge to hold her was overwhelming. I needed to hold her, but she was looking at me with such wariness that I was afraid to move, afraid to face the rejection that was waiting just around the corner. Closing my eyes, I forced my voice to become as calm and even as possible. "Guardians are the ones that you see when the Towers attack. They do the dirty work. They head up investigations and hunt down people of interest for the Towers. They're like the FBI, CIA, and Special Forces, all rolled into one."

"And you're one of them?"

My eyes popped open at the incredulous sound in her voice. I smirked, feeling a little of my usual dry humor start to return. "I'm more of a distrusted junior member. They're sending me out with another warlock to investigate strange things. I'm allowed to use magic in a limited capacity. The Towers are keeping me on a short leash for the time being."

"But you're considered . . . one of them?"

I swallowed a sigh and my smirk died on my lips. "Yeah. I'm a warlock again."

Trixie looked down at her hands tightly clenched in her lap and rapidly blinked her eyes as if she were trying to hold back tears. I couldn't blame her. Leaving the Towers meant that I had reached for something better and achieved it. Going back felt like a betrayal to all the people who still lived in fear. It was a betrayal to the four Tower runaways who were living in hiding and using me as a symbol of hope for a better life. Going back was failure.

"I'm sorry," I whispered. "I didn't tell you sooner because I was still trying to adjust to the idea myself. I can't change what I am. I was born to be a warlock and wield this power. What I can try to control are the people I hurt and who are hurt by the Towers."

"What would have happened if you didn't go back?"

"I would have been killed on the spot."

The silence stretched between us. I stared at my untouched bottle of beer sweating on my coffee table, willing Trixie to say that she was glad that I hadn't chosen death. I needed to hear that she could understand what I had done and that she was glad that I was still here with her. But she didn't speak.

A huge number of her people had been hunted and slaughtered during the Great War. Their numbers had dwindled to a fraction of what they had been. It was all done by the Towers. And I was now a warlock. A killer without conscience. One of them.

I could easily remind her of everything I had done for her. Everything I had done to protect her and her people, but the memory of the Towers loomed between us.

The unexpected knock on the door was a welcome interruption breaking the silence. I jumped up, inwardly praying that it wasn't Gideon on my doorstep with a new task that needed completing for the Towers. Now was definitely not a good time to go running off to my other life.

A woman with short brown hair and light brown eyes smiled nervously at me when I opened the door. "Gage Powell?" she asked.

"Yeah," I replied, leaning against the door. She didn't look like she was selling anything and I couldn't recall anyone moving into the building recently, so she wasn't a new neighbor borrowing a cup of sugar. There was no magic energy signature around her, so she wasn't from the Ivory Towers. She was a rare creature—a normal human being.

"My name is Serah Moynahan and I'm a special investigator with TAPSS."

She flashed her badge at me in one of those leather wallets, but I didn't care. Her mention of the Tattoo Artists and Potion Stirrers Society (TAPSS) had me closing the door in her face. The government agency that monitors and certifies all tattoo artists had been a regular pain in my ass over the years. I had a feeling that it was because a handful knew that I wasn't exactly your run-of-the-mill tattoo artist and they were hoping that I'd finally leave the industry. *Not fucking likely.*

"Not interested," I said.

She stopped the door from shutting by putting her shoulder into it while I pushed. "Please, Mr. Powell. I'm not here about Asylum!"

"Gage," Trixie said in warning.

Frowning, I released the door and stepped back. Serah took advantage of the break and quickly stepped across the threshold as if it meant that I couldn't throw her out. We'd see about that. Serah flashed a grateful smile at Trixie, who was standing beside the couch. Trixie didn't smile back. The elf may be willing to hear what TAPSS wanted, but she wasn't going to pretend to be happy about it.

Serah's smile disappeared as she looked at me while tucking her badge in her pocket again. "The vamps warned me you'd be difficult," she said in a low voice before taking a deep breath and starting again. "I was hoping that you'd be willing to consult on an investigation."

"What investigation?"

"There's been an incident at the Tattered Edge."

"Then you should probably speak with Bronx down at Asylum. He worked there for a short time," I said dismissively at the mention of the tattoo parlor on the north side of town. I wasn't interested in doing TAPSS any favors, particularly if it got Kyle in trouble.

"Someone is already speaking with Bronx."

This made my heart stop for a second before all my protective instincts came surging to the foreground. I stepped closer, backing Serah up. She hit the door, closing it behind her so that she was now trapped between it and me. "Bronx hasn't worked for Kyle Wight in years. You've got the wrong troll if you're looking to draw him in on whatever dirt you're bringing against Kyle."

"Kyle Wight is dead," Serah announced.

I stopped cold. My brain locked up on those few words.

"What?" Trixie asked when I couldn't.

"Kyle Wight was discovered murdered in his shop," Serah said, looking straight at me. "Bronx isn't a suspect. We're talking to him to get information on Kyle. We think he was killed by a customer he had just tattooed. I was hoping you would come with me to the parlor and look over the remains of the ingredients and the design. Tell us what he did for the killer."

Stepping away, I ran one hand through my hair. I hadn't been close to Kyle. We made polite chitchat whenever we saw each other at industry functions or around town. He was an extremely talented artist, but a little too scattered to run a business. Bronx had told me years ago that Kyle wasn't keeping up with his potion supplies and that was why the troll left, before he got drawn into trouble with TAPSS. I had always thought that it would be TAPSS that ended Kyle's career. Not something like this.

"Yeah, I'll help," I murmured. I started to go for my coat in the closet when Trixie's voice stopped me.

"I'm going too."

"Trix—"

Trixie stepped forward, pinning Serah with a piercing stare. "My name is Trixie Ravenwood and I'm a tattoo artist for Asylum. I've been tattooing for several years longer than Gage. I want to help."

"Um . . . yeah. Sure," the TAPSS investigator said, still leaning against the door. "We'd appreciate the help."

"Trixie, you don't have to do this." Stepping into her line of sight, I gently cupped both of her shoulders. "You've already had a long, bad day." *Thanks to me,* I mentally added. "Stay here. Eat something and relax. I'll be there and back again in a couple hours."

"Are you trying to say that I can't handle this, Gage Powell?"

A bark of laughter jumped from my throat and I dropped my hands back to my sides. "You're the most capable woman I know. If you're looking for a fight regarding my opinion of you or your abilities, you're not going to get it."

"Asshole," she grumbled.

I leaned forward and gently kissed her cheek. "I love you too."

The anger dissolved from her face in an instant and her shoulders slumped with weariness. She looked more worn to me now than when she first came through the door.

"Without being a sexist asshole, I am suggesting you stay here and rest. I know you're tired. I'm worried about you."

"I'm going because I knew Kyle. Not well, but I knew him. I also know a lot more about potions. I can help."

I smiled at her, wishing I was looking into the blonde beauty I loved rather than her glamour twin. "I welcome your help."

"Have you two lovebirds got this worked out now? Some of us would like to get home tonight," Serah said, breaking the tender moment, which was probably for the best.

"I'm sure your cats can survive a couple more hours without you," I said as I went to the closet and grabbed my heavy winter coat. When I turned back, Serah was glaring at me and Trixie was trying to glare at me but was failing miserably.

Serah said nothing as she led the way out of my apartment and to her car with Trixie and me trailing behind her. After telling Trixie the truth, this was not how I had expected to spend my evening. I didn't know whether I had been granted a temporary reprieve or if she was storing up her anger for a later date.

Either way, we were headed to the north side of town, where I was potentially going to see my second dead body in a week. I just hoped he still had his head.

CHAPTER 4

Tattered Edge was located in a decent neighborhood about a thirty-minute drive from Asylum. It was on the end of an older shopping plaza next to a place that specialized in Far East remedies and curios. There was also a hair salon, community bank, liquor store, and greeting-card shop. At just past midnight, only the liquor store and hair salon were still open catering to all the nocturnal customers, but the police had the entire area blocked off. Their red and blue lights splashed garishly over the area, sending shadows darting and lunging under cars and around corners.

As I got out of Serah's neat Honda sedan, I pulled my coat closed and stuffed my hands in my pockets against the bitter cold. Winter had moved into the area after All Hallows' Eve and had not let up. We hadn't gotten much snow, but the temperatures rarely ventured above freezing and never for long since the start of December. Glancing around, I spotted an ambulance parked past a scattering of emergency vehicles. Apparently, the paramedics had also drawn morgue duty. What was disturbing was that they were leaning against the ambulance chatting with two people wearing coats with "CORONER" written in large yellow letters across the back. It gave me a sneaking suspicion that they had yet to remove Kyle because they were waiting on us. Fabulous.

For half a second, I thought about warning Trixie, but I kept my mouth shut. Why have my concern thrown back at me as a challenge? I was in enough trouble already and we still had to get through this.

As Serah neared the yellow police tape, a cop reached over and partially lifted it for her. "Thanks, Carl," she said, ducking low. "How are Patricia and the kids?"

"They're good. Everyone's looking forward to the holiday break." Carl's dark eyes swept over Trixie and me, while his arm lowered. "These your experts?"

"Yeah. Trixie and Gage from Asylum, on the south side," she said. The cop nodded and let us duck below the tape. His eyes lingered on me and he took a step back as I walked by, but I ignored him as best as I could. He'd recognized my name and it didn't give me a good feeling.

We paused at the entrance, where Serah directed us to put on some latex gloves and little covers over our shoes. "The police have already been through, dusting, collecting, and photographing, but we need to preserve the scene. Try to touch as little as possible."

Following Serah in, I was disappointed to find that it wasn't much warmer inside than outside. They had turned off the heat and opened doors to keep the smell down. It wasn't working. Kyle's rotting corpse and final bowel movement could be smelled in the small waiting room filled with worn chairs and ragged magazines. A couple large photo albums were left open on a table, displaying an assortment of tattoo designs.

Lifting a gloved hand to my nose, I breathed in the latex, giving my stomach a break from the other gut-twisting scent filling the space. "When was Kyle discovered?"

"About seven o'clock this evening." Serah looked back at us, her brows bunching over her nose. "Coroner estimates that he's been dead three days."

"Three days?" Trixie repeated in horror. "How could no one notice for three days?"

I shook my head, frowning down at the tattoo books. "Doesn't he have anyone else working for him?"

"Two artists actually." Serah paused and pulled out a little notebook from an interior coat pocket. "Nicole Quelsen and Ben Breen," she read when she'd found the right page. "Both have been in San Diego since Tuesday at the Ink Pot Convention." Serah started to continue to the main workspace, tucking her notebook in a pocket, but suddenly stopped. "Is it strange Kyle didn't go with them?" she asked, looking at me.

"No. Kyle hated to travel. He attended only those cons that were within two hours' drive of Low Town." That and the Ink Pot Convention wasn't a big tattoo artists convention. Most on the East Coast used it as an excuse to go out to the West Coast for a vacation under the guise of work.

As we stepped into the main tattooing space, my first thought was at least he still had his head. Unfortunately, Trixie immediately lost her stomach. By the sound of it, Trixie ran out of the room and grabbed a small wastebasket along the way. I was more disturbed by the fact that I didn't get sick. But years of living in the Towers and fighting to survive had pretty much killed my gag reflex. I was growing more detached from it all, as if the violence couldn't touch me.

Kyle's body sat up against a tall mirror that had spider-webbed when he hit it. A large black pool of blood had dried beneath him while his guts were spilled into his lap from where his stomach had been cut open. Kyle's face also was beaten and bruised badly from where the killer had taken a meat tenderizing mallet to it before dropping it at Kyle's feet. What struck me as strange was that the mallet was in the tattooing room, when it normally would have been kept in the back for crushing certain potion ingredients. But then maybe it wasn't so strange. The whole room was a chaotic, haphazard mess of items that had been tossed aside when they were no longer needed.

But the worst for me was seeing Kyle stabbed in the heart with his own tattooing gun. Was this the act of an angry customer? Had Kyle's carelessness finally gotten him killed? If so, he wouldn't be the first and probably not the last. Tattooing was dangerous business.

"Have Ben and Nicole been contacted?" I asked when Serah returned. She had chased after Trixie while I stayed locked to the spot.

"Yes. They're flying back in the morning. Ben is part fey and doesn't travel well at night."

I nodded. Why rush? It's not like they could help Kyle now.

At the sound of Trixie's footsteps, I turned to see her slowly come back into the room looking paler and a little unsteady but determined to see this through. Her eyes flicked to the body for a second before finding my face. Reaching into my pocket, I pulled out a peppermint and handed it to her.

She managed a weak smile as she took it with trembling fingers. "You're always prepared, aren't you?"

"I try." I didn't tell her I used a tiny spell to summon a peppermint from the bag of peppermints sitting on the nightstand in my bedroom. It wasn't important. The peppermint would help with the nausea and the smell.

With Trixie on firmer footing, I turned to Serah. "You had something for us?" The sooner we answered Serah's questions, the sooner I could get Trixie out of this nightmare.

"The design is here." She directed us to a counter with a couple pieces of paper on it. The first was Kyle's original sketch, which was about half the size of a standard sheet of paper and was largely an abstract piece with bold and swirling lines. There were some images, like a knife, embedded in it but it didn't make much sense to me.

"This isn't good," Trixie said in a low voice. Serah and I both looked over at her to find her chewing on her bottom lip in worry as she stared at the design.

"You recognize it?" Serah asked.

"It's used in Alpha Conversion potions."

Using the tip of my index finger, I carefully turned the paper slightly, taking another look at the drawing. My stomach sank as some of the lines finally tugged some memories free in my brain. It was an old and basic technique to change a chunk of a person's inner core, their sense of self. I had done something similar but far more delicate and subtler to my brother. The difference between the two was like the difference between a jackhammer and a chisel. Trixie was right. This wasn't good.

"What's an Alpha Conversion?" Serah asked. She was holding a pen and small notepad now, ready to take notes.

"Most people in the world can be divided into two groups: alphas, which are the bold aggressors and risk takers, and the betas, which are the cautious followers," Trixie explained.

"Like Type A and Type B personalities?" Serah supplied.

Trixie looked at me and frowned. Trixie was an elf and she dealt in nature's laws, not Serah's human constructs of human psychology. When Trixie spoke of alphas, she was talking predators.

"In a basic sense, yes," I jumped in to keep things moving. "The design is important, but the types of ingredients used determine the degree and power behind the change."

"Can this tattoo be prepped and completed quickly?"

"No." I looked down at the design, smeared with Kyle's blood. "The client would have contacted him and discussed it days ago. Probably met at least once prior to tattooing the person."

"How long have you worked for TAPSS?" Trixie asked. I was beginning to wonder that myself. Not all TAPSS investigators have a detailed knowledge of tattooing and potions, but most have a solid working knowledge. Serah was asking some pretty basic questions she should have known the answers to.

"Four months, but I was a cop for five years before that. I know how to run an investigation," she said through clenched teeth. I couldn't blame her for getting pissed, but we wanted to see Kyle's killer stopped and that was unlikely to happen with someone who didn't know the pointy end of a tattooing needle.

"Shouldn't you have a partner or something? Someone with more tattooing and potion knowledge?" Trixie continued.

"I do and even he didn't recognize the symbol." I shrugged. "Alpha Conversions are extremely rare and aren't taught during an apprenticeship. A lot of tattoo artists probably couldn't do one. Not an effective one at least."

"My partner also refused to work with me when I mentioned your name," she said, looking very pointedly at me. "None of them wanted to work with me if I contacted you."

Trixie lifted one questioning eyebrow at me, as if to ask what I'd done to deserve that reaction.

"Don't look at me like that. Bronx was the last one to give TAPSS any kind of shit. Not me."

"I'm sure you didn't help matters," Trixie said with a smirk.

She was right, of course, but I bit back my snide comeback in favor of pressing forward. Spending the evening standing in the dried blood of a deceased acquaintance wasn't my idea of a good time.

"Where's the potion?" I demanded.

Serah led the way to the next room, which wasn't much larger than the bathroom in my apartment. A large cabinet stood open with a chaotic array of ingredients that were stored in jars, bowls, and envelopes, while others just lay out on the shelves with no labels. It was a tattoo artist's worst nightmare. Effective potions for tattoos required fresh and properly preserved ingredients. You couldn't just throw a bunch of unknown shit in a bowl and expect it to work.

The table used to stir the potions didn't look much better. The surface was covered with so much old flotsam and random crap that I couldn't be sure what he'd used to make the killer's potions and what was left over from potions he'd stirred weeks ago.

Trixie shook her head, standing beside me. "This is a fucking disaster."

"Yeah, but we can throw out these bowls," I said,

waving my hand at two crucibles and a butter bowl growing mold and collecting dust. They hadn't been used recently. Carefully picking up the chipped ceramic bowl closest to me, I ran my finger along the interior and then sniffed the residue left behind on the glove. I held it up to Trixie, who also sniffed it.

"I can definitely pick out Woodruff and Saint-John's-wort," she said. She stepped back as if she wanted to mentally examine what she had just smelled without any interference.

I nodded, grateful she had come along. My sense of smell was that of an average human's, while Trixie's elf senses were much keener. She'd have a chance of picking out the exact ingredients.

Peering closely at the remains of the potion in the bowl, I tried to identify the rest of the items. Woodruff was a common herb used as a catalyst for significant changes, while Saint-John's-wort was used for invincibility. "I thought I smelled holy thistle," I added, which was used for strength and protection. It was likely that Kyle had also thrown in a black market item or two such as werewolf sinew or ogre spleen, but I didn't want to mention it and send Serah running after the black market vendors. I had no desire to piss of the guys from whom I still got goods.

"And to bind it all . . ." Trixie picked up a bundle of oak branches that had been bound together with twine. Kyle would have lit one end and let the ash fall into the mix. Not a good sign. Oak was a heavy hitter in the natural world. It was used for a burst of inner strength and power. It was the reason that oak was linked to powerful kings and conquerors through history.

"So, how bad is it?" Serah asked. Her pen was poised over her little notepad, ready to take down my opinion. She wasn't going to like it.

"We're fucked," I said, pulling off my gloves and shoving them in my coat pocket.

"Why?"

"The ingredients were strong, assuming most were somewhat fresh, and the binding agent made it permanent," Trixie said. "The person is now extremely aggressive and focused. Seeing as this isn't the person's nature state, it's likely that it pushed their mental state off balance."

"Kyle created a monster," Serah said.

I sighed and pushed my fingers through my hair, sending it standing on end. "Yes and no. This person had to have the desire or . . . . predisposition toward murder already. He probably just lacked the courage to do it."

"Until now," Trixie added. "The tattoo gave the killer that final shove over the edge and most likely unhinged his mind in the process."

"And he's going to keep killing," Serah murmured, staring down at the notepad in her hands.

"I wouldn't be surprised if he hasn't already," I said. Serah said nothing but I noticed her hands grip her notepad a little tighter, her knuckles turning white. "You think he has already!" I stepped closer and her head popped up.

She opened her mouth and I think she was going to deny it, but then closed her mouth. Her eyes darted thoughtfully from me to Trixie. "Kyle's the first death, but not the last. I think the bastard has killed twice since leaving here. We found two women, one last night and one tonight, with their stomachs slashed the same as Kyle. Both were in their last trimester of pregnancy."

Beside me, Trixie let out a horrible cry. I turned to see her knees buckle and she started to collapse. Catching her, I scooped her up and sat her on the only stool in the crowded little room. She gripped my arms with fierce, trembling hands and raised tear-glazed green eyes to my face. For the first time since I'd met her, Trixie involuntarily lost her glamour spell. Serah was staring at her in shock, but I ignored the human.

Cupping Trixie's cheek with one hand, I kept the other on her shoulder to hold her steady. "Are you okay? Do you want me to get the paramedics?"

"No," she said in a squeak. She cleared her throat and repeated it with more force. "No. I'm just overwhelmed. First, Kyle dying like this and then those women." She paused and looked at Serah. "Did the babies survive?"

"No, I'm sorry," she said gently.

Trixie squeezed her eyes closed. A tear escaped, slipping down her too-pale cheek. "I need to go home."

"Agreed. We're out of here," I said, wrapping one arm around her shoulders as I started to help her to her feet.

Trixie pressed a hand to my chest as her head snapped up. "No! You stay. Help the police and TAPSS. *You* can help them."

A frown tugged at the corners of my mouth. What she meant was that I could find the killer because I was a warlock. I wasn't too sure what I could do using my special warlock powers with Serah on my heels, but I'd figure something out. "Are you sure?"

"Yes. I'll get a taxi to take me back."

"I can get a police officer to take you back," Serah offered, her soft voice startling me. For a moment, I'd forgotten that she was even there.

"I can't trouble them . . ."

"Trust me, it won't be any trouble. A few outside are ready to get out of here."

"Thank you," I said on a relieved sigh before Trixie could argue.

"You just might . . . want to . . ." Serah awkwardly said, motioning toward Trixie's face.

The elf looked at me in confusion and I smiled. "You lost your glamour."

"Son of a bitch," she whispered in frustration, but the brunette was back in place in the blink of an eye.

I pressed a kiss to her forehead before releasing her. "I'll see you back at my apartment soon. I'll bring Bronx with me."

Trixie nodded and then followed Serah back to the parking lot while I walked into the main tattooing room, where a trio of men struggled to get Kyle into a body bag. Not the easiest of tasks with his innards slipping out and threatening to flop all over the place. If I hadn't liked the guy, I might have suggested using a shovel. Of course, I can't say I was overly fond of him. Kyle had gotten sloppy and bad potions made us all look bad. Even so, the guy didn't deserve to go like this.

Watching their slow progress, I saw something that could be useful, but I didn't think the police would let me just walk off with evidence. "Here, let me help," I offered, kneeling down by the body. Dried blood brushed off onto the knee of my jeans, but it wasn't the first time my clothes had acquired bloodstains in the service of others, and it certainly wouldn't be the last. I was getting damn good at laundry since I could afford to replace my clothes every time things got messy.

One cop gave me a brief, grateful smile as I slid one hand under the corpse's left knee, while the other was under its back. I quickly stopped my brain from trying to identify the crunchy and cool gel-like substances my bare hands were encountering. I was an idiot for taking off my gloves and a bigger idiot for not putting them back on.

It was awkward and we were all trying not to breathe deeply as we worked, but we got the body bagged on the first try. As they rushed to get Kyle zipped up, I sat back on my heels so that my body hid the small waste-basket closest to the tattoo chair Kyle had been using when he worked on the killer. In the blink of an eye, I snatched up a blood and ink-encrusted paper towel and stuffed it into my pocket before standing.

The paramedics stood and solemnly marched out of the room, their shuffling feet releasing flakes of dried blood into the air. The cop followed, his head down, looking pale but also relieved. His night in this grim place was almost over.

The tattooing room had always been a place of new beginnings, second chances, and adventure. But this one screamed of death and violence. It was ugly and mocked everything that had drawn me to becoming a tattoo artist in the first place.

Serah moved out of the entrance to let them pass, coming to stand beside me. "Trixie is being taken back by Carl and Ernie. They're good guys and will see to it that she's safe in your apartment before leaving."

"Thanks."

"I had no freaking clue she was an elf," she continued in a low voice despite the fact that we were alone in the parlor. She shook her head as if she trying to dislodge the last of her shock.

"That's how glamour works." I grinned down at her. Serah couldn't have been more than five feet five in her low heels, making her seem positively tiny next to Trixie, but there was a spunkiness to the woman that kept you from brushing her off.

She rolled her eyes and then turned serious. "I promise not to tell anyone."

"She'd appreciate it. She's not hiding any longer, but everyone knows this disguise, so she keeps it just to make life easier."

"She was in hiding?" Serah said, but I was already

shaking my head at her. The TAPSS investigator didn't need to know about Trixie's past. I was already cursing myself for that stupid slip.

"I've not spoken with many elves. Are they usually so sensitive? I wouldn't have expected that."

In general, that was a big NO. From my experience, elves were indifferent to humans because we were inferior. Luckily, my girlfriend had a different opinion. But her reaction was unexpectedly strong. The Summer Court seemed to be the most sympathetic of the three different clans. The Winter Court was cool, distant, and definitely frightening, from my limited experience. And the Svartálfar, or dark elves, were murderous assholes looking to kill or control everyone around them. They weren't quite as bad as the Ivory Towers, but it wasn't for a lack of trying.

"Until recently, the elves have had some reproduction issues. I think Trixie's a little sensitive about babies right now," I said, hoping that was the reason. During my quick visit to see Mother Nature in September, I convinced the old girl to set the elves right again. Of course, there were days I still felt hollow and raw from that visit. Mother's Nature's home had put me at peace and holding my son had been the best experience in the world, but I couldn't stay. There were still too many things I needed to do here.

"Do you have any more insight you can offer on the tattoo or even the killer?" Serah asked and I was grateful she dropped the subject of Trixie and the elves.

Stepping back over to the counter that held the

original sketch as well as the copy used for the inking, I tucked my hands in my pockets to keep from touching anything. "Kyle reduced the size so it can easily be tattooed on an arm or just about anywhere on the body. With this potion, it would need to be on the left side. Preferably on the arm or shoulder—as close to the heart as possible for this to take effect."

"What about on the chest over the heart?"

"Possible but less likely. Kyle hated tattooing on the chest and generally avoided it. Chest tattoos are a pain in the ass because the customer keeps breathing."

"Anything else?"

I shrugged. "Just the basics—check fingerprints, Kyle's schedule, phone records, and the paperwork the client had to sign before the tattoo was done."

"Police are working on it, but I doubt they're going to find much on the paperwork side. I'd heard there are some artists who tattoo without filing the proper paperwork," Sarah added wryly as she tucked her notepad in her pocket. She didn't glance up at me, but I kept my face blank and my mouth shut. Most of us took an off-the-books client every once in a while for the extra money. It was highly illegal and could cost an artist his license if discovered, but we always told ourselves that we were careful. Too few of us every caught any trouble from it. But Kyle was proof that careful didn't count for shit in this world.

Serah's narrowed eyes scanned the room as if she were searching for that one clue the other thirty people had missed when they traipsed through. "Nothing else?"

My shoulders lifted in a small shrug. "Sorry. I'm a tattoo artist, not a miracle worker."

"Then why don't you give back that bloody napkin you grabbed out of the trash?" she said as her gaze rose to my face.

My expression remained unchanged as I scrambled for a reply while silently cursing my clumsiness. I had been so focused on not getting caught by the men moving Kyle that I didn't notice her return. Obviously becoming a thief was out of the question if the tattooing thing didn't work out.

"The police are already checking the blood samples from the tattoo," she continued when I didn't speak. "They say it's a waste of time. The soap, ink, and potion have likely destroyed the DNA. They doubt they'll even be able to identify the species of the killer." When I still didn't speak, she crossed her arms over her chest, making her look like an angry marshmallow because of her puffy winter coat. "Can you do better?"

A smile finally lifted my lips. I *could* do better. I might not be able to get a clear image of the person, but I could get something. There was a spell or two I could use that had nothing to do with DNA.

"Listen here, Powell," she said, poking me in the chest with her index finger. "You're not going after this sadistic fuck because your friend was killed. This is *my* case, *my* collar. Just give me the info."

It was interesting that she said "my" rather than TAPSS or the police. I wasn't the only one with a personal interest in this. Sadly mine wasn't about avenging Kyle's death. Trixie's tear-filled request was driving me. Of course, I didn't think Serah's reasoning figured justice for Kyle either. *Poor Kyle. Killed by a client and no one's promising justice in his name.* It was tough being a tattoo artist in Low Town.

"I've got a couple ideas. I can get back to you—"

"Nope. Ain't gonna happen." She poked my sternum a second time to emphasize her point. "Where that sample goes, I go."

I hesitated, temptation gnawing at me. With magic, I could wipe her mind of this conversation. She'd forget and I'd be safe to pursue Kyle's killer alone. But Serah could give me easy access to police information. Her memory could always be wiped after the killer was caught. And it wasn't like I was bringing more danger into her life. She was enthusiastically seeking it out when she pursued this case.

"Fine," I said and started for the door.

"Wait!" she called, following quickly on my heels. "That's it? Fine?"

"Yep."

"I'm beginning to understand why the vampires don't like you," she muttered, as we paused to pull off the little paper booties and we stepped back onto the sidewalk.

The ambulance and most of the police cruisers were gone. Muddy lamplight washed over the lot rather than rotating red and blue lights, allowing the shadows to return to their proper homes. Smoke curled up from the few cars idling, while people huddled before the heating vents and discussed Kyle's gruesome death. Or maybe they were all talking about their holiday plans, eager to forget about one man's violent death.

For a moment, I wondered if this very scene was waiting in my future. Between my dealings with the Towers, the local mafia, and the fact that I was a warlock trying to live among the people, my life hovered on the edge of a violent end. Were these same people going to be discussing my blood-splattered death scene over a mug of coffee while inwardly wishing they were already home with their spouses and kids? And what were the chances that it would just be my body lying there in pieces? Not good. I couldn't stomach the idea of Trixie or Bronx being killed because of me.

"Why did you contact me?" I demanded a little sharper than I had meant to, as I tried to pull my thoughts back from that dark abyss.

"Because you're one of the best tattoo artists in the area," she quickly said, but refused to look up at me. She kept her eyes lowered and concentrated on pulling off her latex gloves and pulling on fleece winter gloves.

"*One of.* I can think of two damn good artists who live here on north side. You could have just gotten Bronx. He worked here and knew Kyle better than I did," I pressed. "Do you have an axe to grind that I need to know about?"

"Of course not!" she nearly shouted.

I snorted, a blast of white fog jumping from my nose in the bitter cold. "Yeah. You ignore your mentors and every vamp at TAPSS when they tell you to stay away from me. What's the deal?"

Serah glared up at me, her hands balled into fists at her side. I found myself cringing slightly as I waited for her to explode. "You have a sealed file at TAPSS!" Bumping me with her shoulder, she stomped toward the car, seeming to talk to herself. "No one has a sealed file. I can access basic things like training and certification, but all other information is locked up tight. And it's not just that the vamps don't like you. They seem . . . scared of you. And nothing scares them, except maybe the Towers."

"So . . . what? You got something to prove?"

"Yes!" she hissed. She shoved her fists into the pockets of her coat and stopped in the middle of the parking lot. Turning back to me, she looked like she was struggling not to scream. "I spent five years on the Low Town police force and I was a damn good cop. But these fucking vampires treat me like some snot-nosed rookie who doesn't know shit."

I couldn't stop the laugh that bubbled up. "And you're building your street cred with me?"

Serah shrugged, some of the anger draining from her frame as she started for her car again. "Well, that and the cops have started whispering about you as well."

Grabbing her shoulder, I spun Serah around, forcing her to look at me. "What about the cops?" The sealed file wasn't a surprise. TAPSS knew some details about my past, but that was supposed to be locked down and kept secret from most of the agents. The cops weren't supposed to know anything about me.

"There have been rumors recently. Started this past summer."

"Rumors about what?"

"Magic."

My heart stopped for a second and then started painfully again, racing in my chest. This was not a good thing. "You think . . . what? I'm a warlock?"

Serah's head fell back on a laugh. The sound was like little bells ringing in the crisp air. "A warlock?" She laughed again and this time she snorted. She slapped her hands over her mouth, her cheeks turning red in the dim light. "Now you're just being ridiculous. You're a warlock and I'm queen of the pixies."

Pulling her keys out of her pocket, she unlocked her car and got in while I walked around to the passenger side. Relief made me light-headed, but a small nagging part of me was insulted. I'd spent most of my life trying to prove to the Towers and myself that I wasn't like the other witches and warlocks. They were only cold-hearted killers focused on gaining more power while crushing the world. But it was the perverse part of me that didn't like being told that I didn't have it in me to be something. Why couldn't I be a warlock? I shrugged before pulling open the door. My aura must have been wrong. Gideon and the others exuded scary.

Boy, was I about to prove Serah wrong.

CHAPTER 5

Pink Floyd was trickling out of the speakers at Asylum when we arrived, causing my stomach to clench with guilt and worry. "Wish You Were Here" was usually saved for when the troll was troubled. The album *A Collection of Great Dance Songs* had been played a lot in that first month after I'd been drawn back into the Towers. I'd never gotten around to telling Bronx what had happened, but then I hadn't been my usual cheerful self during that time either, so he knew things hadn't gone well.

The troll looked up as we came in the front door and gave a soft grunt of acknowledgment before reaching under the counter to turn down the music. "TAPSS got ahold of you," he said, though I think it was meant to be a question.

"Yeah." I shrugged out of my heavy coat and tossed it onto the wooden bench that ran along the back wall.

"I'm sorry about Kyle."

He grunted again, though this one sounded a little more thoughtful. "I hadn't talked to Kyle in a couple years, but . . . to go like this. I was just starting to think that the Towers were the only thing that we needed to worry about." He turned his piercing gold eyes on the woman standing in the middle of the lobby, looking undecided as to whether she wanted to be there.

"Bronx, this is Serah Moynahan, an investigator with TAPSS."

As he rose to his feet, the troll's relaxed demeanor disappeared like a wisp of smoke in the wind. I could see the muscles in his hard jaw tighten as if he were grinding his teeth. He didn't offer her his hand, which was unlike Bronx since the troll's manners usually put Emily Post to fucking shame, but Serah was TAPSS and no tattoo artist liked the regulatory agency.

"I'm sorry about Kyle," Serah said as she shrugged out of her coat. She didn't seem particularly put off by his cold demeanor, though she was keeping a good distance between them. At over six feet, Bronx was an intimidating figure of muscle and menace. It also didn't help that Trixie had drawn dancing skeletons along Bronx's bare arms using greasepaint. Since a troll's skin was too thick for tattooing, Bronx had Trixie draw different images on his arms every night so that it appeared that he had some tattoos.

"Are you almost done for the night?" I asked, breaking the awkward silence that had settled in the room.

Bronx reluctantly tore his eyes off Serah to look at

me, his expression softening. "No more appointments and I've only got another hour of my shift. Sunrise is in three hours."

"No shit?" I twisted, looking out the front window as if I could use the moon to judge how late it was. But then, the moon was hidden from where I stood and I couldn't use it to tell time even if I could see it. No matter. Between the trip out to Kyle's shop, the investigation, and the drive back, the night had wasted away, when I had hoped to spend it in a more enjoyable manner. Or at the very least, a productive manner in terms of my relationship.

I shook my head in disgust. Life had a way of getting in the way of my plans. "On your way home, would you check on Trixie at my apartment?"

"Sure, what's up?"

"She was with me at Kyle's shop. It wasn't pretty."

"She took it bad?"

"Yeah, and that wasn't the first bad news of the night," I muttered as the look on Trixie's face when I told her I was once again an agent of the Ivory Towers flashed through my brain. I'd never forget that look for as long as I lived. The horror, the fear, the disgust, and disappointment threatened to drown out rational thought. Despite knowing why she couldn't, I wanted her to understand my choices, needed her to understand.

"You finally talked . . ." Bronx's deep voice drifted off meaningfully.

"Yeah." My own voice had become rough with

emotion. I wanted to fucking throw something as frustration welled within me, but a temper tantrum wouldn't fix shit. It would only waste time I didn't have. I just kept telling myself that my relationship was still fixable. "She can tell you or we'll talk later. Check in with her before heading home if you don't mind."

"I got it."

"I appreciate it." And I did. I knew the risk he was taking. Trolls were vulnerable to sunlight, turning to stone at the first touch of the sun's rays. It was a death sentence for them, but Bronx had risked himself for me time and again. My only hope was that I'd be able to return the favor one day.

"You need any help?" Bronx asked me, but was pointedly staring at Serah with a grim expression. I don't know what the troll was offering, since he wasn't the violent type despite his frightening appearance, and would never raise a hand to a woman.

"No, I got this," I said, feeling the first hint of a chuckle in hours. "We think we've got a little of the attacker's blood and we're going to see what kind of information I can get out of it."

Bronx's narrowed gaze jerked back to me and he moved to block the entrance to the tattooing room when I stepped forward. "How?" he growled and I was warmed by his protectiveness.

"Using the bad stuff."

"In front of her?" Yeah, he thought I'd officially lost my mind at last and I certainly couldn't blame him.

Serah snorted. "I'm still here and can hear you," she said in a loud voice vibrating with her annoyance.

Bronx ignored her outburst, keeping his eyes locked on me. "You don't have to do this. You weren't close to Kyle. Let the cops and TAPSS do their job."

My weariness seeped back in and I shook my head. "Trixie asked me to."

The troll frowned and I could almost hear the gears turning in his head. "Why? She wasn't close with Kyle."

What Bronx wanted to say was *This isn't your fight*, and I had to agree with him. I'd been dragged into Trixie's problems with the Summer Court and a fight with the Towers that might have worked out better if I'd just stayed out of the mess to begin with. I wanted to walk away, but the look of fear and desperation in Trixie's eyes was enough to put me on this path. If only to restore her faith in me again.

"Apparently Kyle wasn't the killer's only victim." Learning against the wall, I crossed my arms over my chest and looked at my closest friend. "Based on the evidence at the crime scene, the police think the same person has also murdered two pregnant women. It's likely the person would never have struck without the tattoo. We need to find out who this is and why he's targeting pregnant women."

The troll's expression grew even darker and he swore softly under his breath. "Any leads?"

"None so far," Serah admitted with some frustration.

For the first time, Bronx's expression softened toward Serah. "Have you tried the goblins?"

"Why the goblins? What could they have to do with this?" Serah asked, taking a tentative step forward.

"The area goblins run the baby black market," Bronx volunteered.

The small woman's mouth hung open for a second in shock before her face flushed red with anger. "And people know this is happening and aren't doing anything about it?"

"They're not stealing and eating babies," I said and quickly bit my tongue.

Well, supposedly they weren't stealing babies anymore. In the old days, goblins were quite fond of stealing human children from their cribs. Apparently, young humans are a delicacy. But as times changed, the goblins discovered they could make more money selling babies on a black market. Despite the significant progress we've made in recognizing most races as citizens and giving them access to proper health care, many lawmakers aren't as open about adoption, particularly interspecies adoption.

"The goblins pay women quite well to have babies and give them over for adoption," Bronx explained when she didn't look convinced.

"There are a number of vampires as well as interspecies couples who can't have children and aren't allowed to adopt, so they go to the goblins," I said.

While I'd never personally visited the goblins regarding their wares, I'd learned that once you became involved in purchasing goods in one black market, you tended to be aware of what else was going on in the underground. You never knew when turmoil elsewhere was going to impact your own livelihood.

"You don't think that the goblins are behind the murders, do you?" I asked, drawing my tired eyes up the troll's frowning visage.

"Probably not," Bronx said with a shrug. "They're fond of money and wouldn't do anything to hurt their supply. More likely, they've already started looking into the matter and might be able to give you some information."

"Could be someone they've crossed in the past?" Serah suggested.

"Possible. I'll dig around and see if I can locate a contact after we finish with tonight's little escapade," I murmured.

The troll looked like he was going to argue with my decision to burrow deeper into this mess when I needed to step away from it, but after several seconds, he closed his mouth and nodded. Lines of tension still stretched from his eyes. He was worried.

"If you need anything . . ."

"You've got my back," I finished when his voice faded.

Bronx stepped back and I cut through the empty tattooing room. I kept my head down so that the three chairs skated briefly through the periphery of my vision. The three of us had worked together for nearly three years. Laughter had almost constantly echoed through that room as we tattooed the people of Low

Town. Crude jokes, strange misadventures, and unexpected revelations filled that room and a part of me worried that it was on the cusp of ending.

Pushing aside my personal worries, I concentrated on the soft patter of female footsteps as Serah followed me down the narrow hallway that connected the main tattooing room with the windowless storage room at the back of the building. When she entered, I closed and locked the door as I usually did when I planned to enter the basement. My eyes jumped to the back door, to find that it was still double-bolted.

"What are we doing back here? You know a potion to pull information out of the blood?" Serah demanded. Her voice had grown colder and harder with her increasing anxiety. My veiled conversation with Bronx had only raised her suspicions about me and the situation wasn't going to get any better.

Taking her winter coat out of her arms, I tossed it on the padded table I used when I needed someone to lie flat for a tattoo. "Hand over the gun," I said, holding out my hand.

Serah frowned and took a step backward. "Why?"

"So accidents don't happen."

She didn't budge beyond her gaze hardening on me. "I don't trust you."

"Good. We have something in common. I don't trust me either." I tapped down the urge to use magic to make the gun disappear, but that wasn't the way to win this person over. "Hand over the gun. We're leaving it here."

"Where are we going?"

"Basement."

Her eyes darted from one locked door to the other as she thought it over. "Anyone else have a key to those doors?"

"No."

While not pleased with the idea, Serah removed the gun from shoulder holster under her right arm and popped the magazine from the grip before placing the weapon on top of her coat. The magazine she shoved into the back pocket of her jeans.

"You're left-handed," I observed, talking mostly to myself.

"Yeah," she said slowly, looking at me as if a few of my marbles had just rolled out of my ears.

I flashed her a crooked smile. "I've not met many left-handed people. Parents used to believe that kids who were left-handed would turn out to be a witch or warlock so they tried to train lefties to use their right hand."

She rolled her eyes and muttered, "Superstitious bullshit."

It helped to break the tension a little bit. With a deep breath, I knew it was time to get down to business.

"I've got to set some ground rules before we continue."

"And now I'm worried again," Serah said. Her voice carried some levity as if she was trying to meet me halfway, but it was fading fast. "Why do we need ground rules?"

"For both our protection."

"You know, Gage, if you're going to use some kind of illegal potion, it's unlikely I'm going to recognize it. I want to catch this bastard too." *Ahh . . . dear Serah.* Already willing to bend the rules for me. Of course, she was right. If I'd decided to use a little pixie liver in a spell she wouldn't be able to recognize it. While the ingredient was illegal, she wouldn't be able to tell the difference between it and a shriveled up lima bean.

"It's not a potion."

"Hacking software?"

"No." When Serah looked utterly confounded, I continued, knowing it was better to push ahead than to let her imagination run wild. "First rule is that you will wait here until I call you down into the basement." When she opened her mouth to argue, I pulled the blood-soaked paper towel out of my pocket and held it out to her. "Since you don't trust me, you'll hold this until you join me."

Serah wordlessly closed her mouth and took the paper towel, holding it carefully in her right hand. It was a fair trade. She could be sure that I wasn't trying to pull a fast one on her while I was out of her sight.

"Second rule is that you will remain calm no matter what you see."

"How much illegal crap you got down there?"

I just frowned at her. The shit I had down in the basement wasn't even on TAPSS's radar. Warlocks could do some seriously fucked-up shit, but it often required some really strange and rare items. There was plenty down there that could be considered illegal if all the rule makers ever considered what a person could get their hands on. For now it wasn't illegal simply because they hadn't thought of it yet.

"Fine. I'll stay calm," Serah said in a huff.

"And third, you'll give me a chance to explain anything you don't understand before you consider breaking Rule Number Two."

"Got it. Stay here. Stay calm. Give you a chance to snow me." Serah ticked off each rule on her fingers while glaring at me. "Can we get this going now? I would like to crawl into bed before the sun comes up."

Resisting the urge to flip her off, I turned and pushed a rolling table off the trapdoor in the floor, moving it to the far corner of the room. I didn't care if she was irritated with me. There was a huge potential for disaster by taking her into my secret lair, and I wanted to at least try to cover my ass before descending into this nightmare. I glanced over my shoulder at her one last time to see her still standing across the room with the tissue in her extended hand before turning my attention to the yawning darkness at the bottom of the warped wooden stairs.

Common sense said this was a mistake and I was having trouble remembering why I was doing this, but the die was cast and it was time to get this show on the road.

CHAPTER 6

With ease, I quickly descended the creaking stairs and hit the compacted dirt floor. I blindly grabbed the beaded pull chain overhead and gave it a hard yank as I walked into the center of the room. Grimy yellow light washed over the low-ceilinged room with exposed concrete walls. Deep shadows instantly retreated to peek out from around the three large cabinets that lined three of the walls. The fourth, far wall was empty except for a large symbol I'd spray-painted there. The air in the basement was thick with the scent of dirt, burned ozone, and some other, subtler scent that I had come to associate with the scent of my own magical signature.

Standing in the center of the room, I threw my arms out and then swiftly brought them in again before thrusting them out toward the dark symbol. A rush of magical energy stirred in the room, surging toward the wall, while a separate energy shifted, seeming to make the black paint undulate as if something large were crawling beneath it. Over the years, I'd spent hours staring at the symbol trying to decipher the meaning. Encased all in a large, unbroken circle, there were several other symbols running through it. At times, I thought it looked like a name and that frightened me more than anything else.

The defensive spell I had placed over the basement was a dangerous thing. It attacked with lethal force anyone who entered the basement that wasn't me. It was also a fickle thing, not liking to be turned off as I learned when I let my friend Sofie descend into my private domain. While it hadn't attacked her, the spell hadn't gone into magical sleep mode, which was more than a little unnerving.

It was never a good thing when a spell stopped obeying you. In fact, spells weren't supposed to have a mind of their own, but something was different about this one. I'd used this protective spell for several years and I was beginning to wonder if storing all these magical items near the spell was starting to have a negative impact. It was time to consult Gideon for a new protective spell.

When the last of the magical energies in the room finally settled down, I breathed a small sigh of relief. At least the spell wasn't going to kill us when Serah came down into the basement. I was just hoping the woman wouldn't try to kill me. Walking back over to stand at the bottom of the stairs, I called up to her.

Her footsteps creaked across the wood floor until she appeared at the top of the stairs with a questioning look on her face. "That didn't take long. Finished hiding your stash from the big bad TAPSS investigator?"

"Get your ass down here," I muttered.

As she slowly descended the stairs, I walked over to the high table that was pushed against one of the walls. Its surface was cluttered with random bits of junk that I had collected for use in random spells and potions. A series of crystals hung from ribbons and leather strings along the wall just above the table, while a stack of hardbound journals was piled in the corner. It was a mess, but it was my mess and I knew where everything was. Grabbing my wand out of the carved wooden box, I quickly shoved it up my sleeve. My hope was to ease Serah into this to keep her panic down to a minimum, and wands were panic-inducing things. I scooped up a battered box of wooden kitchen matches and a baby-food jar filled with sea salt, and then paused as my brain ran in circles, trying to figure out anything else that might help give this spell some kick.

"Gage?" Serah's tremulous voice rose up in the silent air. For the first time all evening, she sounded unsure and more than a little afraid. While the room housed cabinets that looked like they contained your typical potion ingredients, the padlocks on the front of each made you second-guess it. The black symbol dominating the far wall also didn't help. Even if you didn't understand magic, the thing held a sinister air as if it was a gateway to something evil. It didn't take an expert in magic to know that she was treading on dangerous ground.

I smiled broadly at her when I turned around to find her standing on the dirt floor near the foot of the stairs. "Almost ready," I said, trying to sound reassuring as I shoved the jar of salt into my pocket.

"What is all this?"

"You remember Rule Number Three?" I asked as I stepped over to the cabinet nearest her. Turning my body so that I blocked her view of what I was doing, I picked up the padlock and ran my thumb across the back while pushing a tiny burst of magic through the mechanism. A chunk echoed through the room as the lock popped open.

"Something about letting you explain," she said, still sounding as if she was about to bolt for the door.

"Yep. Here, hold this," I said, slapping the box of matches into her free hand before I turned my attention back to the cabinet. I squatted down where several plastic jugs were lined up along the bottom shelf with dates scrawled across them in black marker. Grabbing the fullest one, I stood and closed the cabinet doors with my foot.

"What's that?" she asked, eyeing the jug suspiciously.

"Water."

"Isn't starting a fire in the basement a little dangerous, even with water on hand?"

"We're not starting a fire," I said as I carried the

water jug over to the middle of the room and put it on the floor.

"Fine. So what do you have to explain?" Her mind didn't sound particularly open and her tone wasn't what I'd call inviting.

A little voice in my head screamed, *This is a mistake!* But I was already on this course and I'd made enough mistakes in the past by hiding important things from the people I was depending on to help me. It was time to be honest. Unfortunately, a TAPSS agent wasn't the best place to start.

"I want to tell you why my file at TAPSS is locked."

Serah immediately perked up and I had her full attention. She was going to get her hands on something that would give her a bit of clout over some of the other investigators who were giving her shit. *Fantastic.* She was going to hate that she couldn't tell another soul.

Taking a deep breath, I just spat it out. "I'm a warlock."

She stared at me for a second, her eyes wide, before a burst of laughter jumped from her open mouth. The tiny woman was nearly doubled over as she staggered to the side in her mirth. Well, she seemed tiny to me, but then I'm surrounded by six-foot-plus creatures all day.

Shaking her head, she straightened and looked at me. "Geez. You had me going for a minute. I thought you were going to actually tell me something," she said around lingering chuckles.

"I'm being serious."

"Whatever. You're not a warlock."

This had been a lot easier with Trixie, but then Trixie recognized when there was magic shit about that had nothing to do with potions. Serah didn't stir, so she thought my hidden stockpile was for potions, or at worst, she thought I was running a black market for illegal goods.

"Fuck," I mumbled. I had wanted to do this without scaring the shit out of the woman, but she refused to make it easy for me. Reaching up my left sleeve, I withdrew the wand I had hidden there while keeping my eyes on her. Serah stubbornly kept the smile on her face, but it had become a little more forced and sickly. Fear clouded her eyes and I knew I was now edging onto dangerous ground.

"Funny, Gage. Let's quit the joking and get down to business," she said, her gaze locked on the hawthorn wand like I was holding a poisonous snake in my hand.

"Stay calm, please." Pointing the wand at the ground, I murmured some words for the binding spell and a red laser-like beam shot from the end of the wand, which I used to draw a large circle in the dirt. When it was complete, I waved my hand over the circle and a series of swirls and symbols were drawn around the circle as if a dozen invisible children were seated in the dirt doodling.

Serah screamed. I turned back to see her drop the blood-soaked tissue and box of matches. In one fluid motion, she reached behind her and pulled her gun.

It trembled, but I had no doubt she could put a couple slugs in my chest at the blink of an eye.

"Stay back!" she shouted, still trying to sound authoritative while slowly edging toward the stairs.

Apparently she didn't trust me enough to leave the gun upstairs. I knew I should have taken the damn thing instead of leaving it behind. Fear tightly clenched my stomach. I wasn't worried about her shooting me. I could stop a bullet. No, terrified people waving guns around while rational thoughts flew from their brains led to disastrous things happening. I'd asked her to leave the gun behind to protect herself—not me. "Serah, you agreed to the rules. You said you'd stay calm and let me explain." I prayed my own calm voice would help her. It didn't.

"I'm calm." Her voice jumped in panic and the trembling became more pronounced in her gun. "I'm in a basement with a warlock. I know your secret and now you're going to kill me. How could I not be calm?"

I sighed and was almost overwhelmed by a wave of frustration and hatred . . . and helplessness. The Ivory Towers had fucked with people over the centuries. They destroyed families, businesses, and hope so that all that was left now was fear. "If I was going to kill you Serah, I would have done it already." But even as the words left my lips, I knew I hadn't said the right thing.

She snorted. "Like I'm going to believe that."

Kill her.

The low voice rumbled through the basement, sending a chill up my spine. Serah swung her gun around, searching for the unseen assailant. She stopped trying to edge toward the stairs and was now focused on defending herself.

She's a threat. Must kill her.

"Gage!"

"Hold still!" I snapped. My heart was thudding in my chest like a freight train, threatening to explode. I knew where the voice was coming from, but didn't want to believe it. The once-dormant protection spell had awoken when Serah had pulled her gun and was now actively pushing against its restraints in an effort to get to her. This was an unexpected development. But then, this was the first time I had invited someone down, vouching for them, only to have them later threaten me. Apparently my protection spell was more sentient than I had thought.

Fearful that any movement toward her on my part would set her off, I had to quickly defuse the situation from where I stood. Pulling in as much energy as I could from the air around me, I first turned my attention toward strengthening the binding on the defensive spell so that it couldn't lash out at Serah. Once I was sure that it wasn't going to strike my guest, I extended my hand toward the small woman. Despite her tight grip, the gun jumped from her hands and landed on my open palm.

"What the hell!" she said and lurched after her gun until she saw where it landed. She froze, tears glistening in her eyes. Bitter anger rose in my chest to see such fear directed at me. Those looks followed me no matter where I went. I might not have earned them for my actions, but there was no doubt that her life had been touched by the Towers. No one escaped the Ivory Towers.

"I'm not going to hurt you," I said slowly and in the most soothing voice I could muster.

"But . . . the voice . . ."

"The gun pissed off my security system." I forced a little smile as I shoved my wand into the back pocket of my jeans with the hope that its absence would help her relax a bit. "It's a little protective and not very discriminating."

"Oh," she whispered.

Holding up the gun, I took several steps backward and placed it on the table along the far wall, putting out of our reach for the time being. "We're just going to put this here for now. So we're both safe."

"So . . . so . . . you're a warlock." She violently blinked back her tears, fighting to keep them from falling. I admired her for trying to get her emotions under control and it wasn't an easy task. Her face was frighteningly pale and her hands were shaking, forcing her to ball them into fists at her sides so that I wouldn't notice.

"Yes. I am a warlock."

"Do the Towers know?"

A surprised laugh escaped me. I liked the idea that I might have slipped past the Towers' notice all those years ago; not that it was at all possible, but it was a nice thought. "Yeah, they know. I studied in the

Towers when I was a kid before escaping. I've been trying to lay low and avoid their notice but it doesn't always work out too well."

Some of the fear eased from her eyes and her body relaxed as I spoke. "Are they looking for you?"

"No," I said quickly and then scrunched my face up as that didn't exactly feel like the full truth. "Well, some might be, but they're not supposed to be." I groaned and rubbed my face. I was exhausted and the story of my escape was not a quick one. Or an easy one. "Let's just say I got away, but not everyone is very happy about it. I'm here in Low Town pretending to be an average tattoo artist. I'm not supposed to be using magic, but I thought you could use some help to stop this sicko."

"And you're not going to kill me?"

Sadly, that was not the first time I'd been asked that question. "No, it's not my thing."

"Does your girlfriend know?"

Nor was it the first time I'd been asked that question. "Yes, Trixie knows," I said, though there was a little bit more of an edge to my voice. I wanted to get home and snuggle in bed with my girlfriend. That was assuming that my lovely Trixie had decided to stay at my place rather than retreat to her own apartment. Fuck, this had been a long night!

"Shall we get on with trying to identify Kyle's killer so we both can return to our respective homes before the sun rises?"

Serah jerked at my question as if suddenly remembering why she had come back to Asylum with me in the first place. She twisted around, looking for where she had dropped both the tissue and the box of matches. Scooping them up, she hesitantly joined me back at the circle I had drawn in the dirt.

"What are you going to do?" The soft waver was still in her voice, but she was fighting hard to bounce back from shock.

"It's an identity spell. I'm afraid that the blood might be too damaged for an actual tracking spell, but we might be able to get a glimpse of what this bastard looks like."

Reaching over, I plucked the box of matches out of her hand and tossed them onto the ground next to the jug of water. Pulling the jar of sea salt out of my pocket, I unscrewed the lid and handed her the jar.

"Sprinkle the salt over the tissue, but be careful not to get the salt in the circle."

Stepping back from the circle, Serah held the balled-up paper towel out with the tips of two fingers and very carefully sprinkled a few salt crystals on it. I rolled my eyes at the sight. She was acting as if I had just handed her a dangerous acid that was going to dissolve her fingers.

"It's sea salt. It's not going to hurt you if it touches you," I said blandly.

Her narrowed eyes snapped to my face. "I didn't know that! You said you're doing magic. I thought this was dangerous shit."

"Magic *can* be dangerous, but I'm not going to

give you something dangerous after you just held me at gunpoint. Now really put some salt on that thing, please."

After making a face at me, Serah put the paper towel in the palm of her hand and liberally poured the salt over it. "Why am I doing this?"

"Salt is good for nullifying potions and some spells," I explained as I knelt on the ground and unscrewed the lid of the water jug. "Kyle's potion is in that blood and I need to hinder as much of it as possible if I'm going to get to the blood's owner."

"Yeah, but why am I doing this?"

"I thought you'd want to help," I said with a smirk. "That and I don't want the salt on my hands. It could mess with my control of the spell."

"And that'd be bad."

"Real bad," I muttered, watching the salt slip through her fingers and rain onto the floor. I'd have to go through tomorrow and try to pick up most of the salt. I didn't want to risk it coming back to bite me in the ass later when I was casting down here. "That should be enough. Hand me the jar and carefully shake any remaining salt out of the paper towel."

Screwing on the lid on, I shoved the half-empty jar back into my pocket as Serah rejoined me at the circle.

"What are you going to do?"

"Build a killer," I said with a smile that she didn't return. Picking up the jug, I held it out so she could see it. "All living creatures have at least three basic elements. Earth." I paused and pointed to the nice, fresh dirt within the circle. The shit was expensive. It took me two years to have it all shipped in from a remote island in the Pacific. "Water." I held up the jug of water, which had started as snow. This snow water was from the first snowfall of 2011, which turned out to be a heavy snow year. Pouring the water into my cupped left hand, I then sprinkled it over the dirt within the circle. I repeated this three times while whispering the first words of the spell. After a moment, the drops stopped falling and were captured in the air, becoming a mist.

"Whoa," Serah whispered, taking a tiny step backward. "And the third is the blood," she said, holding out the paper towel toward me.

I shook my head, but smiled encouragingly at her. It was a good guess. Putting the jug back on the ground, I grabbed the box of wooden matches and withdrew one. "Nope. It's energy. The closest I can come to reproducing that same energy without blowing the roof off this place is fire." Striking the match, I let it burn for a second so that the flame was as large as I could get it and then dropped it into the center of the circle. Like the drops of water, the burning match stopped falling a couple feet from the ground, flickering within the thickening mist.

The magic energy within the basement thickened, and a strange breeze stirred the hairs on the back of my neck. This spell tapped into something deeper, more basic than what most warlocks and witches ever bother with. It was as close to the old magic as any of us ever got. Old magic, the stuff of the big bang and the start of life, was wild and untamed. It didn't like to be controlled, and the inhabitants of the Ivory Towers were all about control.

I took one last glance up at the back wall and the protective spell that had nearly attacked Serah just minutes ago. It wasn't completely dormant but appeared content to watch us. I was really gonna have to find a new security system for down here.

Plucking the wadded-up paper towel out of Serah's open hand, I whispered the last words of the spell and dropped it into the center of the circle. The air shifted and stirred within the circle as if I had created a mini tornado. The dirt, water, and fire mixed together, spinning around so that the bloody towel was at the center. What I hadn't told Serah was that the blood contained the tiniest bit of the killer's soul and I had just added it to the pseudo-person I had created. Unfortunately, I'd never had a reason to use this spell and I wasn't quite sure what the blood was going to carry into my creation.

After a couple of seconds, the swirling mist started to clear and we could see the beginning of some form. The creature had two legs and two arms, which didn't help to narrow down the species much. Color flushed its pale skin, revealing a human-like complexion, which narrowed the field a little further. The killer was proving to be slighter in frame than I had been expecting, considering it had overpowered Kyle, beaten him to a bloody pulp, and stabbed him in the chest with his tattooing gun.

"Holy shit," Serah whispered.

Following her gaze, my own mouth dropped open. "Fuck." Whoever this was had a really nice set of breasts. I was not expecting a woman to be Kyle's killer. After seeing such brutality, I had been sure that it was a man who'd killed him.

The creature within the circle stirred, lifting its featureless face. Glowing red eyes focused on me and my heart jerked in my chest. The creature was conscious in some way, which shouldn't have been possible since it was little more than a shadow of the original person. But it was aware of me. This was not good, particularly since my protection spell had noticed it as well. Was the protection spell going to think that a third person was now in the basement? *Really not fucking good.* "Serah, I want you to go calmly and quickly up the stairs now."

"Why?"

"Please, do it now."

Too late.

Something had finally snapped within the creature I'd summoned. Its face contorted, as though it was screaming, but no sound came out. It launched itself at me and slammed into the invisible barrier that rose up from the circle. Lurching back, it pounded its fists and clawed at the binding spell, fighting to get at me. At the same time, the defensive spell broke free, ready to shred the creature that was trying to attack me. Unfortunately, the spell was prepared to go through me and Serah to get at my would-be attacker.

Diving into Serah, I tackled the small woman into

the dirt, covering her as best as I could. Pain slashed across my back near my shoulders like someone had taken a hot blade to my flesh. I swallowed back a scream, tightening my hold on the woman beneath me. A black mass circled the bound creature I had summoned. They slashed again and again at each other, but neither made contact because neither was technically there. Only Serah and I were at risk of being killed.

As soon as I could draw in a breath through the pain, I shouted the counter-spell to lock up the protective force in the symbol again. The black mass gave a high-pitched scream of frustration that scraped across my eardrums before diving back into the symbol. The creature in the circle pounded on the wall of its cage a couple more times, but with less force, before disappearing as well. The water and fire were spent. All that was left was a fine ash hanging in the air. Sadly, the killer's features had never fully resolved, so we couldn't make a positive I.D.

Fuck. While the effort hadn't been a waste, it certainly wasn't as fruitful as I was hoping it would be, particularly considering that we had nearly been killed in the process.

With a groan, I rolled onto my side so that Serah could move free of me, while being careful not to press the open wound on my back into the dirt. Dirt was good for spells; bad for gaping, bleeding wounds. Serah didn't move. She stared up at me with wide, stunned eyes; her face was stark white except for a smear of dirt across her cheek.

I tried to smile, but I was suddenly too tired. Muscles twitched and trembled from exhaustion. It had taken a considerable about of energy to summon the creature and hold it within the circle. A second helping of energy had been required to shove my so-called guard dog back in its kennel. I was ready to sleep right where I lay. "Sorry about that," I mumbled, trying to pull myself together for the poor human who was having a rough night.

"Yeah . . . ummm . . . thanks." She sounded shaken, but was holding it together a little better than when she first discovered that I was a warlock.

Clenching my teeth, I pushed to my feet, struggling to ignore the pain that was screaming across my back. "No problem. I'm sorry we didn't get a better look at the face, but I think it's a pretty safe bet that the killer is a human female."

"Maybe. Were the eyes supposed to be red? Is she possessed?"

I stood staring at the circle where I had cast the spell. The ash was starting to settle, but there was still a smell hanging in the air, part burnt ozone and part . . . something else. "No, they shouldn't have been, but she's not possessed. She wouldn't have looked human if she had been, but more like the creature possessing her. The red was a reflection of her soul, her rage. I'm guessing that the potion Kyle tattooed her with has only amplified her strength and her anger."

"Are you sure she's human?" Serah took a step closer to the circle and then appeared to think twice about it as she rocked back on her heels. "There are a number of races that look very similar to humans but technically aren't. Sirens and succubi. Maybe even an elf."

"Maybe." I shrugged and then winced as pain cut across my wounded back. "But there's something about the woman. Just feels human. I'm sorry I can't explain it."

"You sure it doesn't have to do with her boobs?"

I glared at Serah and she glared right back. Sure, I'd noticed the creature's boobs, but then I'd been shocked that they were there in the first place. That's what I got for being sexist when it came to acts of violence.

"Anyways . . . I think we've got a start, though not as big of one as I'd hoped."

"I'm not sure what we can do next." Serah shoved one hand through her mussed short hair. "It's not like we got a good look at her face to get an ID. I also don't think you want me going to the police, describing how I know that it's a woman we're after."

A stiff grin twitched on my lips. "I'd prefer it if you didn't."

"Then what do we do?"

"I need you to do two things. One: try to get another sample of her blood. I want to see if I can come up with a tracking spell."

Serah nodded. "I think I can come up with an excuse to get my hands on another sample. Two?"

"Use your contacts with the police to keep you in the loop on this."

"With the crime being a murder, they have jurisdiction. Not TAPSS."

"I know, but you've still got plenty of friends on the force, right? You can pull some information out."

Her eyes narrowed and she slowly shook her head at me. "That's why you told me. You need me to give you the information that the cops have."

I started to shrug but stopped myself rather than strain the seeping wound. "I can do it myself, but my magic use might catch the attention of the Towers and we need the Towers involved."

"Yeah," she breathed. She turned away from me, her eyes skimming over the basement with a new understanding. This wasn't the realm of a tattoo artist. It also wasn't the realm of the Ivory Towers, but of one rogue warlock. She was somewhere no human had ever tread and lived. When she turned back, I could see all the questions colliding in her brain, fighting to jump off the tip of her tongue first.

Lifting my hand to stop whatever she was going to say next, I smiled weakly at her. "Can we hold off the questions for another time? It's really fucking late and my back is killing me."

"Can I have just two questions?"

"Yeah, I guess." I didn't want to answer any more questions, but I figured she had earned them considering how poorly the night had gone.

"Why are you doing this? I mean, I know you said that you're doing it because of Trixie, but is that really the only reason?"

I scrubbed my hand over my face, sure that I was now rubbing in dirt but I just didn't give a damn. For Trixie, I would do anything, but Serah was right. The elf wasn't the only reason I was standing in the basement just a couple hours before dawn bleeding. "Something she said, that I was the only one who could do this, stuck with me. You've got a killer who has been created based on a powerful potion. You're going to need someone versed in a little magic to track this person down and I don't see anyone else from the Towers volunteering."

She made a little noise of acceptance in the back of her throat and nodded. "When this is over and the killer is caught, are you going to kill me?"

"No, Serah, I'm not going to kill you," I groaned, more than a little agitated that this topic kept coming up.

"I'm serious!" she snapped, looking as if she really wanted to stomp her foot in frustration. "You're trusting me with a big secret. You don't know me."

Anger bubbled from the petite woman, but the protection spell didn't stir, so I took it as a sign that she wasn't violently upset with me. "No, I don't know you, but I trust you not to tell anyone while we're working together because you don't want to see me lynched."

"And when it's over?"

"I'll wipe your memory."

Her face bunched up a bit at that pronouncement as if she were weighing the alternative, which was definitely death in her mind. "Will it hurt?"

I chuckled as I walked back over to the table in the

far corner and picked up her gun. I'd clean up this mess tomorrow. I was too damn tired now. "No, it won't hurt."

At my urging, she preceded me up the stairs. I turned off the light and returned the protection spell to its normal active status before ascending the stairs to the tattoo parlor.

A quick glance at the clock revealed that we'd been down there less than a half hour but it felt like it had been far longer than that. Dawn was only a couple hours away and I was eager to get to bed for a few hours. There really was no chance of salvaging the evening.

"Get some sleep," I said, handing her gun back.

Serah clicked the safety back on before shoving it into her shoulder holster. Reaching in her back pocket, she pulled out her wallet and withdrew a little card. "Here. Call me if you hear from the goblins. I'm going with you."

"Yes, ma'am," I said with a smirk as I shoved the card in my pocket. She was adjusting to the knowledge that I was a warlock pretty fast. But then, most people in Low Town adjusted fast. There was too much weird shit here and if you didn't adapt, you were likely eaten . . . or you just went insane.

CHAPTER 7

Gravel crunched and pinged against the undercarriage of Bronx's Jeep as he slipped off the old narrow road onto a weed-choked pull-off that might have once been someone's driveway. After spending the majority of the day leaning on my few contacts with fingers in illegal activities, I finally had the address to a farmhouse in the middle of nowhere. It was supposedly the goblins' base of operations. Dropping in unexpectedly wasn't smart, but goblins weren't the friendliest of creatures. They weren't going to be happy to see me even if I was there on business, and trying to go through the right channels to schedule a meeting would have taken days if not weeks.

Of course, I wasn't in the best of moods either. Trixie hadn't been waiting for me at my apartment when I returned last night. She'd kindly put dinner into old butter bowls and placed them in the fridge before leaving me a note stating that she'd gone home after talking to Bronx. It had been tempting to go over to her place and slide into bed next to her, but instead I stretched out on the couch and glared at the ceiling until sleep claimed me. She needed her space. Between the news of my return to the dark side and Kyle's death, Trixie could use some time to herself.

I was even proud of the fact that I'd managed to refrain from rushing over to her place first thing in the morning, but rather waited until noon to call her. Her lovely voice drifted through the phone to me, sounding strong but wary as she promised to return to my place that evening to get an update on any progress made in finding Kyle's killer.

But all that self-control had left me edgy and pissed.

The troll turned off the engine and killed the lights. The heavy silence of winter consumed the night, threatening to suffocate us. There were no chirping crickets, no howl of the wind, and no distant hoot of an owl. Just a vast nothingness and the cold gleaming snow set against a black sky.

"How do you want to handle this?" Bronx asked. His seat creaked as he turned to look at me in the passenger seat. Serah's coat rustled softly as she moved closer, ready to join in our little adventure.

"I thought we'd just talk to them. Nothing too strenuous," I said, my eyes skimming over the large white three-story farmhouse rising up like a forgotten sentinel against the darkness. Nothing moved and there was only a faint glimmer of light peeking out of a heavily shaded window on the second floor.

Serah scoffed and flopped back against the back-seat. Glancing over at Bronx, I found the troll frowning at me, his yellow eyes narrowed.

"Have you dealt with goblins before?" Bronx said, sounding more than a little skeptical.

"No. Not directly."

"This won't go well," he muttered.

"Yeah, I've heard that they're a pain in the ass, but they can't be entirely unreasonable." Lifting my left hand, I rubbed my eyes with my thumb and forefinger. A dull ache had started along the bridge of my nose and was creeping through my skull. "They run an underground business. How can you ever hope to have customers if you can't talk with them?"

"The goblins started this little enterprise because they've discovered that they love gold more than they love eating human babies," Bronx explained. "They don't give a damn about seeing that childless vampires are able to have a family of their own. They don't even care if these children go to good homes. They want the money these desperate people are willing to pay."

"And when you're desperate, you're willing to put up with a lot of shit," Serah chimed in from behind me, her soft voice pricking my conscience. Was I some of the shit she was willing to put up with just so she'd get a little respect from her coworkers? Wonderful.

"Look, we find the ringleader and we ask if they've

heard anything about these murders," I said sharply as I grabbed the handle on the door. "That's it. Once we get our answers, we leave. I've got other things I'd rather be doing tonight."

Without waiting for my companions to agree with my poorly thought out plan, I shoved open the door of the Jeep and climbed out. A small wave of relief swept through me when I heard two more doors open and close behind me. I preferred to have Bronx with me during this encounter. He had a knack for pulling my ass out of the fire. I wasn't as confident about Serah. She might have been a police officer for five years, but there was no telling what kind of experiences had filled those five years. Had she ever been in a high-stress, shoot-or-be-killed situation? I wasn't ready to bet my life on that.

"I'm sure I probably shouldn't ask," Serah said as she walked with me on my right.

"Then don't," I snapped.

"But is there any chance you can use your hocus pocus to speed this along?" she whispered.

I fought the urge to roll my eyes. Despite her attempts to be quiet, I was sure that Bronx had heard her. The cold, still air carried her words too easily, but at least she was attempting to keep my secret to herself. When I rolled off the couch this morning, I was partially expecting to find a lynch mob waving torches and pitchforks outside my window. I was mildly disappointed when they weren't there.

"No, I will not be using any hocus pocus, hoodoo,

or voodoo to get us through this interview," I growled, not caring who heard me.

"No abracadabra?" Bronx pushed.

"No."

The silence was punctuated by the crunch of the frozen snow under our feet as we marched up the winding drive to the farmhouse. A couple inches of fresh snow had fallen that afternoon, coating the world in a twinkling blanket of white. It was like living in a cheap, dime-store novelty snow globe. A thin layer of snow underfoot, black sky above, and cliché Norman Rockwell winter scene in the foreground. Of course, I doubted that old Norman ever imagined goblins on the other side of those windows. But I could be wrong.

"You ever try to pull a rabbit out of a hat?" Bronx asked, surprising a laugh out of Serah.

Glancing over my shoulder, I glimpsed the tiny smirk that was lifting one corner of the troll's fat lips. "Keep it up and I'll a rabbit out of your ass." But my threat fell flat because I was struggling not to smile as well. *Bastard.* Bronx always knew how to put a stop to my sulks whether I wanted him to or not.

While trolls were unattractive from a human point of view, I'll have to say that they could have passed for supermodels when compared to goblins. Covered in pasty greenish gray skin that always looked greasy, the goblins possessed long, spidery limbs and narrow torsos, as if they spent the majority of their lives tee-tering on the edge of starvation. Their sunken milky orange eyes glowed, reflecting the light as if you could see the fire of madness burning in their souls. You just prayed they didn't smile, revealing a mouthful of crooked, jagged yellow teeth.

Goblins were the stuff of nightmares and were what you thought of when it came to the monster under your bed or hiding in your closet. If you were unfortunate enough to have something under your bed as a child, there was a good chance that it was a goblin rather than the extremely rare boogeyman. He just wanted to steal a couple years of your childhood. The goblin wanted to strip your flesh from your bones while you were still alive.

Taking a deep breath, I pounded on the front door. A goblin just a few inches shorter than Serah jerked the door open and stared at us in confusion. "Appointment?" he demanded in a high, squeaky voice that sounded like he was dragging his pointed teeth along a chalkboard for shits and giggles.

"No, we don't have an appointment," I replied, wincing. It felt like my eardrums were starting to bleed.

The door slammed shut in my face before I could catch it.

"I believe that was the wrong answer," Bronx said blandly.

Flipping my friend off with my left hand, I pounded on the front door with my right. The door was pulled open a couple seconds later by a different goblin. This one was my height but he was missing his right eye. Unfortunately, he wasn't wearing an eye patch so you could clearly see the poorly healed hole in the creature's head.

"Appointment?" he demanded in a rough voice. I was willing to guess that whatever had taken his eye had also tried to rip out his throat.

"No, we need information," I quickly replied. I took a breath to explain that I wished to speak to their boss, but I didn't get a chance.

"This ain't a library," the one-eyed goblin announced before slamming the door shut.

"Strike two," Serah murmured, earning a chuckle from Bronx.

Oh, this was just fucking dandy! I was so glad that my companions were having fun while I was getting the door slammed in my face. Magic was starting to look appealing, but I'd already proclaimed that I wasn't going to use magic. Growling, I reminded myself that I didn't need it for every little damned thing, and pounded on the door again.

We waited longer this time before the door was pulled open by a third goblin. Taller than his other companions, his large lower lip was split down the middle from where it had been cut and never properly sewn up. What bothered me was the faint light of intelligence that sparked in his eyes, unlike the other two.

"Appointment?" he said.

"Yes," I said with a hearty sigh. My right arm shot out and wrapped around Serah's shoulders before I jerked her against my side in a tight embrace, earning a surprised squeak from her. "We're the Smiths. Gage and Serah Smith."

The goblin's scraggly eyebrows rose on his sloped forehead and he sniffed the air slightly. "You smell like cops."

"Nope," I quickly replied, upping the wattage of my smile in an effort to look even more harmless. "I'm a tattoo artist in Low Town and my wife is a postal clerk." I felt Serah stiffen under my hand but I squeezed her arm through her coat and she flashed the goblin a somewhat manic smile.

"And him?" The goblin jerked his pointed chin toward the troll standing behind me.

"Enforcer for Jack and the Low Town Pack," Bronx explained before I could come up with a viable excuse as to why a desperate human couple had brought along a large troll to a black-market baby dealer. "If you can help them, the pack gets a finder's fee for pointing them in your direction."

"You work for Reave?" the goblin demanded, still sounding more than a little skeptical.

Bronx grunted. "Till the dark elf was snatched by the Towers."

The troll's answer sounded convincing. Of course, Bronx had been a member of the underworld once and had worked for the mob boss Reave, but that had been a long time ago. . . . Well, sort of. He'd given it up until I'd fucked up his life and dragged him back in when he'd saved my life. Yeah, that's what friends are for.

The goblin stepped back, opening the door wide

enough for me to enter the farmhouse first, trailed by my companions. From the foyer, I could see the dining room on my right and the living room on the left, while a narrow staircase led to a dark second floor. The furniture in the living room was ragged, with the stuffing poking out through the rips in the stained fabric. There was a table and a trio of chairs set up in the dining room. A scattering of paper covered the table, indicating that it likely served as some type of office. The rooms I could see were lit by a collection of candles and old kerosene lamps, creating a thick nest of shadows and a low haze of smoke about the place.

"Wait," the goblin ordered, pointing toward the chairs in the dining room.

I nodded, grabbing Serah's hand and pulling her along with me while trying to maintain an appearance of nervous fear and hopefulness. It wasn't hard. Serah just looked anxious, which worked for our lie. I couldn't see Bronx as he continued to stand behind me, but I was confident in his ability to look intimidating. With the mass of a small mountain, the troll had "frightening" down to an art.

"A postal clerk?" Serah demanded in a harsh whisper as soon as we were alone.

"Sue me. I blanked. Be grateful I didn't say swimsuit model or telemarketer."

"Asshole," she grumbled under her breath.

I ignored her comment and turned my head so that I could see Bronx from the corner of my eye. "How many are here?"

"More than three?" Bronx offered.

I was about to snap at him when Serah spoke. "Between two and three dozen on the low side. Goblin clans tend to be very large when they have the space and assurance of safety. This location would have likely been outside of Reave's reach unless they had some kind of special arrangement with the dark elf. Either way, we're massively outnumbered."

I didn't question how she knew about Reave. It was likely that she would have heard about the bastard while she worked as a cop. What surprised me was her knowledge of goblins. They weren't your average criminal and were pretty good about avoiding the notice of the local law enforcement, even if their main business was illegal. In short, goblins wouldn't have been required reading for surviving Low Town's streets.

The TAPSS investigator looked up at me with wide, expectant eyes. "Is it true? Was Reave grabbed by the Towers?"

Even though the dark elf had been killed three months ago, his death wasn't common knowledge yet. There had been no grand announcement, news report, or celebration. To most, he'd simply disappeared— possibly returning to the bosom of his own people, the Svartálfar, but some knew the truth.

"Yeah, he's gone," I mumbled, leaving out the part about how I'd been the one to kill him at the request of the Towers' council. Turning to look at Bronx, eager to forget about Reave, I asked, "Would they keep their supply here?"

Bronx frowned. I was treading carefully here. I didn't want to get involved in the baby black market. Don't get me wrong: I didn't like the idea of babies being in the hands of goblins, but the upside was that these kids were going to people who couldn't have children and didn't have legal options. It had taken the world centuries to give same-sex couples the right to adopt. Vampires were still fucking years away, as well as a number of mixed couples. Who said a banshee and an incubus couldn't be great parents? Or a were-bear and a leprechaun? Hell of a lot better than the Towers.

"Unlikely," he said with a slight shake of his head. "They'd keep them separated from prospective parents in case negotiations went south. Why?"

"In case questioning goes south," I said, turning toward the foyer at the sound of approaching footsteps. If things went bad, I didn't want to worry about the safety of any children who might be on the premises. Even with Bronx's assurances, I was still worried there was a baby hidden somewhere.

Of course, I would have to worry about that later, as footsteps thundered across the bare hardwood floor, sounding larger in number than what should be approaching us.

"Got any more ideas?" Serah asked, taking a couple steps away from me and reaching under her coat to her back. She pulled out the gun she had hidden in the back of her pants and flipped off the safety with her index finger.

"Keep that hidden for now," I said, waving her

behind me. "Let's see if we can still talk our way out of this."

That proved to be wishful thinking on my part. A six-foot-tall goblin strode in, surrounded by more than twenty goblins of all shapes and sizes. The leader's orange eyes glowed like beady fires in his wrinkled face, and pointed at me. "You lie!" he shrieked.

"Whoa! Hold on a second!" I shouted back, holding my open hands out toward him while putting myself between my companions and the goblins. "We're just here to talk. Nothing more."

"You bring a troll and a cop into our nest and you say this is only talk? Lies," he hissed, taking a step closer. Around him, the other goblins brandished knives and vicious claw-like weapons that would do incredible damage if sunk into the flesh.

"Pregnant women are being killed in Low Town by some maniac. We only wanted to ask you if you've seen anything. Have you heard anything?"

"The killer? The baby killer? You know of this person?" the leader demanded, sending a ripple of unease through the gathered goblins. They had stopped speaking English and were chattering amongst themselves in a guttural, sharp language that I couldn't understand, but with each passing second the group was growing more excited.

I took a wary step backward as several started screaming and waving their weapons again. This was really bad. They weren't listening and the situation was quickly slipping out of my control. Or rather, I was finally coming to the realization that I had never really been in control of this situation. I'd gone looking for a shortcut and I was about to pay the price. And in my recklessness, I'd dragged two innocent people along for the ride.

"Look, we're just looking for some answers!" I shouted over the growing noise.

"Have you led the killer to us? Threaten us? Threaten our business?" the leader shrieked.

"No!" I screamed over the din, but no one was listening to me now. The horde of goblins charged, pouring over me to surge toward my companions and fill the room.

For a moment, there was just a tangle of teeth and claws converging on us. They scattered briefly when Serah fired her gun in the air once, but they hesitated for only a breath before convincing themselves that their overwhelming numbers would win in the end.

Dropping down into a crouch, I launched my first attacker over my shoulder, sending him crashing into the table in the center of the room. The wobbly structure collapsed under his weight, scattering paper and pens. The lamp on the table clattered to the ground, splashing kerosene across the floor. The light went out, casting everyone in deep shadow as the faint glow from the next room could only stretch thinly to where we were pinned down.

I grabbed the chair closest to me and swung it into the face of the next goblin to reach me. An ugly crack echoed above the shouts and the wood frame shuddered in my hand, only to give way completely when I brought it down on the back of a second goblin.

Swinging the chair like an enraged lumberjack, I mowed down my opponents, forcing them back as I tried to reach Serah. I glimpsed four goblins writhing on the floor, clutching carefully placed wounds as they howled in pain. The swarm was giving her a little more space. They slowly stalked her, searching for an opening.

"An escape plan would be nice!" she shouted above the din before squeezing off a round into the groin of a goblin who had gotten too close.

I flinched as he went down, his low keening sending the remaining goblins scrambling away from her and over to me. The remains of the chair shrank in my hand with every swing until I was left with a jagged stake. We had been pushed back, while the horde of goblins didn't seem to be waning. For every one that fell, two more popped up to replace him. They were wearing us down.

Dodging another goblin who had lunged at me, I thumped him in the throat before kicking him away. In a second I had between opponents, I found Bronx had been pushed back toward the front window. We had our exit.

"Bronx!" I shouted, catching the troll's attention. "Behind you!" As the massive creature turned sharply, his elbow hit a goblin about to strike, knocking him into the window. The tinkle of glass was a pleasant sound. Bronx smiled and picked up his would-be attacker. With a low grunt, he tossed him through the window, where he bounced across the front lawn.

Stepping over another goblin, I grabbed the sleeve of Serah's coat and jerked her toward Bronx. Unfortunately, I pulled her off balance. She knocked into small side table that had been hidden from my view. Two flickering candles fell to the floor. One went out. Time slowed down as we all froze, watching in growing horror as the flickering candle rolled to the spreading pool of red kerosene that was soaking into the old hardwood floor.

"Shit!" I muttered before pushing Serah ahead of me to the window. The whoosh of the growing flames nearly drowned out the screams of panic. I shoved Serah out the window, hoping she avoided the jagged teeth of the broken glass. Diving after her, I kept rolling for several feet across the frozen ground to give Bronx some room to follow me.

When I stopped to catch my breath while lying on my back, I looked at the house to see that a good chunk of the lower level on the right side was already engulfed and the flames were spreading to the second floor. Panic riding hard behind the rush of adrenaline, I fought hard to slip into my inner center of calm as I gathered together the magical energy in the surrounding air. A quick whisper of words gave me insight into the occupants of the house—they were only goblins. Bronx had been right. They weren't keeping any of the babies in the farmhouse.

The relief that swept through me brought the sting

of tears to my eyes and my hands trembled. Most of the goblins were escaping into the woods to the south, heading away from us. Some would die in the flames, but I couldn't summon up the remorse I was sure I was supposed to be feeling. I was just too grateful that we hadn't accidently killed any children in our poor attempt to contact the goblin black market.

A soft laugh dragged my gaze from the burning structure to find Serah on her knees in the snow, staring at the house. Her laughter grew until she was shaking her head and holding her stomach. Sitting up, I found Bronx watching her with an equally quizzical expression. When she caught our confused looks, she smothered her laugh and pushed to her feet.

"I get why the TAPSS vamps are scared of you now," she said, as I came to stand beside her. When I didn't quite get what she was alluding to, she waved her hand to the burning building just a couple yards away. "We're just going ask a few questions," she said sarcastically.

I looked back at the house. Both floors were ablaze now, creating a massive orange-and-yellow ball of fire in the middle of the open field, pushing the darkness back. The kerosene lamps spread around the old building were speeding up the process, so that we were now sweating in the bitter cold as waves of heat poured from the farmhouse. The roar of the flames had become a ravenous monster set loose on the house, consuming anything within its path. God, I hoped this wasn't a bigger fucking metaphor for the things in my life.

"I guess we should have started smaller," Bronx said, scratching his chin thoughtfully. He lifted one bushy blond eyebrow as he looked down at me. "Just grabbed one goblin for questioning instead of going to the source."

I gave a jerky nod, frustration eating away at my patience. I was accustomed to going to the heart of the matter rather than sneaking around. When I had questions, I went directly to the person who had the answers. Obviously, the direct approach had been the wrong tactic when it came to dealing with goblins. Unfortunately, I was too eager to have this wrapped up so I could turn my full attention to putting a smile back on Trixie's lips. It just wasn't going to be that easy.

"I'll have to remember that," I murmured.

Serah stood and dusted the last bits of snow and dirt from her jeans. "What do we do now?"

Shoving my hands into the pockets of my coat, I led the way back to Bronx's Jeep. We were far enough out in the middle of nowhere that it was unlikely any neighbors would call in the fire, but I didn't want to be around when someone decided to investigate. "We keep digging. I'll see if I can find a new way get info from the baby black market. You need to see if your cop buddies have discovered anything useful."

"And me?" Bronx's keys jingled softly when he drew them out of his pocket as he fell into step beside me.

I paused, trying to think of any possible avenues of information that we hadn't explored yet, when an idea hit me. "Contact Jack."

"Werewolf Jack?" Bronx said, his brow furrowing at my suggestion. "I thought he didn't like you."

"He's gotten over it. Well, mostly." *You turn a guy into a chihuahua and he doesn't like to forgive you for it.* However, this past All Hallows' Eve I helped his pack out at the risk of Trixie's life. We were square. It also didn't hurt that I got his pack out from under Reave's thumb and put him in control of the Low Town underworld.

Pulling open the passenger door when Bronx unlocked it, I raised my voice so he could hear me over the vehicle. "See if Jack's people have heard anything. A psycho killing pregnant women has got to have stirred up some chatter."

Taking one last look at the house as Bronx drove down the deserted country road, I prayed that tonight's botched attempt to get us closer to the killer didn't result in a massive waste of time. The longer it took to find this insane bitch, the higher the likelihood that more people were going to die.

CHAPTER 8

When Trixie walked into my apartment later that evening, my frustration was pushed out the window in favor of gut-twisting anxiety. We hadn't talked about my grand reveal from the night before and I didn't have anything positive to relay from my adventure with Serah and Bronx out to see the goblins. All in all, I was feeling pretty damn useless.

Her smile was strained and uncertain when she stripped off her winter coat and tossed it over the arm of the sofa. And for the first time since we had started dating, I hesitated to hug her. I looked at her and I couldn't tell if she would welcome affection from me.

"How was your day?" I asked, shoving my hands deep into the pockets of my jeans just so I didn't do something stupid with them like reach for her.

"Long. Boring," she said with a shrug as she dropped onto the sofa. The shop was closed on Sunday, but I think she would have preferred to have been working so that her mind wasn't drawn back to the ugly truth. She was dating a warlock. "How about you? Learn anything interesting?"

Shaking my head, I sat on the center cushion of the couch, close to her so that I could easily reach out to touch her, but still with some space between us. "No. The whole fucking thing was a disaster."

"You . . ." she started, but her voice drifted off as she looked at me funny for a second. "That fire I heard about on the news wasn't from you guys, was it?"

I flopped back on the sofa and covered my face with my hands. "That wasn't my freaking fault. We just went in to ask them some questions. They're the ones who decided to launch an attack on us. There were like fifty of them against the three of us! What the fuck! Things got crazy and the fire started accidentally."

My hands dropped at the sound of her soft laughter. She smiled at me, a look of sympathy and amusement dancing in her eyes for the first time in too long. "I'm sure you never meant to burn the place down."

I groaned. "If I had, I'd at least have the balls to admit to it." I dropped my head back against the couch, staring at the ceiling as the comfortable silence settled into the room at last. "Serah is trying to get information out of her police connections. Bronx is going to talk to Jack. Maybe the pack has heard something. It's moving slowly, but with any luck we should have a lead on this woman."

"Woman?" Trixie said with a horrified gasp.

I winced, suddenly remembering that I hadn't yet told her of the spell I had cast in the basement of Asylum with Serah. As quickly as possible, I ran through the events while reassuring her that I planned to wipe the investigator's memory as soon as this was all settled.

"Maybe you shouldn't," Trixie said, chewing on her lower lip.

"What? Let her keep that knowledge? It's a big risk."

"Yes, but if you think you can trust her, maybe her knowing would get Asylum a little more slack from TAPSS. We both know they love to come down on you." The elf gave a little shrug, her wide green eyes drifting away from me. "But you don't have to listen to me. It's your secret."

Reaching out, I placed my hand against her cheek and gently turned her head so that she was looking at me again. "It's not just my secret anymore. You're impacted by those who know about me. It's a matter of your safety as well."

Trixie took a deep breath, her expression growing sad. "And exactly how safe am I, with you back at the Towers?"

"You're safe," I said firmly. "As a member of the guardians, the witches and warlocks don't have a reason to hunt me like they once did. I do a job for them every once in a while. Then I come home and forget all about it. They aren't going to come after me and I won't let anyone come after you."

"But doesn't that mean you'll be forced to kill people for the Towers? That you'll have to hand over people for interrogation? How can you live among these people, pretending to be one of them, only to betray them later?" she demanded, her words growing more desperate so that they tumbled over one another in a rush to escape.

I stared at her, watching her chest rise and fall with each heavy breath, as if she had been running a race. Her words hadn't been tinged with anger or disgust but with fear and worry. She was scared for me, for my safety, and I think even for my soul and sanity. I was living a double life, and the likelihood of failure was high.

"I know there will be times that I can't avoid doing the will of the Towers, but I think most of the time, I'll be able to act as a buffer for the people of the world. I can do a better job of protecting them as an insider than I ever could while I was hiding from the Towers." Trixie started to shake her head, but I grabbed one of her hands in both of mine. "I can. Gideon has done it for years. He was tasked with watching over me, but his real orders were to find an excuse to kill me for breaking the agreement I made when I left. God knows I gave him plenty of opportunities over the years, but he hid the truth, protecting me. It's time I returned the favor."

"But you're a target," she whispered. "Because of who you are, you'll always be a target."

I tightened my hold on her hand. "It'll pass. We're just in a bad time right now. Things will settle down soon."

I hoped I was right. God, I *needed* to be right about this. The past year had been pretty damn crazy. Between the Grim Reaper, Simon, Reave, the Ivory Towers, and even the incident with the Wild Hunt this past fall, we were constantly rushing from one disaster to the next. Every time I thought things were going to go back to normal, something new popped up to drag me back into the thick of things.

"Would you mind if I lay down for a little while? I'm starting to get a headache," Trixie asked, already pushing to her feet.

"No." I hovered close as I followed her to my bedroom. I remained in the doorway, watching as she kicked off her shoes and slid under the blankets.

Trixie was nearly as tall as me and had always been this beacon of shining light and strength, but something had changed recently so that now she felt so much smaller and more vulnerable to me. When she was hunted by her brother, she'd been afraid and hurting, but there had always been an underlying strength and a fire of determination. Something had put out that fire and I was starting to suspect that it was me.

Refusing to let her go without a fight, I started forward with the intention of climbing into bed with her when my cell phone started vibrating in my back pocket. Trixie graced me with a weak smile, indicating that it was okay that I answer it before I joined her.

Stepping out of the bedroom, I paced to the living room. "What?" I snapped into the phone. Any distraction that took me from Trixie was unwelcome, but I was also hoping for some kind of good news that might lift her spirits.

"Well, aren't you just a chipper fellow?" Serah mocked.

"I'm a little busy at the moment. What's up?"

"I talked to a friend at the station. They haven't been able to get anything from the blood and they're very doubtful that they ever will. However, they seem to think they might be able to identify all the ingredients for the potion. I was wondering if that would help you in tracking the killer."

I frowned at the sliding glass doors, watching the haggard man glaring back at me in my reflection. I looked like shit. "I don't know. I don't think so, but it doesn't hurt. Have they found anything in Kyle's records that identifies who his most recent clients were?"

"No. The man kept horrible records. It also looks like the killer might have been smart enough to grab any identifying paperwork before she left. They're still digging."

"I would—" Trixie's scream halted the words in my throat and squeezed my heart in a vise. Instantly dropping the phone, I raced to my bedroom.

I stopped on the threshold of the room to find a goblin struggling to pick up Trixie as she fought him while a second goblin was climbing in the window. They'd followed me. I'd been so focused on getting home to Trixie that I hadn't noticed that I was being tailed by goblins. Scooping up one of the hard-soled shoes I wore while out with Gideon, I launched it at the goblin climbing in the window. It smashed into his ugly face, knocking him back so that he was hanging by his claws on the window frame.

The other goblin roared in pain as Trixie plunged her fingers into his eyes. He released her to cover his face, but she couldn't escape because her legs were tangled up in the blankets still. Leaping over her onto the bed, I grabbed the goblin by his large pointed ears and threw him into his companion in the window. Their collision knocked the one in the window loose. His scream echoed through the silent night as he fell three stories to the parking lot below.

The goblin who had attacked Trixie snarled at me as he threw one leg out the window. "You started this war when you attacked us! You stole members of my clan. I will take her from you."

I jumped down to the floor, keeping my body positioned between Trixie and the remaining goblin. "I didn't start this! I just wanted to ask you some questions! You attacked us," I shouted back.

He thought about this for a second before narrowing his bright orange eyes on me. "We are not satisfied." And then he was gone.

Rushing over to the now vacant window, I looked down to find him helping the other goblin to his feet before they disappeared in the thick shadows of the parking lot. *Great!* Not only was I trying to track down a serial killer, but I had managed to piss off the local goblin clan. Shutting the window, I stared at the wood frame for a second. I needed to lay down some better protective spells. The ones I had used were too specific, aimed at magic users and vampires. I needed something broader that would keep out goblins as well.

With a weary sigh, I turned back to find Trixie sitting in the center of the bed, the sheets a twisted mess around her, tears slipping silently down her cheeks. Dropping onto the bed, I pulled her into my arms.

"Are you hurt? Did they hurt you?" I demanded, my voice rough with worry.

She shook her head against my shoulder as she clung tightly to me. As we sat there, her crying grew worse instead of better, as if the incident were finally sinking in. I held her tight, my hands rubbing up and down her back. "I'm sorry, Trix. I'm so damn sorry. I never thought they'd follow me," I murmured in her hair. I felt like shit, but I could still fix this. "I'll put better protection spells around the apartment and then I'll go to your place and lay them down there. I'll put them down at Asylum as well. Those fucking bastards will never get close to you again."

"I can't do this anymore," she whispered in a choked voice as her tears slowed.

Pulling away slightly, I looked down at her face, my heart stopping in my chest. "What do you mean?" I choked out as my throat started to close on me.

"I can't stay here."

"At my place?" I demanded, but some deep, fear-tinged voice said that she was talking about something far worse.

She shook her head and then raised haunted eyes

to my face. It wasn't just my heart that was breaking. "Low Town. I'm . . . I'm going back to my people."

I released her with a hiss of air and jumped off the bed. Panic pumped through my veins and clouded my thoughts. With a wave of my hand, the overhead light came on so that I could clearly see her now. I stalked away from her to the opposite end of the room, trying to get a grip on my emotions. "Because of the goblins? I can protect you from the goblins. I'll go to them. Settle this misunderstanding. They won't bother you again."

"That's not it."

"What? Because I'm back with the Towers. You're leaving me because of the Towers?" I demanded, my voice rising despite my attempts to remain calm. "I had no choice. It was go back or die. Which do you want me to have chosen?"

"I want you to live," she said, pushing off the bed. She violently brushed away the tears that had streaked down her cheeks. Some of the spark had returned to her vibrant green eyes. "I hate that you're forced to be among them again, but I want you to live."

"Then why?"

"I have to leave because of what you are!" she shouted.

It was like she'd shoved a knife through my heart. I had to swallow twice to get the words past the lump in my throat. "I thought you loved what I am."

"I do." Her voice wavered and tears returned to her eyes. "I love everything about you, but things have changed and I can't stay."

"What's changed? We can fix this. Just tell me what you need."

She shook her head, looking away from me as if she'd already given up. "You can't."

"Please, tell me. We can fix this!" I repeated, desperately clinging to the hope that there was still some way I could mend this rift between us.

"I'm pregnant."

All thought halted with those two words. The world swam and my knees became jelly. I blinked and the next thing I knew, I was sitting on the floor in the middle of my bedroom. Trixie knelt in front of me with a worried expression on her lovely face.

"Breathe, Gage. You need to breathe," she said, holding my face in her hands.

"How?" I wheezed because my brain wasn't completely online yet. I knew the mechanics of how people created children but we had always been careful. Kids weren't in our current plan—not that we really had a plan.

"Sometime after you had your little chat with Gaia," she said with a gentle smile. "It seems our precautions were for nothing. I've heard that most elves are currently pregnant. I guess Gaia's trying to make up for lost time."

Dear Mother Nature had gotten me. I'd gone to her months ago to get her help for the elves after a witch's spell had made them infertile. I thought she'd just make them fertile again, not nullify all attempts at contraception. It was even more startling to find that a human and an elf had successfully bred, since there were very few instances of it in history.

I stared at the woman kneeling beside me. Synapses started firing again. She was carrying my baby. Our baby. Trixie was having our baby. Joy filled my chest, blotting out all prior feelings of despair. We could do this. She was having our baby.

"That's wonderful," I breathed. I grabbed one of the hands cupping my cheek and pressed a kiss into her palm.

Trixie sat back on her heels and stared at me in shock. "You're not upset?"

"Upset? No. I'm stunned and a bit muddled still, but not upset. I'm thrilled actually," I said with a laugh as I pulled her into my arms. "We can do this. We can move in together. Get a bigger place. Maybe something in the suburbs with a yard. We—"

"No!" Trixie sharply cried, pushing violently out of my arms. She stumbled as she got to her feet and moved to the other end of the room. "Don't you understand? I have to leave because of the baby."

"No, I don't understand. You think you have to go to your people because the baby will be half elf? We can raise the baby together here just fine."

"No, I have to go back because it isn't safe to stay with you!"

The rush of pain that returned to my chest left me breathless for a second. This roller-coaster ride of joy and pain was making me nauseous. She was alternately giving and stealing away hope with every sentence she spoke.

"Of course it's safe to stay with me," I said, pushing to my feet as well.

Trixie said nothing, just pointed at the window where the goblins had climbed through only minutes earlier. My stomach twisted and I swallowed back the rise of bile.

"That was an isolated incident," I said evenly, tearing my eyes from the gouges in the wood from the goblins' claws. "I know the proper protection spells. I can keep anything you can think of out of our home. Name it and I can block it out."

"The goblins are an isolated incident, but how many isolated incidents have there been since we've known each other? Vampires attacking and the damn Low Town mafia. The Svartálfar and even the Wild Hunt. And that's all without mentioning the Towers! Even if you don't consider the Towers, there will always be something."

"No. I won't get involved. I—"

"You can't actually believe that," she scoffed, shoving one hand through her long blonde hair. "It's who you are, Gage. It's the man I love. You help people who are hurting. They're drawn to you because they sense that you can help them and you can't say no. But the problem is that the danger follows you and it hits the people closest to you."

"It won't. I'll stop. I'll just be a tattoo artist and nothing more. No getting involved. I'll protect you and the baby," I countered in a rush, desperate to convince her that I could be strong and responsible. I could keep her safe.

"What about the Towers?"

I backpedaled, my brain desperately searching for an answer that would convince her that she was safe with me. But I didn't have one for the Towers. I couldn't escape the Towers, not so long as I was alive. They would always be a part of my life. "I can shield you from the Towers. I wouldn't be the only warlock to have a child or spouse. I can hide you, protect you."

"But there would still be a great risk. . . ."

"Of course there's a risk. There are no guarantees!" I shouted, my temper finally snapping. She wasn't giving anything. She wanted perfection and I couldn't give her perfection. "You'd have to worry about the Towers no matter who you were with. Everyone has to worry about the Towers! There are dangers out there that everyone has to deal with. You can't escape that!"

"Yes, but it is worse because of who you are." Her lovely voice was calm and even, unmoved by my rising hysteria. But then, she'd had plenty of time to think about this. She'd had time to work out all the arguments in her head. "You've had people within the Towers hunting you and it will happen again. When I chose to be with you, I knew that I was a target if they ever discovered our relationship. I happily accepted that risk for myself, but I can't do that with our child."

"Please, don't do this, Trixie," I said softly, but I couldn't put any force behind it because I understood her argument. I couldn't blame her for wanting to protect our child from the danger that followed me like a black shadow waiting to cast its dark pall over those I loved.

"I love you, Gage." Her voice broke and the tears started down her cheeks again. "I love who you are and I'm so proud that you can help people with your gifts. I would never change that about you, but I think this is the sacrifice that we must make for your gifts. I'm sorry."

I stood staring at her for several seconds, my brain locked in a useless loop of trying to find a way around her arguments. I needed a solution, a guarantee that she and the baby would be safe. But there wasn't one. So long as the Towers existed, so long as I was cursed with this gift for magic, I couldn't give her the safety she demanded.

"When are you leaving?" I asked, my voice was raw and rough as sandpaper.

"Soon. Eldon is coming to get me."

A bitter, sarcastic laugh escaped me. "I'm sure your brother was thrilled to hear your news."

"Eldon doesn't hate you. You fixed it so that I am welcome among my people again and your actions have resulted in his wife being pregnant with their second child."

I nodded because I was simply out of words.

"Our child will be happy and safe, I promise you."

"But I will never see you or our child."

Trixie didn't respond because I was right. To keep her and the baby safe, I had stay away from them. I would never hold my son or daughter. I would never see their smile and their first steps. I would never hold Trixie again.

"Will you let me see you one last time before you leave?" I asked.

"Yes."

I don't know which of us cracked first, but in the next second she was in my arms, my face buried in her hair while her nails scored my back in her attempts to get as close to me as possible. Drawing in a shuddering breath to get a handle on my emotions again, I lowered my mouth to hers, but at the first touch of her lips, I knew it wasn't going to be enough. Clothes were torn away, leaving us pressed skin to skin. That night, we made love again and again. Sometimes it was fast and violent, filled with rough and desperate caresses, as if we were in a rush to be merged at last. Other times, it was a slow exploring as if each of us were trying to memorize every inch of the other person so that it was imprinted forever on our brains.

It was shortly after dawn when I lay on my side beside Trixie. She was deep in sleep, her lovely face wiped clean of worry. I placed my hand over the slight mound of her abdomen where my child was growing within her. Was this Squall sleeping inside of her? When I met the little boy's soul at Gaia's, I'd instinctively known that he would be my son one day. I just hadn't expected it to be so soon. Was this him now, so close to me and yet on the cusp of being stolen away?

A small smile tugged at the corners of my mouth. I'd find a way to keep them safe. Even if I had to tear down each of the Ivory Towers brick by brick with my bare hands, I'd keep Trixie and my child safe and at my side.

Part 2

DEMON'S VOW

CHAPTER 1

Gideon appeared on my doorstep less than an hour after Trixie left for her own place. Luckily, I had been expecting him. There was no missing the surge of energy that hit, sending ripples out through the air like waves across a pond while leaving behind a stinging, tingling sensation in the tips of my fingers. Whoever was stirring up this strange magic was getting better at it. And I had an idea as to what this person's purpose was.

"Come in!" I shouted when the warlock pounded on my front door like some disgruntled bill collector. I was tying my tie while sliding my right foot in a shoe when he stepped over the threshold. He looked surprised to see me already in my uniform, but then considering all the bitching he'd endured on our last outing, he probably thought he'd have to dress me himself.

Lying with Trixie in my arms last night, all too aware of the baby growing between us, I had forced myself to face the hard reality that it was time to get my shit together if I was going to keep my vow of protecting her.

The first step was coming to terms with my identity.

"You felt it?" he asked as he shut the door.

"No missing it." Dropping on the sofa, I propped my foot on the edge of the coffee table so I could finish tying my laces. "It felt close. A lot closer."

Gideon grunted. "Charlotte, North Carolina, area. He's moving north."

"You sure the maniac is a 'he'?"

Gideon gave a little shrug. "No, I guess it doesn't have to be."

Pushing to my feet, I grabbed my blazer and cloak from where I'd tossed them over the back of the chair. "I've been burned by that assumption already. A tattoo artist was murdered recently and the killer has gone on to stalk pregnant women in Low Town. A blood spell revealed that the killer was actually a woman."

"Putting aside the fact that you're doing magic that you shouldn't be," Gideon said with a weary sigh. He pinned me with what I'm sure he thought was a threatening glare, but it just didn't work anymore since I was now using magic in his presence to serve the Towers. The whole situation had become too damned complicated to worry about Gideon hauling my ass in for illegal magic use.

"That is a bit surprising," he continued after I gave the required nod indicating that the warning had been received. "Women tend to commit crimes of passion. Stalking is methodical and premeditated. That's very . . . unusual."

"So is the tattoo that has pushed her over the edge." I checked one last time to make sure that my wand was properly secured in the holder on my left wrist and easily accessible through my shirt sleeve. Taking a deep breath, I pulled in a little bit of magical energy to put a charge in the charms and spells woven into the garments. A low level hum surrounded me for a second, but unlike the wave that hit earlier, this was comforting because the resonance matched the energy that came from my own soul.

"Let's do this," I said, expelling a breath I hadn't realized I had been holding.

Gideon said nothing, his expression remaining grim. He put a hand on my shoulder and the world turned dark. There was a slight shifting sensation as we traveled the miles separating Low Town from Charlotte, North Carolina. It lasted only a couple of seconds before we were standing in bright sunlight on the edge of a park. Screams and panicked cries echoed through the still winter air. At first I expected to be faced with the killer creating ugly magical waves, but then my eyes focused on the people rushing away from the park, looks of fear and hatred clouding their faces as they scrambled to put more distance between them and us.

"Do you get used to it?" I asked softly, unable to tear my eyes from the frightened people. Moments ago, they had been walking their dogs and children through the park on a sunny, mild winter Monday.

And then the Towers appeared, reminding them that they were vulnerable to a higher, darker power that could strike them dead in a heartbeat.

"I stopped worrying about them because I had bigger problems. Just like you do."

"Yeah," I murmured. He was right. I did have enough problems on my plate. I didn't need to worry about what other people thought, particularly when I'd never see them again. "Any new clues as to who is doing this or why?"

"No, not yet, but I'm still digging."

"I . . . I have a theory," I said, hesitating to put to words the thought that had been slowly forming in my brain. "I think this person could be human. It's just the purpose of the magic that might be confusing us."

Gideon stopped and turned so that he was facing me. "What are you talking about?"

"I think the person is trying to set Lilith free."

"Lilith who?"

"Lilith *who*?" I gasped. Had he lost his mind? "*The* Lilith. Queen of the Underworld, mother of all monsters, and keeper of those souls paying a debt to magic."

A soft snort escaped Gideon and he turned his attention back to the once-peaceful street in North Carolina. "Lilith doesn't exist. She's a myth."

"She's real. I've met her."

"You've been tricked then," Gideon snapped. "You would have had to die to meet her!"

I just stared at my companion and part-time mentor, watching his face pale as the idea took form in his head. It had been tricky, but I beat death once already, narrowly escaping Lilith's clutches. At our first meeting, she'd argued for me to free her.

Gideon cleared his throat, getting his thoughts reined in. He pointed one long finger at me, holding it so that it nearly touched the tip of my nose. "We have much to discuss. But not now."

"Agreed." It would be best if Gideon knew something about the things I'd done and seen recently.

"But you think she's behind this?"

I nodded. "She's been haunting me for the past several months, trying to get me to free her, but she's never been specific about how I do that." Pushing back my cloak, I shoved my hands into the pockets of my trousers against the frigid air as it nipped at my fingers, making them stiff and sore. The air was significantly colder than Florida, though not quite as cold as Low Town. "I really don't think I'd be her only way out of the Underworld. She's probably working over as many people as possible. Someone is bound to give in to the temptation eventually."

"She's as powerful as the stories?"

"It's certainly the impression she gives. I haven't tried to fight her and I definitely don't fucking want to. Do you think it could be her?"

"I don't know, but the use of death magic would

fit." Gideon turned away from the now empty park and started down the residential street at a brisk pace with me hurrying to catch up with him. "This new wrinkle has left me wishing that we are actually facing a dragon."

"Why the hell would you ever say that?"

A wan smile lifted the corners of Gideon's mouth as he slowed his pace. "We've beaten dragons before. We can do it again. Last I read, Lilith was more akin to a . . . a . . . demi-god, and I don't know how to win against something like that."

It wasn't something either of us wanted to contemplate. Lilith was far better off staying in the Underworld, where she belonged. If some bastard was keen on setting her free, we were better off stopping him before we had to face Lilith.

"Where are we going?" I demanded, turning my attention back to the current problem at hand.

"There. That's our first issue to tackle."

Gideon pointed to a large white Victorian house farther down the block we were on. All the windows reflecting back the bright late-morning sun were covered with heavy shades, while some on the first floor were even covered with metal blinds used by several of the races that were vulnerable to sunlight. Evergreen wreaths with big red bows hung on the tall black metal fence surrounding the front yard. It looked like your average house in a high-rent neighborhood. Except for the thin wisps of black smoke rising from several different points in the front yard and coming down to the sidewalk.

Squinting, I nearly stumbled as I tried to clearly make out the strange scene. "Are . . . are those vampires? What the hell's going on? Group suicide?"

Each creature's steps were slow and jerky, as if their joints didn't properly bend with each movement. They were more like puppets on strings, or worse, zombies from too many late-night horror movies out in search of delectable brains. Despite the excruciating pain they had to be in, not one of them made a sound as their pale white skin blackened in the rays of the sun and then flaked off in papery ash to gently float away.

Recovering from my initial horror, I started to jog toward them, my mind boggled by the idea of several vampires stepping out of their home and into the bright sunlight. They were slowly burning to death. There was no clear plan in my head; just the idea that I had to get them back inside where they were safe from the sun.

When I was still a couple houses away, Gideon grabbed my shoulder, pulling me to a sharp halt. "Wait! This feels all wrong."

"We can't just stand back and watch a bunch of vampires fry in the sun," I snarled, trying to jerk out of his grasp so I could try to help them before it was too late.

Yet before I could get any closer, a Good Samaritan decided to brave the Towers warlocks and try to usher the sleep-walking vampires back into the safety of their home. In a violent blur, the vampire closest to the human lunged at him, tearing his throat out with fangs and claws. It all happened so fast — a devastating combination of blood and black smoke like a demented magic trick on a Vegas stage.

"What the hell?" I shouted, stumbling backward in horror. Recovering from the explosion of violence, I jump into the struggling, instinctively moving to pry the vampire off his victim, but Gideon's hand tightened on my shoulder, holding me in place. Twisting around, I knocked the warlock's hand away. "We have to help them."

"He's already dead," he replied, his eyes never straying from the bloody scene before us.

When I turned back, I found that the vampire had dropped the now lifeless body to the ground, leaving it to coat the empty street with blood. This didn't make any sense. The vampire hadn't even attempted to feed from the poor soul. He just killed him as quickly as possible, like pulling the plug on the TV.

Obviously, the vampires hadn't been driven out of the house to feed. If this was suicide, I can't understand why the creature had taken the time to so brutally kill the bystander. With no one in front of him, the vampire now stood in the middle of the sidewalk, swaying slightly as the sun slowly cooked him. Ash flaked off, rising up into the breeze to dance around him in a macabre ballet.

"We have to do something," I repeated, though I hadn't any suggestions on what exactly that was going to be.

"What? They're already dead."

"Just because they're vampires doesn't mean—"

"No, damn it!" Gideon cut me off. He stepped forward and pointed at the chest of the vampire that had attacked the man just seconds ago. "His heart has been ripped out. He's already dead. There's nothing to save."

My eyes dropped from the face of the poor creature with his flaking flesh to his chest. There was a hole in his Batman T-shirt right over where his heart had been. Dark, thick blood stained the fabric, and when the cold winter breeze ruffled his crusty shirt, you could see the hole extended down into his chest. Hesitantly stepping closer, I looked over all the vampires who dotted the front yard of their home. Each one had a bloodstained chest. Someone had killed an entire nest of vampires during the daylight hours and then . . . reanimated their bodies.

A chill ran through me that had nothing to do with the winter wind. "How?"

"The magic that we felt," Gideon murmured. He shook his head in disgust as he pushed up the sleeves of his jacket and shirt. "We need to put them down before someone else gets hurt."

Clenching my teeth, I balled my hands into helpless fists at my side. I wanted to do something to help them, but it was already too late for that. Once a vampire's heart was staked or removed, life flees the body and there's no getting that back. This stiff, shuffling movement made you want to believe that there was still some life left in these poor creatures, something that could be saved, but it was an illusion.

Magic tingled in the air as Gideon drew energy to himself and began to cast a spell. In unison, the vampires stopped their shuffling and their heads snapped in Gideon's direction as one.

Fear careened through my system, sending my heart pumping. "I think you might want to stop what you're doing," I said, taking a slow step backward.

The warlock focused on the vampires, his eyebrows nearly lifting to his hairline. "Huh." The surprised sound was a massive understatement when it came to this new development. A small flame flickered to life in the palm of his hand. "I guess that answers the why," he muttered to himself.

The smoldering creatures watching Gideon with a frightening intensity were an impressive facsimile of the zombies I'd watched in so many late-night horror marathons. Unfortunately, where the zombies in the movies were shambling, mindless eating machines, these vampire zombies were fucking fast.

The second the flame sprang to life in Gideon's hand, they darted across the yard and through the street to get to us. Shifting from sloths to cheetahs in a flash, the zombies suddenly resembled the vampires they had once been. My pulse doubled at the sight of the merciless creatures charging toward us. Summoning up the same fire spell as my companion, I instantly became a target as well, but at least I was armed.

The first wave burst into bright orange and yellow flames as if they had been doused in gasoline, but the fire failed to slow them down. In fact, we had only succeeded in making the situation worse. Instead of being attacked by mindless zombies, we were now about to be attacked by mindless zombies on fire.

"Any more great ideas?" I shouted as dodged the first one to reach me. The heat from the flames scorched my face and threatened to scald my lungs as I sucked in a breath. Ducking under his arms, I sent a blast of pure energy into his chest. The blow knocked him over and sent him skidding toward the house on his back.

"Catch!"

I dragged my eyes from the zombies for a second to see Gideon throw me a large, black-bladed machete. Gripping the handle, I smiled a little to myself, feeling as if I was regaining control. Gideon had to teach me that little trick before our next outing. There was no way the warlock had a pair of machetes strapped to his body.

Dodging the arms of one zombie as she made a grab for me, I rolled a short distance away. Coming back up on my feet, I swept back with my blade, slicing through her legs with sickening ease. The fiery creature crashed to the ground, seeming momentarily disoriented by the fact that she was no longer standing. Swinging back in one fluid motion, I removed her head as well as the head of another as it charged me.

But both of them kept coming — breaking all the rules of movie zombies. Being headless was supposed to stop a zombie.

Of course, what I wasn't considering was that these zombies had been reanimated with a magic that I didn't yet understand and were given a specific purpose. I was willing to bet that they had been charged with the task of attacking any magic user who drew close. They were going to keep coming so long as their limbs still worked. Sadly, it was going to take a while for the fire to eat through their limbs so that muscles and tendons no longer responded to magical manipulation.

As the former vampires kept coming, I dipped and dodged, keeping out of arms' reach while hacking off bits. Gideon went for a more magic-based approach, setting them on fire as soon as they stepped outside their home and then using a binding spell to pin them to the pavement or the iron fence where they sizzled, burned, and flaked to ash in the sun and fire.

When there was nothing in danger of actually killing me, I stopped and drew in a shaky breath of relief. Looking around, there were pieces of vampire scattered everywhere in the street and sidewalk. The air was thick with black smoke and the horrid stench of cooking flesh. Nearly two dozen vampires had attacked us — likely what had been the entire nest. What a fucking waste!

But it wasn't just the tragic loss of life that twisted my gut. It was the idea that someone had gotten into their protected home and methodically killed each one. While vampires were weaker during the day, they could still move around, they could fight back against an attacker. I couldn't think of anyone, short of a warlock or a witch, being able to do such a thing. If this attack came from someone within the Towers, then we had a bigger problem on our hands. Someone had gone rogue.

The winter wind chilled the sweat that coated my face. Each heavy breath was like swallowing shards of glass. I wiped the back of my hand across my brow, smearing more ash into my pale skin so that I now looked more like a banker who worked part-time as a chimney sweep.

I opened my mouth to ask Gideon about the vampires, but he wasn't looking at the house or even the corpses littering the empty street before us. His attention was behind us. A small group of people had gathered several feet away and were angrily shouting. They called us murderers and butchers.

Rage and hatred twisted their features. Shoulder to shoulder stood humans, shifters, ogres, sirens, and dwarves, shouting at us. At any other time, this motley group barely tolerated each other, but they easily united when faced with members of the Ivory Towers. We saved their lives. If any one of them had approached the bespelled vampire corpses, they would have been torn apart like that one poor soul minutes earlier.

But they didn't care. Or rather, they likely thought that we were the cause of the attack in the first place and the vampires were merely defending themselves. When they looked at Gideon and me, they saw only centuries of oppression, violence, and death.

If only they knew what it was like inside of the Ivory Towers. If only they knew what we were protecting them from. The two separate thoughts whispered through my head, but I quickly shoved them aside.

"Let's go, Gideon. We need to finish this investigation," I growled, turning back toward the house the vampires had exited. Guilt and frustration warred in my chest. There was no convincing them that I wasn't one of the bad guys.

I didn't get more than two steps when pain exploded in the back of my head, knocking me to my hands and knees in the middle of the street. Gravel bit into my filthy palms while a second shockwave of pain surged through my knees. Blinking hard to clear away the stars from my eyes, I lifted one trembling hand to find a massive gash across the back of my skull while blood poured across my scalp.

"What the fuck?" I groaned, trying to pull together a coherent thought through the pain that was making a playground of my body. "What happened?"

"A rock," Gideon answered in an icy voice. I slowly turned my head at his tone and I saw the large stone he was pointing to a couple feet away. I was pulled from my stunned contemplation of the act by the sharp swell of magical energy sweeping through the air. Gideon was summoning up great amounts of energy for a spell.

The air had grown frighteningly still in that frozen moment so that the silence was nearly suffocating. Pushing unsteadily to my feet again, I turned back to find that the crowd was still standing several yards away, but no one spoke. They looked as if they weren't even breathing as they waited to see what would happen. A rabbit trapped by a fox. They waited wide-eyed for their messy end to be delivered by the warlocks they dared to attack.

And Gideon was more than willing to hand out Tower justice. The wind rose, rattling the limbs of the nearby trees, and the sky turned dark with thick black clouds rushing in to blot out the once clear blue sky. The warlock spread his hands wide and blue sparks arced between his fingertips. His black cloak snapped angrily in the wind.

"Gideon," I started in the firmest voice I could muster over the howl of the wind. "Let it go."

"They attacked us!" he shouted at me without taking his eyes off the gathered crowd.

"They attacked me and I said drop it!"

The warlock ignored me, keeping his focus on his spell. A sharp crackling filled my ears and the hair on the back of my neck stood on end. Cursing him and the rock thrower, I gave Gideon a hard shove, knocking him off balance just as the energy was leaving his fingertips. The blast of energy flew wide, cutting through the bare limbs of a nearby tree. People screamed and scattered as debris rained down on the street.

Gideon swung around, turning nearly black eyes on me now that his initial targets had beaten a quick retreat. I fought the urge to grab my wand, knowing that the sight of it would only escalate the matter. My heart was pounding so hard I could taste it in the back of my throat.

"Protecting them only gives them courage!" the warlock roared, waving a hand back at the empty spot where the people had gathered.

"There's no reason to kill more people! They've been through enough!"

"Enough? They haven't been through enough if someone dares to throw a rock at a warlock!"

"Are you saying we haven't earned it?" Stepping forward, I got up in Gideon's face, my temper shredding each word I spoke.

I could feel the weight of my own past with the Towers come crashing through my pain like a rhino. Broken bodies, screams echoing through the long, lonely nights, and the blood on my hands that would never wash off—it was all there in vibrant Technicolor in my brain.

Even after I had left the Towers, there were more deaths I had done nothing to stop. Dolan had been tortured before me because he'd been cutting into the Towers' magical-ingredients supply with his drug trade. Part of Low Town had burned when members of the Towers tried to lure me out. I was sick of it all and ready to rip into anything I could get my hands on.

A cold grin spread across Gideon's lips as he glowered at me and I knew I wasn't the only one. "Let's do this." The warlock clapped a hand on my shoulder and the world went dark.

CHAPTER 2

The vast flat plain was filled with knee-high grass and weeds, while the sun was just starting to peek over the horizon, painting the cold winter sky alternating shades of pink and orange. Gideon had been kind enough to move us at least a few time zones west for a little privacy. The warlock gave me a hard shove away from him as he whipped his wand from his left sleeve.

Stumbling a couple steps, I regained my balance and fought through the wave of nausea that hit. The travel spell, combined with the head wound, was doing a number on my stomach and equilibrium, but I was still too pissed to pay any of it much attention. Rather than grabbing my wand, I held my hands open and out to my sides, my fingers slightly curled as if they were dug into globs of magical energy just waiting for my use.

"I've been waiting so fucking long for this," Gideon

muttered under his breath as he slung his first spell at me.

Yeah, me too. We had been at each other's throats for the better part of ten years. Ten years of this asshole harping about not using magic. Ten years of listening to how the council wanted to remove my head because I was a worthless excuse for a warlock who didn't deserve the air in my lungs.

Pulling up the energy around me in the form of a shield, I blocked his attempt to turn me into a box turtle and reflected it right back at him in the hopes of cramming it down his throat. The warlock brushed the spell off and came back with a second before I had a chance to formulate my own offensive strike.

"Why fight back?" Gideon taunted as he began weaving another spell. "This is what you wanted, wasn't it? You want to be the whipping boy for the Towers." A trio of long thick icicles formed in the air around him, dancing in the air like crystalline daggers. With a flick of his wrist, the first one whistled through the air before shattering against my shield.

"You want to be a martyr, dying for the sins of the Towers."

A second icicle sliced through the air, exploding in a fine mist just inches from my heart.

"Dying might ease your conscience but it won't save a single soul."

The third icicle screamed through the air and stopped in the air just an inch from my forehead. It had gotten through my defenses because I'd let his words distract me. I gasped, my heart freezing in my chest as I stared at the weapon that very nearly killed me.

"Time to get off the cross, Gage, and find a real answer to our problems."

I wanted to scream. In that moment, I hated him, but I hated myself more. Rage pumped through my veins, but Gideon didn't give me a chance to unleash any of that anger on him because he quickly continued his assault. Each time, I managed to block his attack or unravel the spell, but each one was growing more and more complicated.

Any idiot would have known that I would be outmatched if I had to actually fight Gideon. He had more training, more experience dealing with other warlocks, making him better equipped. But instead of calling a truce, I was becoming more frustrated with each spell as his words hammered against my brain.

There was no question that I was skilled when it came to using magic. I could pick apart charms and curses I had never seen before in a matter of seconds. There was a part of my brain that simply understood the workings of magic even if I didn't entirely understand the why of it all.

Yet, when it came to a fight with magic, I couldn't just go on gut. A wrong move on my part and I was dead. Or Gideon. Or some innocent bystander four towns away who was just trying to get to his first cup of coffee of the day.

Damn it! All this raw potential and I couldn't fucking tap it!

With a shout, I tore apart Gideon's last attack and tossed a blast of energy at him, rocking him back on his heels. The warlock blinked, looking stunned. Running the short distance that separated us, I plowed my shoulder into his sternum, tackling the taller man to the ground.

While he might have been surprised by the physical attack, it didn't take him long to recover. My fist slammed into his jaw, snapping his head to the side before he brought both of his fists down on the top of my head. Stars burst before my eyes while sharp pain sliced across my brain. I nearly crumpled. My stomach tried to eject its contents then remembered at the last second that it was already empty, leaving me choking for air.

Gideon rolled away from me, pushing to his feet first. The bastard tried to give me a swift kick to the ribs, but I caught his foot. With a hard jerk, he landed on his ass, disappearing in the high yellow weeds.

Pushing to my feet, I swayed but remained standing. The warlock sat up, frowning at me. I smiled as I kicked him, catching his chin so that his head snapped back. "That's for ten years of kicking me around," I shouted.

"That the best you got?" he snarled, wiping blood from the corner of his mouth.

"Fuck no!"

Magic forgotten, we were back at each other in a heartbeat, exchanging kicks and punches like a pair of teenagers in the schoolyard. I don't know how long we went at it, but when I was finally on my back, my body an intricate web of aches and pain, I noticed that the sun was now fully above the eastern horizon but was doing little to remove the deep chill from the air.

Slowly, I pushed myself into a sitting position, a low groan escaping from my split lips before I could catch it. Looking around, I noticed that in our struggle we'd managed to flatten most of the high grasses close by, so that I could now see Gideon's long body stretched out just a few feet away from me. His chest rose in short little gasps as if taking a deep breath was too painful. I thought I had cracked a couple ribs when I slammed my knee into his side.

"Fucking asshole," I mumbled, but it was missing the heat I had felt earlier. Right now, all I could feel was pain.

The warlock pushed into a sitting position as well, deep lines of pain cutting through his lean face as he moved. A sharp hiss of air squeezed through his clenched teeth and he pressed on hand to his side. Yep, I'd broken a rib or two. *Man, his wife was going to kick my ass.*

A bark of laughter jumped from my lips at that errant thought and I followed it with a groan as new pain lanced through my temples.

"What's so funny? You look as bad as I do," Gideon said. He tried to glare at me, but he was failing miserably since one eye was already swollen shut and the other wasn't far behind it.

"Yeah, but I was just thinking that your wife is

going to kill me when she sees you and I'm more scared of her than I am of you."

Gideon snorted, his shoulders moving slightly with silent laughter. "It would serve you right." But even as he said it, he called his wand to his side from where he'd dropped it in the tall grass. With the oak wand lightly held in his right hand, he whispered a healing spell over and over again while moving the wand from his feet slowly up his body to his head. As he did it, I could see cuts close, discoloring fade, and swelling reduce as if I were watching time spin backward. By the end, his body looked loose and comfortable again, while his voice had regained its usual strength and tenor.

Taking my own wand in hand, I started to repeat the spell Gideon had used. I had never used it before. The healing spell I had always relied on was far cruder and couldn't do much to reduce pain. It was simply something to keep me from dying so that my body could finish naturally healing on its own.

"No!" Gideon said sharply, halting the words in my throat.

I stared at the warlock in surprise. Was he really going to stop me from using magic to heal myself? Sure, it was technically against the rules, but I was pretty damn useless as I was and we still had to finish our investigation in Charlotte.

To my utter shock, Gideon rolled to his feet and squatted down on my right. Carefully, he adjusted my hold on my wand, corrected my pronunciation of the spell, and even changed my breathing pattern for optimal use of the spell. He taught me magic.

In all my years at the Ivory Towers, not once had anyone taken an active role in making sure that I knew how to properly replicate a spell. It was monkey see, monkey do at the Towers. You learned to mimic what you saw if you wanted to stay alive. It was only after you survived your apprenticeship that you went back to try to understand why the things you did and said worked.

Under his guidance, I managed to easily replicate the healing spell he used, wiping away cuts, fractures, bruises, and pain. When I was done, I felt better than I had in a long time and a little sad. How many kids would be alive today if they had been taught magic with patience and care? The faces of so many dead zipped across my mind for a second that I thought I was going to drown but I pushed them back into the shadows for another time.

When I looked up at Gideon, there was a sadness in his own expression that made me believe a similar thought was crossing his mind. Which style of teaching had guided him through his apprenticeship? Or worse, which style waited for his daughter should she prove to be magical in nature? Of course, that was assuming he found a way to hide the fact that he was her father.

"I wasn't going to kill them," he said as I stood again. His voice was dull and flat. He refused to look at me. Gideon was hurt by the unspoken accusation, though he'd choke before he admitted it aloud.

I opened my mouth to say that I hadn't thought that, but I quickly shut it again with a click of my teeth. The truth was that I didn't know what the warlock was going to do to the crowd. I hadn't really thought about it. The only thing I had been sure of was that he was using magic on people and it wasn't going to be the nice fluffy bunnies-and-rainbows kind of magic.

"They've suffered enough," I simply said.

"I agree."

"Then why?"

Gideon finally looked down at me, frowning. "What would have happened if Simon Thorn had been hit with a rock?"

I cringed at the thought of that crowd striking back at my old mentor. "Fuck," I whispered as horrible images of death and smoldering carnage flickered through my brain. I could think of any number of gruesome and painful spells that he would have used to slowly kill each of them, and then it was likely he would have leveled most of Charlotte to teach the rest of the area that he was not to be disrespected.

"Exactly," Gideon said as if I'd spoken. "If they strike at one of us and we do nothing, then it could give them the courage to strike at another. The only problem is that the next one could be like Simon. You scare them. Give them what they will consider a close call and it should stop them. Otherwise, you're guaranteeing they will die the next time."

I nodded, hating it but recognizing the truth behind his words. I had fought Reave and sacrificed my own future to crush the same kind of hope that Gideon was talking about. The dark elf had gotten information on the locations of the Towers, hoping to spread it to the world so that a war would start. But a frontal assault on the Towers would lead only to catastrophic death. The witches and the warlocks couldn't be beaten like that.

"So we continue to take away all hope?" I said miserably. Some of the frustration I had lost in my fight with Gideon was starting to seep back into my voice, leaving me clenching my teeth.

"No." Gideon paused, waiting until I looked up at him before he continued. "We let them have the hope that if they avoid us, they will live. We let them have the hope that they can live most of their lives without ever encountering a witch or a warlock. They have to understand attacking a warlock will end in death because that's how most of the Towers see it."

I shook my head, knowing that he was right, but it didn't help solve my bigger problem: convincing Trixie that I could keep her safe. "Nothing changes that way."

"I don't think the outside world has a chance at stopping the Towers. The change has to come from within."

"That's not fast enough!" I snapped as I jumped to my feet. Pacing away from him, I clenched both my hands in my hair. There had to be another answer, something that we were overlooking that would flip the switch, topple the Towers, and let me live a normal life with a girl I loved and a good job. But even as I thought that, I knew there wasn't a quick fix and what fix there was required years and a lot of death.

"What's happened?"

I flinched at his question and swallowed my first impulse to tell him my latest bit of news. "You mean other than the fact that the world is being worn away by the Ivory Towers? Or that people are scared and desperate? Or beside the fact that there's a monster out there killing vampires and reanimating their corpses to use as guard dogs?"

A mocking smirk lifted one corner of Gideon's mouth and I could see some of the playful youthfulness that Gideon kept locked down at all times. "Yeah, I mean other than all that."

"Trixie is pregnant," I whispered, closing my eyes as the words left my lips. "She's leaving me because I'm a danger to my own child."

Pain crushed my heart and lungs, making it impossible to breathe. It was crippling. My brain just went around in useless circles trying to find ways that would make her and the baby safe. Were there places we could escape to? Spells that would hide her and the child for the rest of their lives? Anything so that I didn't have to watch her walk away.

Minutes ticked by and I slowly became aware of the wind as it flew across the field. The tall grasses bent and swayed like golden waves in the sun. I breathed deeply and slowly. In and out. The pain tumbled away, steadily becoming more manageable.

"I understand," Gideon said.

Not *I'm sorry* or *Congratulations*. No false wishes or hopes.

I understand.

If there was anyone in this world, Gideon was possibly the only person who could understand. We both wanted a different world, and this man had taken several big chances in trying to attain that goal. Gideon had broken one of the Towers' most basic rules. He fell in love and got married. He'd even taken it a step further and dared to have a child. Every day he had to be haunted with the terror that if his wife or daughter were discovered, they'd be executed, but only after extensive torture.

The idea that Gideon understood my dilemma helped more than I would have expected. I wasn't alone.

"Let's get back to Charlotte and finish up," I said, glancing over at him. "I've got better things to do with my day than to freeze my ass off in the middle of Nebraska."

"Idaho," Gideon corrected, coming to stand next to me.

"Whatever."

He put his hand on my shoulder, but the world instantly didn't blink away as it had before. The warlock stood beside me, staring forward at the sun rising above, in a sky laced with thin white clouds. There was an unexpected look of peace on his face.

"I've been meaning to thank you for having your little chat with Mother Nature this past fall," he said out of the blue. "It seems it had farther-reaching implications than anyone could have foreseen."

"What do you mean?" I asked, a cold chill already crawling up my spine.

Gideon looked down at me, a wide grin stretching across his face while joy filled his eyes. "Ellen is pregnant as well."

If the man felt any fear about their newest little one, it did nothing to cloud his obvious happiness. There were no worries about being discovered by the Towers or about his daughter developing powers. There was only the promise of a new little life that would one day join his family.

"Congratulations," I said in a rough voice.

He nodded. "I think this one will be a boy."

And for a brief flash, I envied his sense of peace and acceptance.

CHAPTER 3

Upon returning to North Carolina, we stopped at the house that belonged to the vampire nest. Our return caused the police who had cordoned off the area to retreat as we resumed our investigation. They didn't look pleased by our arrival, but no one spoke as we slowly picked our way across the lawn to the massive, three-story house. Not surprisingly, law-enforcement agencies around the globe quickly learned not to oppose the Towers when something interested them. They simply stepped back and waited for the Towers to leave.

The doors were left standing wide open, allowing the sunlight to pour in. The old wood floor creaked as we entered. A quick look around revealed that nothing was disturbed or out of place. There was a mix of antique and modern furniture around the place, as well as the requisite flat-screen TV and sound system.

Books neatly filled shelves.. But what else would you expect?

It was well known that upon conversion a vampire became instantly allergic to the sun and all foods and liquids besides blood. What a lot of people didn't know was that the vast majority of vampires also developed obsessive-compulsive personality disorder. For some reason, nearly all of them became as neat as a pin and compulsively organized, particularly about objects. There was some speculation that it had to do with how their brain handled the information it was now receiving through newly heightened senses. No one knew for sure, but it meant that every nest and vampire house I had ever been in was incredibly orderly. It was fucking creepy.

We continued through the house until we finally reached the sleeping quarters and located numerous bloodstains in the sheets. They had been attacked while they were sleeping.

"I don't get it," I said as I walked out of the third bedroom behind Gideon. "Not one of them made a sound? Not one heard a noise and woke up? No one fought back?"

"Maybe they couldn't fight back." The warlock stopped in the middle of the hall and rubbed the fingers of his left hand together as if he had gotten something on them, but I hadn't seen him touch anything. "There's a residue left here."

"Yeah, I feel it too. It's from the dark magic spell we came to investigate."

Gideon shook his head, continuing to stare at his fingertips as if he could actually see the magic. "No, it's under that. It's almost sugary . . . like cotton candy or cooked caramel." When I frowned and only shook my head, he pointed to the stairs leading to the third floor. "The scent of the blood is masking it. Go to the stairs."

Following his orders, I started to climb the stairs, but stopped on the third one. It was there, so subtle and soft that you could catch only the barest whiff before it was lost in the other magic hovering in the air. He was right. It was like walking into an old-fashioned candy shop or the midway at some amusement park.

"It's . . . almost fey," I whispered as I tried to analyze something that I was getting only the faintest hints of. "But the fey rarely have a quarrel with vampires. The bloodsuckers don't prefer them for prey so they're not a threat. And this . . ." I paused, waving back toward the bedroom where the murders had taken place. "The fey wouldn't be involved in something like this."

"Except for maybe the dark elves."

"Yeah, well I wouldn't put much past the dark elves, but their magic doesn't feel like this. It's grittier. Maybe a brownie or a pooka? A red cap?" I suggested, but even as the words left my mouth, I knew they were wrong. The magic felt as if it should be fey but it wasn't like any fey I had ever encountered.

Gideon shook his head, letting his hand finally fall limp at his side. "We should keep looking."

All the vampires that had been in the house were now bits of ash out on the street. There were no corpses in the house, vampire or otherwise. Our killer hadn't conducted the spell within the nest, which didn't surprise me. I could feel the energy here, but not as strongly as when we walked through the apartment where the first spell was cast. That energy had crawled across my flesh and left me feeling dirty.

My companion didn't seem particularly surprised that we didn't find anything either, but we had to search the house for any evidence. We had so few leads to go on as it was; we couldn't risk overlooking any possibility now.

"Where do we go now?" I asked when we were standing in the backyard. It wasn't very big, but the grass was neatly trimmed and the flower beds were carefully edged with smooth river rocks. It probably would have looked beautiful in the summer, but right now it was all dead and barren.

Gideon led the way across the backyard and through the gate to the neat redbrick house on the right. All the windows were covered with blinds and there hadn't been a peep out of the occupants despite all the chaos that had whirled about the neighborhood. I could feel the eyes of the cops on us from the street as we strode up the front porch and entered the house without bothering to knock. Not that a warlock or witch would have knocked. *Crap*. Acting the part of a Towers asshole was a lot harder than I had ever expected it to be.

We didn't have to go far before we found four headless bodies sitting around a large dining-room table. The glossy finish was now splattered with blood and bits of brain matter. While it was hard to gauge without heads, the four victims looked younger than the killer's first. Their bodies were smaller and their clothing made me think that he'd grabbed four kids from the local middle school. My stomach lurched at the sight and it was a struggle to get my feet to move forward into the room. How much horror did I have to wade through before we finally caught up with this bastard? He tore through an entire nest of vampires, and now . . . kids.

Gideon frowned as he carefully circled the table, picking up his robe so that the hem didn't drag through the growing pools of blood. "Go check the rest of the house. Find the owners," he barked without looking up at me. His voice was gruff but emotionless. He seemed cold, but it was a lie. There was a tightness around his mouth and his jaw looked hard as if he was tightly clenching his teeth. The warlock had packed his emotions away so that he could find the killer that much faster, relying on the sharp focus of his mind to see him through the grisly scene around him.

I needed to follow his example, but I was just grateful to be away from the nightmare in the dining room. The living room was empty except for an ugly floral-patterned sofa and love seat set placed around a coffee table heavily laden with magazines. As I wandered down the hall, the smell of rotting flesh hit me. Raising the sleeve of my jacket to my face, I pushed open the first bedroom door. The remains of an elderly couple still in their flannel pajamas lay in the queen-sized bed.

Judging by the degree of decomposition, they had been dead for several days at the very least.

The couples' throats had been slit while they slept. It wasn't the fastest or most painless way to die, but they hadn't been the target of the killer's latest spell. He had just needed their house in which to work.

Continuing down the hall, I drew in a somewhat clear breath of air while I explored the rest of the first floor. A quick inspection took me through a spare bedroom, a bathroom, and a tiny eat-in kitchen. Most of the house was untouched. The kitchen had some empty food containers and broken dishes from where the killer had obviously ransacked the owner's goods, but he hadn't stayed here long.

After a couple tries, I finally found the door that led down to the basement and I kind of wished I hadn't. There weren't any dead bodies waiting for me, or even reanimated vampires looking to tear out my throat. No, it was more of the strange writing.

The lower level had been turned into a family room/entertainment area with a massive sectional couch placed before a large TV. Upon taking over the house, the killer had pushed everything to the far side of the room and ripped all the pictures off the wall, throwing them onto the pile. He then covered three of the walls with more of the writing that was part of the spell this asshole was determined to perfect. It looked even more ghastly and horrifying that he'd written it on top of wallpaper laced with delicate rosebuds.

The meaning of the writing was still lost on me, but

I didn't need to understand it to feel sick when looking at it. Pulling my cell phone out of my pocket, I snapped more pictures of the words, adding them to the ones I had taken at the first apartment. Someone somewhere had to be able to understand this stuff. Though I was beginning to feel like I didn't want to meet the person who could read this shit.

Footsteps echoed on the stairs as I returned the phone to my pocket. I turned to find Gideon standing on the bottom stair as his eyes skimmed over the writing on the wall. He looked a little paler than when I'd last seen him, but then he'd spent a lot more time with the victims.

"I found the owners," I said, breaking the silence. "He killed them while they were sleeping. They've been dead several days, allowing him time to set up the house as he needed it before doing the spell again."

Gideon said nothing as he walked over to the nearest wall covered in the cryptic writing, his brow furrowed as he examined every inch of it. I stayed silent as I watched him move from wall to wall, waiting for him to finally make an announcement of how he figured it all out so that we could catch this bastard.

"He's getting better," Gideon murmured as he reached the last wall. His voice had been so low that I wasn't sure if he was talking to himself or if he was talking to me.

"Less mistakes," I replied, noting that the killer had marked out fewer sections than at the Florida apartment.

The warlock gave a little grunt of agreement before turning back toward me. "You realize that he chose this house for a reason."

"Because it was owned by an elderly couple?"

Gideon shook his head. "Whoever this is, he's strong enough to take out vampires. A pair of humans, regardless of their age, isn't going to trouble him. No, he wanted this house because it was close to the nest. He used the spell this time to raise the corpses."

"If the goal was to raise the vampires after he killed them, why didn't he just do it over at the nest house? Why here?"

The warlock looked back at the wall. He had pulled his wand out and was slowly rolling it between his fingers with both hands in a sort of nervous gesture. It wasn't the first time I'd seen him doing that. Whenever the warlock was thinking deeply or anxious, he preferred to have his wand in his hands, as if it could help him focus his thoughts—or maybe it just gave him a sense of control.

"I think it was a time factor," Gideon said after a minute. "He needed time to prep. This type of magic isn't easy to harness and even harder to control, from what I've managed to learn. I think he also needed the corpses to be relatively fresh. Vampires don't keep well after they've died. Well . . . died a second and final time."

"He killed the old couple so he could have the house next to the vampires. Killed the kids to fuel the spell. Killed the vampires . . . to what? Raise the dead?"

"And to send us a message." Gideon shoved the wand back into the holder up his sleeve. "He knows that we're hunting for him."

"Of course." I gave an indifferent shrug, shoving my hands into my pockets. "Anyone would be able to guess that if you use magic, you're going to catch the attention of the Towers."

"Yes, but you were the first to notice that the dead were trained on anyone using magic. Prior to me casting the spell, they only attacked if you got too close to them, which I think was more of a reflex left from their prior state." Gideon gave a little shake of his head as he stepped closer to me. "No, they started violently attacking only when we used magic. They were commanded to attack any witch or warlock who appeared in the area."

I gave him a little smirk, though I wasn't quite feeling so amused. "He's sending the Towers a warning? That takes some balls."

"Or he's just insane."

"I thought that went without saying," I grumbled.

"Or . . ." Gideon said, pausing as he looked over his shoulder at the wall again as if he were rereading the writing there, even though I was sure that it was just gibberish to him as well. "He knows something that we don't know."

"And what's that?"

"I have no idea," Gideon said with a frustrated sigh.

Groaning, I walked over to the pile of furniture and pulled out an old metal folding chair the owners had probably saved for family holidays. Setting it on its legs, I sat down and crossed my arms over my chest. "Fine. Tell me what you do know."

"It's not much." Gideon walked a short distance away with his hand resting loosely on the top of his head.

"You've got to give me something. I'm working blind here and it's not a feeling I care for if this asshole managed to take out an entire nest of vampires."

Gideon stopped in front of one of the walls of writing, dropping his hands back down to his side. When he finally spoke, his voice was barely over a whisper. "I think this is Death Magic."

"Death Magic? What the hell is that?"

Turning back to face me, Gideon looked at a loss for words as he tried to formulate his answer. He started to pull out his wand again, but shoved it back into his sleeve in frustration as if he'd caught the nervous tick. "The magic we do, what nearly all creatures use, it's based on the energy generated from living creatures. It's why there's so much energy available around us, but there's a limit to how much and how quickly a creature can draw in that energy to use for a spell."

I nodded, agreeing with his explanation. Leaning forward, I balanced my elbows on my knees. "And Death Magic?"

"The user pulls the energy straight from the life of a person who has been killed quickly and violently. I think it's also necessary for the user to have caused the death, but I'm not completely sure about that aspect."

"I don't understand. How can the power drawn from one life be tempting in comparison to what is around you? And why does he keep going after kids for the spell?"

"Two reasons. The power comes from the number of years that a person has left in their life, hence his choice of victims being kids. More years equals more power."

"Okay." It was perverse and disgusting, but I could understand it.

"And because all that power comes to you all at once. I'm getting the impression that there are no limitations to how much you can take in. It can be more powerful than what we use."

"Who the fuck came up with this style of magic?" I shouted.

"No idea."

"Then who was using it before it fell out of fashion?"

Gideon gave me a look saying that he wasn't amused by my question. "Again, no idea."

"Then what's the purpose of this magic? Other than being unbelievably brutal, immoral, and reprehensible, why stop using it? As you said, it's more powerful."

"Most likely because it is difficult and limited in its application." Gideon turned around to face me, his hands dropping back down to his sides. "Death magic, as far as I can tell, is only used for raising the dead."

"Okay, so this shit fell out of favor ages ago. If no one has used it for a long time, that really kind of limits who might know about it." This time it was my turn to pause because I really didn't want to voice this fear aloud. "Could this be someone from the Towers? Someone gone rogue?"

"You mean, like you? Or those runaways we took so much care getting properly settled and protected this fall?" Gideon asked snidely.

"Not quite," I said, clenching my teeth. "I was thinking someone more along the lines of Darius Courtland."

It was the first time I had brought up the warlock's name since my appearance before the council that resulted in Reave's death and my being named a guardian. The guy was a fucking prick who left me with a sick feeling in the pit of my stomach. He'd love to see the council wiped out so that he could place himself on a throne to lord over the entire world.

"There are plenty in the Towers like Courtland," Gideon conceded with a shake of his head. "I don't see how using Death Magic would help him achieve his goal. There are easier ways to amass power."

"But everyone in the Towers knows about them," I countered. "It would be a lot harder to fight him if we don't understand what he's using. Besides, if this magic can raise Lilith to this world, she might have promised him something that he couldn't walk away from."

Gideon paced back and forth in front of the spell, tapping his wand against his jaw. "That is a frightening idea, but I don't think we should limit our search to just the Towers."

"Then who could be doing this? I mean, Death Magic isn't common, so it's likely that it has to be someone who has been around long enough to have seen it performed or at least hear about it. Right?"

"Yes, making it one of the long-lived races," Gideon agreed.

I glared at him and got to my feet. "I hope you're not about to point a finger in the direction of the elves. They've been through enough because of the Towers and this kind of thing isn't their way."

"They have been through a lot, which would give them an excellent reason to strike back at the Towers. Raise Lilith, and they'd have all the firepower they need to strike back at the Towers."

"Except that this isn't their way," I argued, pointing at the words that seemed to radiate evil.

"True." Gideon frowned and made an exasperated sound. "Well, except for the dark elves. There isn't much that I would put past them."

"True, but since Gaia's gift, I think all the elves are more focused on increasing their numbers the old-fashioned way."

"Then what are we left with?"

"There are others out there that could remember it, but I don't know who would take this ugly path," I said, flopping back in the chair.

"We can't pursue this line of thinking anyway," Gideon said with disgust. He stood with his fists balled at his sides, facing the writing. It was like he thought he could pull out the killer's secrets if he could just intimidate the writing enough. "What if we figure out a race or two that could be capable of this? What then? Tell the council so the Towers can launch another genocidal purge like what happened to the dragons, unicorns, and too many other races to count? We can't allow that, not when I'm sure that this is only one person acting."

"I agree, but we haven't been able to find a thing from these sites that would identify the killer. We don't know who he is and we are only guessing that his goal is to free Lilith. And he's been killing kids as he works his way north," I listed, anger increasing in my voice with every word. To say I was frustrated would be an understatement. It felt like I was wasting time chasing after a guy I couldn't anticipate while another killer was running loose in Low Town . . .

"Oh fuck," I gasped as the thought finally clicked into place. "Fuck! Fuck! Fuck!" I flew to my feet, my hands clenched in my hair as my brain attempted to sort through the newest horror to dawn on me.

"What?"

"He's heading to Low Town," I whispered.

"How can you be sure?"

"The serial killer in Low Town. She's killed at least two pregnant women. They were in their final months of pregnancy and the babies died as well."

"Oh shit," Gideon said in a low voice.

"I don't think she knows about the Death Magic user, but the killings in Low Town have been making the national news because of the victims. *This* killer has to have heard about them," I said, pointing at the wall covered in spell notes. "What if he's making his way north to Low Town so he can meet with her? What kind of power is he going to stir up if these two meet up?"

"We need to keep these two apart, Gage," Gideon said with a frightening urgency.

"No shit, Sherlock! But how the hell are we going to manage that if we can't catch this guy?" I snapped.

"I guess you just need to catch the female."

I nearly smashed my fist into his face. If it was that fucking easy, I would have done it days ago. Settling for flipping him the bird, I stomped across the room to the stairs leading to the main floor. Of course I needed to catch the bitch who was terrorizing Low Town. It was all part of my plan to keep Trixie safe. There was no doubt that she was feeling particularly vulnerable now that she was a target, even though you couldn't tell she was pregnant if you looked at her. And then Ellen was pregnant as well, making her a potential target. Damn, I had to catch this psychopath!

Halfway up the stairs, I stopped and turned to find Gideon standing on the bottom of the stairs, ready to ascend behind me. "Can you get me into a library in one of the Towers?"

Gideon jerked back in surprise at my request. "Why?"

"I need to know more about this Death Magic if we're to figure out who is trying to use it now. I need to know who created it, who used it, and who put a stop to its use. I also need to know how it's used." Gideon frowned at me, looking less than enthusiastic about my stepping foot inside the Towers again. "We're at a disadvantage here, not knowing shit about what this bastard is up to. The more we know, the faster we might be able to identify who or what this is. It's not like I'm going to start using it. I just want to know what we're up against."

The warlock nodded slightly, his frown starting to fade. "I agree, but your induction into the guardians was a . . . provisional thing. You don't have the full rights of a warlock. I'll need to do some checking to see if I can arrange something. If I can get you in, it's not likely to be a comfortable thing."

"Nothing ever is where the Towers are concerned," I said with a sigh. "Just see what you can do."

"I will." I started to walk up the stairs again when Gideon's voice stopped me. It was one of the few times I had ever heard him sounding hesitant and unsure. The warlock was always so confident in everything he did and said, I was a little taken aback. "If you think you can tolerate it, I'd also like to teach you a few things. Spells. Wards. A few charms. Protection items that would help make your life a little safer."

I smiled, though he couldn't see it because I wasn't looking back at him. He was actually afraid that I'd turn him down. That was laughable. "Bring it on. I'll take all the help I can get."

CHAPTER 4

Something inside of me relaxed when I stepped over the threshold of Asylum just after noon that day. The quiet in the parlor was absolute. Standing in the center of the front lobby, the silence crept into my soul, settling the raging frustration and building sense of helplessness so that I could draw my first deep breath in days.

Asylum Tattoo Parlor was mine. It was my refuge. It was my castle. It was my domain. TAPSS slithered in every once in a while to throw their bureaucratic weight around, but they could not tear down these walls. And so far, the Towers had yet to find me here, even though Gideon's shadow had crossed the doorstep on more than one occasion.

The world made sense when seen through the large front window of Asylum. The people who came through my door wanted ink or they wanted a fix for their problems. They needed help with their love life or illness or luck. They needed something to give them an edge in a world where humans weren't the top dog. And I could do it with a potion.

It was just ironic that I didn't know the right potion that would fix all the problems in my life.

After resetting the antiglamour spell I had carved in the floor of the lobby and replacing the large area rug, I jacked the heat back up and put away my winter coat. The daily routine of opening the shop—checking the ingredients and other supplies, turning on lights, reviewing my schedule as well as the schedules of my employees so I knew who was due when—helped to settle my ragged nerves more than any number of Jack Daniels shots could have. I'd had Asylum for several years and I could go through all those motions without a thought, which I welcomed. The empty hum in my head allowed my subconscious to churn away, turning over my current problems, looking for an obvious answer I had not seen yet.

Before flipping the sign over to OPEN, I pulled my cell phone out of the back pocket of my jeans. There were no messages for Bronx, Trixie, or Serah. I tried to take this as a good sign. No news was good news, right? Not really, but I could really use some fucking good news.

The parlor wasn't typically open on Monday, but I'd recently started keeping limited Monday hours in an effort to make some extra money and catch up with clients after I'd been forced to repeatedly cancel due to some other obligations. I left it to Trixie and Bronx to decide whether they wanted to work on Mondays and was only a little surprised when they decided to join me at their usual times.

The first couple of hours were quiet, with a few people stopping by to schedule appointments for later in the week after I finished an initial sketch of what they wanted me to do or acquired any of the ingredients that I might need for the potion. While I had a solid stockpile of items, there were just some things that were better if they were as fresh as possible. I'd recently learned that the hard way when dealing with a luck spell.

For the most part, the local ingredients shops around Low Town provided what I needed, but occasionally I had to contact some less-than-legal sources to get the item. Those tattoos were quite pricey and required upfront payment. Those didn't happen often, but when they did, you could smell the desperation on the client.

When Trixie strolled into the shop around five o'clock, I had completed two small tattoos and the outline for another that would require several visits due to the level of detail. It was nice when a customer came in just for a piece of art. I glanced up from the guy's bicep at the sound of her heels across the hardwood floor. I had been in the middle of inscribing a protection potion into an abstract piece I had completed a few years earlier. Flashing Trixie what I hoped was a reassuring smile, I clamped down on the nervous fear that was clawing at my heart. It was the first time I had seen her since she dropped her bombshell on me and I didn't want working together to suddenly become awkward.

"Hey, Trixie," Gary called, waving with his free hand while I returned my attention to the man's arm.

Gary was one of my regulars. A bouncer for a seedy bar down on Main Street, he came in once every six months like clockwork to have the protection potion touched up. The potency of the potion faded with time and he relied on it to help keep a knife out of his back. He was a good guy, always paid cash, and had a strong work ethic. He'd been bouncing for more than a decade and with his experience, I wasn't sure that he actually needed the protection potion, but I guess he was willing to accept any kind of help he could get if it could get him through his shift alive and in one piece.

"Hey, Gary. How's things?" she asked as she stowed her bag in one of the cabinets near the floor and shrugged out of her heavy coat. Her glamour was in place, so that the world once again saw her as the human with rich brown hair and a heart-shaped face.

However, because of the antiglamour spell I kept on the shop, her brunette image was reduced to a shadowy ghost over her real appearance so that I could see both worlds. This was the way I'd always seen her.

"You know, just more of the same shit, different day," he said with a wide grin.

The two amiably chatted as I continued to work and Trixie set up her station for the day. Unfortunately, I finished with Gary's potion touch-up ten minutes later and he was out the door a couple minutes after that. Trixie and I were alone.

The tension in the parlor immediately ratcheted up so that I was massaging the stiff muscles in the back of my neck while I stood behind the glass case in the front lobby. I felt like a coward lingering there when I had no reason to, but I didn't know what to say to her. Was I supposed to pretend that everything was normal and that our relationship wasn't crumbling before my eyes? I didn't want to say anything that would drive her away faster, but we couldn't sit all day in this uncomfortable silence.

"Nine Inch Nails, huh?" Trixie called from the main tattooing room.

A reluctant smile tweaked the corners of my mouth and I turned around to face her. Music had always been the easiest way to determine the mood of whoever was controlling the MP3 player hooked up to the speakers. When Bronx was troubled, it was Pink Floyd, and when he was happy, it was Cage the Elephant and Foo Fighters. When Trixie was in a good mood, she opted for Dropkick Murphys, and switched to Tool when she was upset. And when I was in a bad mood, I listened to NIN. Oddly enough, when I was in a good mood, I frequently put on show tunes, but that was only to torture my coworkers. If I was alone, it was Shaman's Harvest.

"I've got a lot on my mind," I admitted, desperately holding on to my smile.

"I would imagine." The elf sat on the little rolling stool beside the tattooing chair she preferred, her hands folded on her knees. She looked exactly the same to me despite the fact that she was carrying my child. There was no extra fullness to her, no extra luminescence that shown out from her soul. She was still Trixie. Beautiful, sarcastic, intelligent, perfect Trixie.

"I heard on the news that there was fight between a pair of warlocks this morning down in North Carolina. Would you know anything about that?" She lifted one brow to me in question while fighting her own smile.

"Two warlocks fight and you automatically assume I've got something to do with it," I teased, waving my hands about dramatically. I crossed the room and dropped onto the tattooing chair I usually used. "You know I hate to get out of my bed in the morning."

"True, but I thought it might be you since there were no reports of anyone being killed by the warlocks," she pressed.

"Oh," I murmured and I could feel a light blush staining my cheeks. That was something of a dead giveaway. Beside the fact that warlocks won't fight in public, it was rare for them to not at least maim someone. "Yeah. Gideon and I were checking something out. It didn't go as well as we might have hoped and I guess we needed to blow off a little steam."

Trixie shook her head, a hint of a smile showing on her face. "At least you didn't get yourself killed."

I flashed her a smile that felt more genuine the longer we talked. "I'm harder to kill than a cockroach."

"And just about as charming," she muttered.

I snorted and rolled out of my chair so that I was standing before her. "I think you've found me plenty charming," I said, wagging my eyebrows at her. "You know, considering you've got a little Gage growing in you now."

Trixie chuckled softly. "Like I said, as charming as a cockroach."

Bending down, I pressed a gentle kiss to her lips while she was still laughing. For a heartbeat, I was lost in her lovely scent drifting around me. A thousand memories surged to the front of my mind so that I could clearly remember every time I kissed her, touched her, and held her. I remembered every laugh and I could count the tears that had slipped down her face. It was all there and I wanted a thousand more instances just like those, but I was afraid that they weren't in our future.

When I pulled back, the laughter was gone from her eyes and she looked as worried as I felt. There was no dancing around the obvious when we were alone together. This tattoo parlor wasn't big enough to house us and the elephant in the room.

"How are you feeling?" I asked, taking a step back so that we both could breathe.

"I'm good. A little more tired than usual and my stomach gets a bit touchy at times, but the doctor said that it's normal."

"You've been to a doctor? What did he say?" Without thinking, I sat on the tattooing chair next to her and then leapt back to my feet, worried that she didn't want me that close when we talked about this, that she might prefer a little space.

"Sit, Gage," she said with a tender smile, patting the seat I had just vacated. She waited until I was seated again, her hands clasped in both of mine. "Yes, I've been to a doctor. She said that everything is progressing just fine and that I'm in good health. She doesn't think I'm going to have any problems despite my age."

"Despite your age! What the hell is that supposed to mean? Does this quack know that you're an elf?"

"Yes she does." Laughter tinged her words at my outburst, while I was barely managing to keep my seat. I was fighting the urge to call of this so-called doctor and give her a piece of my mind. *Despite her age!*

"You're still incredibly young."

"I'm almost six hundred years old, Gage," she said patiently.

"Sure, but that's young for an elf."

Trixie gave a little shrug. "Reasonably so, but it is somewhat old to be having a baby. At least a first baby."

"*Pfttt*. You're in perfect health. Age has nothing to do with it. You and the baby will be fine." But even as I uttered the words, a chill ran through me. What if she wasn't? What if something went wrong and the pregnancy hurt her? The worry must have shown on my face because Trixie placed her hand against my cheek, drawing me back from my dark thoughts.

"You're right. We will be fine," she reassured me before pressing a kiss to the tip of my nose.

I took a deep breath and slowly released it, pushing those fears away. There was no reason to go borrowing trouble, as my mother used to say. I had plenty of trouble already on my plate that needed taking care of.

"Do you know what it is?"

"I'm pretty sure it's a baby," Trixie teased.

"You know what I mean, woman! The sex. The gender. Are we having a boy or a girl?"

She laughed at me, the wonderful sound rising up to fill the entire parlor so that I was laughing as well. When she could catch her breath again, she shook her head at me. "It's still too early. Another month."

I wanted to ask her more about the baby in general, and if there was anything she worried about because the child would be part elf and part human. I wasn't ready to think about the prospect of the baby inheriting more from me than just my blue eyes and big feet. The child was likely to be magically inclined already, due to its elvish heritage. With any luck, that would be enough to mask anything that might catch the attention of the Towers. Unfortunately, a chime echoed through the parlor, indicating that someone had come in the front door. A glance at the clock revealed that it was likely to be Trixie's first appointment of the night. We'd have to circle around to this later. Right now, it was time to get some work done.

It was just the two of us for a couple hours and then Bronx joined us at seven thirty. With it getting darker sooner, the troll had shifted his hours as well, taking advantage of the longer nights to make some extra cash. He paused in the doorway and also commented on my choice of music when I looked up from the dwarf I was tattooing. I swore under my breath, and made a mental note to change the music as soon as I was finished with my customer.

We settled into our easy routine without batting an eye. Trixie was kept busy with her client and I was relieved to be busy as well. December wasn't usually a big tattooing month, as most people chose to use money for gifts and holiday celebrations, but people were making exceptions this year. My calendar was full for the next couple of weeks and it looked the same for my companions. I welcomed the brisk pace, as it meant that I couldn't spend time worrying about things I couldn't fix.

As I bandaged up my customer and walked him to the lobby, Trixie started pulling out her greasepaint as she chatted easily with Bronx. When I returned to the tattooing room, she had dragged her chair over and was already drawing on his left bicep. It was a tradition that had gone on almost nightly for more than two years. Trolls were impossible to tattoo because of their thick, rhino-like skin. Being a tattoo artist, Bronx felt odd not having a tattoo, so Trixie used greasepaint to draw pictures on him.

Tonight, it was a flashback to a classic I had never seen her draw before. A large red heart outlined in black covered his bicep and across the center of the heart was written MOM in large white block letters.

"Interesting choice," Bronx said, his deep voice a low rumble.

Trixie didn't look up at him, but just smiled. "Gage says that you always know everything before he tells you. This shouldn't be a surprise either."

His large eyebrows bunched over his large nose, shadowing his deep set yellow eyes. "What do you mean?"

Trixie looked up at me and smiled before she leaned over and whispered in his ear. Leaning against the doorway with my arms crossed over my chest, I watched the impressive display of emotions cross his face. Joy, horror, amusement, sorrow, and even a little fear – they all flickered through over his usually stoic face before he finally got control. And then it was just uneasiness as he couldn't decide whether congratulations or condolences were in order.

"We're happy about it," I announced, letting him off the hook.

"And I am happy for you both as well," he said before pressing a kiss to Trixie's temple. "Have you started discussing names yet?" he asked conversationally as Trixie started to clean up her paints.

"No. She hasn't even told me what we're having yet," I said.

"It's no mystery, Gage. It's going to be a baby," Bronx said in a dry voice, echoing Trixie's wry words.

"Smart-asses. I'm surrounded by fucking smart-asses," I muttered, feeling lighter to hear Trixie laughing again.

"Will I get to be the godfather?" Bronx asked.

"Only if you promise not to eat the little tyke," I said snidely, earning a deep laugh from the troll, no doubt recalling a similar conversation we had a long time ago about trolls and their young.

A chime announcing the arrival of a customer stopped whatever comment was on his lips as I turned around to greet whoever had walked in. However, the greeting became lodged in my throat at the sight of Jackson Wagnalls. The shifter was all sleek movements as if his joints were kept well oiled. That, or his inner wolf was riding high with the rise of the moon, even though it was still several weeks away from the next full one.

"'Sup, Houdini?" he greeted, flashing a grin full of sharp teeth.

"Watch it, dog. I could have customers in here," I snapped irritably.

The werewolf was one of the few around Low Town that knew about my past in a somewhat limited capacity. The bastard had even gotten to experience it firsthand, when I changed him into a chihuahua for a couple weeks. In my own defense, he was about to attack me and I'd done it in as an act of protection. The spell had put me on his shit list for a while, but the removal of Reave from Low Town and giving him some help with the Winter Court at All Hallows' Eve had gotten me moved to a list of people he tolerated.

"Do you have a customer back there?"

"Not at the moment."

Jack leaned across the glass case that separated us, getting up in my face. "Then I repeat: 'Sup, Houdini?"

It was a struggle not to laugh. I couldn't blame Jack for wanting to have his fun. He knew I was a warlock and it was his only chance to tweak the temper of one without fear of being turned inside out. But then, his good mood also helped to lighten the load on my shoulders. When we'd first met, the werewolf had a major chip on his shoulder and was looking to tear out anyone's throat who got too close. The removal of Reave meant that he got to rule his pack like a true alpha. Killing Reave also put most of the Underworld into his paw, which I think he was enjoying as well. He'd even been nice enough to confer briefly with me when he ascended to his new position of power. My only request was that his people didn't deal in fix. The drug was made from livers taken from pixies and resulted in the death of too many creatures. I knew I'd never stop it from being dealt in the area, but I was happy to just slow down its availability.

"Nothing. How's the tattoo?" I asked, dropping my eyes to his neck.

Jack's grin widened and he straightened, pulling away from me as he moved the collar of his leather jacket and T-shirt away from the side of his neck to flash the tattoo I had completed just a few weeks earlier. "Healed and looking good."

I glanced at it, then frowned at the poor lighting in the lobby. "Come on back. I think I need to touch up the red a little."

As the werewolf greeted my coworkers and shed his jacket, I grabbed what I needed and started to prepare my area for a quick touch-up while we talked. Werewolves were great to tattoo because they healed quickly, had a high pain threshold, and their skin tended to be flawless, if a little hairy. With the removal of Reave, Jack's entire pack had been in for a clan tag I designed, involving an oak tree and the initials L.T., for their home turf. It had turned out pretty damn good and I was pleased that nearly all of them had returned more than once for additional ink, keeping me and my employees busy.

"When are you going to let Trixie tattoo me?" Jack demanded as I snapped on a pair of latex gloves and picked up a disposable razor.

"The day I've heard that you've been neutered," I replied, tilting his head to the side. I carefully shaved away the little hairs that had grown through the tattoo, giving me a clean canvas to work on. In the improved overhead light, I could clearly see where some of the red coloring in the letters hadn't completely filled in. There were also a few spots where I needed to touch up the black.

"This should only take a couple minutes," I said, throwing away the razor and preparing the tattooing gun.

"That's fine. I came in to talk to you anyway."

The werewolf settled in and I stepped on the pedal, sending a soothing buzz through the shop. I went over the black first, touching up some of the outline and making some of the lines thicker before cleaning up the red in the letters. Over the buzzing, I could hear some of the conversation Trixie and Bronx were having. While light, their words were strained and distracted, as if they were waiting for whatever news Jack had brought.

I spent more time on it than I should have, but there's something soothing about working on a client who doesn't squirm and flinch with every touch of the pulsing needle. I think I also needed to get lost in the work to find my center. My thoughts and worries slipped away with the buzz, my eyes locked on the living canvas before me.

"What news do you have for me?" I asked when I finally put the gun down and cleaned the excess blood and ink from the tattoo.

"Bronx asked that we keep our ears out for the serial killer, but we haven't heard anything yet," Jack said.

I frowned, placing a pad of gauze against his neck. "That sucks."

The shifter shrugged. "Whoever this bastard is, he's not passing through our territory. He's other side of the tracks."

Cutting off a couple pieces of tape, I secured the pad. "The killer is a woman."

"Doesn't change anything." Jack sat up when I finished, his hand smoothing over the tape to make sure that it was in place. He'd only need it for an hour or so to keep the area clean. "I've got all kinds of lowlifes and scum trekking through my domain. Not a whisper, but it's probably for the best. I know of four shifters in Low Town who are pregnant and these killings have got the entire shifter community on high alert. If this bitch isn't caught soon, someone is going to get killed when tempers finally snap."

"All werewolves?" Trixie asked.

Jack shook his head, all smiles gone. "Two werewolves, one were-panther, and one were-bear. But I've heard that the were-bear family has headed out of town for the winter. I think they're going to hibernate through the bulk of her pregnancy."

"Fantastic," I muttered under my breath. The tension that had slipped away with our joking in the tattooing room had come back, tightening in my neck and shoulders.

This was turning into an ugly situation. It wasn't just that we were dealing with an insane killer on the loose in Low Town, but we also had shifters growing edgier the longer she was on the streets. Powder kegs were popping up around the city, waiting, primed to explode. People were going to end up dead, and I didn't think that the killer was going to be the first in line.

"I also hear that you've managed to rile up the goblins," Jack said with a knowing smirk.

"There was . . . an incident," I hedged.

The werewolf laughed, his head tipping back so that his long canines flashed in the dim light. "An incident? Word is that you burned down their house outside the city."

"Oh, that's bullshit! They attacked us first. We went

there to talk. The fire was an accident if anything. I didn't start shit with them!"

Jack snorted, covering up the last of his chuckles at my plight. "Yeah, well . . . it seems they talked to a couple ogres that are still in my employ who remember you very well. They didn't come out and say what you are, but they apparently hinted around enough to imply that you're a dangerous man to fuck with. They might have also hinted that you had something to do with Reave's disappearance, so the goblins are at least taking you more seriously now."

My eyebrows jumped at this unexpected development. "You think this will make them willing to talk?" I asked, hoping to use this shift to my advantage.

The werewolf shrugged as he pulled on his leather jacket. "Don't know. Goblins are a pain in the ass on a good day. If you managed to put the fear of God in them, they might answer your questions. But that's assuming you can corner them again."

"Thanks." I sighed. That sounded to be about my luck with things anymore.

Jack waved at me and called back to my companions before slipping out into the night to rule his little empire. All in all, the werewolf was proving to be a good guy, even though he specialized in needling me. Most of his activities might be illegal, but then I couldn't throw stones. I'd completed plenty of tattoos in my years that were off the record and then there was the whole warlock thing. Sure, it wasn't illegal, but admitting it to the wrong people would definitely see me lynched for it.

Ambling back into the main tattooing room, I started to sit down in my chair again when the front door chimed. Customers poured in for the next few hours, keeping my mind away from my latest worries and focused on the job at hand. I welcomed the distraction while I had it. When I was tattooing, I felt like I was actually accomplishing something good with my skills. That feeling didn't happen often when I was faced with problems that involved the Towers.

After tattooing two sirens and a leprechaun, I finally hit a lull. Standing up, I stretched my arms above my head and yawned. The clock said that it was nearly eleven, which explained why I was starting to drag so badly. I was usually out of the shop before ten, even on my busiest of days. But I didn't want to leave. The atmosphere was good, reminding me of the days before my companions knew about my past and trouble was pounding on our door. The jokes and teasing flowed freely through the air, keeping my mind off of darker matters.

But there was no more putting it off. It was late and I needed to get a few hours of sleep if I was going to be of any use to anyone during the next several days.

"You heading out?" Bronx asked as he turned back from the lobby after showing out our last customer.

"Yeah. I'm beat," I said around another yawn. Reaching up, I rubbed my hands over my face, trying to clear my thoughts. A slow and steady snowfall had started to coat the city during the past hour and I needed to be clear for the drive home so I didn't end up with my SUV wrapped around a telephone pole.

"Gage, I think we need to discuss how we're going to divide up my schedule," Trixie said softly.

I dropped my hands back to my sides, my brain finally coming back online with her words. She was still intending to leave.

"Can you give me more time?"

"Gage—"

"No, wait. Hear me out," I said firmly, holding up my hands as if they could stop her words. Closing my eyes, I drew in a deep breath, while packing down the initial wave of panic that threatened to consume me. Losing my shit wasn't going to convince her to stay. When I opened my eyes, I forced a smile on my face in an attempt to at least look reassuring. "You've known about this for a while now, had plenty of time to make up your mind, and line up your arguments. I haven't and that isn't fair to me. We're in this together. Correct?"

"Of course, but I have to think about the baby's safety first."

"I know and I agree. I have to keep you and the baby safe. What if I can do that? What if I can find a way that will keep you both safe from harm? Will you stay?"

"I don't know," she said softly, seeming painfully unsure now that I was being calm and reasonable.

"You said your only reason for leaving was an issue of safety. Is there something else?"

"No."

"Then if I can keep you safe, will you stay?"

"I don't know. I guess. How are you going to make it safe for the baby?"

"You and the baby," I corrected with a warm smile. Some of the panic subsided as I managed to get that tiny concession. "I don't know yet. I'm still trying to figure that out. I want you to give me more time. Can you wait?"

Trixie shook her head. "I don't know. It's winter. The longer I wait, the more dangerous it becomes. It's better if I leave soon."

"I understand. I just want you to give me a chance."

She gifted me with a little smile that didn't reach her sad eyes. "I'll try."

Quickly closing the distance between us, I gave her a swift kiss. "And you promise not to leave without telling me?"

"Yes."

"Thank you," I whispered, pressing my forehead to hers. My heart ached to see her so troubled, but I appreciated that she was at least trying to give me some time to protect her and the baby. I just had to figure out how in the world I was going to accomplish that.

Grabbing my coat, I stepped out into the bitter cold, my mind turned to figuring out a way to permanently extricate myself from the Towers. Or at the very least, create a buffer that would protect Trixie and the baby from their notice.

But I didn't get far.

Gideon was standing in the middle of the sidewalk, waiting for me.

CHAPTER 5

Sometimes, there's no escaping it.

I stopped several feet from Gideon, watching the snow swirling through the air to land on his black suit. His cape flapped slightly in the breeze, as if to flick away any tiny flakes that might spoil his dark aura. While the warlock never looked pleased to see me, he was looking grimmer than usual tonight.

"Is it too much to hope that you've caught the bastard and I can return to my normal life?" I asked, stepping around him to walk down the alley beside the parlor. I had parked my car out front, but I didn't want to risk anyone seeing me talking to a warlock. It was bad for my image of a harmless tattoo artist.

"Yes, it is," he said, following a step behind me.

"So what's new? Been out scaring little kids?"

"The council has decided to let you use the library in Dresden," Gideon said in a low voice.

I stopped walking and jerked around to look at him in shock. "Really?" The Ivory Tower in Dresden was home to the largest collection of spell books and magical history tomes of all the Towers. I hadn't expected them to allow it, let alone decide so quickly.

"On one condition," he added, causing my stomach to knot.

Dropping backward, I leaned my shoulders against the wall of the building and shoved my hands into my coat pockets. "I knew it." The council was never one to do anything the easy way.

"They will let you use the library as much as you like on the condition that you remove the protection spells on Simon Thorn's rooms."

My mouth dropped open at the mention of my old mentor. The bastard's body was now buried under the street in a crappy part of town while his soul now served as the ferryman for the dead in the Underworld, thanks to yours truly. I couldn't feel bad for him though. He'd tortured me while he was alive and succeeded in handing a chunk of my soul over to Lilith. At least he could say that he had steady employment for the rest of eternity.

"The spells are still active?" I'd killed Simon months ago. Someone should have figured out what he was using to protect his shit ages ago.

"Three have gone in. None have come back out."

"Is the council sure they're dead?" But even as the question left my lips, I knew it was stupid. This was Simon we were talking about. The man was a murderous psychopath on a good day. It was only made worse by the fact that he had been a warlock, giving him carte blanche to raise whatever the hell he wanted without fear of retribution.

"If their screams are anything to go by, then yes, they're all dead."

Sighing, I leaned my head back against the wall and stared up at the sliver of sky I could see between the buildings. It was an ugly orangish black as the lights of the city hit against the heavy black clouds overhead, leaving you with a claustrophobic feeling like you were trapped in a bell jar with all the other insects.

I wasn't thrilled with the idea of going back to the Towers in the first place, particularly the Dresden Tower, since that's where all the horrors of my life actually took place. But I needed to research Death Magic, not to mention a few other things that Gideon and the council didn't need to know about.

Adding to my dilemma was the fact that if anyone could get into Simon Thorn's rooms, it was most likely going to be me. I had studied under the bastard. I knew the spells and wards that he favored. Hell, I used half of them to this day. I learned to unravel most of them so they wouldn't kill me in my sleep each night. The only concern was whether Simon had bothered to change all his spells after I left the Towers when I was a teenager. If he hadn't, there was a good chance I could get in quite easily. If he had, I was so fucked.

But what choice did I have?

"Let me head home and get changed into something Towers appropriate," I said with a sneer as I turned back toward the main street and my car.

"You don't have to do this," Gideon said, catching me with a hand on my shoulder.

"We both know I do," I grumbled. "If it's not this, then it'll be for some other reason. Everyone knows I'm their best shot at getting in there, and I'm sure there are some nosy pricks who are dying to know what the hell Simon was up to."

"Then we go now." As he spoke, a biting chill swept down my body like icy hands sliding over my flesh from my shoulders to my feet. I tried to jerk away but Gideon held tight to my shoulder. Glancing down at myself, I found that I was now wearing the uniform of the guardians, leaving behind the guise of the mild-mannered tattoo artist with the charming disposition.

"Warn me next time," I snapped before one last shiver claimed me.

I thought I heard Gideon give a derisive snort, but the world blinked out and there was no sound at all — only the all-consuming silence of the nothing we traveled through to get to Germany in the blink of an eye. A rise of panic had me clenching my teeth because it felt like there was no air to breathe in the emptiness, but even as that frantic thought formed in my brain, we were in Germany. I had to shield my eyes for a second against the glare of the moonlight coming off the snow after the darkness that had consumed me.

The Dresden Ivory Tower rose up like a pale, bony finger against the thick velvet night sky. The forest that surrounded the structure had been pushed back as if even nature feared to draw too close to the witches and warlocks that lived inside. My heart gave a couple hard thumps at the sight of the structure and my breathing grew ragged around the lump that had formed in my throat.

The last time I had seen this Tower I had stood before the council waiting to hear if I was to be killed for my rebellion against my mentor and my attempts to escape. Obviously, I was allowed to live, but there had been a price. And in the end, whatever concessions I thought I had won proved to be false because I was right back here ten years later. Only this time, I had asked for entrance into their bloodstained halls.

"I brought us in this way because I wasn't sure if Master Thorn had a secret entrance that you could use," Gideon said when I no longer sounded like I was at risk of hyperventilating. There was no missing the note of hope in his tone.

"If he did, I don't know about it." My voice sounded like it had been dragged across the concrete. I never thought I'd find myself back here. And when Simon had been killed, I'd hoped I would never have to think about him or my past again. It's amazing how fucking wrong I can be at times.

Clearing my throat, I took a step forward and then another one, relieved to find that it grew easier as long as I kept my mind on the task at hand. Getting into Simon's rooms meant my getting into the library, which meant that I was closer to finding the killer and finding a way to keep Trixie and our baby safe. Now I just had to enter Simon's rooms without having my organs pulled out through my belly button.

Gideon wordlessly commanded the massive double doors to open and we stepped inside the Tower, escaping the bitter cold for something that felt so much worse—a heart-sickening familiarity that was almost comforting. Ten years had passed and it all looked the same. The floor was covered in cold gray marble and the walls were a deep charcoal gray, while smoky white globes of light dotted the walls at regular intervals. There was a hint of burnt heather in the air along with a whiff of lavender, both of which just barely failed to mask the coppery tang of old blood.

But it wasn't the scents or sights that nearly had me gagging. It was the fact that something in my body relaxed upon returning. I had lived here for nine years—longer than I ever lived with my real family, who loved and treated me with kindness. This Tower had become my life, my future, and my entire world. No matter the horrors I survived, the people I had killed, or the times I had nearly died myself, something in my psyche called this place home.

"I can go up to Thorn's door with you, but I can't help you beyond that," Gideon said, breaking the silence after allowing me a couple of minutes to merely stare at my stark surroundings.

"No. I'll meet you in the library after I'm done," I said once I felt that I had a firm handle on my emotions.

"Gage, you don't—"

"Yeah, I do." Glancing over my shoulder at his, I flashed him a twisted grin. "Don't worry. I remember the way."

Striding across the open main hall, I stopped before a quartet of large black openings along the wall. They were like car-less elevators that could take you to any location within the Towers. You just had to have the balls to use them. Or maybe you had to be a little insane.

I sucked in a deep breath and forced myself to step into the open black pit. My heart clenched as my foot fell a couple inches, pulling my entire body down before it hit a solid floor. I stepped the rest of the way into the opening, so that it looked as if I were hovering in open air. Without needing to close my eyes, I thought of the location of Simon's old rooms and my body was thrust upward at a startling rate by an unseen force. The openings for the other floors flashed by in a splash of white light before I suddenly stopped just a couple floors from the top.

As I stepped off into the foyer of the floor, a terrified scream echoed up through the empty chamber, sending all the hairs on my neck to standing on end. The scream came from a child, likely a new apprentice who had yet to grow accustomed to this mode of travel through the Tower. I'd seen too many warlocks and witches push their new wards into the tunnels so that they could wring a scream out of them. Travelling up wasn't so bad as you had a base to start with. Descending to the lower levels almost always left you confident that you were going to smack into the hard paving stones at the bottom, shattering every bone in your body. It took years for that fear to finally subside. Luckily it only took a few months for a new apprentice to stop screaming. But at that point, the mentor usually gave them something new to scream about.

The empty shaft opened into a short narrow hallway that led to the main foyer of the floor. The circular foyer was surrounded by four doors that led to the private rooms of four different warlocks or witches. A dim light glowed in the center the foyer, lacing all with a thin gray shadow.

Everything was silent as I stood there, looking at the other doors. It was nearly five in the morning in Dresden and soon the apprentices would be stirring from their tiny cots and uncomfortable pallets to prepare the morning meal for their mentors. I tried to move silently, but I was sure they had already heard my footsteps across the stone floor. The smart ones learned not to sleep too deeply. There was no telling what would sneak up on you when you were at your most vulnerable.

With some reluctance, I finally dragged my gaze off to the left, where Simon's door stood. The shadows were thicker there, as if whatever malevolent spell he'd set on his rooms was leaking out into the main foyer in search of fresh territory to conquer. Closing my eyes for a second, I took a deep breath and pushed my memories of the bastard to the back of my brain. Simon Thorn was dead. I had killed him and sent him down to the Underworld. He wouldn't hurt me any longer.

I needed to stay focused on unraveling the spells that lay before me.

Stepping closer to the door, I put out my hand and immediately snatched it back. I was right. The protection spell was starting to leak out. The air wavered slightly and there was a tingling along my skin like little needles digging into my flesh. Apparently if you left whatever he had created running too long, it decided to expand its reach. That or it was affected by all the magic that hung in the air within the Towers because of all the damn magic users. I had heard of incidents where spells went a little wild because of the errant magic, but hadn't personally encountered it until now.

With a frown, I decided the best course was to start with the easy stuff that I knew he'd still have in effect. Patting down my pockets, I located a piece of white chalk I had started carrying with me at all times. On my knees outside the door, I put the chalk to the bottom of the frame and whispered a cleansing spell. After a couple seconds, writing along the frame shimmered into view. Simon was fond of using invisible chalk to inscribe some of his wards. I just had to go back over them in reverse to undo each of them.

As I completed the last one, there was loud cracking sound as if part of the wooden frame split. I leaned close to inspect the door frame when something large and angry slammed into the back side of the door, causing the heavy barrier to rattle in the frame. I jumped back, my heart launching into my throat as I stared at the door. Claws scratched against the wood, as if the creature was trying to climb through it to get to me. What the fuck had Simon set loose in there?

I crabwalked backward until I was seated in the middle of the dimly lit foyer, waiting for the scratching to cease. There were no other sounds coming from the room besides the claws on the wood and stone floors. No growling or snarling. There were any number of creatures you could summon up that loved nothing more than to snack on weaker creatures, but I should have heard some other noises. None of them were mute. They were also a bitch to control and I didn't think even the strongest witch or warlock would be insane enough to use one.

When the clawing had ceased, I pushed to my feet, trying to ignore the shaking that had crept into my hands. The attack didn't resume when I approached the door again, but I didn't take that as a sign that the creature had curled up in its little bed and gone to sleep. It was waiting for me to enter.

Inspecting the door and the frame again, I was disappointed to find that there weren't any other spells guarding the entrance. There was no more stalling. Shoving the chalk back into my pocket, I pulled out my wand and carefully erected as many shields and protective wards as I could on myself before uttering the unlocking spell.

Soundlessly, the door swung open. I tried a lighting spell, knowing that there had to be lamps or candles in there to push back the darkness, but nothing happened. *Wonderful.* I either stepped into the black pit of death or gave up on saving my relationship with Trixie. *Man, I was an awesome boyfriend!*

Calling up a ball of white light, I stepped over the threshold with it hovering just over my shoulder. It did little to cast light over the room. The shape of a chair a few feet in front of me and what might have been a table cluttered with books were barely discernible within the gloom.

And then something moved. It crossed from right to left, as if circling me. I didn't see it so much as felt the movement within the darkness, as if it were nothing more than a ripple of energy. Twisting around to try to keep whatever it was in view, I tightened my grip on my wand. My heart was pounding and my palms were growing sweaty, making me feel as if my wand was going to slip right out of my hand.

The door slammed shut, cloaking the room in darkness. My body tensed, waiting, but the creature didn't attack. It moved around me again, drawing a little closer as if testing what I'd tolerate. The only sound in the room was my breathing as it broke past my lips in short gasps. There were no sounds of claws on the stone floor, no shuffling sounds of cloth or the rub of fur. I couldn't even hear it breathing.

That's when it dawned on me that this was no living creature I was facing. As I had feared, this thing was similar to what I had guarding the basement of Asylum. But even as my heart ramped up with this sickening idea, I was confused as to why it hadn't attacked yet. The spell at Asylum launched itself at anything that just partially descended the stairs, ripping the poor fucker to shreds. If this were the same thing, I should have been dead before clearing the threshold.

It was watching me. Waiting.

Praying that my shields would hold, I pulled together the same spell I used to disarm the protection spell at Asylum. As I did, the creature in the darkness drew closer on my left. I couldn't see a shape or any defining features. It was just the sense of a massive force that was a little darker than the unyielding blackness of the room.

Why are you trying to lock me up?

The words drifted through my brain, but it felt as if they had been hissed in my ear. I lurched back a step, trying to put some distance between myself and the darkness. But there was no getting away. The force was everywhere in the room, crowding close but still not harming me. Was it toying with me? Playing with its food out of boredom? That couldn't be because that would mean this wasn't just a spell. This dark energy was a thinking, feeling creature.

"Why haven't you attacked yet?" I asked, trying to make sense out of what I was faced with.

She's asked me not to kill you.

"She? She who?" I barked.

The thing laughed without making a sound. I could feel its amusement, leaving behind the feeling of oily sludge sliding down the back of my throat. The darkness rippled and the little light I had created winked out. I couldn't see anything, not even a strip of light leaking into the room from under the door. I wasn't even sure I was still in Simon's rooms but was now floating in nothingness.

The one you've been promised to.

"Lilith?" I breathed as my hearted threatened to explode in my chest.

It didn't answer. It didn't have to. Besides the fact that Simon had handed over a chunk of my soul to the Queen of the Underworld, I had killed two people using magic. I owed magic two years of my life and when it came time for me to pay up, Lilith was the one I went to serve.

The creature laughed again and I fought the growing wave of nausea threatening to send what little I had eaten that day up my throat. Clenching my teeth, I drew in air through my nose and slowly released it, pushing back against my twisting stomach. Puking now would break my concentration and I'd lose all the protective spells I was clinging to. I certainly didn't trust this thing not to attack me just because Lilith had asked nicely.

"You're one of her monsters then," I said when some of the queasiness had passed.

What twisted amusement I had felt from this thing disintegrated in a heartbeat and it was instantly on me, knocking me to the ground. Even without a body, it felt as if the creature was crouched over me, pinning me to the cold hard stones.

Not hers! Demon, not *monster,* it snarled.

I flinched, feeling as if the thing was grinding my brain cells between its molars. "Fine! Sorry! Demon.

Not monster," I shouted, ready to concede anything so it would give me a little more breathing room.

The demon's anger receded with my words and it retreated. I was slow to get to my feet. My knees were jelly and couldn't hold me. Sadly, I think the demon had also fried my common sense, because I still couldn't keep my mouth shut. "Fine, Demon Not Monster. You're following Lilith's suggestion, but she doesn't control you. Why bother listening to her request?"

If it was going to give me a free pass at breathing, I wanted to know why. The hope was that if I knew the real reason, then I was likely to find the boundaries of its good will. A stupid hope, I was sure, but I was afraid of running into the situation where if it thought too much about its decision to let me live, it might discover that its reasons weren't all that good after all.

Why would I kill the one who lets me out to play?

A chill ran down my spine, raising the hairs on my arms. I opened my mouth to argue that I had no dealings with demons but something shifted slightly in the creature as it drew away from me and it suddenly felt . . . familiar. The same feeling that had hit me when I first stepped into the room.

"Shit," I hissed, stumbling backward. The demon moved, closing the distance between us to push against my back to keep me from falling on my ass. I jerked away from it, but didn't take any additional steps. My head was spinning. The protection spell in the basement of Asylum, the energy I set loose to attack anyone that entered my private domain, was a demon.

I cursed myself and my stupidity for ever trusting a powerful protection spell I copied off of Simon. It should have been no surprise that the warlock has been messing with things no sane person would have used. Everyone said demons couldn't be controlled. They'd tear your heart out just for laughs and slurp up your soul as a cocktail. All they knew was pain and destruction.

Pushing back the panic, I tried to focus on the fact that the demon that was guarding my basement as also guarding Simon's rooms, which meant that I could actually put it back into lockdown mode. It would take a whole hell of a lot more energy than I normally needed to use, because it had consumed not only Simon's rooms, but its energy was also starting to leak out into the hall.

"It's the symbol," I murmured, not sure if I was talking to the demon or myself. Any fear I had felt instantly disappeared as a rush of understanding swept through me. Adrenaline pumped through my veins and I nearly laughed. "It's the symbol. It's not so much a spell as it is a doorway for you. The only reason you listen to me is because I control whether the door is open or closed."

True . . . partially.

"And the reason your powers are leaking into the hall?"

The one that lived here, the one that you killed . . . the door has been left open for too long. It has allowed me to push against the boundaries he set for me.

"And if I lock the doorway again?"

I would not be pleased.

Yeah, I could have guessed, I thought but kept my mouth shut. The key was that the demon didn't say that I couldn't close the doorway again. Sure, I certainly didn't want to piss off a demon, but it wasn't like I could leave it running around loose in Simon's rooms.

Or maybe I could . . .

"If I leave this doorway open, will you allow me to come and go in this room unharmed?"

You control my door. I must.

I frowned. That was only partially true. It was hard to believe, but demons couldn't lie. They could bend the truth. They could tell you partial truths, leaving out key information that would get you killed later. But they couldn't say "no" when the truth was clearly "yes." Funny enough, there were also stories that angels could lie to you and did frequently in the name of keeping the balance preserved.

"I control the door back at the tattoo parlor, but I didn't draw this door," I murmured. It wasn't fooling me. I knew exactly where the leash ended for this thing and it was well before I walked into Simon's rooms.

True. But you could.

The first ripple of temptation washed through me. Setting the door here, I could enter Simon's rooms without having to worry about anyone else from the Towers mucking around in here. I would have access to all of Simon's books and notes. I'd also have all the magical items that he'd collected during his life. While I wasn't keen on the idea of leaving the demon running around the rooms, as long as I strengthened the boundaries again, the only people that it would be a threat to were the witches and the warlocks of the Tower. I wasn't going to lose a lot of sleep over that thought.

"I need light to work in," I announced.

Immediately, the lamps in all the rooms came on, filling the chambers with a soft yellow glow. Some of the queasiness returned to my stomach and it had nothing to do with the demon. The chambers were almost unchanged from the day I left so many years ago. The main room held a massive wood table that was about chest high and covered in books, glass beakers and jars, and a sundry of potion ingredients. Papers were scattered everywhere with Simon's nearly illegible scrawl, where he had been making notes on whatever the bastard had been working on.

Stepping around the table, being careful not to touch it, my eyes slipped over the stuffed chair beside the fireplace. More books were stacked beside it, with one lying open across the arm as if Simon had been pulled from his reading to deal with me.

The main room led into the small kitchen with an old-fashioned iron stove. A fire sprang to life as I passed through and I jumped. The damn thing was still tuned to me, as if Simon couldn't have been bothered to erase my memory from half the spells that still littered his rooms. There was a complete collection of shining copper pots hanging from the ceiling. Two blocks of knives were on the counter—one for potions and another for cooking. I'd spent most of my time in this room. I slept on a pallet beside the stove and cooked all of Simon's meals as well as prepared his hot tea throughout the day while he worked.

The final room, off the kitchen, was Simon's bedchamber. I rarely visited this room during my apprenticeship. I popped in once a day to quickly make the bed and pick up his clothes for the laundry before quickly scurrying out again. Now, there were dirty clothes piled everywhere and his sheets were a tangled mess as if his last sleep had been an uneasy one.

The black mass was gone, becoming invisible to the naked eye, but I could feel it following me from room to room. It hovered close with ill-concealed glee as if excited to have a new playmate as I explored the Tower rooms.

I packed away all my bitter emotions associated with these rooms. Even after all this time, I couldn't conjure up an ounce of pity or remorse for my old mentor. The world was better off without him and I would soon wipe his memory from these rooms as well.

But the first step was to locate the symbol that Simon had drawn so that I could put some of my own blood into it. It was all part of the agreement you made with what I had thought were the powers of the protection spell. I had been more than a little wrong on that one. Apparently that agreement was made with a demon in return for some degree of control over it.

Unfortunately, after a quick search of the rooms, I hadn't found the symbol. In fact, I couldn't remember ever seeing where Simon had placed the symbol. I had stolen it from a book in Simon's collection. How could Simon have hidden the symbol in his rooms? As far as I knew, the symbol had to be at least five feet across. Not something that was easily hidden. He also couldn't draw it with his invisible chalk.

Walking back into the main room, I carefully inspected the walls but still didn't see anything that resembled the demon's doorway.

You're getting warmer.

The demon's voice drifted in a singsong tone through my head, sending chills down my back.

Gritting my teeth, I stood off to the side of the room and raised my hands out in front of me as I slowly summoned up a little energy before sending it seeking the symbol. The only reason I was able to do this was because it was part of the spell that closed the doorway. If you didn't know the symbol was there or how to close the door, you'd never be able to feel it.

The demon shifted a bit nervously near me, but didn't give any other indication that it might be agitated by what I was doing, which was a relief.

The energy left my body and instead of flying off toward one of the walls, it went straight down to the floor. I stepped back, staring at the stones for a second before the obvious finally dawned on me. Instead of putting the symbol on the wall and then hiding it from view, the bastard put in on the stones that made up the floor. Crafty. Simon Thorn had always been an extremely crafty devil.

Stepping back toward the kitchen, I gathered up more energy, no longer fearful of the demon that was still hovering close. There was a feeling of gleeful excitement coming from it that did nothing to settle my mind. I wasn't fond of the notion that I was doing anything that pleased the creature. Of course, I didn't want to do anything that might piss it off because that might give it a reason to remove my head.

The burst of energy I sent out wrapped around everything that rested on the floor of the main room. Items trembled briefly before rising steadily into the air. Glass tinkled and papers shifted, but nothing fell from the massive table as it rose. When everything hovered two feet above the floor, I waved both hands in a circular motion toward my body as if I were rowing a boat while whispering a simple spell I had used when folding laundry.

Like flipping over dominoes, the stones in the floor tossed over so that they were now lying on the backs. One after another rolled over and resettled into its proper place in a gray wave until the symbol was revealed in the stones. A gasp escaped me and I took a step forward before I remembered that I was holding two spells together and didn't need to be distracted.

When all the stones were flipped over, I gently lowered everything back to the floor and knelt down. Simon had been intently focused on the protection of himself and the items in the room. The warlock hadn't merely painted the symbol on the stones. He had chiseled it in so that there was no removing it short of destroying the stones in the floor.

Add your blood. Make it yours.

As the demon hissed the words through my head, a dagger shot across the room and landed point first between a pair of stones less than a foot from my hand. I jumped back, watching the blade shiver there in warning. That could have very easily been my chest or the back of my skull.

I wasn't crazy about the idea of closely tying this demon to me a second time, but putting my blood in the symbol in Simon's rooms meant that I could more easily close the doorway. I could control the demon in a manner of speaking, though I knew I was lying to myself if I thought I could control a demon. The only concern was that if I didn't agree to make this doorway mine, then there was a good chance the demon was going to kill me for the irritation. I might let it sulk in the basement at Asylum, but it had a lot more free range in Simon's rooms.

Unfortunately, what won out in the end wasn't the idea of being able to lock the demon away more effectively. It was the notion that Simon's rooms would now be mine and I could use the demon to keep out the warlocks and the witches who might want to take over this space. My gig as a guardian wasn't going to last. They'd reach a point where they'd tire of the game and finally kill me for using magic. But before that, they'd revoke my right to visit the Dresden library. I was easier to kill if I knew less magic than they did.

With Simon's rooms, I could study in secret. I could review his notes and read his books, expanding my knowledge and finally getting the one thing the bastard owed me—an education in magic. I'd give the demon a little bit of my blood if it brought me one step closer to gaining control over my life, a step closer to evening the score at last.

Picking up the dagger, I sliced the palm of my left hand, pain drawing a hiss of air through my clenched teeth. The pain was good. It cleared my head, brought me out of the past and secured me in the present. I held my hand open, waiting for the blood to well up, before squeezing it into a fist over the outer line of the symbol. The symbol didn't need to be entirely filled with my blood, just three key lines required a small smear.

As my blood dripped into the last of the lines, a surge of power jumped into my body, knocking the breath out of my lungs and causing my heart to skip a beat. I shook my head as if to clear it, but the buzzing wasn't in my head. It was the energy in the room and I was suddenly tapped into it all. But the energy wasn't coming from some old spell that Simon had created. It was from the demon.

"Gage!" Gideon shouted outside the door. "Gage! Are you in there?" His hard-soled shoes echoed across the floor as he ran toward Simon's old rooms.

"Fuck," I whispered.

The demon snarled in my brain and I could feel it gather up its energy as it launched itself across the room, slamming into the door with enough force to make the thick wood barrier shudder in its frame. While I couldn't see the creature, fresh gouges appeared in the wood as it fought its way toward the other warlock.

"Stay out, Gideon!" I shouted back. "I'm alive! Stay out!"

Not trusting my companion to listen to me, I tried to use the same spell I used in the basement at Asylum to lock the demon back in the symbol, but the creature was stronger in these rooms than I was accustomed to. It turned the energy it was using on the door toward me. I raised my shields at the last second, but it still plowed through. Pain slashed across my cheek as it tore three long slashes through my flesh with its talons.

"You're not touching him!" I snarled, putting more energy behind the locking spell as I dropped my shields completely.

Glass exploded on the table and the lights winked out again, but I didn't need the light. I couldn't see the demon with the lights on, and the darkness actually helped me focus my magic. As the demon turned, preparing to rush me a second time, I changed tactics. It was lost in a rage, determined to hurt something now that it had been denied access to its prey. When it crossed above the symbol toward me, I directed the energy to reach up from the floor and grab it as if the hands of the dead were trying to pull it back toward the Underworld.

No!

It shrieked in my head, the sound so deafening that I didn't hear the glass breaking, but I could feel it raining down on me from around the room.

"Enough!" I bellowed. I halted the spell, but didn't disperse the energy releasing the demon.

"Gage? Are you all right?" Gideon shouted from the other side of the door, but I ignored him.

"We need to come to an agreement. You attack who I say or I will close the doorway and destroy the stones," I said in a low voice.

You need me, the demon howled.

"But you need me more," I said. "I can find another way to get what I want. Are you willing to wait for someone else to come along to set you free?"

I have an eternity ahead of me.

"Yeah, or you can make a deal with me now."

The silence stretched for several seconds. Sweat beaded on my brow and my arms started to tremble under the weight of holding the spell in a state of limbo. I was giving this thing another two seconds and I was shutting the doorway down. If I had any sense, I'd do it anyway. Dealing with demons was too dangerous and I was beginning to wonder about my own sanity if I was willing to go down this dark road. But it was right. I did need it.

What are your requirements, Master? the demon hissed at last, surprising me.

Master? This was a development that I wasn't expecting. *Master* couldn't be a word demons tossed about lightly. It couldn't actually interpret this bargain I was trying to wring out of it as my beating it. But then, maybe I was beating it. I was forcing the demon to do my bidding.

"You will attack only who I say," I commanded softly, trying to be careful in the event that Gideon was listening at the door. "You will not attack Gideon."

Anyone else forbidden?

"Trixie, Bronx, and Sofie as well." I didn't expect my companions to walk through the door in the Towers, but I had to cover my ass in the event that some fucking witch or warlock got crafty. Besides, Sofie might be stuck as a cat, but the old witch did pop back to the Towers on occasion for information. I didn't think she'd ever dare come into Simon's rooms, but I didn't want to risk her life.

Any other wishes?

"Back off. These rooms are mine now."

The demon was quiet for a moment as if pondering my requests. The fierce, ruthless anger I had felt coming off it just seconds ago had diminished completely and all I felt was a kind of pensiveness.

Am I to be locked up completely like in your other rooms?

It was referring to the basement. The spell down there kept a much tighter leash on it, but then I'd been afraid of the power creeping up through the floorboards and attacking a client in the middle of a tattoo. Unexplained attacks and gruesome deaths were always bad for business.

"If you can agree to not attack me or those I have listed as untouchable, I will allow you to remain freer than at Asylum."

Agreed.

As if to show that there were no hard feelings, the

lights popped on around the room. Glass that shattered in the face of the demon's rage drifted gently across the room, and reassembled into beakers, vials, and other sundry items as if nothing had ever happened. Not allowing myself to be distracted by the elegant display of power, I completed part of the closure spell I had started, trapping some of the demon's powers. In comparison to what I had erected at Asylum, I was willing to estimate that the demon was now operating at only half power. Or rather, I hoped that it had access to only half of its powers.

My legs wobbled when I released the energy and I started to collapse toward the floor, but a cushioned ottoman shot across the room and caught me before I could hit the floor. This was just too weird.

"Gage?" Gideon called, reminding me that the warlock was waiting in the hall.

"I'm alive," I shouted back. My body ached as if I had pulled several muscles trying to lift something I had no business lifting. But then, I guess that was only natural when you went a couple rounds with a demon. No, that was wrong. You go a couple rounds with a demon, and your intestines get strung up around the room like Christmas lights. This was what it felt like when you went a couple rounds with a demon that needed you alive.

I heard the rattle of the door handle as the warlock tried to open the door. My hand shot out and I reinforced the lock, keeping him barred from the room. "Don't come in. I can't shut down the spell. Simon still has it tuned to me so I can be in here, but anyone else coming in will be shredded."

"What kind of spell? Maybe I can help unravel it," Gideon offered.

"I'm not sure. I need to dig through his notes and try to find it," I lied. Closing my eyes, I drew in a deep breath, pushing down the self-loathing that rose up like bile in the back of my throat. "I've got it so it can't leak out of the room anymore. Go down to the library and I'll meet you in a few minutes."

I waited in the tense silence, listening to the pounding of my heart in my ears. I was terrified that the warlock was going to force his way in. The demon might say that he wasn't going to attack Gideon, but I could still feel it coiled just past my shoulder as if waiting to launch itself across the room. Demons couldn't lie, but they were great at half-truths and finding loopholes in agreements.

"Five minutes, Gage," Gideon warned.

I breathed a sigh of relief when I heard his footsteps retreating as he headed back toward the open shaft in the far wall that would take him to the basement level where the library was located.

You're sure you don't want that one killed?

"Yeah," I snapped. "I'm sure."

The demon chuckled and I shook my head. Exhaustion was taking its toll and the bed in the next room was starting to look appealing. Of course, I'd have to burn the sheets first, but I had a feeling my new little friend would be only too happy to help with that task.

Fuck it. Even with fatigue leaving me trembling where I sat, I wasn't sleeping here. I had a bed waiting for me that wasn't watched over by a demon.

"I need to get out of here," I muttered, slowly pushing to my feet.

Looking around, my eyes landed on the bookshelves in the far corner and some small bit of energy returned to me. If I was to have any hope of finding some spell or at least learning more control that would give me an edge over the Towers, there was a good chance it lay in Simon's books. Unfortunately, I didn't have the time or energy to go searching through them tonight to find what I was looking for—not that I even knew what I was looking for at this point.

"How long did you watch Simon?" I asked as I walked over to the bookshelves. None of the books looked familiar to me, but then the bastard hadn't let me touch his books while I was his apprentice. He believed that the best way for a young apprentice to learn was through watching and mimicking.

Time is difficult for me to judge, but I was here before you arrived as a child.

I nodded. "Could you help me find something? I need . . ." I started, but my words quickly drifted off, unsure of how to phrase my request.

Power, the demon whispered with a gleefulness that bit at my nerve endings like a jolt of electricity. *You wish to take down the Towers. You wish for control and power. You wish for protection.*

"Yes."

Two books slid partially out from there they had been shelved, one at chest level and the other on the very top shelf. Grabbing both, I took them over to the table and looked at them. The first looked to be a spell book, but upon flipping through it, the spells all appeared to be extremely aggressive and lethal. The book was old, older than even my former mentor. Simon had either taken this from the library or stolen it from a colleague many years ago.

The second book was the disturbing one. It was all about demons.

"Why this one?" I looked up in the direction that I felt the demon hovering even though I couldn't see it. "More information will give me the ability to control you better. Improve my edge over you. Wouldn't that make it harder for you to eventually kill me?"

The demon's amusement increased and it was like I could feel it smiling at me. Its presence drew closer so that it was surrounding me, but I didn't feel crowded.

It is like a chess game.

"And I'm a pawn?" I growled.

No, in this case, I am the pawn.

"What?"

I have allowed myself to be taken so that greater things can happen in the future.

My heart started pounding as some part of my brain desperately scrambled to find a way out of the mess that I had created. "What are you talking about?" Had my attempts to ensnare and control the demon gotten me into an even bigger mess that I couldn't escape? It was a hidden skill with me to constantly make things worse when I got involved.

She will claim her time with you soon. And if you're not prepared, she will break you.

Lilith. When I'd encountered her in the Underworld this past summer, she'd been adamant about my being able to free her so that she could wreak havoc on the rest of the world.

"Why me?"

You have potential.

"Fabulous," I muttered, suddenly feeling bone weary as hope of getting to the bottom of this dilemma quickly deflated. This conversation was getting me nowhere. I already knew that Lilith wanted to use me. I could only assume it was because she saw some kind of weakness within me that she could exploit.

Yes, it is. But as you will learn when you read, demons can read the future in the waves of magic.

"The future?"

Possible futures, it corrected, with a hint of amusement. *And there is one that I have seen with you that interests me.*

"And what is that?" I asked, though there was a part of me that didn't want to know.

The one where you defeat Lilith.

My blood ran cold at the demon's words and my eyes dropped back down to the book before me. I could defeat the Queen of the Underworld. But to do that, I was going to need the help of the demons. *What the hell had I gotten myself into?*

CHAPTER 6

Morning came too damn early. I groaned and rolled over onto my stomach, trying to escape the sunlight pouring through my open curtains. I forgot to shut them before falling into bed last night. No, this morning. The sun was already tinged with sunlight when I stumbled across the threshold.

Gideon and I spent hours digging through the archives of the library for books on Death Magic. There hadn't been a lot there, but what we found was not reassuring. The books made no mention of the creatures that first used magic, but it had been linked to several groups over time. Of course, all those groups had been wiped off the face of the earth by time and war, so we couldn't point fingers in their directions for our killer. Gideon had also been right in that the magic was only good for raising the dead, though most of the time the dead returned zombie-like rather than having any real resemblance to their former selves. I wasn't sure if Death Magic could be used to free Lilith from the Underworld, but it was the only logical reason I could come up with for someone playing with it.

All in all, my trip to the Dresden Tower proved to be a waste of time when it came to the investigation. But in Simon's rooms? Now in the bright light of day, every instinct screamed that I should have locked down the demon and destroyed the symbol etched into the floor. And when I was done, I should have gone straight to Asylum and destroyed the symbol there.

Did I?

No.

I was playing in something just as dangerous as the Death Magic killer.

But what if I could use it to protect Trixie and the baby? What if I could use it to stop the Towers and protect the world? Wasn't something like that worth the risk?

Closing my eyes, I started to drift off again when a persistent ringing forced my eyes open again. It was my cell phone, which explained why I had woken up in the first place. Some asshole was calling at this ungodly hour.

"What?" I barked after fumbling to answer the call. My fingers weren't working yet. I needed more sleep.

"Gee, you're a cheerful guy in the morning," Serah said.

Twisting around and propping myself up on my side, I looked at the alarm clock on my cluttered nightstand and groaned. "It's eight in the morning. I've been asleep only two hours. What the hell do you want?"

"The cops found another body."

"Fuck," I whispered, flopping onto my back. I was definitely awake now. Rubbing my eyes with my left hand, I tried to order my thoughts, moving them away from demons, Trixie, and even the psychopath with his army of the undead vampires. I needed to catch this bitch before Low Town fell apart. "How long ago?"

"The victim was found about an hour ago in an alley behind a Dumpster. Her husband reported her missing last night." Serah paused. I could hear her breathing and she sounded tired. I wasn't the only one losing sleep. "I talked the cops into letting us see the scene before the coroner takes the body, but we have to get down there now."

Which meant that I needed to move my ass now. "Yeah, I'm moving. Where?"

"Actually, it's not far from your apartment. I'll swing by and pick you up. Be there in ten." Serah ended the call before I could reply, officially starting the clock.

With a sigh, I swung my feet to the floor and sat up. I was still in clothes I'd worn to work the previous day. The only thing I'd managed to do when I came to bed was kick off my shoes and drop my wand on the nightstand. I felt grimy as hell and would have killed for a shower, but there wasn't time. Pulling the shirt I was wearing off over my head, I grabbed a semi-clean shirt off the floor and a fresh pair of socks. The jeans would have to do for another day.

In the bathroom, I inspected the three long cuts on my left cheek while I brushed my teeth. Both Gideon and I had tried a number of healing spells to remove them, but nothing worked. In the end, the warlock gave me a worried look before he walked silently away. He likely suspected what had caused the cuts and that wasn't a good thing.

A car horn beeped twice from the parking lot while I shoved my shoes on. On an impulse I grabbed my wand before pulling on my coat and heading out the door. The world was falling apart around me. It was best if I didn't step out the front door without being armed.

As I fell into the passenger seat beside the TAPSS investigator, she held up a large cup of coffee from the gas station about a block from my apartment complex. I felt a lump grow in my throat at the sight of that glorious container of hot liquid caffeine.

"You know, you're going to make some guy an amazing girlfriend," I murmured before sucking down a quarter of it.

"Awww, you're making me teary," she sarcastically said, pulling her gaze from the three long gashes on my cheek. She kindly didn't comment as she pulled the car out of the parking lot. "I need you focused and awake. The cops are getting edgy about letting us play in their sandbox so we're not going to get much time to look. We've got one shot at this."

"Got it, boss," I murmured between sips of coffee. Serah sent me a dirty look as she paused at a stop sign, but otherwise she kept her comments to herself.

The coffee was going a long way to getting my brain functioning, but it would only last a couple hours. I needed sleep desperately, but it looked like I wasn't going to get it since I needed to be in the parlor by noon to open up. This was going to be a really long and ugly day.

The crime scene ended up being halfway between my apartment building and Asylum. When we arrived, the cops had the street blocked off with cars and yellow tape, keeping the few gawkers a good distance off. I scanned the people gossiping and straining to see the body, but there wasn't anyone there who I thought could be our killer, not that I was sure what I was looking for. I just thought there might be something powerful buzzing in the air when she was close or an ugly redness to her aura. Of course, I could be wrong about that.

When we walked under the yellow police tape, the officers were far less accommodating than the men we'd encountered outside of Kyle's shop just a few days earlier. Either Serah hadn't worked the day shift or these guys were just assholes by nature. I was leaning toward the latter.

A large man in a wrinkled button-down shirt and stained brown tie glared at Serah as we approached. He hefted his large bulk in front of the mouth of the alley, a toothpick clenched between his teeth. "Moynahan," he growled, trying his damnedest to be intimidating.

"Curtis," Serah replied, looking completely unmoved by the man's attempts.

"You know TAPSS doesn't have any jurisdiction

here. This is a police matter. You need to let the real authorities handle this."

"I thought the police would be smart enough to accept help from an expert since this perp has slaughtered three women and one man on your watch. Last I heard, you didn't know shit about who was doing it." She gave him a sweet smile that only made me think that she was looking for an opportunity to rip his eyeballs out of his fat skull.

"Expert? Him?"

"Gage Powell, owner of Asylum Tattoo parlor," I introduced, not caring about the fact that the man was looking at me like I was a bug he'd just scraped off the bottom of his shoes.

"Yeah, well the victim didn't die from a shitty tattoo."

"You'd be surprised," I muttered under my breath, already wishing that I was back in Serah's car rather than standing in the frigid air that was already biting through my jeans.

"Look, Curtis. It's fucking cold and I'm sure the meat wagon would like to pack up so everyone can get out of here," Serah broke in. "Let us have a look and then we can all get the fuck out of Dodge."

"Ten minutes," the fat detective snapped before stepping out of the way of the entrance.

Serah snarled something softly to herself that I didn't quite catch. She was a feisty little thing who didn't take shit from anyone, even me, which was more than a little surprising since she knew exactly what I was. I was beginning to think that Low Town had become a poorer place when she left the police force. TAPSS would never be challenging enough for her. It was just one of those moments when being a barely above five foot adorable woman was a hindrance in this world of chest-beating, hairy monsters.

My mind quickly shifted from thoughts of Serah's rough lot in life to the crime as we walked up on the corpse. My heart broke a little at the sight of the woman carelessly slumped against the Dumpster. There was a hole in her chest where she had been stabbed in the heart, while a second slash had partially opened up her stomach. Her hands were still pressed to her abdomen as she had tried to protect her baby in her last seconds of life, but her attempts didn't save either of them in the end. Her head lolled to the side and her eyes blindly stared straight ahead with a yellow tint to them.

"Fuck," I murmured, shoving one hand through my hair as I paced a couple feet away.

"What?" Serah demanded, grabbing the sleeve of my coat to stop me.

"She was a shifter, probably werewolf. You're going to have a war on your hands soon if this bitch isn't caught soon."

"Fuck," Serah whispered. She looked over her shoulder at the woman, her wide brown eyes looking teary.

With a deep breath, I turned back to the body and knelt down a few feet away. The pool of blood had spread far from the body and had frozen on the dirty asphalt, keeping everyone a distance from her as if a moat had been erected in her final defense. A pair of forensics detectives was still collecting bits of evidence while another was photographing the scene. Several more people stood near the mouth of the alley, discussing the case or maybe just what they planned to do later that night. Regardless, there were just way too many people around for me to do any magic and that was all I was good at. I had no special forensics training that would give me insight into this crime scene.

What I needed was someone who could do magic out in the open. But he was going to be pissed at being called so early after the late night we had.

Jumping to my feet, I pulled my cell phone out of my pocket and pressed it to my ear like I had just gotten a call. I quickly walked toward the entrance of the alley and shoved past the fat bastard who had given us shit when we arrived.

"I need you here," I said aloud, even though there was no one on the phone. What the world didn't need to know was that I had used a little spell that had connected telepathically to Gideon. It was something that I had very rarely done with Gideon and only after I'd returned to the Towers as a guardian. As I had expected, I woke the warlock up and he was not happy with me.

And what's to keep me from killing you when I get there? Gideon growled in my head, sounding as if he was still half asleep.

"I've got a body left by the Low Town killer that you need to run a couple spells on," I said in a low voice so I couldn't be overhead while still trying to keep up the pretense that I was on an important call.

Do it yourself.

"Too many cops here. Come be your charming self and do the spells. It could help us catch up with at least one of these damn psychopaths."

I could both feel and hear him sigh. *I'll be there in a few.*

"Now!" I nearly shouted before shoving my cell phone in my back pocket again. Gideon was going to make me pay for this later, but someone needed to use a spell or two to track down this killer before it was too late.

"What the hell?" Serah hissed at me as she gave my shoulder a hard shove so that I was now facing her. "Why'd you walk away to take a phone call? This is a little more important!" What she wasn't saying was that I had made her look bad in front of the police who were closely watching us.

"My girlfriend is pregnant. I just needed to check on her," I said loudly so that anyone listening in on our conversation heard me.

"Oh," Serah said, instantly deflating. "Sorry. I—I . . . we need to get back there."

I forced a little smile, trying to show that I appreciated her concern. I didn't want to think about Trixie while I was dealing with this mess. Shoving my hands into the pockets of my coat, I started toward the alley with the intention of trying to find some way to stall being kicked out of the crime scene by the cops, but

I didn't even get that far. Detective Curtis stepped in front of the alley, an ugly grin splitting his face.

"Time's up," he announced.

"It hasn't been ten minutes," I growled, resisting the urge to shove the man out of my way. Yeah, the Towers were having a very bad effect on my people skills and how I handled confrontation. At least I hadn't reached for my wand, but I figured that it was only a matter of time.

"You walked away. We thought you were done with your little investigation," the man continued in a condescending manner that had me grinding my teeth. "Now why don't you run along back to your tattoo parlor and let the big boys deal with this."

"Cut the crap, Curtis," Serah snapped, shoving past me to get in the man's face. It wasn't the easiest of tasks since the tub of goo in the rumpled clothes had a good twelve inches in height on her, but she got an "A" for effort. "We've got work to do. I'd hate for my boss to call your boss. You know how fucking grumpy vamps are when you wake them in the day."

Curtis flushed bright red and opened his mouth to start railing at her, but the sound remained trapped in his throat when a loud bang of thunder broke across the city. Everyone froze, their eyes jumping to the clear blue sky overhead.

"Shit," the detective hissed, his face going from tomato red to snow white in a heartbeat. It was lucky that an ambulance was sitting nearby because this man was going to have a heart attack any second.

A second crack of thunder tore the sky and Gideon appeared in the center of the street, looking dark and sinister. Even I gave a little shiver at the sight of him, but then I knew he was pissed at me for dragging him from his nice warm bed where he had probably been wrapped around the soft body of his wife.

The warlock didn't look directly at anyone as he strode wordlessly across the street toward the alley. Everyone scrambled to back away from him, while those standing by the police tape ran for the safety of their homes. As Gideon entered the alley, the cops that had been left with the body ran out the other end of the alley, probably heading down the street to circle around. That or they were just going to run back to the police station several miles away.

From where I stood near the mouth of the alley, I could see Gideon looking over the corpse before turning back. He looked significantly paler than when he'd first appeared, but I doubted that any other bystanders noticed it. They were too busy being scared shitless. Standing at the edge of the sidewalk, he finally looked over the surrounding people as if suddenly noticing that he wasn't alone. Using all his imposing height, the warlock stepped close to Curtis so that the man was nearly curled into a ball of quivering fear while still standing.

"Leave," Gideon said in a cold emotionless voice.

"B-b-but . . ." Curtis started to say as if he meant to argue with the warlock. Gideon only had to arch one eyebrow in question. "S-sorry. Yes-s-sir." And then

Curtis was running as fast as his legs would carry him back to his car.

It was like an official's starter pistol had been fired into the air. Anyone who had lingered was now running toward their cars and fighting to get them started. Even I took an unconscious step backward but Gideon's hand snaked out in a vicious flash and he grabbed the front of my coat before slamming me against the nearest wall.

"You're with me, potion stirrer," he said, leaning close enough that I could see that he had his teeth clenched.

"No!" Serah screamed and then clamped both her hands over her mouth as if she had meant to catch the words before they flew free of her lips.

Gideon ignored her as he proceeded to drag me down the alley with him so that we were now standing in front of the poor dead woman. Twisting my coat in his fist, he shoved me against the wall.

"Thanks for the wake-up call," Gideon grumbled, keeping his back to where the cops were still scrambling to leave the immediate area.

"I couldn't try to do a tracking spell with an audience. It would kind of blow my cover," I replied, remaining pressed against the wall even though my expression wasn't what you'd call fearful. Most people would have called it irritated, but then I'd spent the better part of a lifetime getting roughed up by this asshole. It was getting really old.

"Your cover?"

"You know, mild-mannered tattoo artist."

Gideon said nothing, just rolled his eyes at me before returning his attention back to the problem at hand. "It looks like she was killed last night. Probably grabbed off the street and dragged back here, judging by the marks in the asphalt."

"Shifter, right?"

Gideon nodded at my question.

"The attacker had to have been strong to take on a shifter and win, particularly a scared and desperate one," I continued.

"And you said the attacker was a woman?"

"Human female from what I've been able to tell. It's from an Alpha Conversion tattoo." The warlock turned to me, looking a little confused, and I frowned. "It's based on the *fuoco selvaggio* spell."

"What!" Gideon shouted. Now he was angry and in my face with all his Tower-inducing terror. "Are you responsible for this mess?"

"Hell no!" I shouted back, no longer worried about keeping up any pretenses. I gave him a hard shove, pushing him away from me so that I had a little breathing room. "Tattoo artists have been doing a potion and symbol version of *fuoco selvaggio* for centuries. It's not quite as strong as the spell and it's a hell of a lot harder to control the results."

The warlock just shook his head in horror as he looked back at the dead woman. "What the hell," he whispered.

"The Towers are in for an ugly wake-up call if they

keep thinking they're the only ones who know how to do some scary magic shit," I snarled.

Gideon stepped close, his hands balled into fists. "Is that a threat?"

"No, it's a statement of fact." I was more than ready to go a few rounds with the bastard.

Gideon froze. "We still have an audience," he said in a low voice.

"How many?"

"One. It's the woman."

"Serah?"

Gideon paused as he quickly searched her mind. "Yes."

I breathed a sigh of relief. "It's okay. She knows." Pushing away from the wall, I walked to the center of the alley and looked back toward the street. "You can come down, Serah."

"She knows?" Gideon demanded, though I noted that the earlier heat had left his words. "What happened to your earlier complaint? Your precious cover?"

"It's a long story," I muttered, watching as Serah poked her head around the edge of the building before slowly making her way toward us. Now that we weren't snapping at each other I was starting to feel like an ass. But then, short tempers were to be expected from two men standing over the body of a dead pregnant woman. No matter how hard we tried, we were each thinking of someone else who could too easily become a target. "I'm sorry . . . about earlier."

"Yeah," Gideon grunted softly.

Which I took more to mean: *You're right, Gage. I'm sorry I acted like such a total dick. Please forgive me.*

"Gage?" Serah said as she reached me, pulling my thoughts back to the issue at hand.

"It's okay. He's not going to kill us right now," I said, flashing her a weak smile. "He came to scare your old buddies away so we could get some work done."

"Wish I could do that trick," she said, trying to sound friendly, but there was still a lot of fear in eyes.

"I wouldn't advise it. Warlocks don't like mornings."

"Shut up, Gage," Gideon muttered and I closed my mouth. While Gideon was a good warlock, I didn't want Serah to get the idea that she could just give him shit anytime she wanted. If anyone else saw, he'd have to peel off a few layers of skin just to prove to the world that he wasn't going soft.

We stood back and watched as Gideon looked over the dead woman from a distance. There was a slight tingle in the air from the warlock, using some smaller spells as if he were trying to rewind time to see the crime as it happened. After more than a minute, he shook his head as if to clear it and sighed.

"I'm not getting much," he said with more than a little frustration.

"What about a tracking spell? The aura is still strong in the air," I suggested.

"The aura? From the killer?" Serah quickly asked. She took a small step forward, her curiosity finally overcoming her fear.

"Gage isn't referring to a person's aura, but rather

the energy left behind by the violent event," Gideon responded evenly and I bit back a smile. There was just something in him that was a natural teacher. He couldn't help himself. He had done it with me and now with Serah. It made me wish the man could get away from the guardians and mentor an apprentice or two.

"Really?" she said, sounding a little skeptical.

"The theory is that violent events, particularly those that lead to death create ripples in the magical energy around us," Gideon explained. "With the right spell, that disruption, or aura, can be read to reveal what happened." The warlock started to pat down his pockets as if he was looking for something.

With a smirk, I unzipped my coat and reached into an inner pocket and pulled out a handful of multicolored chalk. Gideon just stopped and stared at it for a moment in shock before looking up at me, his expression turning grim. "It's a wonder you weren't executed years ago."

"You're welcome," I said as he picked up a purple chalk from the palm of my hand. He was right in so many ways, but now was not the time to get into it. I had a long habit of carrying chalk around for spells I wasn't supposed to be doing in the first place, but it had gotten considerably worse since I'd been sucked into the guardians. Now I was doing magic whether I wanted to or not.

The warlock started drawing symbols on the sides of the buildings around where the woman had been killed. I wasn't familiar with the spell, but I had heard of it. Gideon was attempting to create a type of magic bubble in which to rewind time. Within the bubble, he would replay the events, putting us solidly on the trail of the attacker. Judging by the symbols he was drawing, it was a complicated spell—one that certainly didn't have a chance of replicating without a lot of help.

And yet, aspects of it looked similar to other things I had done and seen before. A part of me was dying to ask him about it, to pick his brain about this spell until I understood its every aspect, but I swallowed back the words and tamped down the excitement. Where Gideon was a natural teacher, I felt born to be a student of magic for the rest of my life. I wanted to learn everything I could about magic, but it wasn't meant to be. For now, I had to content myself with picking up scraps of information any chance I could.

When he was finished, the warlock pushed a large chunk of energy into the symbols as he spoke the invocation. The air shimmered like fine diamond dust had been caught on the wind and was now reflecting the sunlight. Yet, as it clarified, everything within the bubble took on a slightly red hue. I turned back toward the mouth of the alley as I glimpsed movement out of the corner of my eye in time to see the outline of the killer walking toward the street. It looked like she had been leaning up against the wall, waiting for her prey. The center of the figure was completely transparent so that her face was only a vague impression of features, but she looked to be the same shape and size as the creature that had appeared in my basement.

"What are you looking at?" Serah whispered, jerking my gaze back to her.

I frowned. Apparently only magic users could see the results of the spell. "Gideon has recreated a shadowy image of what happened. I'll fill you in if I see anything helpful."

"Well, this sucks," Serah muttered, folding her arms over her chest as she leaned back against the wall closest to her.

Turning my attention back to the scene unfolding in front of me, I still found myself flinching when the killer lunged forward, wrapping her arms around her prey from behind. The pregnant woman struggled as she was dragged backward into the alley. Her movements were awkward with the heavy winter coat and extremely large stomach. The attacker held her victim with one arm so she could pull a long knife from somewhere on her person. Raising the knife high, the killer drove it down into the victim's chest in one swift motion. Gideon and I stepped back, moving out of the way as the shadowy images swept past us. The killer tossed the woman down behind the Dumpster and stood unmoving over her for a second before slashing her across the abdomen with the same blade.

I was glad that Serah couldn't see this. No one should have to witness such a thing, let alone have to go through it. Horror and rage pumped through my body, leaving me trapped between the need to puke my guts up and rip this murderous bitch apart.

The killer stepped back, tucking the knife back into the holder as she looked down at the pregnant woman, watching the life slowly drain out of her. The were-wolf's last bit of strength was used to hold her child inside of her, trying to protect the baby a little while longer in the desperate hope that someone would come.

Cars passed by the mouth of the alley, not more than a few yards away, but no one saw her. No one came to her rescue. The snow fell and the seconds ticked by slowly as her blood drained from her body to pool on the frozen asphalt. The mother and child died in a freezing, dirty alley with only the murderer standing watch.

The tattooed woman turned and started to walk back down the alley as if she was heading for the main street, but she paused just across from Serah. Was there something on the wall behind the TAPSS investigator that we hadn't seen before?

"What?" Serah nervously demanded as both Gideon and I stared at her. "What do you see?"

Before either one of us could speak, the eyes of the shadowy killer glowed bright red and she lunged at Serah, wrapping her hands around the woman's neck. Serah gasped, her hands jumping to her throat as if she were truly being strangled. Her lips formed my name, her feet slipping along the ground as she struggled to escape her invisible attacker.

Lunging forward, I tried to grab the shadow fig-ure's hands to pull them off Serah's throat, but there was nothing to grab. "Gideon!" I screamed. "Kill the spell."

"This shouldn't be happening," the warlock said in wonder from where he stood just behind me.

"No shit! Stop the spell before it crushes her throat!"

I felt a rush of energy from Gideon, but the shadowy killer didn't stop attacking Serah and disappear. "I can't kill the spell. The residual aura is still feeding it."

Swearing under my breath, I shoved away from Serah, whose face was now bright red from her struggles, and palmed a piece of black chalk. Racing back down the alley to where Gideon had created the spell, I let my eyes dance over the symbols that Gideon had drawn just seconds ago. Without a thought in my head beyond saving Serah's life, I started drawing on several of the original symbols, warping them, linking them in ways they should never have been. As I drew the last line, a dark energy jumped from inside of me and tore through the shadowy killer. When Serah sucked in her first gasping breath, I changed a symbol, closing off the power I had summoned so that it couldn't return to prey on anything else in this alley.

"What did you do?" Gideon snarled at me as he knelt down next to Serah. She sat on the cold dirty ground, coughing and wheezing as she tried to fill her lungs with air.

"I'm not sure," I whispered. That wasn't true. I knew what I had done. I had summoned up a sliver of the power from my new friend watching Simon's old rooms. What had me scared shitless was that I had no idea where that knowledge came from. With a wave of my hand, I pulled the bits of chalk from the wall and ground, causing the little particles to dance in a small black and purple cyclone in front of me before sending it off into the air. No one needed to see what I'd drawn.

"What the hell did *you* do?" Serah rasped, pinning Gideon with an angry glare.

"Sorry," the warlock said, looking a bit sheepish. "That should never have happened."

"I should have warned you," I said, walking over to help Serah back to her feet. "We had a similar experience when we did a blood spell. The tattoo potion has given the energy surrounding the killer an unexpected level of awareness."

"That would have been helpful to know!" Gideon snapped, appearing a little more shaken that I would have expected.

It was my turn to look sheepish, as I muttered a quick apology to the warlock. Honestly, I hadn't thought of it until the image attacked Serah and then it was simply too late. I shouldn't have been surprised. Magic had been acting strange with this killer since we started the investigation and I just chalked it up to the potion the person had flowing through her veins. What if the other killer making his slow way north to Low Town was also having an impact?

"Is there any way you can track this psycho bitch?" I asked as I zipped my coat up again. "I haven't had any luck and we need to catch her for more than one reason."

"I agree," Gideon murmured. He turned and looked back at the dead woman in the alley, a brief sadness passing through his eyes. "I'll see what I can do."

"Here," Serah said. Reaching into her coat pocket, she pulled out a clear evidence bag that had a small piece of a bloody paper towel. "I took another small piece of the killer's blood from the evidence lockup. I was going to see if Gage had another spell he could try."

Gideon accepted it with a nod. And then he was simply gone.

"Geez!" Serah said, releasing an enormous sigh as she slumped against the wall. "I hope I'm never that close to one of them again."

A loud bark of laughter jumped from me, nearly knocking me back against the wall with her. There was some part of my brain that knew Gideon was intimidating, but it was hard to remember when I was up to my armpits in other crazy shit and the warlock was keeping me alive through it all.

"You're pretty damn close to one right now," I reminded her with a smirk.

Serah blushed and gave my shoulder a shove as she pushed back to her feet. "Yeah, well, you don't count because you don't act like them."

"Or look like them. Or sound like them. Or slaughter huge swaths of innocent bystanders like them," I listed, getting a giggle out of my companion.

"Yeah, that too." She started to walk down the alley back toward her car when she stopped and looked back. The amusement was gone from her expression and the dire seriousness of our situation had crept back in. "What about her?"

"Call Curtis. Tell him he can crawl out from whatever rock he is hiding under. The Towers have retreated."

Serah gave me a quelling look, but there was still a sparkle of laughter in her eye. She was going to enjoy this conversation whether she wanted to admit it or not. Tossing me her keys, she stood on the street and called the detective while I walked over and started her car, allowing it to warm up.

A few minutes later, she was driving me back to my apartment, where I was hoping to catch just a couple more hours of sleep before dragging my sorry carcass into the shop. I had half a dozen appointments scheduled for the day and I couldn't cancel them because they were all appointments I had been forced to reschedule once already due to Towers bullshit.

I was dividing my time among the Towers, the parlor, and freelancing for TAPSS. Sadly only one of them was paying my bills, which meant either someone else needed to start forking over some cash or I was going to drop one of my non-paying obligations very soon. Unfortunately, I didn't see the Towers offering me an hourly wage. Their argument would be that I should just be grateful that I was still alive. Damn warlocks. Fucking witches.

I missed my girlfriend.

CHAPTER 7

Upon arriving at my apartment, I discovered that I was not going back to bed anytime soon. Sofie was curled up in the middle cushion of my couch, looking for all the world as if she slept there every day. She did not. The witch-turned-cat lived with Trixie.

"Where's Trixie?" I demanded, slamming the door shut behind me.

The cat blinked wide greenish-yellow eyes at me and yawned. I was ready to shake the answer out of her when she finally spoke. "At home in bed."

"Then what the hell are you doing here? You scared the shit out of me!" I snarled, collapsing on the sofa beside her with my coat still on. As the adrenaline rushed out of my system, I found that I was so tired my body had begun to shake. The world had become a nonstop roller coaster and I longed for nothing more than a turn on the merry-go-round. Leaning my head back, I closed my eyes, willing my body to relax just a bit before I dragged myself back to my nice dark bedroom.

But I wasn't going to get the blissful nothingness for a couple hours. Sofie moved beside me, her small, lithe body barely making indentions in the cushions as she walked over. She climbed into my lap and sat on my legs. Out of habit, I lifted my hand and gently scratched the top of her head. It had taken a little while, but I'd finally gotten over my hang-ups about treating the witch like a cat. If she was going to eat out of a cat food bowl on the floor, use a litter box, and lounge across every surface like she owned it, I was going to scratch her head every once in a while.

"What's going on, Gage?" Sofie demanded, half purring her question.

"There's a lot going on, Sof," I sighed, dropping my hand back to the arm of the couch. "You're going to have to be a little more specific than that."

"Trixie. The elf. The woman you're attempting to date, and rather poorly I might add."

I glared down at the large Russian blue feline in my lap and briefly thought about punting her across the room. Even as a cat, the witch could get on my nerves. Hell, I think she'd gotten better at it since she'd been cursed by another witch. Stuck living among the rabble of the world, Sofie had seen it as her lot in this existence to manage my life—particularly my social life.

"What about Trixie? Did she send you here to talk to me?"

"No. I came to talk to you because she refuses to tell me what's going on." The cat rose up on her hind legs while pressing her front legs against my chest so that her face was now inches from mine. "For more than a week, she has made all these strange phone calls and been packing up her things. I've stuck by my promise to you to stay out of her head, but you need to tell me what's going on."

My stomach sank a little at her description, but then I wasn't that surprised to hear of her preparations. I had hoped that Trixie might give me a little more time, but things kept getting worse instead of better. Could I really blame her? *No,* I thought, mentally sighing. "Trixie's pregnant."

"Oh!" Sofie looked genuinely surprised, or rather as surprised as a cat could look without the same human features. "Is that because of Gaia fixing that mess I made?"

"I like to think that I had something to do with it as well," I snapped, but my anger slipped away almost as quickly as it appeared. "But yeah, Mother Nature helped too." God, I was tired.

"Well, I'm sure this was something of a surprise, but it doesn't seem as if either of you is particularly happy about it."

"No, actually, we are happy."

"Then is she planning to move in with you? Is that why she's been packing?"

"No."

"I don't—"

"Trixie is planning to go back to her own people. She's leaving Low Town."

"I don't understand. Why? I'm sure the doctors here could handle a pregnant elf just fine."

"It's not safe," I murmured, wishing this conversation was finally over. It was like Sofie was determined to pull small strips of my flesh away with every question she wanted me to answer, and I was so exhausted from thinking about this.

"Low Town is safe enough." Sofie dropped back to sit on my lap and I could easily imagine her frowning up at me. "Well, it'll be safe as soon as the killer has been captured."

"No, it's not safe because of me." Groaning, I picked up the cat and dropped her on the couch beside me before getting to my feet. I wandered into the kitchen and started preparing the coffeemaker. It was becoming clear that sleep was not going to happen today.

"Gage?"

"It's because I'm a warlock. It's because . . . I'm working for the Towers."

"She can't hold that against you! She knew what you were before you started dating," Sofie argued angrily as she trotted into the kitchen after me. She jumped up on the counter. I immediately picked her up and put her on the floor again. Witch or not, I wasn't going to have a cat on my kitchen counters. It was bad enough she liked to sprawl across my coffee table while watching TV.

"Yeah, well it's different when it comes to a baby.

She's willing to take the risk herself, but not when it comes to the life of our child," I explained as I filled the carafe with water.

The coffeemaker was old and one of the most basic models. No frills and no fancy gadgets to let me grind my own beans or whatever people did. All the same, I loved my coffeemaker because when I needed it, it produced liquid love filled with scalding heat and caffeine.

"But what about your rights? Don't you have a say? Are you just going to let her leave?"

"I don't know what I'm going to do yet. I see her point. It's been dangerous to be around me. The Grim Reaper, Simon's attacks, the half dozen Tower attacks this fall, Reave, and now I'm involved in two different murder investigations. My life has become a natural disaster. The president is going to send in the National Guard at any second!" I took a deep breath and hit the on button. "You can't safely raise a baby in a mess like that."

"So you're just giving up?"

I flashed her a weak smile as I reached up into the cabinet to grab a mug. "I never said that. I'm still trying to figure things out. I need to either fall off the Towers' radar completely . . ."

"Or?" she prompted when I fell silent.

"Or I get rid of the Towers."

"Even if I thought you could get rid of the Ivory Towers, I don't necessarily think that it would fix everything. What about all those kids born with abilities? Part of the reason the Towers were erected was to give some guidance to those kids for their own safety."

Bracing both my hands on the counter in front of me, I stepped back, stretching the muscles in my legs and my back. After I was sucked back into the Towers in September, I'd started going to the gym again, more as a way of burning off some of my anger and frustration than to get in shape. The recent chaos was keeping me away from the gym now and I felt stiff. If I could spend an hour on some of the machines, the fog from my head would finally clear.

"I don't have any answers, Sofie. I wish I did, but I don't." I straightened and folded my arms over my chest as I watched coffee slowly drip into the carafe. "But I'm looking."

"Is there anything I can help with?"

I hesitated. This wasn't something I could take to Gideon. Sofie was far from the straight and narrow, doing some nasty things in her past with magic. She might have my answers.

But she was trying to mend her ways. She had even shown remorse about trying to kill off all the elves by making them infertile. The cat was also becoming far too tight with Gideon and I didn't need her running off to tell Gideon what I was sure he had already begun to suspect.

It didn't change the fact that I needed answers and I couldn't exactly trust the source that I was using. Demons might not be permitted to lie in some strange twist of fate, but they were tricky bastards.

"I have a question about the symbol you saw on the wall down in my basement," I started, trying to sound nonchalant. I kept my eyes on the steadily filling carafe while watching Sofie out of the corner of my eye.

The cat stood in the doorway to the kitchen and gave a little shudder. "That's some nasty business, Gage."

"You've said that before. What kind of nastiness am I dealing with? I got the symbol from Simon when I was studying under him. What kind of magic was Simon dealing in? Something forbidden?"

The cat sat on the carpet for a moment and then stood, pacing away from the kitchen and then back. If she had been a normal cat, it would have looked like she was begging for her bowl to be refilled, but Sofie killed that image when she opened her mouth. "There are few things that are forbidden within the Towers. I'm sure you know that."

"Suspected it, but I liked to think the council had enough sense to draw the line somewhere," I muttered.

"There are a couple forms of magic that were forbidden, and in general no one mucked around in them because they were too hard to control."

"Death Magic."

Sofie stopped, her head whipping around to face me. "Yes, but how did you know about that?"

"Long story. What about the symbol? It's not Death Magic."

"No, it's not and it's not *technically* forbidden. But

it is extremely dangerous. I've heard of more witches and warlocks getting killed for messing with it. It never ends well."

"You're stalling." Grabbing my mug, I filled it with freshly brewed coffee and sipped it. The precious liquid burned my tongue, the roof of my mouth, and all the way down my throat like I had just sucked down lava, but I welcomed it. The warmth seeped into my limbs, fighting back aches and pains. In a few minutes, the caffeine would start turning the gears in my brain. By the time I finished this cup, I'd be back to human status and could actually take a shower without drowning.

"The symbol opens a sort of doorway for a demon. That's what's guarding your basement," she said cautiously, as if she was expecting me to freak out, and maybe I would have if I hadn't already done that at Simon's.

"Is it capable of coming all the way through the doorway?"

"No, it's more complicated than that. It can't come into our world, but it can send bits of its power through. It remains tied to the symbol. From what I've read, the demon's power fills whatever open space it has. The larger the room and the longer the doorway is left open, the more powerful the demon becomes in our world. Your basement isn't too large, so you've been able to manage it with minimal problems. Anything larger and I'm sure that it would have killed you."

Unless it wanted something.

Simon's rooms were easily three times the size of

my basement and the demon had been running loose in those rooms for months. It would have been able to crush me in a heartbeat if it had wanted to, but it didn't because it needed me to do something. It needed me to destroy Lilith.

"Gage, are you listening to me?" Sofie snapped.

I shook my head and smiled down at her before taking another drink of coffee. My mind had wandered for a second. "Sorry, Sof. I drifted off."

"I said you need to get rid of that symbol. Change it to close the door permanently and then paint over it. You don't need to be messing with that stuff. It's dangerous."

"More dangerous than dealing with the Towers every day? More dangerous than hunting down some psychopath bent on murdering pregnant women?" I demanded, nearly shouting.

Sofie didn't flinch. She didn't blink. "Yes. Yes it is."

I made a dismissive noise as I topped off my mug and carried it into the living room. She didn't understand. I was risking my life every day to maintain some semblance of peace and quiet in Low Town while people were constantly fighting to tear it apart. I was on the cusp of losing the woman I loved as well as the child she carried. I needed to make this city safe for her. And the power I'd been searching for was finally at my fingertips.

There had to be a way to tighten my control over the demon so that it couldn't lash out at me. There had to be a better way to tap that power so that the

Ivory Towers could finally be taken down. I just had to figure out how I was going to do it, preferably before Lilith came to steal me away.

"What would happen if you put the symbol in the middle of a street?"

"Chaos. Total destruction. I can't imagine there's a warlock or witch powerful enough to shut the door again once it was opened."

I nodded, holding my mug between my hands as I sat on the edge of the couch. I'd suspected as much. This had a high likelihood of ending in disaster if I went down this path. Sofie was right in that I needed to close the door at Asylum and at Simon's before I made things worse. But just the idea of walking away from this choice left me wanting to scream. If I could control the demon, I could finally get rid of the Towers and keep Trixie. Yet, if I lost control, I'd destroy the world.

"You'll get rid of the symbol, right?" Sofie demanded, hopping up in the coffee table so that her face was now only inches from mine. Her wide eyes stared into mine and I could even feel a small push in my brain as if she were either trying to read my thoughts or simply give me a mental shove in the right direction.

"Yeah, I'll take care of it. As soon as things settle down."

"Sooner than that, Gage," Sofie said in a warning voice. "Go to the parlor early today. It won't take long to shut down the spell and cover it up. Less than an hour. I can help you."

"Yeah, I've got it," I murmured as I raised my mug to my lips again, draining half its contents. "Look, I've got to jump into the shower before I head to the shop. You can just stay here today. Or move in. Whatever," I finished with an absent wave of my hand. Pushing to my feet, I started for the kitchen. I'd fill up one last time before hauling my sorry carcass into the shower.

"You're giving up?"

Turning, I gave the cat what I hoped was my best cocky smile. "Me? Give up? Never. I'll figure something out."

Sofie didn't look particularly reassured, but then emotions are hard to read on a cat. What she looked was worried. But what was there to worry about? I could handle this. So what if I had to take down the Ivory Towers in order to have my own personal happily ever after?

I had hung myself in my living room so I could beat the Grim Reaper. I'd spent an afternoon with Mother Nature and held the soul of my son so I could save the entire race of elves. I could find a way to stop two killers from destroying Low Town while keeping my girlfriend and our unborn child safe. The only problem was that I had to find a way to do it without involving demons.

CHAPTER 8

Pushing through the day with only two hours' sleep was no easy thing. My body ached in a dozen places, my eyes burned, and my concentration was shit. I was beginning to think that my age was catching up with me a little bit. I was a whole hell of a lot closer to thirty now than I was to twenty. When I'd first opened Asylum, I could tattoo from midday until three in the morning, and then go drinking with Parker and Bronx until about sunrise. I'd catch a few hours of sleep on the couch before jumping in the shower so I could do it all over again.

Now I was dodging too many creatures eager to kill me while worrying about my girlfriend and paying the bills. *Dear God, I was even starting to sound old.*

The first few hours in Asylum passed slowly, but I was grateful that my scheduled appointments were on time. I'd completed the sketches earlier in the week so all I had to do was actually stir any required potions and fire up the tattooing gun. After a while, the combination of the steady buzz of the machine and the inane chatter that drifted about the shop as I worked settled my frayed nerves so that I found a shallow pond of inner peace to sink into.

I loved tattooing. Well, maybe not as much as using magic, but there was a comfort in holding the tattooing gun in my right hand and etching a design I'd created along someone's flesh. I think at first I'd pursued it because potion stirring was something that I was good at. During my time in the Ivory Towers, I had learned a great deal about the magical properties of different ingredients. When it came to stirring a potion for love or luck or just good old-fashioned revenge, I was a natural. It was the actual artistic side of the tattooing that I was forced to work at. That challenge combined with the idea that I was actually helping people with my magical knowledge made it possible for me to finally accept that I'd been born a warlock.

After I opened my own place, a deep sense of security and peace hit me. But it lasted for only a few days. The temptation to set up a secret spot in which to do magic was overwhelming and the basement was perfect. While I'd managed to hide it from my tattooing mentor, I'd never been able to completely stop using magic despite my initial belief that I'd be able to stop cold turkey with no problem. Geez, the world had crack addicts with more self-control than me. I'd gotten better, but it was a struggle every day to not tap into the energy in the air to do the simplest of things.

And now I was back with the Ivory Towers working as a spy and a part-time guardian. I couldn't even spot where I'd veered off my original path anymore. Hell, I couldn't even see my original path from where I stood.

Serah popped into the shop around three in the afternoon, carrying two large coffee cups from the coffee shop down the block from Asylum.

"Come on back," I called as I let up from the pedal for a moment. I watched on the little security camera as she stepped around the glass case before I started the tattooing gun buzzing again, turning my attention back to the siren's hip I was working on. Charise was one of my regulars. I had completed a series of roses and vines along her lower back, placed the kanji for love on the back of her neck, and now I was doing a pair of dragonflies on her narrow hips.

"Oh! Sorry! I didn't realize!" Serah gasped as she entered the main tattooing room.

Lifting the tattooing gun from Charise's flawless pale skin, I looked up to see Serah blushing brightly, quickly turning away to head back toward the lobby. I swallowed back a chuckle. What the TAPSS investigator had not been ready for was the fact that Charise was wearing a little pink tank top and matching pink bikini-cut panties so that I could easily get at her hips.

"It's okay, honey," Charise said in a voice that poured into your ears like expensive champagne. "You can stay. He's almost done."

"Another ten to fifteen minutes," I said, putting the gun down so that I could smear a little more petroleum jelly along her skin.

"Oh, are you sure? I can—"

"Stay!" Charise said with an almost child-like giggle before turning to me. "Isn't she just the cutest thing? She's embarrassed."

I smirked up at Serah, who was torn between embarrassment and anger at being laughed at. "Yeah, she's adorable."

"Ah, honey, I used to be a dancer down at Diamond Dolls. I'm not embarrassed, so you shouldn't be either."

And that was why I liked doing work for Charise. It's also why she got a discount. That and she got a number of her coworkers to come to Asylum for tattoos as well. Charise felt no embarrassment or shame regarding what she did for a living. She knew the value of the service that she was providing and she wouldn't allow anyone to make her feel bad about it. There was an inner strength in her that I didn't see in women who pulled down six figures a year, drove a Mercedes, and had a closet full of designer clothes.

"Is one of those for me?" I asked, saving Serah from the mire that she was starting to sink into. Her eyes snapped to the two cups she had in her hand as if she had forgotten that she was carrying them.

"Uh . . . yeah," she said, extending one toward me.

"Put it on the counter," I directed with a jerk of my head toward the counter on my left while I picked up the gun again. The scent of the coffee was heavenly, though my stomach was starting to rebel a little bit. I'd sucked down a pot of coffee already but hadn't followed it up with anything that actually resembled food. My stomach wasn't pleased.

"What are you having Gage tattoo on you?" Charise asked as I started working again. I inwardly cringed a bit. That was the one drawback about Charise. She didn't have some of the boundaries that most people had. Most customers knew better than to ask what they were having done because there was a good chance that it was something very private between you and your artist. But you couldn't fault her. She was just trying to make polite conversation.

"I haven't decided yet," Serah said. She set her cup of coffee down on one of the empty folding chairs I kept for clients or friends of clients while they waited. She stripped off her coat and tossed it over the back of the chair. Pausing for a second, she then continued to strip off her bulky cable-knit sweater. The heat in the shop was higher than usual because Charise was wearing so little. Once she left, I'd have to turn it back down again so the damn gas and electric bill wouldn't be through the roof.

"Have you let Gage tattoo you before?"

"No, I haven't."

Charise gave an excited little clap and I had to pause as I waited for her to settle down again. "You have come to the best shop in all of Low Town. Gage is a genius!"

"My coworkers are very good too," I interjected.

"Yes, of course, but you're the best," she said, nearly purring as she gave me a little pat on the head.

"Rein it in, Charise," I warned. Sirens were tricky creatures. Their voices can ensnare a mind and hypnotize a creature into doing whatever they want. In general, they've got great control over their gift, but I've noticed that when Charise is really happy, her control slips a bit.

"Oh, you're fine," she said, pooh-poohing my warning as she turned her attention back to Serah. "Do you know if you want a potion with your tattoo? That could limit what you get. I just went with some art and some light cosmetic potions that Gage is just brilliant at."

"I think I'd want just art," Serah said slowly as if she was getting more into the role she was playing for the benefit of Charise. I had no doubt that she had an update to give me on our investigation, but she wasn't going to say a word about it until we were alone. For now, she was just another customer in Asylum Tattoo Parlor.

"You know, I bet you'd look good with a little bluebird on your ankle or a butterfly on the top of your foot."

"The top of your foot is more of a summertime tattoo," I said, not bothering to look up from the canvas stretched before me. Too often people came in with this idea of what they needed to have right that moment without thinking about the long-term aspects. Like the fact that flip-flops were great when letting a tattoo on the top of your foot heal, but they sucked during the winter.

"Oh, that's true. What about your shoulder? That's a good spot for a tattoo."

"What do you think I should get, Gage?" Serah asked.

I looked up briefly to see an expectant look on her face, but I just shook my head at her. "There's a large flip book under the chair next to you that has a lot of designs. Check that out. I'm almost done with Charise."

Every tattoo artist around the world was asked that question and I was pretty sure that every last one of us longed to smack that customer a time or two. To me, a tattoo was a reflection of who you were. It should be something important to you or some aspect or philosophy that you valued. As a total stranger, I could no sooner pick out that one thing that you cherished than I could pick the perfect name for your firstborn child or locate your soul mate in a police lineup. Whenever I was asked that, I was tempted to tattoo the person with the contact info for my parlor. If you're going to leave it up to me, I was going to use your flesh as advertising space, because you obviously didn't give a shit.

Charise and Serah chatted amiably for the next few minutes as I finished up some shading details on the dragonfly I was doing. Serah flipped through the book of designs she had picked up and was sharing them with the dancer as if she were actually planning to get the tattoo. I appreciated her making the effort to keep the atmosphere relaxed despite the fact that I was itching to know what information she had brought me.

As soon I was finished bandaging up the tattoo on Charise's left hip, I stripped off my latex gloves and snatched up the cup of coffee that Serah had brought. There was no holding back the moan of delight that rumbled up my throat as the double-shot espresso poured into my body. The caffeine gave me a nice jolt as if getting those last pistons firing in my brain. I had been starting to drag.

"You're an angel," I murmured while Charise sauntered across the tattooing room to pick up the tiny skirt she had folded and placed on another tattooing chair. The woman had to be freezing when she walked out the door, but it wasn't my problem.

"The guy at the coffee shop said you usually ordered that," Serah said, keeping her eyes locked on me while the other woman got dressed.

"Bill," I grunted. Bill was one of the baristas down at the local coffee shop, though if you called him a barista you risked getting a face-full of steaming-hot coffee. He was usually making my order by the time I walked in the place since I almost never deviated from my usual. There were perks to being a regular customer.

With half the coffee gone, I walked Charise to the front lobby, where we briefly set up her next appointment so that she could get the matching dragonfly done on her other hip. I had offered to do both today but she just smiled and said that she liked to have a reason to come back to see me. I accepted the compliment and the impersonal hug before she strode out of the shop, her high-heeled shoes clomping across the hardwood floor like a draft horse pulling a heavy load.

I hesitated at the glass case, some part of me not wanting to return to the tattooing room. Charise represented everything that was normal about my life, everything that it was supposed to be. I'd wanted a life of bullshitting with people about everyday things that didn't really matter. Life was supposed to be creating art and helping people. I was supposed to be worried about bills and whether I needed to get a new set of tires for my SUV so I could get through the winter snow.

But all that was slipping away in the face of darkness that was crowding my life. Reaching down to pick up my MP3 player, I switched the music over to a playlist of movie scores. It matched my darkening mood and was easy to talk over.

"I think I'd like this tattoo," Serah said, finally pulling me into the tattooing room.

Stepping over the threshold, I leaned forward a little to see that she was pointing to a picture of a Japanese koi. I smiled, impressed by her selection.

"Nice choice. Do you know what it means?" When she shook her head, I picked up my coffee cup and sat down in the tattooing chair that Charise had vacated just moments ago. "The koi is popular among young men, but some women have started getting it. It's the symbol of a person's journey. A sign of growth, courage, and strength. There's an old fairy tale that I don't remember, but apparently the final evolution of the koi is a dragon, the most important of all the Japanese symbols."

"You make it sound like you have to be worthy of attaining a tattoo of a koi," she said softly as she closed the book and set in on the chair next to her.

"Only the person getting the tattoo can decide if she is worthy." I paused, waiting for her to meet my eyes again. "Are you?"

She lifted her head, her shoulders straightening a little, and met my gaze without flinching. "I am."

"Good answer."

A little laugh escaped her and she shook her head at me as we both brushed aside the momentary soul-searching. There was a lot I didn't know about the TAPSS investigator but I respected her. She worked hard and believed in what she was doing. There were a lot of people in this world who weren't doing half as much as she was.

"Thanks for the coffee," I said, holding the empty cup up to her before I placed it on the counter.

"I thought you could use it. You said that you were functioning on only two hours of sleep. The parlor forcing you to keep such long hours?"

I shook my head. "I've got some other problems that I'm dealing with at the moment."

"Earlier, when you told me that your girlfriend was pregnant," Serah started and then paused, licking her lips. "You weren't serious, were you?"

"Trixie is pregnant."

"Oh," she whispered.

"Which explains her reaction to your announcement the other night at Kyle's shop," I added, watching as my companion visibly paled. Yeah, telling a pregnant woman that other pregnant women had been killed by a psychopath was not something anyone wanted to do.

"Is she okay?" she gasped.

"She's a little shaken, but okay."

"I'm sorry."

"No problem. I just found out recently myself. We're happy, but the timing could have been better."

I suddenly found myself wishing I had something stronger to drink than coffee. There was a bottle of Jack Daniels stashed around here somewhere, but I still had a few more hours of work ahead of me and I never drank while I was inking. And while Serah and I were working together, she was still a member of TAPSS. She wouldn't let me drink while I was on the clock. TAPSS frowned on drunk tattoo artists.

Roughly rubbing my hands over my face to clear away the last of the cobwebs, I took a deep breath and turned my full attention back to Serah. The dark blue jeans and pale blue T-shirt made her look soft and approachable while keeping her professional air.

"I'm guessing that you've found something out," I said, figuring that it was as good a start as any.

"A few things actually." Her demeanor instantly brightened and I hoped that this meant that we were actually making some forward progress at last.

"Good news?"

"Good news and some bad news."

"Give me the good news first," I sighed, crossing my left foot over my right foot as I stretched out in the chair. "I can definitely use some good news."

"Well, we found some similarities between the victims. I spent the morning down at the station. One of the detectives reported that two of the women went to the same obstetrician."

"And the third?"

"She didn't use that doctor," Serah said with a shake of her head. "She was a phlebotomist at Low Town Mercy Hospital. But here's the link." Her excitement was palpable in the room as she wiggled to the edge of her seat. "The obstetrician's office is in the tower just across the street from Mercy."

"So you think our killer was stalking his victims at this particular obstetrician's office and she just got lucky when she picked up the third victim as she left work?"

Serah nodded. "It fits. We haven't found any other links besides the fact that both women were in their third trimester." Turning, she reached into her back pocket and pulled out a little notepad. She quickly flipped through it until she found the page that she was looking for. I thought it was cute that she preferred paper over the little memo-pad app that was on her phone.

"The women lived nowhere close to each other," she continued. "They didn't shop at the same grocery store or go to the same pharmacy. They wouldn't have encountered each other in any other way besides the doctor's office."

"I'm guessing that the cops are going to stake out the office building," I said, arching one eyebrow at her.

"That and they've got two detectives working undercover in the office to keep an eye out for anything suspicious."

"Are there other doctors' offices in the building?"

"Yes, and all the offices are being checked. Every woman in the office is being checked for a tattoo. In addition, they are also checking all the businesses to see if anyone has suddenly disappeared or quit their job in case the killer might have worked in the building."

"It looks like they've got all their bases covered." Threading my fingers behind my head, I could feel myself relax a little. The cops might actually be able to catch this person without needing my interference. That would be a nice change of events for once.

"I think it's a good start," Serah conceded, but her happiness was already starting to fade.

"What's the bad news?"

"Four pregnant women have disappeared."

My hands clenched into fists and I fought the urge to pick up the phone to call Trixie. She was fine. She had to be fine. No one knew that she was pregnant. She wasn't showing yet. No one knew. She was safe.

"How?"

Serah shook her head, tightly clutching the little note pad in both her hands. "We don't know. They simply vanished into thin air. Three of them disappeared in the middle of the night from their own beds. The fourth disappeared after dropping off her other two kids at school."

"Was there any kind of evidence of forced entry?"

"None. The police swept each house for DNA, but found nothing. There were no unlocked doors or windows. No evidence of a struggle. The women are just gone."

A chill swept through me. While our Low Town killer had the benefit of a powerful tattoo giving her a boost in strength and confidence, she didn't have any additional magical gifts. At least, the tattoo wouldn't have given her any. She would never have been able to pull such a kidnaping off without leaving behind massive amounts of chaos and destruction.

This was someone new. Could the killer Gideon and I had been tracking north finally have arrived in Low Town? Only someone with magical gifts could have pulled off a stunt like this. We were running out of time to save these women and to stop these killers before they unleashed something even scarier than what was already hunting Low Town.

"Were all the women taken last night?"

"And early this morning."

"Any of them shifters?"

"No. Human."

I breathed a small sigh of relief. It was bad enough that pregnant women around the city were no longer safe, but I didn't need to add to it the fact that all the shifters were in an uproar, though they were already going to be foaming at the mouth about losing one woman.

With my elbow on the arm of the chair, I dropped my head into my hand as I shoved away thoughts about the problems that Jack and his pack were going to cause. I just couldn't get drawn into the mess. Besides, I didn't need to go looking for trouble; I already had plenty in my lap. The easiest way I could help the city was to stop this maniac.

"We need to get ahead of this woman. As it is, we're staying one step behind her so that we're constantly tripping over dead bodies," I muttered, talking mostly to myself.

"I was kind of hoping that you'd feel that way."

My head jerked to Serah, the little hairs on the back of my neck standing on end at the nervous little smile straining her lips. This was going to be bad. "Why?"

"The cops want to set up a sting."

"And what? They chose you to be the bait?" I snapped.

"I volunteered."

"Shit," I swore softly, a rant already rising up my throat detailing her stupidity, but I never got a chance to speak my mind.

"Listen, Gage!" she said sharply, pushing to her feet so that she was towering over where I sat. "There aren't a lot of women on the force in Low Town. I've at least got some experience dealing with some of the lowlifes that lurk down the dark alleys. Believe it or not, I can take care of myself."

"I have no doubt that you've managed to put down a rowdy incubus or a shifter at the end of a full-moon cycle, but this is different—"

"Don't you dare condescend to me! Just because you're some hotshot warlock doesn't mean I haven't learned to protect myself. Or is your issue the fact that I'm a woman?"

I jerked back as if she'd hit me. Is that what I'd just done? *Dear God, I had!* If my mother were here, she would have smacked me and then washed my mouth out with soap. When had I become a condescending prick? *Oh, about the time your friends starting getting hurt because you're a warlock and hell's fury made a habit of knocking on your door.*

"I'm sorry," I said softly.

Serah took a step back, looking absolutely stunned. Yeah, I was feeling a little stunned myself. Not so much because I apologized. I had a lot of practice at that. Too fucking much. It was more to do with the fact that I had stopped seeing people as capable of handling a situation without me. Maybe this is why things got so out of hand with the witches and warlocks. Or at least started out this way.

"I'm serious. I'm sorry. I know you're very capable. I guess with everything going on, I don't want to see you get hurt as well."

"Thank you." Serah returned to her seat and blinked a couple times as if she were trying to get her brain functioning again. "I appreciate your concern."

"There is an element of magic involved here that

makes me uncomfortable leaving you solely in the hands of the police." I shook my head, trying to watch my words but still impress upon her the danger that she was walking into. "You didn't see what Gideon and I saw. The potion has made this woman stronger and faster. If she manages to surprise you, you're not going to have more than a second to escape."

"That's why I'm kind of hoping that you have a trick or two up your sleeve that might help," she said, her smile returning.

"On one condition."

"What's that?"

"I want to be there. Stick me with whichever cop is going to be following you or protecting you."

"I'll see what I can do."

"What time are you heading out?"

"I'm going into the O.B.'s office at five, where they are supposed to have a fat suit for me as well as some maternity clothes. From there, I'm supposed to walk over to the hospital for an 'appointment,' " she explained, making air quotes with her fingers. "After that, I'm to walk six blocks to a grocery store known for its dimly lit parking lot."

"They're going to make a pregnant woman walk six blocks in the cold? Heartless," I joked, though the thought of her route was making me ill. Even without the threat of a serial killer, this wasn't the best neighborhood that she was trudging through.

"Ha. Ha," she said blandly. "We're hoping that the killer took advantage of an opportunity rather than stalked these specific women. Otherwise, we're shit out of luck."

"True. What about backup?"

"There will be an unmarked car following and additional backup at the three-block mark in the alley as well as at the grocery store."

"That's pretty fucking thin," I complained.

Serah gave a helpless shrug. "I'm not the only one acting as bait."

My stomach twisted anxiously with guilt. I wasn't planning to do a damn thing for those other women because I simply couldn't. Anything I attempted would give away the fact that I was a warlock. Of course that raised the sticky question of whether protecting my secret was more important than protecting the lives of these women. I hated ethical quandaries. If the world found out my secret, I lost my value to the Ivory Towers and I was dead. Of course, if the world found out, it's likely the world would rush to kill me or use me against the Towers.

For half a second, I thought about contacting Gideon to see if I could get him to help, but I knew what the answer was going to be—NO. Two warlocks couldn't save the world. But then I didn't want to save the world. I just wanted to save a few women in Low Town.

"Where do you want me to meet up with the cop following you?"

Serah frowned at me, not looking the least bit pleased that I was going to be tagging along. I was sure this ex-cop just saw me as a potential liability and someone who was only going to get in the way. That was a possibility, but I also had a good shot at keeping her alive.

"I'll tell him to stop by for you in a few hours," she finally conceded.

"Thanks." I swung my feet over the chair and to the floor. "And now I've got a little something for you." Walking over to the counter, I started pulling open drawers, searching for something small; something that could be easily concealed on her person but if found wouldn't be seen as suspicious.

After coming up empty, a brilliant idea struck me between the eyes. Slipping past her to the glass case at the entrance to the main tattooing room, I reached back into the shelves and pulled out a large mason jar of buttons. I poured out a handful onto the glass counter and sifted through them until I came to a large black button that looked as if it belonged on a winter coat. With my back still turned to her, I said a whisper of words while sketching a design in the air over the button in the palm of my hand.

Once the spell was in place, I turned around and offered her the button with a smile on my face. She looked at me as if I had lost my mind.

"What is it?" she asked cautiously.

"What does it look like? It's a button," I said, still holding it out to her.

"Yeah, but what did you do to it?"

"I put a tracking spell on it." When she didn't take

it, I grabbed her right hand and laid it in the palm. "Keep it on you at all times and I'll be able to find you."

"I don't need it. I'm going to wear a wire and a wireless device so that I can be heard at all times."

"Yes, but they won't know what you're feeling. I'll be able to tell if you're suddenly afraid or panicked due to being unexpectedly attacked. That could give me an extra second or two on your companions, which could make a hell of a lot of difference when it comes to this bitch."

"And what if I don't want you to know what I'm feeling?"

I arched one eyebrow at her and gave a little sigh as I flopped back down in my chair. "I can read your emotions. Not your thoughts. Right now, you're suspicious and anxious, with a small hint of pissed. You wanted a trick or two to help. This is it."

"Fine," she muttered, shoving the button in her front pocket. With the button, there was no hiding the sense of relief and even a bit of disappointment. There was no doubt in my mind that she'd been hoping for something a little more, something flashy.

"I can't do anything bigger to protect you. With magic soaked into this killer, I'm not sure what she can sense or what might be a trigger. We can't risk scaring her off."

"Oh, no. Sure. I totally understand. This is fine," she quickly said, her disappointment evaporating in an instant.

"I'll have your back, Serah," I said, extending my hand to her.

She hesitated, an odd little smile lifting the corners of her mouth as she looked at it. "You know, I never thought I'd be comforted by the thought of a warlock watching my six, but I am," she said as she shook my hand.

"Most people wouldn't, but I promise, I'm not like them."

Serah gave a snort as she released my hand and twisted around to scoop up her coat. "Something tells me you're worse."

I didn't say anything as I walked her to the door. I certainly didn't think I was worse, but then I wasn't sure how many witches and warlocks were using demons to guard their shit. It certainly wasn't something that placed me with the good guys. But what about the ends justifying the means? My intentions when it came to the demon were to take down the Towers and make the world a safer place for everyone. Wasn't that a good thing? Did it really matter how I got it done?

A sigh slipped from my parted lips as I shut the door behind Serah and watched her walk down the street toward her little blue sedan. Too many questions and I didn't have any of the fucking answers.

CHAPTER 9

Eddie was a pain in the ass.

Detective Edward Lebeau appeared at Asylum just before seven and promptly informed me that he thought it was total bullshit that some con man tattoo artist had been forced on him during a sting operation. In fact, the loudmouth prick didn't hesitate to give me his opinion on tattoos, tattoo artists, and women on the police force—none of which was positive.

I naturally took some pleasure informing him that he wouldn't only be accompanied by me, but by Bronx as well. As soon as Serah left the parlor, I was on the phone to my friend, informing him of the plan. Bronx was eager to help, but it had all depended upon the cop showing up after sundown. For once we were lucky.

The troll's massive bulk and dark expression helped to intimidate dear Eddie, but it was a small bit of hypnosis on my part that finally changed the asshole's mind about not letting Bronx tag along, which was a good thing in the end. Serah's anxiety was already on the rise as I was sure she was either at the doctor's office or on her way. I didn't need to be distracted by the beanpole with attitude to spare. There was already plenty to worry about.

Eddie reached over and turned up a crackling police radio that was tuned to the operation. A stern voice was giving a quick update on a woman who had left the hospital and was headed toward the main southern transfer station for the Low Town bus service, putting her in the opposite direction from Serah.

A couple minutes later, he whipped the twenty-year-old Chevy Malibu with rust spots on the doors into an opening halfway between the medical offices building and the hospital. The position gave us a clear view of the path that Serah would take while the growing darkness helped to keep us hidden. I didn't have high hopes that we would keep such a clear view of her the whole time since we wouldn't be able to follow closely without raising suspicion.

"I need my feet on the ground," Bronx suddenly announced as he pushed open the passenger side door and slid out.

"What the fuck!" Eddie snarled, starting to lean across the seat to grab for the troll, but Bronx moved a lot faster and smoother than a person might expect. Eddie never touched him. "You're going to blow our fucking cover!"

Before he could continue ranting, I tapped my index

finger in the dead center of Eddie's forehead and the man froze. His mind dropped instantly into a hypnotic trance, his entire body locked up as if someone had hit the pause button. It was a shame I couldn't keep him like that indefinitely.

Ignoring Eddie for now, I slid out of the backseat and joined Bronx on the sidewalk. The troll didn't bother looking down at me, his sharp yellow eyes continuously sweeping the area, trying to spot if anyone was watching us.

"Bronx?"

"It's a feeling. A kind of warning that I can't explain. After working for Reave for years, I learned to trust it. Kept me alive through some bad stuff."

"Got it," I murmured, my mind already working. I dug through the pockets of my coat, looking for something I could charm, but I didn't have much on hand. Just my wand, a handful of chalk, and a couple peppermints. You never charmed food. Stupid accidents always followed when you charmed food.

"How about this?" Bronx suggested, pulling on the collar of his wool coat to draw my attention to the onyx stone in a silver setting pinned to the lapel. When the stone caught the light, I saw there was a protection symbol etched into it. It was the first time I'd ever seen Bronx wear anything like it. The troll wasn't religious and didn't buy into protection symbols, but I was willing to bet that being my friend had convinced him that having such a thing certainly wouldn't hurt.

"I knew you were a mind reader," I joked, pulling

the pin a little closer to me as I traced the same tracking spell on the onyx stone that I'd used earlier for Serah.

Bronx gave me a little smirk. "Nope. Just guessed that you'd like to keep an eye on me as well."

"Definitely." I drew a second spell over the stone, turning it into a two-way radio. "Talk and I'll be able to hear you."

"Will I be able to hear you?"

"Yep, but it's got only about a six-block range." I released the pin and stepped back, letting the troll readjust his coat.

"Like a walkie-talkie?"

"Better. I'll also know where you are and that range is pretty damn far. Try to stay close and hidden all the same."

"Not a problem." Bronx gave a little salute and then turned away, trudging down the street with his head down and hands in his pockets.

After less than a minute, he became little more than a massive black shadow, disappearing into the growing darkness. The troll had spent time working for the local mafia boss, Reave, before he could finally escape that life to become a tattoo artist. He rarely spoke of that time and I never got the impression that he enjoyed it. Unlike most of his kind, Bronx had a finer sensibility. He had the soul of an artist and, while his size and strength might lend itself to brutality, he wasn't a violent creature.

Even knowing that, when shit got crazy, Bronx never turned away from me. He was always there to help at the risk of his own happiness and life. I hated a part of myself for constantly drawing him into danger and darkness. And yet, he was the one who I relied to watch my back. Trixie was my heart, but Bronx—he was my rock.

Jumping into the front passenger seat of the car, I took a moment to close my eyes and focus on the two threads of emotion that were attached to my brain now. Serah was anxious with a hard edge of determination. Bronx was a Zen pool of calm. The troll was a master of control, his own worries and fear locked down so that he could focus on the job before him.

With my companions taken care of, I turned my attention back to the cop. I shoved Eddie so that he was sitting back in his seat with his eyes staring blindly forward. "You told Bronx to talk a walk and find some shadows to hide in so he could watch for the killer. He just left to follow your instructions," I said and then tapped his forehead again.

Eddie blinked a few times and looked around a little confused when he spotted me in the passenger seat beside him. "That troll gone?"

"Hiding, like you said."

He grunted and relaxed in his seat, accepting what I said. With his eyes on the building, Eddie pulled a pack of cigarettes out of his ragged coat pocket and I quickly lowered my window a few inches rather than allow him to fill the warm stagnant air with smoke.

"Not a smoker?" he asked with a sneer. "I thought you tattoo artists were into all the vices."

"I've got a few," I mumbled.

"What? Knitting pillows and collecting salt and pepper shakers?" he mocked.

First I was worthless slime and now I was a pussy. The guy was getting on my last good nerve and I hadn't been with him for more than fifteen minutes. I bit my tongue. I figured drinking and casting hexes were bad enough vices. I was pretty sure that I didn't need another. It didn't matter. I had nothing to prove to this asshole.

"So I gotta know something," Eddie said after an extended silence in which he listened to the radio and glared at his dwindling cigarette. He paused and took another draw off his cigarette before rolling down his window a couple inches to pitch the glowing butt onto the street. "You were the guy that bastard grabbed, right? Why didn't he kill you?"

I sighed and rubbed my burning eyes with my thumb and index finger. The lowered window hadn't helped much when it came to the smoke. "You're going to have to be more specific. I know a lot of bastards."

Eddie turned a little in his seat to look at me. He had unbuttoned his coat to reveal an old Iowa State sweatshirt that looked as if it had seen better days. But then so had this guy. The lines on his face and sprinkling of gray in the dark brown stubble on his chin said this guy was closing in on forty, but there was a youthfulness in his voice that made me think that his job and lifestyle were sucking the years out of him like some medieval torture device.

"You know, that Towers bastard who appeared at the site of the last killing," he pressed.

I finally realized that this asshole had been at the crime scene that morning, but I hadn't noticed him. Of course, I'd been half asleep when I strolled onto the scene and couldn't remember anyone besides that lard butt detective and the dead woman.

"The warlock?"

"Yes! Why the fuck didn't he kill you?"

I gave a shrug, turning my gaze from the detective to the street just past his shoulder, looking for Serah. She should be exiting any moment now, and I was anxious to get this show on the road.

"I don't know. He asked if I knew anything about the potion that had been tattooed on the killer. I told him what little I knew."

"And . . ." he prompted when I fell silent.

"That's it." He pushed me around a little and then . . . nothing. Guess he had better things to do with his time than kill me."

. . . *Subject 2 is descending the elevator to the ground floor. Eyes on in two minutes.*

"That's her," Eddie said stiffly as he shifted back into cop mode. He turned in his seat so that his body was facing forward but his eyes were on the hospital. "One of these days, we're going find a way to beat the Towers. Don't ever doubt that," he started, his voice low and soft so that it was creeping across the car toward me. "And when we do, we're going to line up every last one of those bastards and bitches. We're going to kill them slowly, make them spend the rest of their miserable lives in pain so they can pay for everything they've done to us."

"And what about the kids in those Towers? Do they get to go home?" I asked despite knowing I should just keep my fucking mouth shut.

Eddie gave a snort and shook his head. "Nope. They're no different. Why let them go so this can start all over again? We gotta snuff out all magic use so we can be free."

"Those kids haven't done anything."

"Not yet." Eddie tore his gaze away from the empty street to stare at me. "But they will. Don't let yourself go soft on them just because one fucker didn't kill you on the spot. I promise you, the next one will."

He was probably right about that, but he didn't recognize that Gideon had made a conscious choice to not kill me. He made it sound like warlocks and witches had no choice how they behaved. It was just hardwired into their DNA to be psychotic murderous assholes. Sure, I had met plenty who made me think that could be true, but I'd also been through their training, heard their rhetoric. They taught the apprentices that violence and cruelty were the only options if you wanted to survive in this world. And then they backed up their claims with horrific brutality.

A little compassion and understanding and this all could be stopped.

But Eddie didn't care about that. He wanted to

see Gideon staked in the middle of a field while his skin was stripped off with a potato peeler. This asshole didn't give a shit about the fact that Gideon had saved countless lives through his secret protection of the people. They didn't care that he had a wife and a daughter whom he loved deeply. Hell, they'd kill the man's daughter in a heartbeat just to avoid the risk of her one day growing up to be a witch. Probably his wife too because she'd be viewed as a traitor.

A sickening shaft of fear sliced through my heart and I clenched my teeth against it. It wasn't his suggestion that I was afraid of. It was the idea that most people in the world probably thought just like him. At one time, I could have almost excused it. I'd watched from a front-row seat as the Towers tortured and slaughtered the people of world. I understood their hatred and their fear.

But they couldn't see the good within the bad; the so-called diamonds in the rough. If it was magical, it was bad and needed to die. And once they succeeded in tearing down the Towers and destroying all the witches and warlocks, what was next? The elves, because of their natural magical abilities? Or maybe the tattoo artists of the world because we knew how to mix potions?

Was this the world I was trying desperately to save? I'd be trading one horror for another.

I wanted to be sick, but couldn't. Serah had just stepped out of the medical offices building and was heading toward the crosswalk.

She moved slowly, sort of waddling from the front door of the medical offices building and down the sidewalk toward the corner. She was wrapped in a heavy coat with a knit hat pulled down low to cover her ears as well as the Bluetooth device that was there. The only thing that looked somewhat out of place was the fact that she wasn't wearing any gloves. One of her bare hands rested on the large stomach protruding in front of her while her other hung loosely at her side. I was willing to bet that she had a gun in her pocket and gloves would have made it impossible for her to pull the trigger.

While her shape was accurate, she didn't quite act like a pregnant woman. There was a tension humming from her body as if she was expecting to be attacked at any second. Then again, it was likely that most women in Low Town were acting that way now that news had hit of a third murder. Staring out the front window of my shop today, I'd noticed that lone women in cars and walking down the sidewalk were few and far between. They were traveling in packs now and usually had a man close at hand.

Low Town had always had a bit of an edge to it. Maybe not like Chicago or Los Angeles, but it had its dangers. Yet, this recent turn had gone to a sickening extreme.

"What the fuck?" Eddie grumbled. "She supposed to be having twins?"

For once, I had to agree with him. Serah did look particularly stuffed between the pregnancy suit she was in and the heavy winter clothing adding a second thick layer.

"It's like she got knocked up by the marshmallow man," I murmured as she shuffled across the street when the light finally turned in her favor. Eddie's wheezing laugh filled the silence as we waited.

After a couple minutes, Serah was safely inside the hospital and we all breathed a sigh of relief. I could feel the tension rush out of Serah. Her hands were probably shaking. Inside, a nurse was showing her to a private room where she would wait for approximately thirty minutes before she would set out on her long walk down the block to the grocery store.

Reaching over, I tapped Eddie's forehead again, putting him into the trance. "Serah is safely inside the hospital. She'll move again in thirty," I said aloud for Bronx.

Saw her. I'm good, Bronx replied in my head, more for my own peace of mind than anything.

Telling myself that my companions were still safe, I tapped Eddie again, waking him up. We were as ready as we were going to be.

There was a part of me hoping that the killer would strike tonight. I didn't want to think about Serah being grabbed by this psycho bitch and me not reaching her in time. But if she struck tonight and we caught her, it was all over. The threat to the women of Low Town would be over and we could all return to our pseudo-normal lives. If not, we'd have to do this over and over again until we did catch her.

I wasn't sure I could take another night of this, let alone a string of them.

Eddie and I sat without talking, listening to the police radio as the stern voice detailed the movements of the other three women who were acting as bait. I was beginning to worry that this wasn't going to work. What if the killer knew? What if she knew which women were being watched so that she was now off somewhere else killing? What if she decided to take a night off? She hadn't killed every night since the tattoo, right? Even psychopaths needed a break.

There was no snow tonight. A clear sky sparkled overhead with starlight, allowing the temperature to drop close to zero. Was it too cold for the killer to venture out from her nice warm home? I prayed that Bronx was wearing enough layers to tolerate the cold.

Time slipped away from me as the night dragged on with only the sounds of other cops to keep me company. One group was moving to a new location to get a better view. Another was freezing his ass off on some roof across town and wanted coffee. Another stopped to check out some movement down a dark alley along Serah's route. I held my breath, waiting to hear that Bronx had been discovered. It was only an ice pixie chasing a rat, the cop reported back moments later. The world was quiet.

And then Serah was on the move again. Her fear spiked as soon as she stepped out of the bright embrace of the hospital into the night. From our spot across the street, I could see her flinch as the bitter cold slapped her in the face. Shoving one hand in her pocket while resting the other on her false stomach, she slowly started forward, heading north toward the grocery store.

When she was a block from the hospital, the sidewalk became empty. It was nearly eight in the evening, but the freezing temperatures had driven everyone inside for warmth. Only members of the Winter Court and the random Yeti would have found the evening air inviting.

By the second block, it looked as if someone had knocked out most of the street lamps. The darkness had grown thicker so that the navy blue coat Serah wore was nearly invisible. I wasn't sure if the cops had prepared the street to be dark ahead of time or it was just our luck.

Eddie grabbed up the transmitter from the dashboard. "Number Four preparing to move to Location Two," he quickly said. Returning the microphone to its spot, he turned the key. The car shook and growled to life again. He waited.

Serah stopped midstride as she was passing beside a dark, narrow alley. Her entire body was frozen as she turned her head toward the darkness.

"She heard something," I whispered, leaning forward on the edge of my seat so I could try to see a little better. But the combination of the darkness and the distance made it impossible. I could practically taste her fear in the back of my throat while her heart pounded over mine. There was now a low growl in my head from Bronx. The troll had noticed Serah pause, and we all waited.

Eddie snatched up the radio and relayed that Serah had stopped for something. Everyone was on alert. One second stretched into an eternity, and then Serah gave a shake of her head, as if waving off the sound as nothing. She took one step down the sidewalk, resuming her long trek to the grocery, before she was yanked back into the yawning darkness.

I gasped as her fear flooded my veins, blocking out everything else. For a second, I couldn't think. There was only her terror and my own fear for her drowning out all rational thought. Sucking in a deep breath, I felt my heart start again as Eddie gunned the car out of our parking spot. He clipped the bumper of a parked car and cut off another as he raced down the two blocks. Out of the corner of my eye, I thought I saw a large, black mass charge out of the shadows toward Serah's location.

Serah's terror quickly became replaced with anger and I found that I could breathe again. Centering all my powers on her location, I started to form a protection spell for her in my mind and then she was gone.

Poof.

Gone.

As if she had never existed.

I jumped out of the car before Eddie brought it to a screeching halt. He was shouting into his radio for backup as he followed me. Bronx was only a half step behind us. We stood gaping into the darkness, but there was no one there. Swearing softly to myself as my breath broke from my throat in hard gasps, I conjured up a ball of light and threw it into the alley to try to push back the darkness. In my desperation and haste, I'd forgotten about Eddie, the magic hater.

"Fuck!" he shouted, followed by a loud clatter.

Twisting around, I found that he'd dropped the radio on the concrete and was now holding his gun on me with both hands while backing himself against the wall. In the thin light I'd cast, I could see that his face was now ghostly white.

"Y-You're one of them," he said. "You're one of them fucking warlocks!"

"Yeah, but I don't have time for you," I said.

Before he could squeeze the trigger of his gun, I sent a little pulse of energy into his brain. The man collapsed, falling to the ground like a wad of dirty laundry. I wasted another second wiping his memory of the past ten seconds so that the last thing he remembered was racing to this alley with me.

With the cop taken care of, I turned my attention back to the alley and Serah's disappearance. This wasn't the work of the killer who had been stalking pregnant women the past several days. Could it be the asshole who was working the Death Magic? God, I hoped not.

After a couple steps inward, I spotted the button I had given to Serah lying on the ground. If it hadn't fallen partially on an old piece of paper, I would never have spotted it against the black asphalt. Whoever had taken her had been smart enough to remove the charmed object that was tracking her.

"Who took her? The killer?"

"No," I whispered, my mind turning over my options.

Bending to pick up the button, I froze as a whiff of magic drifted to me. Not the same as what I sensed with the Death Magic user. This was a different kind of magic, smelling of stagnant water and mold. It made me think of dark, damp places hidden from the sun. This was a different creature entirely. I wasn't quite sure what had grabbed Serah, but I was starting to get a pretty good hunch. But that didn't matter. The important thing was that the magic had left a trail I could follow.

Taking one last look back at the bastard on the ground, I grabbed Bronx's arm and we winked out of sight before the next cop appeared around the corner. We had a friend to save.

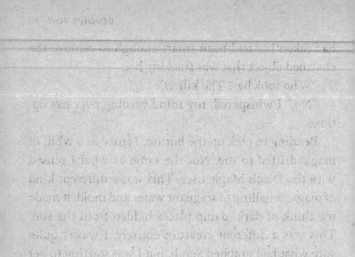

Part 3

INNER DEMON

CHAPTER 1

They were waiting for us.

Darkness blotted out everything when Bronx and I arrived at what I thought was Serah's final destination. Before I could summon up a light spell, they were on us. Pain slashed across my arm as if someone had taken a knife to my flesh. A blunt object crashed into my side with an ugly cracking sound indicating that a couple of my ribs had broken. One of my assailants jumped on my back, wrapping his long, thin arms around my throat, cutting off my air supply.

Over the screeching of my attackers and skittering of claws across pavement, Bronx released an eardrum-shattering roar followed by the sickening thud of his fists pummeling soft flesh. As my eyes adjusted to the darkness, I could start to make out the troll as he picked up his smaller adversaries and threw them across the room.

Sucking in a slender thread of air as I tried to fight my way free, I tapped the energy in the air and sent it out in a raw, angry blast. Some small part of my brain prayed that Serah wasn't in the direct path of the energy, but I was too oxygen starved to give it much thought. I just knew that Bronx would be able to survive it.

Panicked screams filled the air as my enemies scampered away. Someone new shouted above the din and the screams immediately stopped. I didn't recognize the language that was encased in the howl, but it didn't sound friendly.

A twisted spell glowed in the forefront of my mind. I didn't know if I had glimpsed it in a book or if it was the conjuring of my own panic, but the feel of it was dark and violent. My stomach churned at the thought of letting this loose, and yet I still gathered together the energy. I wanted the death and destruction to stop. I wanted the violence to end. I might not have started this fight, but I was ready to fucking finish it.

"Stop!" Serah shouted somewhere to my right. "Everyone stop! It's a misunderstanding!"

"Light!" I barked, throwing out my right arm. The only sound in the suddenly dense silence was the soft patter of my blood raining from my arm as I moved it.

Several balls of white light jumped from my fingertips and elegantly floated upward until they reached a ceiling two stories above us. A quick glance around revealed that we were in an old theater and surrounded by goblins. Fuck. This wasn't good at all.

Serah was being held by the back of her thick coat by the tallest of the goblins, his orange eyes reflecting with a sickening menace as he glared at me. The TAPSS investigator didn't look as if she had been harmed. Only her knit cap was a little askew.

Bronx was leaning on one knee to my left. His heavy wool coat had been shredded by the goblins and there were several cuts on his body that were slowly bleeding. Looking over at me, he gave me a small nod to indicate that he was okay. Trolls could take a beating, but no one wanted to take on a horde of goblins. They weren't strong or even particularly smart, but they had numbers on their side. Take out one, and three more were waiting to take his place.

"It's a misunderstanding," Serah repeated, trying to keep her voice calm now that we were no longer trying to kill each other.

"What's going on?" I demanded.

Another goblin stepped forward, slighter in build with long, stringy black hair. I had a feeling that this one was a female, though there was still nothing attractive about her appearance. However, she quickly settled all doubts when she opened her mouth, revealing a hauntingly melodious voice. "You're hunting the pregnant women of this city."

I had to give my head a little shake as if to clear it before I could bring myself to respond. Her voice was so strangely contrary to her appearance. It was like listening to a nightingale's song leap from the snout of a warthog. "I'm not. I'm trying to protect them."

"Lies," the goblin holding Serah shouted. "You attacked us! Set our home on fire!"

"I didn't! You attacked us first!" I yelled back. It was much easier to argue with this asshole. He sounded like he was aching for a fight and I was more than ready to give it to him.

"You lied to enter our home," the female pointed out.

The next words died in my throat. There was something about the sound. I didn't want to argue with her. It was almost a compulsion. This goblin could have given the sirens a lesson or two about control.

"We tried the truth, but your people kept slamming the door in our face," Serah explained while I fought to untangle my tongue. "We came to discuss the murders with you. We wanted to know if you had heard or seen anything." She unzipped her coat and reached into an inner pocket to produce the little leather wallet that held her TAPSS badge. "We're trying to catch the killer."

The female frowned at the badge. I couldn't tell if she just wasn't impressed with it or if she was more concerned about the fact that Serah represented an officer of the law. TAPSS might not have any kind of jurisdiction over the kinds of illegal activities that they were involved in, but goblins didn't care for anyone within the law-enforcement field.

"And you are working with a warlock?" she inquired after a moment of silence.

Serah sighed, shoving the badge back into her pocket. "It's complicated."

No shit.

"We're just trying to track down the person who has been killing pregnant women." Bronx broke in, once again sounding like the voice of reason. "Do you know anything? Have you seen her?"

I wanted to smile at my old friend. His questions, at least briefly, distracted them from the guy performing magic who was clearly not a part of the Towers regime. I'd already been blackmailed by one bastard who knew my secret. I had no intention of going down that road again.

At this point in our investigation, I'd take a good description of the woman. With all my spells and Gideon's, we hadn't even managed to get a good look at this bitch. Our big breakthrough was that the killer was a woman and likely human. *Fantastic.* That only narrowed it down to a few thousand occupants of Low Town.

"We've not seen her that we know of," the female said, lifting her angular chin a bit. "The killings have scared the women we have working for us. Two have left Low Town, threatening to break their contract with us."

"Wait! You hire women to have babies for you?" Serah demanded. She struggled to twist around so that she could look at the pair of goblins beside her, but the male was still holding her slightly off the ground by the back of her coat.

I groaned and rubbed my temple with my left hand. We didn't need to get into this now. The ex-cop was well-informed when it came to many things about the occupants of Low Town, but apparently there were holes in her education.

"Where did you think they got the babies?" I murmured.

The look she gave me made it clear that she thought they had been stolen from their cribs. While that was their old way of doing things, the result was that they had the cops hunting them down, which was really bad for business. Now the goblins just hired poor women with few options when it came to making any kind of good income. When it came to the actual conception of the babies, that's where my own knowledge fell short. I didn't see these guys paying women to go to a sperm bank for artificial insemination.

"We have heard that the werewolves are planning to go hunting for her tonight," the male said, ending the awkward silence.

"Whispers are that she hunts on the south side because that is where she lives," the female goblin added.

I dropped my hand back to my side and nodded. It was what I had been expecting. "Can you confirm her race?"

"Human," she said firmly only to have the word whispered in an eerie echo through the building. The other goblins that surrounded us shifted, their nails scratching along the concrete as if they were circling me. The tension that had slipped from me started to return, funneling into the lights that still hovered above us. I hoped they weren't getting into position to have another go at me. They knew I was a warlock, which meant that I could kill most of them in the blink of an eye. The only problem was that those I couldn't kill in that breath were likely to kill me in the next breath.

"I'm confused," Serah announced suddenly, snapping everyone's attention back to her. "If I wasn't grabbed by the killer, why did you grab me?"

She had a good point. I hadn't been expecting to encounter the goblins tonight. With the police making the hunting of this killer such a priority, the goblins had taken a big risk in drawing attention to themselves by getting involved.

"We're protecting you," the female said. She grinned at Serah, intending for it to be reassuring, but her wide mouth of sharp, jagged teeth made her look almost like a piranha swooping in for a bite. "We can keep you safe. She won't find you with us."

"Fuck!" I shouted, jerking everyone's eyes back to me. "They're behind the disappearances!" I waved my good arm at the goblins surrounding us, disgust filling me.

I should have been relieved that the other bastard that Gideon and I had been chasing hadn't gotten them, but this whole escapade had turned out to be a giant dead end. We went out searching for a psycho-killer bitch and instead we got a bunch of goblins snatching women so they could be locked away for safekeeping. The only thing in that arrangement that had me worried was that they might be pressuring the women they were protecting into giving up their babies as payment.

"What?" Serah gasped.

"We had to do something to keep them safe. The cops had failed," the male goblin argued, giving Serah a little shake. "And we will keep you safe too."

I cursed under my breath. This day just kept getting worse.

"I don't need your protection!"

"Of course you do. The killer will get you."

"No, she won't. I'm not pregnant. This was all a police sting operation, and I was bait. We were trying to catch her and you grabbed me before we could find her." To further prove her point, Serah completely opened her coat and pulled up her loose shirt up to reveal her padded stomach. The goblins looked utterly flabbergasted for a second. The male released her, shoving her away from himself as if she were diseased.

"Hand the other women over. The cops will place them in protective custody. They'll be safe," Bronx said, pushing to his feet to tower over the goblins that surrounded us.

"The police can't protect them!" the female screamed. The pitch of her voice sliced through my brain so that I curled against it while clenching my teeth.

When I was sure that my ears weren't bleeding, I opened my mouth to argue, but the words stopped in my throat at the sound of approaching sirens. The police were racing toward us and I arched a questioning eyebrow at Serah.

"There's a tracking device somewhere in all this padding," she said with a shrug.

The goblins took that as their cue to run. Or rather, disappear. One by one, the goblins surrounding us in the old warehouse vanished, slipping backward into the shadows as if they were made of them. The female glared at me, seeming to hesitate in decision.

"Keeping the women means that police will start to hunt you as well. Bad for business," I said evenly.

"The abandoned Sleep Tight Inn outside of town," the female growled at me before she disappeared.

With the immediate threat gone, the pain in my arm and ribs came back to me. I was suddenly sore, exhausted, and cold. Sighing, I dropped to the dirty concrete, too tired to keep moving. I knew I needed to use the healing spell that Gideon had taught me to fix my ribs and close the gash on my arm, but I was just too damn tired to move.

"Gage!" Serah shouted, rushing over to kneel beside me. "How badly are you hurt?"

"It's not that bad. I can take care of it," I said. Wincing, I lifted my right arm to look at where the goblin had sliced through my coat and shirt. Blood had soaked through the cloth, which had helped to slow the bleeding.

Bronx limped over the last few feet and dropped on the ground next to me, looking exhausted and a little ragged as well. But he graced me with a small smile and a chuckle. Yep, this was a normal night for us.

"It might be too late for magic," Serah said against the sounds of screeching tires and slamming doors.

I cursed my luck and doused the magical lights hovering close to the ceiling. I didn't have the strength in me to teleport Bronx and myself to another location. Between the pain and the bone-grinding fatigue, I wasn't sure that I'd be able to get up off the floor. I was just ready for this day to finally be over.

"Did you hear what the goblin said? The abandoned Sleep Tight Inn," I pressed. I knew that as soon as the cops swarmed on us, we'd be swept off to the hospital and I didn't want the kidnapped women to be overlooked.

"Got it. I'll tell them as they arrive."

"Good. If anyone asks, tell them that the goblins grabbed Bronx and me too," I whispered to Serah as the first cop burst through the door with his gun drawn.

"What?"

"Just do it," I replied, tucking my right arm against my chest while trying to find a position that didn't make the pain in my side worse. I hadn't yet had the chance to fill her in on what I'd done to Eddie and how I'd gotten there. She was going to have to do some quick explaining about how we'd managed to beat the cop and I didn't want anything too sketchy to come out of her mouth. There wasn't enough energy left in me to erase any more memories tonight.

In the next couple of minutes, close to thirty cops poured through the various doors spread around the building. Some quickly ran over to us while others conducted a search of the old building. They weren't going to find the goblins. They were long gone now. Years of surviving in the shadows had taught them how to effectively elude the law.

Of course, they'd had their own troubles with the Towers, but then so did everyone. Many of the warlocks and witches didn't care for their ability to travel via shadow across vast distances. According to the history I studied while I was an apprentice in the Towers, a large number of goblins were tortured by being kept in a constantly sunny room. Death by dehydration and sunburn was not an enjoyable way to go.

Serah, Bronx, and I were questioned by Detective Curtis about the incident. I'll admit that I managed a small mind-reading spell just so I knew what Serah and Bronx told him. My story needed to be pretty damn similar. I used the same spell on Eddie when he wandered over, looking a bit uneasy when he stared down at me. The prick didn't remember my using magic on him, but he also didn't remember my getting grabbed by a goblin. He was also feeling unclear about how he got knocked out in the first place. It certainly didn't recommend him to his superiors, when he was supposed to be protecting Serah. Regardless, my secret was safe from this asshole.

Unfortunately, that didn't help me when it came to the goblins. Fuck. Fuck. Fuck. The leaders of the local goblin clan knew that I could use magic. Sure, an ogre from the local mafia might have mentioned it, but it didn't mean that they had to believe him. All doubt had been wiped away when I starting tossing around spells like party favors.

While I didn't think that they were going to link me with the Ivory Towers, I was worried that they might try to leverage that valuable information, much like a dark elf that was now dead. And what was my answer to this new problem? To kill them? To kill all the goblins that that been present? Or to kill all the goblins in Low Town?

God, this was really starting to feel like an unending cycle of death, spiraling down the toilet that was becoming my life. I tried to help the people that I cared for, I tried to save a few lives, and what did it get me? More trouble. More death. If anything, today had proven to me that it would have just been better if I hadn't bothered to get out of bed.

And to add to my fun, I was now being forced to go to the hospital so I could get stitched up. I'd rather the goblins come back and rough me up some more than go to the hospital, where I could wait under the glare of blinding white lights in a too-cold room.

There had been no hiding my bloody arm when the paramedics arrived. Gritting my teeth, I let them help me to my feet while shooting a glare over at Serah. They hadn't discovered my broken ribs and they weren't going to. It was one thing to get a few stitches and maybe a nice painkiller. I wasn't going to wait through a bunch of X-rays that my shitty HMO wasn't going to pay for in the first place.

At the same time, Bronx was carefully helped into another ambulance. After making a loud fuss, I got them to promise that Bronx and I would be taken to the same hospital. I'd gotten Bronx into this mess and I was going to keep an eye on him, even if I was forced to do it from a hospital bed. One look from Serah made it clear that she thought I was being a big baby. I didn't care. I was broken, bleeding, exhausted, and no closer to finding the killer.

Damn. I needed a drink.

CHAPTER 2

In my first trip ever to the emergency department of a hospital, I discovered that blood makes a difference in how quickly you are taken to see an actual doctor. Apparently, moaning and whining about the pain will get you triaged and sent back to the waiting room until a doctor is available. Dripping or gushing blood will get you ushered back with a bevy of nurses, physician assistants, and even a doctor or two will poke his head in while people with mops remove the trail you've left on their nice clean floor.

I was covered in blood, not all of it mine, but I didn't need to explain that. They were content to deal with all the blood that was still leaking out of me. Happily, it was a flesh wound that just needed a bit of stitching up. While I was being bandaged and hooked up to an IV that unfortunately didn't contain painkillers, another person was asking me a barrage of questions that were all necessary for billing purposes.

With a bit of a struggle, I handed over my insurance card, though I had no idea why. My insurance wasn't going to cover a goblin attack. At least I'd taken the time to use what little energy I could pull together while in the ambulance to mend my fractured ribs. This little production was already taking long enough.

On the plus side, I got to close my eyes and relax a bit when someone finally gave me a painkiller. Muscles all over my body relaxed and my eyes slid shut on a sigh. The past several days had been hell and they didn't look to be improving anytime soon. I was tired down to my soul. Sleep sounded so good. And not just a good night's sleep. I wanted to sleep for months. I wanted the world to drift away and I wanted to float in a black blanket of silence that covered everything.

"Gage?" A soft, tentative voice drew my eyes back open to find that the doctor who had been stitching me up had left and Ellen, Gideon's wife, was standing in the open doorway. A look of concern furrowed her brow as she took in my disheveled appearance.

"Hey." I smiled, extending my good arm to her.

Closing the door, she quickly crossed the distance between us, taking my hand in one of hers while her other gently brushed back the hair on my forehead. She was a natural mom.

"Are you okay? I heard someone say your name and I had to check. I hope you don't mind."

I squeezed her hand and let my eyes drift shut again. "It's fine. I shouldn't have been brought in, but there were too many people about."

"Of course you should have been brought in. You're covered in blood."

"It's not all mine." A lopsided smile lifted my mouth as I opened my eyes again to look up at her. Yeah, this was a great painkiller the doc had finally given me.

"I'm not surprised." A frown replaced her smile.

"I've been through worse."

"It doesn't mean you don't need help every once in a while," she said tartly. I wondered if she ever used that tone of voice with Gideon.

"Thanks," I sighed, letting my eyes drift shut again. With my wounds taken care of, they were likely waiting for the painkiller to wear off a little more before finalizing my discharge. Not much more time to enjoy this relaxed feeling before reality came crashing back in.

"Gideon told me your news," she started, her voice dipping to a whisper as if she was afraid someone else might be listening even though we were alone in the private room. "I'm so sorry, Gage."

A different kind of pain intruded on my blissful, relaxed peace. Being on the run, chasing after one killer or another had helped me push back my troubles with Trixie and our baby. But it all came crashing back with Ellen's sweet concern.

"Why did you stay?" I asked when I could swallow past the lump in my throat. "Particularly when you were pregnant with Bridgette? What did he do to make you feel safe? To protect you?"

Ellen regarded me silently for a minute, her hand gently brushing my hair back in a soothing caress. "I stayed with Gideon because I loved him and I thought he was worth the risk. I knew the dangers and there is no protecting against all of them. You take your chances. I'm grateful for the time we've had together. It could all end tomorrow or we could have another fifty years ahead of us. It doesn't matter. All that matters is that we appreciate the time we have right this second."

"But you're not scared?"

"Of course I'm scared." She shook her head at me, making feel as if I had asked why the clouds couldn't be covered in purple polka dots. "Only a fool wouldn't be scared. Even after all this time, I still wake up some nights, terrified that something has happened to him. I can't count the number of times I've run to Bridgette's room; sure that someone has stolen her from us. But then I reassure myself that we're as safe as we can be in this world and we just trust that God is watching over us."

"Do you feel guilty for risking Bridgette's life by staying with Gideon?"

"Guilty? No, I'd feel guiltier for denying them the right to be together and know each other. Gideon loves his daughter and will give his life to protect her. What more can I ask for?"

"Safety? A long life."

Ellen gave me a sad little smile. "I understand Trixie's reservations. I really do. But I've worked as a nurse for a long time. I've seen countless people die. I've watched patients who lived nearly a century waste away in pain the last few years, their memories a blur. Was their life better for having lived those last years in pain? I've watched children die far too young, but happy for the joy they experienced in their short time. I'm a firm believer in quality over quantity. Bridgette's life is better for knowing her father, even if it means that it could be shorter for it."

I squeezed the hand I was still holding. "Thank you for your honesty."

"I'm sorry I don't have the answers you're looking for. I do understand her point of view and can't fault her for it, though I wouldn't wish this pain on you." Giving my hand a gentle squeeze, she released it and stepped away. "Get some rest tonight. I'll go check on your discharge. They should have you out of here soon."

"Thanks, Ellen."

She reached for the door and paused before turning back to look at me. "All that being said, I do want my daughter to live a long life. If the quality Gideon provides stops outweighing the potential quantity, I would take her from him. Bridgette's life and happiness are my first priority."

I smiled at her, once again impressed by her quiet strength. Ellen was a fierce woman and Gideon was a damn lucky man. "I never doubted it."

Serah peeked into my room after Ellen stepped out, her arms wrapped around my coat, which she was holding to her chest. She looked pale and worried when she had to no reason to be. Sadly, all I could think was that I had all these women looking after me and worrying about my health, and not one of them was the one I wanted most to see pass through the door. But I appreciated it nonetheless. A warlock could do worse.

"They're discharging Bronx now. He just needed a few stitches," Serah reported. I'd sent her to track down the troll as soon as the doctor arrived. I wanted to be sure he was getting the care he needed. Some people were anxious around trolls when they were injured—they weren't the most tolerant patients. "I also just got a call from a friend on the force. He said all the missing women were discovered safe and unharmed at the inn, like the goblins said. After some questioning, they'll be headed home."

"Glad to hear it."

"How are you?"

"I'm fine," I said, holding up my bandaged arm to her. "A few stitches and a prescription for some decent painkillers. Not the good stuff, but then you can't hand out the good stuff for a minor goblin attack."

A reluctant smile briefly tweaked the corners of her mouth as she stepped into the room. "I know. I just don't handle hospitals too well. I've known too many people who went in, but never walked back out again."

"Towers?" I asked, only to silently curse myself, wishing I had never spoken in the first place.

Her smile returned, and this time it looked as if she was trying to reassure me. "Not as often as you'd think. I knew a couple people on the police force who were killed by the Towers. One during the attack this past fall down by Diamond Dolls."

I swallowed back the bile that rose in the back of

my throat. I had been there and walked away because Gideon had convinced me to. Those witches and warlocks had been searching for me, hoping to draw me out by creating chaos. It had nearly worked. There were times I thought I had been wrong to listen to Gideon, but then it was likely that I'd be dead now if I hadn't. Or more people would be dead now if I hadn't.

Looking back solved nothing.

"But being a cop in Low Town is always dangerous. My old partner was killed by an ogre high on fix. I had a friend in college killed by a vampire she was dating. It was an accident. He took too much one night. I had some neighbors killed a couple years ago by some trolls during a turf war on the west side."

"Tough city," I murmured.

"That's just it, Gage," she said, drawing my gaze back to her face when I had looked down at my hands. "The Towers have taken the blame for a lot of our problems, and they've earned a good chunk of it, but the Ivory Towers aren't the only thing that's wrong with this city. You've got to stop thinking that you're to blame for everything that goes wrong."

"You think that's what I'm doing?"

"Yeah, I think you're beating yourself up when things go wrong and most of the time it has nothing to do with you or the Towers."

The speech was starting to sound far too similar to something that I'd already heard from Gideon. If I was a smart man, I'd pay attention to their words.

"Well, this time the goblins beat up on me."

Serah frowned at me and started to open her mouth to say something about my glib response, but the door swung open behind her, forcing her farther into my room as a tall vampire glided inside. For my first hospital visit, this was turning into a party, though the presence of the vampire wasn't what I'd call a good thing.

He pinned me with a dark look as he pressed his lips into a hard, thin line. If he kept it up, he was going to pierce the interior of his mouth with his fangs. "Powell, you're recovering," he softly drawled. His words were supposed to be a question, but they certainly didn't come out sounding as such.

When he spoke, it finally dawned on me why he looked so damn familiar. The asshole worked for TAPSS and had stopped by Asylum to put the so-called fear of God in me when I opened my parlor to the public years ago. It had taken more than a little arguing and hoop-jumping to finally get my license for the parlor. The whispers had already started about me in the upper levels of TAPSS and I was forced to spill my secret in an effort to get my license. This schmuck knew the truth.

"Hello, Harvey. It's nice of you to visit me in the hospital, but it's really unnecessary," I said with a wide grin. I know, *Harvey*. A vampire named Harvey! A name like that really ruined your ability to be afraid of the man despite the fact that he was over six feet and was as wide as a lineman.

"It's Weston," he hissed, his fangs flashing at me as he clenched his teeth. "I'm sure it is unnecessary, considering, but I didn't come to see you." He turned his dark glare on Serah, who took a nervous step backward toward my bed.

"Mr. Weston," she said firmly. She was trying to sound as if she wasn't intimidated, but I don't think anyone in that room was convinced. Other than his name, he was a frightening creature and we could only hope he'd eaten before visiting the hospital. The scent of blood hung in the air and I had no desire to see his more predatory instincts triggered.

"What's going on with this investigation, Ms. Moynahan? I was expecting much better results by now."

"We're getting closer, sir. I was involved in a sting operation this evening to try to catch the killer now that we've identified a link between the victims," Serah eagerly explained.

"You were involved in a police operation. Not a *TAPSS* operation. I shouldn't have to remind you that you are no longer a police officer, but a *TAPSS* investigator. This inquiry that you are pursuing is outside of our jurisdiction."

"But this woman killed a tattoo artist. She's become a danger to the people of Low Town because of a tattoo."

"All of which should have been clearly documented and turned in to your superiors and the Low Town police, as needed," he snapped, his sharp voice like a whip cracking across her skin. "Hunting down this killer is *not* your responsibility. It is a job for the police."

"But the tattoo—"

"Documented and catalogued. Nothing more."

"Sir, we can't let this woman remain loose. I've been working with Gage to track her down and—"

"I'm fully apprised of the fact that you've been relying on Mr. Powell's skills to track this person down, and it stops now. You have other duties you have been neglecting. You will cease your association with this man and resume your other duties."

"Mr. Weston, she's killing pregnant women!"

"Leave it to the police. Continue this investigation and not only will you be fired, but I will also hand you over to Low Town police personally on obstruction charges. Do I make myself clear, Ms. Moynahan?"

"I understand, Mr. Weston," Serah said in a low voice while meeting his narrowed gaze.

I couldn't see Serah's hands as they were buried in my coat, but if her shoulders were anything to go by, they were balled into tight fists as she fought the urge to brain the vampire with the nearby computer monitor.

The asshole was bringing down hell on her head when she was risking her own life to save a few others and get a killer off the street. Did he have a point about the fact that hunting this killer wasn't in her job description? Sure, but hunting down murders wasn't in my job description either and I was still doing it. Maybe this world would be a better place if more people stepped up like Serah and tried to help instead of stepping back and arguing that it wasn't their job.

The vampire continued to glare at her for another second before gliding silently out of the room. He never gave me another look, as if he wanted to pretend that he hadn't been in the room with a warlock the entire time.

I waited several seconds for Serah to say something or at least relax her shoulders but it never happened. She just continued to stare straight ahead at the closed door. If it were me, I would have been running through all the things I would have liked to say to the asshole. But then, if it were me, I probably would have said more of them out loud. I guess it was a good thing that Serah had more restraint than me.

"You gonna keep looking for the killer?" I asked, but it sounded more like a statement.

"You better fucking believe it," she growled.

With a grunt, I slid my legs over the side of the bed and sat fully upright on my own. "Call me when you need me."

Serah twisted around suddenly, looking surprised that I was still willing to help her. "You know I'm not officially doing this as a TAPSS investigator, right? I can't make you help me."

I laughed, rocking back a little. Exhaustion, blood loss, and painkillers were combining to make me loopy. "You couldn't make me help in the first place. I was never doing this because you're a TAPSS investigator."

"You weren't? Why then?"

I shrugged, plucking my coat out of her arms. "My girlfriend asked me to. My *pregnant* girlfriend."

"Yeah, I guess that would do it." Her brief smile quickly died and she took a step back away from me.

"But Weston could take away your license if you continue to help me."

"True, but I don't think I would lose it for long. I've got ways of being very convincing when I want to be."

"True," she said with a little sigh. "Let's see if we can get you out of here then, scary magic man. You look like you're about to drop and it's too damn expensive to stay the night here."

"I'd never sleep," I said as I slid to my feet. She looked skeptically up at me, knowing that she saw a man who could barely keep his eyes open as he swayed on his feet. "I'd be too afraid of them removing a kidney or something while I slept. You can't trust the fucking hospitals. They're the true source of evil in this world. Not the Towers, the hospitals."

Serah giggled as she pulled open the door and led me toward the nurses' station. Someone had to know what I had to do to get out of this joint. Once I was free, I'd grab Bronx and the three of us would make a run for it.

"You're ridiculous." She chuckled.

"I'm serious. You ever seen a hospital bill? They'll steal your arm and your leg."

"Idiot," she murmured, but she was smiling.

I was relieved to see her happy, already shaking off Harvey's comments. It was better this way. There was no use in trying to convince her that she should listen to the blood sucker and stop her hunt before she got hurt. The woman was on a mission to stop this killer and to prove something to her peers. I just prayed that whatever it was that she had to prove wasn't more important than her life.

CHAPTER 3

I stomped my feet on the welcome mat, knocking off the snow that was clinging to my shoes before I pushed open the front door. Warm air brushed across my cheeks, chasing away the cold and bringing a sigh from my lips. The house was quiet except for the soft murmur of the television in the living room—someone was watching the evening news. Holiday decorations were carefully placed on the small table and cards were taped to the large mirror hanging on the wall.

The quiet was welcome after the chaos that had consumed my life. So far, I was lucky that the Towers hadn't found my parents. That ugly part of my life had yet to leak into their home on the north side of Low Town. Common sense said I shouldn't come here, but I couldn't help myself. It was the only way I knew to maintain my sanity.

"Hey Dad!" I called as I stripped off my coat and

hung it in the hall closet between my mother's and father's. "Did you catch the score for the Warriors game last Sunday?" Low Town was lucky enough to field its own professional football team, though it had been a long time since we'd had an actual shot at a championship game.

A frown puckered my brow when no one responded. I thought I was loud enough to be heard through most of the house. Hell, at least one of the boys should have heard me and come banging down the stairs to greet me as they usually did. My parents had generously agreed to take in a pair of runaways from the Towers and were keeping them hidden while trying to give them some semblance of a normal life.

Walking down the hall, past years of family pictures, I stopped in the living room to find it empty. The small television was on in the corner with the evening news signing off in favor of a game show. My father's favorite glass sat on the side table next to his chair, half filled with iced tea. I stood in the center of the room, straining to hear any sounds in the house, but it was as silent as a tomb. There should have been something. My parents were always home in the evening. Hell, they should have just finished dinner and the smell of my mother's amazing cooking should have filled the air. But there was nothing.

"Mom?" I called, turning toward the kitchen.

My heart stopped as I took my first step. Lilith stood in the open doorway, a haunting smile playing with her nearly black lips. Her gray skin took on a somewhat pearlescent shine in the soft lamplight and her black dress clung to her curves like a second skin.

"What are you doing here?" I demanded, forcing the words out past a lump of fear in my throat.

"I thought we could take some time to chat," she purred, taking a step toward me. I could see her legs moving as she approached me, but her motion was so sinuous I was sure she was slithering.

"Where are my parents?"

The Queen of the Underworld smiled, but it was all sharp teeth and fangs. "Occupied."

"Where the fuck are they?" I roared, my temper snapping in the face of nearly crippling fear.

Lilith was on me in a second, her face less than an inch from me. Her smile was still in place but it looked all the more menacing now that all I could see was her teeth and bottomless black eyes. "Don't forget yourself," she snarled. "I have a piece of your soul. You also belong to me for two years of your life and I don't have to return you to the land of the living if I don't want to."

I swallowed back my own angry retort and straightened. There was no need for the reminder that I was headed straight into her hands at some point. The thought of my parents being in her clutches was enough to make me shut my damn mouth.

Stepping back, she arched one pencil-thin brow at me in question, but I didn't say a word. "Good. What I want to discuss with you is this association you've apparently struck up with one of Simon's playthings."

The demon. This was not something I wanted to talk about with her. Not when this demon planned for me to destroy Lilith.

"I want you to stay away from it," she continued, slowly strolling back toward the kitchen. "I've got it under control so it won't kill you, but demons are nasty things full of lies. I don't want it whispering things in your ears, filling your head with tales that will only get you destroyed. It's only looking out for itself." She flashed me a soft smile, trying to appear as if she was actually concerned for my safety.

"It's only looking out for what it wants."

Her smile widened. "Exactly."

"Like you," I added.

Lilith's smile melted away like heated wax. Her long bony fingers curled into fists, but she didn't rush me like I expected. No, she did something worse.

"You forget who the true power within the Underworld is, Gage," she hissed. The lights in the kitchen blinked out so that the shadows in the dimly lit living room lengthened. "My reach includes both this world and the next. Stay away from the demon or face the consequences."

Lilith slithered backward into the kitchen so that she was instantly swallowed whole by the darkness. A second later, I heard a voice that shot straight to my gut.

"Gage?" My mom's frightened voice warbled from the blackness and my knees nearly gave out. A low growl rumbled after my name, followed by a crash of broken furniture. A woman's terrified screams cut through the silence, slicing my soul in half. I plunged into the darkness . . .

And sat straight up in bed on a strangled cry.

Blinking and fighting the twisted blankets around my legs, I struggled to get my bearings. I was in my room. In my apartment. Safe. The fucking bitch had invaded my dreams . . . again. Covered in a cold sweat, I tamped down a sob of equal parts fear and relief while I tried to find a peaceful center in which to think. My hand was shaking as I pushed it through my tangled hair.

Despite my attempts to reassure myself that it was only a dream, I snatched up my phone and called my parents' home. My mother's sweet voice danced across the distance after the second ring and she only laughed at my concern. Everyone was fine and safe. Nothing had happened. I got off the phone as quickly as I could, not wanting to worry my mother since I was struggling to get my emotions under control.

Dropping my cell phone back on the bedside table, I fell back into bed and ran my hands roughly over my face as I tried to organize my thoughts. Serah had dropped me off at my apartment at just before ten the night before, after taking Bronx to Asylum. I had stripped out of my filthy, bloody clothes and collapsed in the bed. I had no memory of falling asleep. But then, I think I was out before I'd finished pulling my blankets up around me.

The alarm on my phone had me jumping a couple

minutes later. It was time to start my day whether I wanted to or not.

Sliding out of bed, I snatched up my phone and turned off the alarm. But I stood there, dumbly staring at it for several seconds. There were no missed call or text messages from Trixie. I had seen her briefly last night when she arrived at the shop for her shift just before Bronx and I left with Eddie. But she'd never called to check on the progress of the sting or if everything was okay. The distance between us was growing by the second and I no longer knew how to close it. She was pulling away so that it would be easier to return to her own people.

Was I going to let her go without a fight? Not a fucking chance.

I kicked the coffeemaker on before jumping in the shower to scrub away the dirt and blood I hadn't bothered to get off myself the night before. Clad in some nearly clean jeans and a T-shirt that had only one small hole it in the side, I grabbed some white chalk, my wand, and a mug of black coffee as I walked into the living room.

Putting down the coffee, I inspected the twelve stitches I'd received the night before, closing the wound the goblins had given me. The skin was red and puckered around the dark thread. It looked so barbaric and medieval compared to the neat and tidy touch that magic was capable of. Lightly holding the wand in one hand, I concentrated on the healing spell that Gideon had shown me. The power flowed easily through me and up the wand to hit my arm with laser-like precision. The wound closed and healed before my eyes while the stitches slipped from my flesh, leaving the thread coiled on the coffee table. In a matter of seconds, I had completed what would have taken weeks of natural healing. Magic had some positive purposes and I was going to show Trixie that.

Putting my wand down on the table, I picked up the piece of chalk and cleared a large open space in the middle of the scarred coffee table with my arm. I drew a large circle on the slightly uneven surface and then decorated the edge with a series of symbols, linking the circle to a specific location within Trixie's apartment on the other side of town. With the circle grounded and locked against any potential intrusions, I put down my chalk and picked up my wand again.

Holding the hawthorn stick and my free hand up before me, I paused to draw in a slow, deep breath. My eyes slipped shut and I relaxed the muscles in my shoulders. The energy in the air seeped in through my flesh and flowed through my veins so that my soul was now bound to the energy of the world in a deeper way. In my mind, I created the image of a tall crystal vase filled with colorful flowers. I could see purple and yellow irises, pink carnations, and orange birds of paradise.

As I released the breath I had been holding, I pushed the energy out through the tip of the wand, directing it toward the circle, building the image in my head up from the bottom. The crystal and the water in the vase caught the light coming in through my blinds and bounced it about the room. The flowers formed in a colorful profusion, overflowing from the vase.

When my creation was complete, I spoke a word, activating the connection I had drawn with the circle. There was a flash of light and the vase of flowers was gone. If I had done it right, the vase was now resting in the center of her dining-room table. She'd see it when she walked to the kitchen to brew her first pot of coffee for the day. If I had done it wrong, it was very likely that I had created a large mess in her apartment.

After sending the flowers, I swiped my hand over the top of the table, smearing the chalk so that the writing was no longer legible and the spell couldn't be tapped by another. Feeling confident and a little more at ease, I finished getting ready and left for Asylum.

Something was wrong.

Stepping over the threshold at the Asylum parlor, an odd tingling crept over my body. Something felt wrong about the place. Locking the door behind me, I sent a series of seeking spells through the building to see if anyone was hiding or if any spells had been left on the place that I hadn't put there. But nothing turned up. I used more aggressive spells, but still nothing turned up. I restarted the antiglamour spell and searched every inch, including the second floor apartment and the basement.

It was only when I stepped into the basement that I finally relaxed. And I realized why something felt wrong when I stepped into the lobby. The tattoo parlor was my home; the one place I was sure I belonged in this world, but it wasn't helping me find my center any longer. The sickening part was that the cellar now gave the peace I unconsciously longed for.

The symbol spray-painted on the far wall rippled as the demon shifted, its powers stirring to life with my presence. I couldn't sense its emotions or feel the contact with its thoughts like I could in the Towers. The spell that bound it at the parlor kept it more tightly locked down, but there was no question that it was watching me.

Pulling my phone out of my back pocket, I checked the time. It was barely after eleven. I had nearly an hour before the parlor was supposed to open and my first appointment of the day wasn't until two. I had some time to myself. Time for research.

Turning off the lights and leaving a sign on the door that I'd open the shop at two, I teleported to just outside the Dresden Tower. The memory of Lilith's nightmare haunted my thoughts, but I wasn't going to let her put me off. I could keep my family safe from her. I needed the secrets hidden in Simon's rooms if I was going to find a way to protect Trixie.

An uneasiness crept through me, squeezing my chest until it became difficult to breathe. It was early evening in Dresden. The warlocks and witches would be about in the Tower at this time. There would be no avoiding them. But I had an easy excuse. I was unraveling the defensive spells on Simon's rooms. I was also a member of the guardians, sort of, and had a right to be there.

There were a couple gasps and murmured comments when I walked through the front door. I didn't stop as I walked straight to the empty tube and rode it up to Simon's level. The dark energy was no longer present in the hallway and there was no resistance when I entered the pitch black rooms.

The door slammed ominously as I stepped in as if it had been caught by an errant wind. Elation surged from the demon to hit me in the chest. I had returned. I had come back without its coaxing, because it thought it had me. Sadly, I wasn't too sure that it wasn't right about that.

The rage and anguish that had plagued me on my first visit were noticeably subdued this time. The childhood memories that constantly followed me, whispering of pain, blood, and betrayal were silent. I knew if I continued to visit and study here, I'd succeed in chasing Simon's ghost away at last and these rooms would become mine. And there was some small part of me that was excited with the thought.

"Lights," I said in a firm voice.

In an instance, lights flared to life around the main room and then on through the kitchen into the bedroom. A fire crackled in the hearth while the magical orbs glowed warmly overhead. And still the eagerness from the demon didn't wane at the idea of being commanded by someone it considered to be inferior.

Not inferior. Just poorly trained.

The demon's cool voice whispered through my head, making me more than a little uneasy that it was picking apart my thoughts.

"And you're planning to change that."

If you let me. . .

"I've got a few hours to do some reading," I said, walking over to the table in the center of the room, where I had left the two books the demon had pulled aside for me. The first one looked ancient and I suspected that Simon had "borrowed" it out of the Dresden library and never gotten around to returning it. The book on demons was more disturbing because it looked as if most of the handwriting was Simon's, though the first few chapters were in a different script. Simon's mentor?

Picking up the general magic book, I carried it over to the large, overstuffed chair in front of the fire and tossed it on the seat while I pulled off my coat. When I turned back, the demon book was in the chair.

"I don't think starting with demons is the best idea when I'm weak in too many other areas," I grumbled as I turned back to the table to pick up the other book.

But I can help you in those areas until you grow strong.

"Or I can just grow dependent upon you and never learn those things for myself," I snapped irritably.

That works too.

The demon's amusement never wavered.

Grabbing the book I wanted, I dropped the demon book on the floor beside me and flopped down in the chair, putting my feet up on the footstool. I flipped open the old tome and started skimming over the topics laid out before me. A lot of the information was familiar, though it gave some background that I had been sorely lacking. Yet it wasn't long before I was craving a notepad and pen so I could make some notes.

The thought had barely occurred to me when a hardbound journal appeared at my elbow along with a black pen. I stared at it for a moment, surprised that it looked identical to the ones I had been using for years to make notes regarding spells and potions I uncovered since leaving the Towers. When I picked it up, I got a whiff of a familiar scent, marigolds and blood.

"Did you get this from my basement at the parlor?" I demanded, sitting up with a jerk.

Of course. You needed to make some notes.

"You can bring things from one place to another?"

As long as they're connected.

As the words crossed my mind, there was a soft shifting of the stones in the center of the room that contained the demon's symbol. Simon's rooms were connected with the parlor because I had drawn the same symbol that Simon used.

"Did he know I used the same symbol?" I asked softly, suddenly wondering if he could have used the same connection to walk right into my parlor during the past several years.

No.

"Can you bring through larger items?"

Size has no bearing.

"What about a person? What if Bronx or Trixie

walked into the basement? Could you bring them here?"

It would not be . . . healthy for living creatures.

I could feel the demon's amusement at the thought and a chill pricked along my flesh.

"It would kill them," I said, crossing off the idea as a potential way of getting my friends immediately out of danger should the need arise.

No.

"But . . . ?" I prompted when the demon chose not to elaborate.

Their minds would break under the burden of the journey.

Before I could question the demon about what it meant, the book at my feet opened with a snap and the pages flew until it found the proper entry. With a grunt, I picked up the book and placed it on top of the one I had been reading. A quick glance revealed that the original writer of the book had done quite a bit of research on the region where demons resided, or rather where their corporeal form resided.

It wasn't a pretty place by the sound of it, making the Christian version of Hell look like a summer retreat for girl scouts. Not a place I wanted to visit. Luckily, Lilith had something entirely different planned for me, though I doubted it was much more pleasant.

A groan slipped from my lips as I sat back in the chair again, when I realized that I'd turned the page twice since picking up the book. I wasn't supposed to be reading this one, but my mind immediately starting soaking up the information, as if it had been starved for too many years. And maybe it had been. It had been a decade since I'd been permitted to study any kind of magic, leaving me eager to study anything I could get my hands on.

"Look . . ." I started and then stopped when I realized that I had been about to use the demon's name, but didn't know it. Hell, I didn't even know if demons had names. Did they need them?

Zyrus.

I flinched at the hissed sound. It was like someone had stabbed a red hot knitting needle through my frontal lobe.

Say it.

"Why?"

Say it.

"Why? Will it give you some kind of power over me?"

The demon chuckled. *No.*

"Will it give me power over you?"

You mean more than you already have? No.

I hadn't thought so. There was no power in the name. If you wanted power over someone, you needed a bit of their blood. Or better yet, a chunk of their soul.

"Then why do you want me to say it? I didn't think that demons had names."

The pages in the book started flipping again to stop on another section that Simon had written about demon names. There wasn't much there, but there was no mention of any danger inherent in speaking a demon's name. A few other demon names were listed there, but I found it interesting that the demon that guarded Simon's rooms wasn't listed.

"You didn't tell him?"

No. Say it.

I could feel that its amusement was fading and it was growing more irritated, but I wasn't going to be cowed by this creature. It had said that it needed me, that it was the pawn that I had claimed in this game. I wasn't going to follow its directions without a damn good reason.

"Why didn't you tell him?"

Say it first.

I frowned, not liking the fact that it was trying to bargain now. Looking down at the book in my lap, there was no warning about saying the demon's name and I was confident there was no power in a name. Could there be any real harm?

"Zyrus," I said between clenched teeth.

Zyrus, the demon repeated, correcting my pronunciation while sending a fresh stab of pain through my head.

"Zyrus." I winced as I hissed the name. With his voice in my head, the "U" became more of a soft "I," sounding like "ZEAR-ris."

Zyrus.

But something frightening happened this time when it said the name. The pain was gone. I could still sense the demon's emotions, like its pleasure and amusement at my saying its name, but the nausea that always accompanied it was gone. I was also starting to get thin snatches of the creature's thoughts.

"What the fuck?" I demanded, lurching to my feet while dumping the books in my lap onto the footstool.

I could feel the demon organizing thoughts to formulate a response. It was all murky and gray, but I could actually feel it more clearly now as if we were connected. Yet before Zyrus could explain, a heavy pounding echoed through Simon's old rooms as someone demanded entrance.

"I know you're in there, traitor!" the warlock shouted as he pounded on the door.

Excitement built in Zyrus as it moved from hovering close to me to the door. It was hoping the warlock would force his way inside the rooms. This creature was not on my list of people it could not kill. The thoughts were coming more clearly now as the demon was focused on the intruder. It had been far too long since it had killed something. It had been feeling frustrated since it had failed to kill the magical intruder in the basement at the parlor and was eager to rip into the flesh of something.

"Wait!" I said in a low voice, trying to tighten the leash on the demon without needing to actually lock it away within the symbol. Putting the demon away meant that I would be on my own against the warlock if he did come into the rooms.

The demon pulled back slightly and was far from pleased about it.

He means to do you harm.

"I don't doubt it."

Let me protect you, Master.

Even with our new connection, my skin still crawled at that hissed word. There was a layer of malevolence to the word I hadn't sensed before. Zyrus wasn't pleased with its newest yoke, but was willing to accept it if it got it closer to its goal.

"The council has tasked me with dismantling the defensive spells on Simon's rooms," I shouted back at the warlock while trying to push down the demon's thoughts and desires.

"You gave up your right to have access to his books and notes, traitor! Come out of there!"

"I'm not finished with defenses in here. I'm having some trouble unraveling them all," I lied.

"Let me see what kind of mess you've made," the warlock grumbled as if he were dealing with a particularly slow child. I knew he didn't give a damn about me and cared only about getting access to Simon's work.

There was a rattle of the doorknob and for a breath, time stood still. I hung on the edge of the abyss with Zyrus floating just over my shoulder. This warlock was invading these rooms and meant me harm. He was eager to get his hands on Simon's research, though I wasn't exactly sure what interested him. It irked him that I might be touching it, a traitor to the Towers and my mentor.

I exhaled. My heart beat once. Twice. "Be quick," I whispered.

The door started to swing open and total darkness

consumed the rooms again. I sat down in my chair as the door slammed shut. The warlock muttered something in surprise and then there were only his screams.

I felt myself being torn into two pieces. A part of me was sick at the sounds of ripping flesh and organs, accompanied by the high-pitched screams of terror and pain that finally gave way to low moans that followed the warlock into his death.

The other part of me was swept up in the demon's glee. There was such joy in its triumph, in the shredding of the warlock who had meant to cause me pain and possibly even death. *Traitor.* The warlock called me a traitor, and I knew he had no intention of sharing Simon's research with his brothers and sisters of the Ivory Towers. He had killed countless people in his years as a warlock and Zyrus had put an end to it at last. The world was better off with this monster gone. With the help of Zyrus, I had made the world a little bit safer.

When the room was finally silent, I relaxed in my chair, waving my hand toward the fireplace so that flames jumped to life again. Zyrus circled back to me, practically purring in its contentment, as if it expected me to give it a little pat on the head as a reward.

"Clean up the mess, please," I said, trying to suppress my own conflicted feelings.

As you wish.

Zyrus rushed off toward the mutilated remains of the corpse while I picked up the book on demons I had been reading. I had only a couple more hours to get some research done and then I had to return to Asylum. There were people in Low Town who needed tattoos and potions.

I also needed to get away from Zyrus for a few hours so I could think clearly. The demon offered a tempting solution to my problem. Could I use it to pick off the warlocks and witches of the Towers one by one until the world was finally safe? Was it wrong to use a demon to save the world? I wasn't sure anymore.

For now, I had access to Simon's books and I knew I was safe while I did my research on magic. There had to be a way to take down the Towers. There had to be a way for me to keep Trixie and our baby safe.

I returned to the back room of Asylum just after one thirty. There was too much on my mind after Zyrus had killed the warlock for me to continue reading. Too much in my life was changing and slipping away from me no matter how hard I worked to hold it all together. Zyrus had presented me with an option that I still wasn't sure I should jump on, yet it was almost guaranteed to be the one thing that fixed everything. Wasn't that what I wanted? Wasn't I willing to sacrifice myself in order to keep Trixie and the baby safe?

As soon as I arrived, I realized that I wasn't alone in the parlor. The energy zipped to my fingers without a thought, an aggressive spell at the ready on the tip of my tongue when the person called out.

"Gage? Is that you?" Trixie asked from the main tattooing room. Her heels clicked across the linoleum floor as she approached the back room.

With a heavy sigh of relief, I released the magic and walked down the hall to meet her, a smile growing on my face.

"What are you doing here so early?" I asked, pressing a quick kiss to her pursed lips. She wasn't happy. Had she not seen the flowers that I sent?

"You mentioned yesterday that you wanted to do inventory, so I came in early to help. Where were you?"

"Shit!" I slapped the heel of my hand against my forehead. "I am an idiot. I'm sorry. Yesterday was so insane. I completely forgot."

"I noticed," she murmured as she returned to the main tattooing room and sat on her little stool. "Where were you?" she repeated, giving me a very pointed stare. "I checked the basement."

My heart leapt into my throat and I couldn't breathe. "I said never to go into the basement without me!"

"I didn't go down. I opened the door and saw that the light was out. I called down there. I figured unless you were lying dead down there, you weren't in the basement. Where were you?" Her voice was growing sharper with each word.

I forced a casual shrug. "Nowhere important. I was doing a little research on the many problems that are in my lap at the moment."

"Am I one of those problems?"

My eyes narrowed on Trixie and I felt my teeth clenching. My dear girlfriend wasn't usually so combative, but there was no question that the woman was looking for a fight. Something had upset her and now

I wondered if it was something I had specifically done or if I was just getting the brunt of her anger because I was convenient. Or maybe it was hormones? Pregnant women were emotional. Did that apply to elves as well?

"Trixie, I don't see our situation as a problem," I said calmly, hoping to diffuse her anger before we were embroiled in a fight.

The lovely elf just shook her head and sighed. "You went back to the Towers, didn't you?"

Confusion furrowed my brow and I forced myself to sit down in the chair across from her. "You know I did. I told you about that already."

"No, I mean that's where you were just a minute ago. You went to one of those damn Towers to do your research."

Blood froze in my veins at her words. How could she possibly know about that? I hadn't told her about going back to Simon's rooms or the fact that I had done any research at the Towers in relation to any of my current problems. "How did you know?"

When Trixie lifted her green eyes to me, there was a world of disappointment resting in those sad emerald orbs. "Gideon told me."

"What? When did you see him?" I demanded, jumping to my feet.

"He was here a little while ago. He's worried about you."

"Bullshit," I muttered, shoving one hand through my hair so that it was now standing on end. I started to pace, but there wasn't a lot of room for moving around because of the various chairs and little tables filled with tattooing supplies.

"He is and so am I. What are you doing there?

"Research."

"The only kind of research you could be doing at the Towers is magic. What are you doing with magic, Gage? You're not supposed to be using it."

"Things have changed. I told you that. The Towers have backed off from that edict," I said with an absent wave of my hand.

"Not so much that using magic just willy-nilly is safe," she snapped. "You created those flowers with magic and sent them to my apartment with magic."

"You could tell?"

"I'm a Summer Court elf, Gage! I could smell it. Those flowers aren't real."

"Of course they're real."

"No, they're not. They were created by magic, not nature. I can smell and feel the difference. Those flowers have no soul. They never lived. They were never connected to the earth and they never spent a single day in the sun."

"I'm sorry. I wanted to give you something nice. Prove that magic could be used for something positive and pretty," I shouted. My volume was rising with hers and it was becoming harder to get a hold on my emotions so that I could keep this conversation from exploding.

"I appreciate the sentiment, but hate the fact that

you're using magic more." Brushing some hair from her face, Trixie pushed to her feet so that she could more easily look me in the eye. "When you were hiding from the Towers and the world, you were careful about your magic use. You made sure that no one saw you, no one knew. You found other ways to get the things you needed. Now, it seems like magic is your first choice for everything."

"Only because it's the more efficient way of getting things done." I paused and took a deep breath, reminding myself that she was just worried about me. I should feel pleased by her concern. "Look, I'm using magic because it's the only way to accomplish what I need. The Towers aren't hunting me any longer, so there's no danger."

"But don't you see? Using magic is a danger in itself. You're becoming dependent upon it. Nothing good ever came of using magic that frequently. It warps things. Twists it."

"That's not true."

"The Towers," she said quickly before I could continue.

"I'm not the Towers! I'm not one of them! I'm not a killer!" But as the word left my throat, I felt myself pale and my heart stutter to a halt in my chest. I wasn't a killer, right? That was the line I had always drawn in the sand that separated me from the assholes in the Ivory Towers. Yet, I had let Zyrus kill that warlock. I had let goblins die in that fire when I could have stopped it. I had clung to that rationale for years; used it as a reason for leaving the Towers. But it wasn't true. Not anymore.

"I know you're not a killer, Gage," Trixie said gently, pulling my horrified gaze back to her face. "But I'm afraid of things going too far and you not being able to stop yourself. You're using things that are bad."

"What are you talking about?" I whispered.

"There's something . . . some magic that you're using now that is . . ." she paused, wrinkling her nose as she tried to find the right word. "It's like . . . it's tainting you. You smell different and you feel different when I'm near you. It's not good and you need to stop whatever it is. It's gotten worse from last night to this afternoon."

Zyrus. She could feel my association with the demon, though she didn't know exactly what it was.

"I've got everything under control. Nothing has changed," I said firmly, though I don't know if I was trying to reassure her or me.

"No, you don't. You're using magic—"

"Of course I'm using magic. I'm a warlock. You knew that before we started dating. You knew who I was before our first kiss. Do you regret it now?"

"I knew *what* you were before we started dating," she corrected, evading my question. She stood, her hands balled into fists at her sides as she stared at me. "But I don't know *who* you are anymore."

"I'm Gage Powell, father of the baby you carry and the man who has been tasked with making you and this city safe so that you won't run! I'm doing this all for you!"

The air crackled with magical energy that I was barely holding in check. Whenever my emotions slipped past my control, magic followed eagerly behind it so that I ended up destroying light bulbs and glass containers without even trying. A part of me wanted to hear something explode or shatter. I wanted to see something eaten away by snapping flames. But the tears Trixie was struggling to hold back were enough to keep me from letting loose completely.

"I never asked you to change," Trixie said, her voice wavering with each word as it pushed aside the thickening silence. "I love you as you are and would never change you."

Her words were a balm on an old, ragged wound that refused to close. The electric charge of energy drifted away and I took a deep breath, reining in my temper. Something in me still longed to cut the magic loose, but I could feel the urge coming from outside of me more than in my own soul. Zyrus was restless in the basement as it undoubtedly sensed the anger and frustration growing within me. But I wasn't going to give in to the demon. I was in control, not the demon. It called me master and I would be the master in this situation.

"I'm not changing," I said as calmly as I could manage. "I'm using more magic because I am constantly being thrown into situations that demand I use it. The people I am up against are using magic and I have to use it to stay alive."

"The flowers?"

I clenched my teeth against the spike in my temper and waited a beat before speaking. "That was a mistake. I see that now. I'm sorry." I wasn't sure I actually agreed with her on that point. But I could see that the flowers had unnerved her and I didn't want to upset her further. Unfortunately, the look in her eyes made me think that I wasn't entirely convincing.

"The magic has to stop."

"You tasked me with ensuring your safety so that you will stay. Magic is the only way I can do that."

"Magic only makes things worse."

She was being stubborn and ridiculous. Yes, I understood that the Ivory Towers had hunted down and slaughtered most of her people. I understood that the Towers still had a deep distrust and hatred for all elves. But that did not mean that all magic was bad. Magic could be used for good and that was what I was doing now. I had protected her and Bronx and countless other lives in Low Town with my magic over the years. Yes, I was using it more frequently now but I wasn't afraid of the Towers removing my head because of a little cloaking spell or a memory charm.

I opened my mouth, not really sure what I was going to say, but I knew my tone was creeping back toward shouting. The words never had a chance to leave my tongue. A sickening wave surged through the parlor, moving from north to south, leaving me feeling like I'd been hit by a truck.

Gasping, I collapsed to the floor on my hands and knees, my heart struggling within my chest to start beating again. Dragging in a breath, I felt the air burn down my throat, like acid on my lungs. I choked, coughing and unwilling to take in a second breath, but I couldn't fight it more than a few seconds. The next was easier, though still painful.

Across the room, I could hear Trixie coughing and choking as well. I slowly turned my head to look at her and winced. It was like my brain had been reduced to sludge and was now free to slide around in my skull. Trixie stayed on her feet, but was leaning heavily on the counter behind her. Her face was pale and sweat was streaking down from her temple.

"Are you okay?" My voice was like brittle autumn leaves, cracking and breaking at the slightest touch.

She nodded, slowly easing back onto her stool. "You?"

"Getting there." I still didn't feel up for standing, but I needed to get up and move.

"What was that?"

Fear rippled through me. There was no mistaking it. "Death Magic."

"What? What's that?" she asked and I was surprised. The elves were a long-lived race. I was sure that she would have heard of it. Of course, the Summer Court was the least likely to use something like that since they so highly valued life. Maybe she didn't know about it because it was something that had never touched their lives.

"A dark kind of magic." Reaching up, I grabbed the edge of the counter and pulled myself back to my feet. I stood still, swaying a bit as the last of the dizziness and nausea started to fade. "I've been tracking this killer for the Towers the past couple of weeks with Gideon. It's why I've been away so much. We're trying to catch this bastard before he destroys more people."

"Is this the same person who killed Kyle?"

I shook my head, a part of me wishing they were the same person just so I didn't have to find a way to catch two lunatics. "No."

"You need to go?" Trixie said it as a question, but it didn't feel that way. We needed to talk more. To work out this issue she was having with my use of magic, but it had become obvious that we were just going around in circles. Maybe it would be best if we just walked away right now so that we could both cool off and think clearly. Truth be told, I was beginning to wonder if I could think clearly being so close to one of Zyrus's doorways. I hadn't thought the demon could influence me, but the creature's emotions were starting to tangle with mine and that couldn't be a good thing.

"I need to catch this asshole before he hurts more people," I said, careful not to add that this killer was now in Low Town and things were on the cusp of getting nasty if he found the other killer stalking innocent women.

"It's okay. Go. I'll keep an eye on things here."

I hesitated, staring down at the wide-eyed elf who was still too pale. For a moment, I thought about loosening the bonds on Zyrus so that it could protect the first floor of the tattoo parlor and watch over Trixie, but it was far too dangerous. I couldn't trust the demon to properly guard her and I doubted the elf would welcome the protection of a demon.

Trixie's safety had become a tenuous thing. A demon was an easy answer as nothing could stop the creature but me. Yet, there was a tiny voice in the back of my head that was slowly getting louder. It was saying that Trixie and the baby would be safest with her own people. But I shoved that voice back down into the darkness.

Trixie couldn't leave me. There would be nothing left of me without her.

CHAPTER 5

The street was silent as the sun sank toward the horizon, casting long shadows across the snow-crusted lawns. A crisp, bitter wind swept through the neighborhood, rattling the bare tree branches and reminding me that I was an idiot for not pausing long enough to grab my coat, though I was beginning to think that I had left it in the Towers rather than the parlor. Damn, my mind was anywhere but where I needed it to be.

Prior to leaving Asylum, I slapped on a cloaking spell to hide my sudden appearance from the normal residents of Low Town, but it wouldn't have hidden me from the person working the Death Magic. I didn't have anything in my bag of tricks that would help me on that front. Gideon and I had been two steps behind this asshole for too long. Now that he was in Low Town we had to act fast, which meant there wasn't time for fancy Towers suits or better cloaking spells. I was just grateful that I had started carrying my wand with me at all times.

My heart stopped upon arrival. The neighborhood reminded me too much of where my parents lived. I knew the tracking spell had taken me to the north side of Low Town, but I couldn't have told you my exact location. Twisting around, I took in the street of two-story brick homes and evergreen shrubs, willing my heart to slow down. It wasn't my parents' street. The killer wasn't close to my family. Relief made me light-headed while my hands shook from something other than the cold. It was enough that I was constantly worried about Trixie. I didn't need something new to throw on the fire.

Farther down the street, a car rumbled to life, the sound echoing off the buildings before it pulled sharply from the curb and headed away from me. I reached out, sensing the air, but the magical energy didn't follow the car, so I didn't think it was possible that the killer was escaping that way. The tang of death was heavy. I was hoping that I had acted quickly enough and he was still here.

Crossing to the sidewalk, I crunched through the frozen snow. The cold bit at my fingers and I fought the urge to shove them into my pockets. I needed my hands free if I suddenly found myself faced with the killer. Without Gideon at my back, I felt like I was at a distinct disadvantage against this insane fucker.

The thickest concentration of the energy was only a few houses down from where I'd arrived. It wasn't as bad as when Trixie and I were initially hit at Asylum, but it was heavier than either of the times Gideon and I had shown up at the other two locations. My stomach lurched and churned, trying to force out its contents, while my heart hammered in my chest. An aching throb had started in my temples, threatening to split my skull. Whatever this magic was, it didn't agree with my own magical inclinations and body chemistry.

A ripple of energy slipped down the street from behind me and I jerked around, my feet nearly slipping out from beneath me on a patch of ice. Gideon stood in the middle of the street, his cloak waving around him like a pair of ebony wings. The warlock looked pale in the fading light, probably feeling just as shitty as I did. Prior to the great revelation of this past summer, I had always thought that the warlock spent most of his time in his assigned Tower, but I was coming to the understanding that he actually spent the majority of his time here in Low Town to keep a close eye on me as well as to be close to his family.

Gideon took an unsteady step forward, his wand clenched in his left hand while his other hand was open and held out before him as if feeling the waves of energy shifting through the air. It actually took him a few seconds to notice me. At first, I would have been little more than a waver in the air before he pushed the cloaking spell aside to reveal a ghost-like image of myself.

Dropping his hands to his sides, he swiftly closed the distance between us. "You weren't going to wait for me?" he inquired, looking around at the nearest houses.

"Neither were you," I pointed out.

The warlock gave a nearly imperceptible shrug of his narrow shoulders. "I was confident that you would catch up." He paused and looked over at me, frowning. "Though I thought you'd at least have the sense to change clothes."

I grunted and continued down the block, heading toward the house from where the magic emanated. "I didn't want to waste the time. We've been too close and just missed him." A large two-story Georgian-style red-brick house with dark evergreen shutters rose up in the middle of the block. The front windows were dark, but dim light glowed from the back of the house, possibly the kitchen, and was leaking down the main hall. "Besides, we're still in Low Town. Someone could recognize me."

"If anyone happens to see us together, I promise to knock you around," Gideon said with a little smirk. "Wouldn't want to ruin your precious cover."

"Fuck you," I growled as I stepped around the smug warlock and walked up to the front of the house. I was just ready to get this done. I knew there was no chance of Trixie and I finishing our discussion until we were both done working for the night, but it would be nice to go back to her with news that at least one psychopath had been stopped.

The house looked empty. Of course, if the killer had murdered everyone on the premises like he did the last time, then the place would look empty.

"Do you know where the local nests are located?"

I shook my head. "One of them is on the west side, but I don't know about the other one." Vampires were notoriously secretive about where they slept during the day. But then, if you burned away to ash in the sun and were significantly weaker during the day, you'd be a little paranoid too.

Gideon swore under his breath, taking another look around the silent street. "We'll just be cautious then. No magic if you can help it."

"Whatever you say, boss."

Gideon glared at me for a second as he tucked his wand back up his right sleeve. "You take the back door. I'll go in the front. We'll search from bottom to top."

With a little wave of my hand, I started around the side of the house, heading toward the gate in the six-foot wooden privacy fence that lined the backyard. The fucker had picked a pricy neighborhood in which to settle. He couldn't have spent much time here because the neighbors would have definitely noticed something strange going on in the house. It had been my experience that the more money a person had, the more attention they paid to what their neighbors were doing. Or maybe that was just the neighborhood my family lived in when I was a kid, living in an upper-middle-class subdivision littered with houses just like this one. You couldn't sneak out of your bedroom window without someone being there to call your mom two minutes later.

The gate creaked as I pulled it open on frozen metal

hinges. At the same time, a security light flashed on, flooding the back lawn and stone patio with harsh white light. I blinked a couple times, my eyes adjusting to the bright glare after walking for so long in the fading afternoon light.

A high-pitched laugh drew my eyes to a tall, thin man seated on the swing of a child's playground set. He had hair as white as snow and his skin had a strange gray cast to it. His lank, stringy hair fell forward, covering most of his face, but one glimpse of his eyes revealed madness burning in their liquid black depths.

"I can seeeeee you, warlock," he called in a singsong voice. Using his feet, he pushed off the frozen ground, swinging slowly while his bare hands gripped the metal chains on either side of him.

"Who are you?" I took a couple cautious steps into the yard while letting the gate close behind me. Was I finally faced with the madman who had been slaughtering people as he traveled north? He certainly didn't look as if he was in his right mind. Could the Death Magic have driven him insane? There had to be a chance of that, but then didn't you have to be insane to kill children in order to raise the dead?

"You've been following me," he continued. His voice had a strange melody to it, as if it would be extremely pleasing if it weren't entirely creepy at the same time.

"You're the psychopath who has been murdering those children."

The white-haired man cocked his head to the side

so that his eyes were completely covered, but I wasn't willing to bet that he was blind. "Psychopath? That's not a nice word. But warlocks aren't very nice. You've killed so many."

"Like you."

His laughter rang out, echoing through the silent neighborhood. There was a sickening child-like innocence to that sound, which twisted in my stomach. The man kicked his feet out and lay back as he swung higher. His white hair fanned out behind him in a cascade of starlight, shining in the glare cast by the security light.

I pulled some magical energy together, preparing to defend myself. I didn't know where Gideon was in the house, but the warlock would realize that I hadn't entered yet and would come looking for me. Right? He was my backup. And I was going to fucking need it. This guy was definitely not human. He wasn't an elf, a siren, an incubus, or a shifter.

"No need for that, warlock," he called as he straightened, his hair falling back over his face when he leaned forward. "I'm not going to kill you yet. I need you alive to see my final creation. My moment of triumph."

"But maybe I'd rather see you dead now," I muumbled before sending out a debilitating spell meant to incapacitate the fucker but keep him awake for questioning. One of the few spells I'd picked up from Simon during my studies.

The madman laughed again, the sound like needles prickling along my arms. The spell just washed over him as if he wasn't even there. My heart stumbled and for the second time I wished that I felt more secure in having Zyrus watch my back, because it would know what I was faced with.

Gideon! I mentally reached out for the other warlock.

"Calling for help?" he taunted with a soft giggle.

"What are you planning?" I demanded, hoping to distract him long enough for Gideon to join me.

"Oh, I can't tell that now. It would ruin the wonderful surprise."

"Never been a fan of surprises myself."

"No, warlocks aren't." The man's voice changed suddenly, becoming cold and biting like a sharpened blade slicing through the fatty tissue around your stomach. The singsong mocking was gone. "You don't like anything you can't control and manipulate."

"No, we don't," I said, grinning broadly at him. The boiling anger that lay just below the surface was something I could use. If I could get him pissed, then I might be able to get him to make a mistake. Lord knows I'd done that often enough in my life.

"Your time is coming. We're going to destroy you all," he snarled.

I gave an indifferent shrug. "And who is 'we'? The Towers have got a lot of enemies."

The man chuckled. It had become a low and ugly sound as it tumbled across the lawn toward me. "But that would be giving away the surprise." And then it was like he'd flipped a switch. His high-pitched laughter returned as he started swinging again. "Nice trick, warlock, but you're not going to get me." His singsong voice had me clenching my teeth.

At the sound of the back door opening, the man was consumed in a brilliant flash of white light. When I could finally see again, an enormous white owl was perched on the wooden beam that held the swing. The owl watched me and Gideon, who was now standing on the patio just past the back door of the house, and then the owl extended his massive wings and took to the air.

I started to form a new spell that would pull the bastard back down to the ground. There was no way in hell I was going to let this prick out of my sight. I'd find a way to get some answers out of him. But I never finished the spell . . .

A surge of raw energy blasted through the back-yard, similar to what I had felt at Asylum earlier in the evening. The power of it threw me backward, tearing through the defensive spell I had erected like it was wet tissue paper. Pain exploded in my spine as I slammed into the wooden fence. Boards creaked and splintered under the impact, but I didn't go through it. I collapsed in a heap in the yard, my face down in the dirt and snow. My organs clenched and burned while my brain felt like it was melting in my skull. My cheeks were wet, but I couldn't tell if I was crying in pain or if my eyes were bleeding.

It took all my energy to roll partially onto my side so that I could throw up without choking on my own vomit. When I had flushed both the coffee and old pizza I'd had from my system, my stomach decided that it needed to rid itself of stomach acid and then blood. Sheer exhaustion was the only thing that finally stopped the massive purge.

Gage. . .

Gideon's voice drifted weakly through my head and I cringed. He didn't sound any better than I felt. With some effort, I rolled onto my side, curled into the fetal position as I prayed for the pain to stop.

Promise me I'm going to die, I sent back to the warlock. I hurt so bad in more ways than my brain could comprehend. I just couldn't accept the idea of living much longer with this pain.

You will . . . if you don't tap into the magic around you.

"Good," I whispered. There was an end in sight.

Do it, Gage. Pull in just a little energy. You'll feel better. It helps.

I lay there. The pain was growing worse instead of subsiding. My bones were being slowly ground into dust and my lungs weren't pulling in enough air. I couldn't catch my breath. Too much pain. It was burning through me. I just wanted it over.

Tap the magic. Or do you want that killer hunting Trixie?

Gideon's comment was barely enough to snap me out of my wallowing. Clenching my teeth, I released my last breath and opened up the little door inside of me that allowed the energy to flow in. Gideon lied. It made the pain hundred times worse.

I screamed. My legs jerked straight out and my

back bowed off the ground, but the energy rushed in. I gasped, sucking in my first deep breath since being hit. My heart pumped and life flowed through my body, shoving out the dark magic that the bastard had hit me with.

It felt like I was on the ground, covered in sweat, tears, and blood for hours, but only a few minutes passed. My arms trembled when I pushed myself into a sitting position and looked around. The yard was a little darker now that the strange man was gone. Gideon had made it to his feet, but he didn't look all that steady as he leaned against the side of the house. He was ashen and his face was streaked with what was probably both sweat and tears.

"What the fuck was that?" My voice sounded like I'd been gargling broken glass for cheap thrills. With a grunt, I pushed myself to my feet and immediately fell back against the fence when the world violently shifted around me.

"The bastard forced the Death Magic into us. The energy was trying to take over our bodies. It would have killed us."

"And then what? Zombies?"

"Don't know. Possibly."

I closed my eyes and concentrated on breathing while my mind turned over the bastard who had tried to turn me into a brain-munching, shambling horror show. He'd appeared pretty confident that he wouldn't kill me, but I couldn't agree with him. If Gideon hadn't known what to do, I would have been quite content to let the Death Magic consume me in the hopes of death relieving my pain.

When I was sure I had my bearings again, I opened my eyes and pushed away from the fence to stand on my own. My cloaking spell was gone, and I just didn't have the strength to put it back into place. I was still using the energy I had pulled in to heal my damaged body.

"What the hell was he?" I demanded, starting to slowly walk toward Gideon. I prayed that the neighbors didn't pick that exact moment to look out their windows. Of course, I seriously doubted that anyone in this neighborhood frequented my parlor, but then I was taking enough chances in life, I didn't need to add to my troubles.

Gideon straightened, his eyes slipping back to the swing set. "I don't know. I didn't see him long enough to recognize any distinguishing traits. I also didn't sense anything in his magic use that would have identified him. Did you?"

"No," I grumbled.

Frustration was building. If I had finished my schooling in the Towers, I might have been able to recognize what the bastard was, but my knowledge was considerably lacking. As it was, I could only recognize most creatures if I'd met them in the past.

Raking my fingers through my hair with a groan, I turned back toward the house. "On the plus side, I don't think he's planning to leave town. He mentioned having a surprise, a final triumph that he wanted me to witness. He's sticking around to perform his final show here."

"Wonderful," Gideon muttered. "Did he mention what exactly that would be?"

"Nope."

"He give you an address of where he was staying?"

"Nope."

"Then I guess we do some digging here before I report back to the council," Gideon said as he turned back toward the door he had exited minutes earlier.

"Why report back? We don't know who or what this asshole is. We also don't know what he's planning."

"True, but they need to know if something bad is about to happen. We can call in more guardians to search the area."

"Is that really a good idea? Do we want more witches and warlocks running loose in Low Town? How many people do you think they'll slaughter in their so-called search for this prick? A few hundred?"

"And what choice do we have?" Gideon shouted back at me, throwing the door open. "I don't like the idea of it any better than you, but this guy has to be stopped before he opens up hell beneath us all."

And maybe that's exactly what this asshole was planning to do if he was hoping to free Lilith. I shook my head. "We've got to figure out what this guy is and what his plans are before we tell the Towers. We saw what the guardians did to Indianapolis when they felt threatened. They'll do it all over again, but this time it'll be Low Town that's a smoldering pile of rubble."

The warlock stood in the open doorway with his back to me, his head lowered. We were trapped. We needed more help, but the Ivory Towers' preference for blowing things away and asking questions when the smoke cleared would result in too many deaths and not enough answers.

"Let's look around the house and do some more digging," I said calmly, trying my best to sound reasonable rather than desperate. "Something helpful might be found in there, giving us an edge that we didn't have before." Anything so we didn't have to call in more warlocks and witches.

It was with considerable reluctance that Gideon nodded his head and continued into the house. I followed behind him, clinging to what little hope I could muster that we might actually get ahead of this prick and stop him before the Towers leveled Low Town.

What we found didn't help our cause.

CHAPTER 6

After a quick search through the ground level, where we found nothing, we descended the stairs into what appeared to be a family room and play area for the kids of the house. As with the other sites, the psychopath had been kind enough to leave behind some bodies in the basement. The only thing different was that he'd changed his style of murder, which left me torn between crying and wanting to level the city myself.

In the center of the family room, we found children tied back to back in a pair of wooden dining-room chairs. The little boy looked to be about four years old and the girl was six or seven. It was easier to guess because they both still had their heads. The fucker had punched into their chests and ripped their hearts out.

Their young faces were still streaked with tears from where they had cried for their parents before being murdered. Their horror was a palpable thing, seeming to suck the oxygen from the air. Where were their parents through this? Had the children been forced to watch their parents being murdered before they finally met their own grisly end? Or was it the other way around?

Gideon cleared his throat, dragging his gaze away from the tortured pair. "No writing this time." His voice was rough and I pitied my companion. Sometimes I could almost understand the Towers' edict against warlocks and witches having children. Bridgette had to be on Gideon's mind, haunting him while he stood in the blood of children so close to her age.

"He's not experimenting anymore," I murmured, trying to find my own voice through the sadness and rage.

"No," he said, shaking his head. "He knows what he's doing now. I think he perfected what he was attempting with the vampires."

"Then why do this?" I waved a hand at the two children, starting to lose my grip on my temper.

"To get our attention. To taunt us. To bring us out so that we could finally meet, letting him show us that he's not afraid of the Towers."

I sighed, rubbing my head as I turned away from the kids to trudge back up the stairs. "The Ivory Towers have pissed off every race on this planet. You care to take a guess as to which one has figured out how take on the Towers and win?"

Gideon followed me up the stairs to the kitchen. The room was nearly spotless. There were a couple glasses and a plate with bread crumbs in the sink. A roast was defrosting on the counter. Someone had planned ahead for dinner that night. Our killer hadn't resided in this house. No, he'd just stopped by to kill the kids so that we could meet at last.

"You think there's a reason he chose this house?" I asked, turning around the island in the center of the room to face Gideon. "I mean, he took some risks coming here in the middle of the day. People would have noticed someone strange in the neighborhood."

"Possibly. Of course, he could have been using a cloaking spell just like you."

I shrugged. "Maybe, but I don't sense any of the magic residue from him like I did at the first location."

Pulling out his wand, Gideon started for the front of the house. "Let's finish our search. The owners are around here somewhere."

I hope they're dead. It sounded horrible in my head when I thought it, but I really didn't think they'd want to know how their children died or why.

I got my wish, but there was a price for that. We found the parents on the second floor, but one look at them confirmed that our killer now had a partner. The bitch who had been stalking pregnant women had been here and worked her horrific skills on the parents.

The parents were found in a nursery. The husband was tied to the rails of the baby bed while the wife was across from him, leaned up against the dresser. She had been killed in the usual way; stabbed in the chest and slashed across the stomach. However, judging by the blood crusted to the man's wrists and the broken rails, he had been forced to watch the death of his wife before our killer took him out with a long cut across the throat. His death had been slower.

Looking at how the two victims were arranged so that they could clearly see each other, I was sure that this murder had been personal for our female psychopath. In all the other deaths, they had been terrible but relatively quick and completed in secrecy, taking limited risks. She picked the location, not the white-haired weirdo.

"They found each other," Gideon said emotionlessly from behind me.

What he meant to say was, *We're fucked*.

"Tell the council," I said past the lump in my throat. Something big and nasty was bearing down on Low Town and we needed help. "Just try to keep them from destroying the city."

"I'll do what I can."

Shaking my head, I stepped around Gideon and started back toward the first floor. "I've got to call Serah. She might be able to figure something out that we haven't thought of."

"You think?" Gideon asked skeptically, following me down the stairs.

"I'm telling your wife you said that. Humans are pretty damn resourceful and you know it."

"True," he conceded, sounding more tired with each passing minute. This investigation was wearing us both down.

"I really doubt that we'll be able to track the magic

user, but the woman chose this place. Serah might be able to pull some info out of the cops that would allow us to track down the other killer."

"Agreed."

Gideon went quickly around the house and into the backyard, wiping away any evidence that we had been there, while I stepped outside under a cloaking spell to call 911 to report screams and a strange man at this address. The second call was to Serah to tell her the whole story.

As I pulled up her number in my cell phone, I hesitated. She'd been warned away from this case. If she kept pushing, she would lose her job. And yet, I still completed the call, because she wasn't the type to walk away. I'd met few people more determined or tenacious than she. Serah was not going to stop until the killer was caught and dragged in front of a judge.

With the scene reset to look as if we hadn't been mucking about the place, Gideon disappeared. I could only assume that the warlock was heading to one of the Ivory Towers to report to the council. I dreaded the idea of more witches and warlocks getting involved in this hunt for a madman, but Gideon and I were a step behind and outgunned when it came to taking these assholes down. We needed help, but I was afraid that we were getting the wrong kind. I wanted someone to act with the precision of a surgeon wielding a scalpel, not a five-year-old with a chainsaw and too much sugar.

I hesitated, trying to decide where to go. It was with some disgust that I found myself standing in what had been Simon's rooms within the Dresden Tower. I at least had the excuse of wanting to pick up my coat, but as I stood there holding it in my fists, I knew that the truth was that I didn't want to go back to Asylum. There was too much unsettled business between Trixie and me, but I didn't have any new answers for her.

Throwing the jacket down, I slumped in a chair with my head in my hands. Zyrus danced around me, excited by the scent of death clinging to me like a second skin. In my desperation, I even tried asking the demon if it knew what I was up against, but Zyrus was unable to help. It recognized the magic as Death Magic, but it didn't know who had cast the spell or even why.

Shoving myself out of the chair in frustration, I paced over to the bookshelf on the far wall, but I didn't pull anything down. What creature existed now that might be old enough to know what Death Magic was? What creature would be powerful enough to use it as well as have a vendetta against the Towers? The Dark Elves? Definitely, but that man didn't look anything like a dark elf. His hair made him similar to the Winter Court, but that was the only similarity between them. The stranger's features had been softer, more rounded than the Winter Court elves.

My mind kept going back to the first trip Gideon and I took to investigate the magical disturbance. The magic we had sensed there had been different. Extremely different. Something I had never encountered before. It wasn't fey and it wasn't shifter, despite the man's ability to easily change forms.

Could Gideon be right in that this creature, this man, was one of the Lost Ones? They certainly had a bone to pick with the Towers, since it was believed that all of their kind had been wiped from the Earth centuries ago. There were a few species out there that were on the cusp of being categorized as Lost Ones, but the only groups who had truly earned the title were dragons and unicorns. Had I just seen one of those?

I shook my head. Couldn't be. I wouldn't have survived an encounter with either creature if it had been. Then again, I had barely survived the encounter as it was. Gideon had pulled my ass from the edge.

Fuck.

And what if it was one of the Lost Ones? What was I supposed to do? Kill him, officially destroying the last of his kind. That's what I wanted to be known for! Gage, the man who slaughtered the last unicorn. Gage, the dragon slayer.

I roared with rage. Twisting around, I blasted energy through the room, shattering every glass vial, jar, and beaker in its path. Papers scattered, flying through the air.

What the fuck happened to just being a tattoo artist? When had my life gotten so damn complicated? I rubbed my eyes with the heels of my hands and tried to clear my thoughts, but they kept getting pulled along the timeline of my life. Was it when Simon came back, hunting me? Should I have not killed my mentor to survive, but let him kill me that night last summer? It would have gotten me out of the Towers' hair, but it would have landed me solidly in Lilith's hands, which couldn't possibly be a good thing.

Was it when I faced down the Towers and saved my

brother's life? No witch or warlock likes to be shown up, and that was what I accomplished by outmaneuvering them. Or maybe things went off-balance when I solved the elves little reproduction problem?

Trixie blamed magic for all my problems and magic was involved in all those incidents. But what would have happened if I hadn't used magic? My brother would be dead, Low Town would be a smoking crater in the earth, the elves would be going extinct because they couldn't have babies . . . oh, and I'd be dead. Sure, magic had caused all those problems in the first place, but it had fixed it all as well. Where did you draw the line? How did you stop the cycle?

Flopping back in the chair, I stared at the mess I'd made across the room. Glass glittered in the pale light while scattered paper soaked up the liquids that were spreading across the table and onto the floor. I didn't know the answer. It felt like I was left with only two choices. On the one hand, I could let the Towers kill me. That would stop them from bothering Trixie and our child. But, in my opinion, that was a really shitty choice.

On the other hand, I could use the magic and information that filled this room and many like it in this Tower to take down the witches and warlocks, dismantling the Towers and all their power. Removing the Towers meant removing the threat from Trixie and the world. That road was long, treacherous, and unlikely to lead to a happy ending for me.

"Is it even possible to get rid of the Towers?" I murmured, talking to myself.

Of course you can. The man who destroys Lilith can do anything in this world.

The demon's words reminded me that I had another task waiting for me that I'd rather not think about. Zyrus still had its little black heart set on me destroying the Queen of the Monsters. I wasn't sure how the fuck I was going to accomplish that feat, but that seemed a little more possible than the road I currently faced against the Towers. I might just be reassured by the idea that Zyrus had already read in the future that I had the ability to take Lilith down. It was too much to hope that such a thing was possible.

"And become a murderer in the process," I muttered, dropping my head into my hand.

Murderer for some, but savior for your world.

I would happily give my last breath to save the world for Trixie and my child. But then dying was easy. Was I willing to become a murderer for my love?

Serah called, jerking me from my dark thoughts. She said it was safe to return to the scene of the crime now that the cops had arrived and locked the place down.

Glancing around Simon's old room, I sighed. I needed to stop spending time here. It wasn't good for my state of mind. I also needed to stay focused on the problems directly in front of me. If I could catch the killers, the city would be safe and I could turn my full attention to Trixie. Maybe then it would be time for me to part ways with Zyrus. It might not be too keen on the idea, but I didn't think hanging around with a demon was good for my health.

CHAPTER 7

Night had claimed the city when I crawled back to my apartment. The investigation at the crime scene had taken longer because of the changes made by the killer. I kept my mouth shut about the fact that they were now looking at the chaos created by two separate killers. The Low Town police didn't need to chase after the other asshole. I was still trying to figure out how a pair of warlocks was going to take these lunatics down. Humans didn't have a chance.

When Serah dropped me off, she promised that she'd follow up with me as soon as possible. She was confident that we'd get closer to the killer now because she was sure she could establish a link between the victims and the killer. I just pitied them. How could you piss someone off so much that *this* was the result? The world had enough of pain and death already.

Rubbing my eyes, I shoved my key in the lock and

froze. Someone was in my apartment. I could feel them on the other side of the wall. Their energy was warm and inviting, though the occupants felt agitated, as if they were anxious about my arrival. Very carefully, I probed the room to find that Trixie was in the living room along with . . . her brother.

My heart stopped for a second and I leaned my head forward to rest it against the door. I didn't want to move forward. Hell, I wanted to back away and go hide at Asylum, where I could bullshit with Bronx and pretend that my girlfriend wasn't leaving me. But they would have heard the key going into the lock. They could probably hear me breathing. I didn't get the choice of acting like a coward.

Turning the key in the lock, I stepped into my living room to find Trixie sitting on the edge of the couch with her hands folded tightly in her lap. Her brother Eldon was prowling my dining room and kitchen, a scowl on his face. I scowled back at him. We'd never actually gotten along. I think it had to do with the fact that I was a warlock and that I was the reason his sister had chosen to stay in Low Town rather than returning to her people. Of course, I was the one who had saved their race, so you'd think he'd cut me a little slack, but not this prick.

Carefully closing the door behind me, I walked over to the dining room table and draped my coat over the back of one of the chairs. Eldon had stopped pacing and out of the corner of my eye I could see Trixie now standing beside the sofa. I wracked my brain for the perfect words to say: the words that would win her and convince her to stay. At that moment, I would have promised anything. If she wanted, I would give up magic. I would find a way to be a normal guy who did normal things that didn't attract the attention of murderers, thugs, and the Towers.

But the words I needed in that instant would be a lie, and we both knew it.

"I thought you were going to give me more time," I said softly, breaking the tense silence that had grown in the room.

"It's too dangerous," Eldon said in clipped tones. My head jerked up and I clenched my teeth, fighting the urge to snap at the man.

"Don't, Eldon," Trixie sharply said, surprising me. But then I had no doubt that she could sense that I was just about to crack. Trixie always knew how I felt. "Just let me talk, please."

Without breaking his gaze, Eldon nodded stiffly. The elf leaned back against the wall across from me, folding his arms over his chest.

"I thought it would be best if I left now," Trixie said. Where her brother's voice was like a sledgehammer beating against me, Trixie's sweet voice was a blade, slicing through my heart as if to remove it completely from my chest. "The weather has been getting worse and we've heard whispers that the Winter Court is planning for heavy snowfall at the start of the new year. It would be safest if I leave now."

A sigh slipped from my parted lips. I dropped my head to stare down at the top of the table before turning to face her. "You know that's not the reason. If you're going to leave with my child, the least you could do for both of us is to tell the truth."

Tears glistened in her wide green eyes and I almost wanted to take the words back. My first impulse was to take her into my arms and tell her that it would all be okay and that I understood why she was doing this, but I couldn't. I was hurting too and I didn't understand why she had to do this when it was killing us both.

"Low Town is too dangerous." Trixie paused and cleared her throat, though her voice wasn't any less rough when she continued. "You've become too dangerous." When my gaze narrowed on her, she started speaking much faster as if she was trying to head off my next words. "You're messing with some kind of magic that is just bad. I don't know what it is, but you're changing. You're becoming more reckless. The Towers are demanding more of you, and I'm afraid that you'll never be able to escape again. I'm afraid for you, Gage. I'm afraid that if they keep demanding, eventually you're not going to want to leave. "

"I'm fine—"

"No, you're not. You've been hunting down two different killers while still keeping up with your hours at the parlor. You're spreading yourself so thin that you're barely sleeping, barely eating. It's affecting your control over magic. Most people wouldn't notice, but there's a change in the air wherever you go. It's like waiting for lightning to strike."

"I've got it under control. I'm f—"

"No, you're not!" Trixie closed the distance between us and cupped my cheeks in both of her hands. "Please, you have to realize that you're not fine. We're not fine. You need help. You need to stop and get away from the Towers."

Tears slipped down her pale cheeks when she blinked, but she didn't wipe them away. She kept her hands on me and I was at last shaken by her fear. Her crisp fresh scent floated around me. If I closed my eyes I could see a spring rain on a green glade filled with wildflowers. I could hear birds singing and I could feel the cool water hitting my face. The feel of her, of her own gentle magic, broke through the sludge of darkness that had coated me for so long.

"I just wanted to keep you safe," I said, struggling to get the words past the lump in my throat.

"I know, my love. You have tried so hard, but what we wish for will take more time and more power than either of us possesses. So long as the Towers exist, they'll haunt us. I'm afraid of bringing a child into that kind of life."

"What if it were just you? Would you stay?" I asked. It was a stupid question to ask because it didn't reflect reality any longer. But something irrational in me had to know that she would have fought for me if she had only herself to worry about. Somehow, I thought knowing that would help ease the pain that was suffocating me.

"Yes," she said in a rush. She stood on tiptoe and pressed her lips to mine in a kiss made damp by her tears. She kissed me a second time and then kissed my chin as she stood flat-footed on the floor again. "If it were just me, I'd stay. Damn the Towers and the danger. If it was just me, I'd stay with you. I would fight for you and I would win."

Reaching out, I pulled her against me, wrapping my arms tightly around her as I squeezed my eyes shut against a sudden burning. I didn't know if her answer made me feel better or worse. I'd loved Trixie for so long, and we'd had so little time together. We didn't start dating until after she'd found out the truth about me. I respected her too damn much to take a chance on a relationship without her knowing that I was a warlock. Now I was losing her.

"Trixie," Eldon said, reminding me that the elf was still here. My arms reflexively tightened around Trixie as if he'd tried to pull her out of my arms. Maybe in a way, he had. He was reminding us both that it was time to go.

It was an inner struggle but I finally loosened my hold on her and took a step back, even though I kept my hands locked on her forearms. I looked down at her, confident that I'd always remember what she was wearing at that moment. She had on her favorite worn blue jeans with the small hole in the right knee. Her pale blue sweater reminded me of the summer sky on a cloudless day. Beneath the sweater, she wore the black T-shirt I'd randomly picked up for her as a joke. It had a picture of an animated ninja cat on it because I complained that she moved so quietly around my apartment.

I placed my right hand over her lower abdomen, which was only now starting to show a little bulge. "Do you know what it's going to be yet?"

She placed her hand over mine, holding it there. "Not yet. Another month. Maybe a little longer. Do you have any suggestions for names?"

"I do," I said with a fragile smile, my head popping up to look at her. Releasing her, I knelt down before her so that my face was directly in front of her stomach. I gently placed my hands on either of her hips, my thumbs brushing against her stomach. She was so small and slender in my hands. I'd never get to see her grow large with our child. I shoved the thought away and clung to the happy moment I'd held just a second ago.

"I never told you this, but when I went to see Mother Nature, I met several souls who were living in her . . . place," I started, struggling for the right words. Mother Nature lived in a sort of energy crossroads, having largely abandoned Earth because of the warlocks and witches making a mess of everything. "There was one soul in particular. He was so very small, so very young. When I saw him, he had curly blond hair and blue eyes. He was beautiful, Trixie. And the moment I held him, I knew he was mine."

"You met your son?" Trixie asked in a hushed whisper.

I looked up to see her expression filled with surprise and wonder. I smiled at her, loving the feel of her hand as her fingers slid through my hair in a reassuring caress. "I think I met our son. The soul of the child I held, I knew he would one day be my son, but I didn't know who his mother would be. But if the baby you carry is a boy, I think it will be the soul that I met."

"I hope you're right," she said in a strained voice.

"When I was with Mother Nature, I called him Squall. Could you . . . ?"

She nodded, wiping away fresh tears with her free hand. "I'll honor it."

"Thank you." Leaning forward, I pressed a kiss to her abdomen while inwardly praying that this wasn't the closest I ever came to kissing or holding my child. I stayed there for a second, my forehead pressed against Trixie's stomach as I blinked back the tears and swallowed past the lump that was choking me. My throat was raw and the ache in my chest left me feeling as if my heart had been passed through a meat grinder.

After several deep breaths, I stood again and took a step back. Trixie was crying openly now, while trying to keep a smile pasted on her lips as if she could reassure me that this was for the best.

"I'll send pictures and letters somehow. I'll keep you updated on everything, I promise," she said in a wavering voice.

"And I will find a way to make it safe. Even if it means tearing down the Towers one by one. It will be safe for you and our child. We'll be together one day, I promise you that."

"I know we will," she said and then turned quickly and hurried out the door. The sound of her sobbing could be heard echoing down the hall as she descended the stairs.

Eldon moved to follow after her, but I grabbed his shoulder and slammed him against the nearest wall. The elf glared at me, his hand going to his side like he was going for a weapon, but I was already there in his face.

"You will watch over her. Keep her safe with your people. Do you understand me?" I snarled.

"Yes," he hissed as me through clenched teeth.

"No one bothers her. No one goes near her or upsets her."

"My sister is in enough pain. I would not have her suffer more."

"And our child—"

"I will protect the child as if he were my own," Eldon replied, his tone softening slightly for the first time.

"I don't what him to suffer because of who his father is."

"The child will not." Eldon paused, looking a little uncomfortable. "While I might not be fond of you, the people of the Summer Court know what you have done for our race. You are . . . respected. Your child will be held in high esteem."

With a nod, I released Eldon and stepped away from him. The elf gave me a small bow of his head and slipped out the open door. The silence of the empty apartment was suddenly overwhelming. I closed the door with a loud slam and leaned against it with my hands over my head.

"I will keep you safe!" I screamed, the desperate shout reverberating through the emptiness. "I will destroy them all! I . . . I will keep you safe."

And then I let the pain consume me.

CHAPTER 8

I woke up lying half under the dining-room table, staring into the kitchen. I had no idea how I'd gotten there.
It was only extreme discomfort that finally drove
me to sit up. Sun poured through the open window
blinds, casting the dusty living room in a golden light
that was almost sickening considering the state of my
life. Trixie was gone and I felt like I had no reason to
ever move again. There was no reason to get up, make
coffee, take a shower, or breathe.

Leaning back against the wall, I placed my elbows
on my bent knees and roughly rubbed my face. My
eyes felt like they had a pound of sand in them and
my throat was raw. The throbbing ache in my head
was getting worse the longer I stayed conscious. It was
tempting to call up a snowstorm to blot out the sun
while I crawled into my bed to stay for a few days.

But what would that have accomplished? I groaned

and leaned my head back until it banged against the wall behind me. Trixie would still be gone. The killer stalking pregnant women would still be free, murdering more people. The other psychopath would be preparing his final triumph and Gideon would not be able to stop this asshole alone. And the Towers needed to be taken down permanently.

If I stopped the killers and destroyed the Towers, Trixie would come back. The world would be safe. She'd have to come back. I didn't know if I was right or even if that was the sanest thought to cross my mind that morning, but it was a start. It was enough to get me to my unsteady feet. I had to hold on to the hope that I could get her back—that I could prove to her that I could create a safe home for her and our child.

I started the coffeemaker, creating more noise than substance in the process as my brain was having trouble getting my hands to obey commands. With the dark liquid brewing, I climbed into the shower while the water was still ice cold to clear my head and shock myself awake. I needed all the cylinders running if I was going to figure this one out.

Serah would be hot on the trail of the tattooed killer and I fully expected her to call me with information at some point during the day. But the other murderer was out of her reach. The police might be able to identify the woman, but I needed Gideon to perfect the tracking spell with the blood he'd gotten from Serah. The only problem that was left was identifying the other killer. Gideon and I needed to know what the fuck we were up against before we met for the final showdown. He'd nearly killed us once. I didn't think we'd be able to escape a second time.

Unfortunately, Zyrus couldn't identify the fucker from the magic or the description I had given it. I'd kind of hoped that the demon had been around enough to be able to recognize every creature that walked the Earth. I guess there were still a few that escaped its notice.

I needed someone who knew a little bit about everything, particularly the dark side of this world. Someone who had his nimble little fingers in everything. And there was only one man in this city who knew everything that happened within the bounds of Low Town, and maybe even beyond.

Chang. The black-market dealer had his withered hands in everything, especially those rare, impossible-to-get items. He knew freaking everything without being told. And if I was lucky he'd know exactly what I'd need to do to defeat this asshole. I generally didn't go to Chang for information, but rather for that rare item to complete a complicated potion or to save my ass from a nasty lunatic.

Turning off the water just as it was getting warm, I jumped out of the shower and toweled off the majority of the water still running down my body while hurrying to my bedroom. My heart was racing. I finally had a shot at getting one up on this bastard. It was a big first step in getting Trixie back.

Hell, if I could get rid of these two assholes today, I could maybe convince her to stay. Trixie and Eldon couldn't have gotten too far from Low Town. I could use a tracking spell to find her and convince her that it was safe to come back.

I made a complete mess of my bedroom, or rather an even bigger mess than it already was, as I searched for something that was in the gradient of mostly clean. It had been weeks since I'd last bothered to take a pile of clothes down to the laundry room in the basement of my apartment building. For the past several days, I had been surviving on clothes that weren't covered in blood, ripped to hell, or smelled like spoiled milk and feet.

The faded black jeans I pulled on were my last pair of clean pants. I'd either have to do laundry or wear shorts tomorrow. For most people, the choice would be clear considering that it was December and the temperature hadn't climbed above freezing in more than a week. Sadly, as I pulled up the zipper, I found myself praying that I didn't get blood or a new hole in these because I would be wearing them tomorrow.

Sucking down one cup of coffee, I filled a travel mug with more and left for Chang's. It wasn't too far from the parlor, but it was a long drive because of the slow morning traffic that was struggling to pick its way through yet another blanket of snow. These damn Winter Court fey needed to back off with the fucking snow. Low Town wasn't so far north that usually we got several feet of snow each winter. But now it was nearly every other day that we were getting a fresh coat, giving residents just enough time to dig themselves out before it started all over again.

By the time I found a parking spot more than a block from the entrance to Chang's, my head was throbbing and I was trying to push down an ugly case of road rage. I'd nearly been hit by a bus when it slid into my lane while trying to stop for a light. Taking a deep breath, I sipped my coffee and waited until I was calm before stepping out into the bitter cold that failed to be alleviated by the bright sunlight reflecting off the piles of snow.

Burrowing down into my heavy wool coat, I walked briskly to the site of the burned-out Diamond Doll strip club. I paused in front of it, frowning at its blackened walls and boarded-up front door. The Towers did this. Fourteen people had died that day and several dozen had been injured in their attempts to escape. Most of the buildings on the block were boarded up, while others were simply vacant, the previous owners having left in search of somewhere safer to live. The gods only knew where that was.

With a shake of my head, I continued past the strip club and turned down an alley beside it. Taking a quick look over my shoulder to make sure no one noticed me, I entered through what looked like another boarded-up door; but the boards were only there for show. Chang still had a business to run regardless of the chaos the Towers created. This was probably a better cover for him than the strip club.

I walked quickly across the fire-scorched concrete floor past broken chairs and shattered glasses. The bar was almost completely gone and I smiled wistfully at it. I missed seeing Jerry Caskey, the owner of Diamond Dolls. We'd talked on a number of occasions as I waited for my turn to talk to Chang. I'd even gotten into the habit of picking up a coffee for him at a nearby cafe before coming in. A mocha-coconut coffee with nonfat milk, whipped cream, and toasted coconut flakes. I felt like an ass ordering it most of the time, but it made Jerry smile.

But the Towers had ruined that, like they had ruined so many other things in this world.

Cutting through the main room of the club, I entered a narrow hallway that had led to the washrooms. I put my shoulder into one of the blackened doors and it opened slowly without a sound. This room was untouched by the fire. The floor, ceiling, and walls of the small room were all completely done in a bright white. There was no smell of burned wood and as I walked across the floor, I left behind no sooty tracks on the perfect floor.

This was the first time I'd visited Chang since the attack on Low Town, but I knew that he would still be here. His place would be untouched by the Towers. The man had survived too long, acquired too many things, and knew too much to ever be caught by a warlock or a witch.

But his dogs were missing. Named Patty and Cake, the two Doberman pinschers were the most frightening dogs I had ever seen, and I didn't even know if they were real. There was so much magic circling the old man that I was never quite sure what was an illusion. When it came to the dogs, I wasn't willing to take a chance on their teeth.

Pushing the call button for the elevator, I was a little surprised when the door immediately slid open. Still no dogs waiting for me. I stepped into the elevator and hesitated. One of the dogs always pushed the button, knowing exactly where to find its master at any moment. Of the four floors besides the ground floor, I usually met Chang on the third floor of the sub-basement, but the last trip had taken me to the first floor, which housed a giant underground Garden of Eden. With a growl of frustration, I pushed the button for the third floor, hoping to find the old man in his usual spot.

When the doors opened again, a familiar but unhappy sight was waiting for me. I found the dogs. They stood just beyond the open doors, their teeth bared as they growled. I stepped back until I hit the far wall of the elevator, my open hands raised before me. Every muscle in their lean bodies was tensed, waiting for a command from their owner to tear my throat out.

"Whoa!" I shouted, already mentally pulling together a defensive spell. "What the hell, Chang? I need to talk to you."

To my surprise, the little old man stepped out from behind a shelf piled with his goodies. He wasn't happy. "You're not welcome here! Get out!" he shouted, waving his cane at me.

At the same time, the doors started to shut. Stretching my right leg out, I pressed the "open door" button with my toe. I kept it pressed there while balancing on my left foot. The dogs flinched and my heart stuttered in my chest. *Holy shit! These dogs were going straight for my freaking nuts if Chang gave the command to attack!*

"Listen, Chang. I need your help," I said, trying to sound calm and not half as desperate as I felt.

"Go away, Gage Powell. You're too much trouble." Chang gave an irritated wave of one hand before he started to walk farther into the room and away from me.

"Damn it, Chang!" I swore as the little old man disappeared behind some shelves. I glared at the dogs, who were still growling at me while eyeballing my crotch like I was smuggling doggie treats down there. Reaching behind me, I pulled my wand out of my back pocket and waved it quickly at the dogs before they could react, inwardly praying that these were real fucking dogs and not some nasty spell. The moment the sleep spell hit them, they blinked a couple times, gave jaw-cracking yawns, and then lay down outside the elevator.

Sighing, I dropped my foot from the button and lunged forward, catching the doors before they could close. I carefully stepped around the sleeping dogs, figuring that I had close to an hour before either one of them stirred. More than enough time to talk to Chang and get the hell out of there. I had no idea what had crawled up his ass and died, but I was getting to the bottom of this. Chang had always helped me in the past and he had to know something of use now.

Once I was past the dogs, I hurried my pace to a jog and darted around the shelves I had seen Chang cut down, but he wasn't there. Fuck, that old man could move fast! I paused, trying to guess where he'd gone when his voice drifted above the collection of objects.

"Get out of here, warlock. You're not welcome here."

"Come on, Chang! We've worked together for years," I shouted back, trying to get a fix on his location from the sound of his voice. My eyes danced over crystal prisms holding snippets of actual rainbows, treasure maps under glass, and what looked to be Excalibur half hidden under a stack of fast food napkins and ketchup packets. "I need a little information and then I'm gone."

"The last time you were in this part of town, the Towers burned half the neighborhood."

"That wasn't my fault! I didn't lead them to you. Hell! They still don't know about you, old man."

"How do you know they're not following you now?"

"They're not, Chang. They're not interested in me anymore."

The old man stepped out from a shelf, his muddy brown eyes narrowed on me. "Yes, that's because you're one of them again. You are not welcome here, Gage Powell. Get out."

"Oh for fuck's sake, Chang!" I snarled, shoving both of my hands through my hair. "You know I'm not one of them. I had no choice but to go back to work for the guardians. They were going to kill me if I didn't."

The black-market dealer didn't look convinced and I swore, briefly looking for something to kick in my frustration. That certainly wouldn't have endeared me to Chang. "I'm still trying to protect the people of Low

Town from the Towers. That's a lot easier to do if I know what the Towers are planning, right? It's better than working blind like I had been."

"I'm not convinced."

"Do you seriously think I would be part of a group that nearly wiped out my girlfriend's people? Do you think I would willingly be part of a group that would hunt down my child if they found out about him?"

For the first time since I'd met him, Chang looked surprised, but that was understandable since the man made it his business, a very lucrative business, to know everything that was happening. "You're having a baby?" he whispered.

"Trixie is, yes," I said in a sigh, my shoulders slumping under the weight of the thoughts as well as the renewed ache at her loss. My anger flashed to life again in the next heartbeat. "And if you tell a goddamn soul I swear I'll give you something to fucking worry about."

Chang's dark expression eased a little as he stared at me, possibly weighing what he knew of me. I had been going to Chang for several years after being introduced to the old man by my tattooing mentor Atticus Sparks. It should have been no surprise that I would end up with a tattooing mentor who liked to color outside the lines of what was legal from time to time. And Chang's goodies definitely wouldn't have been on TAPSS's list of approved ingredients for potions.

I never said one word to Chang about being a warlock. He'd sold me things to get past suicidal vampires and crazed warlocks. He'd even helped me escape the

Grim Reaper once. I thought we had a good understanding, but the fact that he believed I could willingly return to the Ivory Towers hurt. It hurt more than I would have thought it could.

"Come on," he grumbled, motioning for me to follow him as he shuffled along a winding course through his massive warehouse of unique goods. I smiled faintly when we walked over the flying carpet still pinned down on each corner by a stack of books. Apparently Chang hadn't been successful in getting rid of it yet.

As we walked, I filled Chang in on what had happened in the Towers that saw me returning to the fold, as it were. He nodded, his free hand absently touching his various treasures as he passed them, as if their presence comforted him. Chang moved a little slower than he usually did. He looked older too, as if he'd aged a few years since my last visit, at the end of summer.

On the last turn, we stepped into a large open area that had a little kitchen setup, with a refrigerator that looked like it was straight out of the fifties. Off to one side sat a small dinette set with four chairs arranged around it. A heavy sigh slipped from Chang as he sank into one of the chairs and stretched his legs out in front of him.

"You doing okay, Chang? You're not looking so hot."

The old man snorted and looked me up and down once. "You're not looking so hot yourself," he said irritably.

"Trixie left," I murmured as I sat in the chair that put me on his left.

Chang nodded. "Not surprised. It's dangerous up there," he said, motioning toward the ceiling. Reaching into his pocket, he pulled out a slightly crumpled packet of cigarettes. While not a smoker, I was surprised that I didn't recognize the label on the front. The picture was of a woman who looked like a Bettie Page pin-up girl holding a cigarette and smiling. But instead of perfect white teeth, her mouth was full of sharp fangs. Holding one cigarette between his thin lips, Chang started to pat down his pockets as he searched for either a lighter or matches.

With a little grin, I snapped my fingers on my right hand, creating a teardrop of a flame on the tip of my index finger. As I held it out to him, Chang leaned forward and took a couple draws, getting the cigarette lit. Satisfied, the old man leaned back and smiled at me. "How long have you been waiting to be able to do something like that in front of me?"

"I haven't been," I said, waving my hand to extinguish the flame. "Smoking is bad for you."

"Not as bad as you'd think," he murmured cryptically. We sat in silence for a couple minutes as he puffed pensively on his cigarette while I tried to ignore the acrid smoke hovering in the air around us. I appreciated the companionable silence. Too much had happened recently to fill the void with needless chatter. Chang also knew that he wasn't going to be able to sell me any of his random knickknacks today.

When he was half finished, Chang ground out the cigarette in a little black plastic ashtray in the center of the table and pushed to his feet. "More is wearing on you than your girlfriend troubles."

"There's this crazy bitch killing pregnant women for a reason I can't even guess," I said, watching as he pulled open the yellow door of the rounded refrigerator and started digging through the drawers. "And then there's this other psychopath. He's killing kids and . . . and . . ."

"Death Magic," the old man murmured. He straightened, holding oranges held in either hand.

Chang handed me one of the oranges before easing back into his chair. I smiled as I turned it around in my hand. It was a sanguinello, a blood orange; the same type that Chang had sold me a couple years ago when I had been trying to help my vampire ex-girlfriend out with a problem in her nest. It was the same time that I met Trixie.

"You do have a way of getting yourself into trouble," Chang murmured, slowly peeling away bits of the thick orangish-red rind.

"Tell me about it." I put the orange away from me, setting it against the ashtray in the center of the table so it wouldn't roll around. "I think we've got a good lead on the woman. She's human, with an Alpha Conversion tattoo. It's made her insane, but in the end, she's still just a human. My problem is the other asshole. I have no idea how to catch this guy. Fuck, Chang, I don't even know what he is! How am I supposed to stop him if I don't know what he's capable of?"

"He is the one who is using this Death Magic?"

"Yes," I sighed. Jumping out of my chair, I paced into the kitchen area and turned back, running my hands through my hair. "When we started tracking the guy, he was putting all this strange writing on the wall, like he was experimenting. Gideon seems to think that he didn't quite know what he was doing. But as he moved farther north, he got better at what he was doing. He slaughtered vampires and brought them back as zombies."

"Death Magic is very old," Chang said slowly, nodding. "I don't even remember the last time it was used. The Ivory Towers destroyed all the spell books years ago. This man would have to experiment if he was to accomplish what he was seeking."

"Yes, but who or what is he? Who used the Death Magic in the first place?"

"Humans."

"What?" I said, stopping sharply. "That's impossible!"

"Why?"

I opened my mouth, but no words came out. These crimes were so horrible that I didn't want to think about my own people being responsible for them. But then, the Towers were still humans and they were responsible for all kinds of atrocities. I guess I just didn't want the humans to be responsible this time. I needed it to be someone else.

"It was a very long time ago. They were a sect splintered off from either the Picts or the Vikings that had settled in the region. They were fighting very bad wars and had lost many people. They wanted a way to raise their dead so that they could continue to fight. They started stealing the children of their enemies and killing them so they could bring back their dead." Chang sighed, staring down at the orange in his hands. "They had some help. Goblins stole the children. There were also some Dark Elves who helped to twist the magic."

"But as you said, it's been a really long time. Who the hell remembers?"

"There would be a few. Not many. What did this man look like?"

I frowned and resumed my pacing. "Tall and thin, he had white hair and large black eyes. There was a kind of . . . luminescence to him. It reminded me of the fey, but he was . . ." Turning back to face Chang, I stopped and stared at the old man. He was sitting perfectly still, his head down so that I couldn't see his face, but there was a new tension in his lean frame.

"You know," I said in a low voice. "You know who this bastard is."

"Yes."

"Are you working with him? Damn it! Are you what he is, Chang? I know you're not human. You're too damn old and know too many damn things. You do magic. Are you one of these things?"

"No!"

"Then what the hell are you? You seem to know all my secrets."

When Chang looked up at me, his dull brown eyes were gone, replaced with bright red eyes. The irises were narrow, vertical black slits like those of a cat. The old man smiled, revealing a row of sharp, pointed teeth, while a thin stream of smoke curled out of the corner of his mouth. I took an unsteady step backward away from Chang as he smoothly pushed out of his chair, displaying an ease of movement that I'd never seen in him before. He waved a hand at me that was now covered in red scaly skin and tipped with black talons.

"You would put me in league with that creature?" he growled. His voice had become deeper as if his chest was massive. "Have I ever done anything to make you believe that I would kill the innocent for my own gains?"

"No, Chang, but we've both got our secrets."

His smile widened and he gave a little shake of his head as if he pitied me. I was beginning to feel like I deserved a little pity but that thought was lost to me in the next second as the air tingled with a rush of magic. A bright light engulfed Chang like it had the white-haired man, and my heart stopped for a second in my chest.

Where the other man had transformed into a large white owl, Chang was larger and far more frightening. When the light waned, I blinked my eyes, trying to get them to adjust to the normal light levels of the room, but I immediately wished I hadn't. Standing before me was a dragon.

I tried to take a step backward but I simply fell on my ass, staring up at the massive creature. He was huge in the small, confined space. His wedge-shaped head nearly brushed the two-story ceiling and his long tail was wrapped around his body to keep it from crashing into any of his shelves of treasures. His entire body was covered in dark red scales and his black-and-red wings were folded against his back. Lowering his head to me, he cocked it slightly to the side as if to say "Happy now?" No. No I wasn't. I was so much better off in the fucking dark on this one.

"I thought all the dragons were gone," I said in a rough voice.

It was probably the most inane comment I could have made, since Chang really didn't need to be reminded that all the dragons had been killed by the Towers, but then my brain wasn't working properly. There was a voice in the back of my head screaming for me to attack or at least put up some kind of defensive spell, but I couldn't. And it wasn't because I was faced with a dragon, one of the most magically powerful creatures in the world. It was because this dragon was Chang. I'd worked with Chang for years. I wouldn't necessarily call him a friend, but I had never gotten the impression that Chang hated me either.

"No, we're not all gone," he replied, his voice a deep rumble that shook the ground beneath me. "But our numbers are very few."

Chang exhaled and a cloud of smoke swirled around me. I coughed and waved one arm in the air before me, trying to clear it away. When the smoke finally thinned, I found that we were no longer in Chang's underground warehouse of goodies. Now we were in the middle of a green field with snowcapped mountains rising up in the distance against a pale blue sky. At first I thought it was all an illusion because it didn't feel as if we'd traveled across any great distance, but I could feel the warm sunlight on my face, and the sweet breeze ruffled my hair.

I looked over at Chang to ask him where we were, when he lifted his head toward the sky. Following his gaze, I gasped and nearly fell back against the ground to see dozens of dragons soaring across the sky, their massive wings spread on the wind and their brilliant scales reflecting the sun.

"There was a time when our numbers were great. We filled the sky and made the earth tremble with our roar." Chang's voice was a deep rumble as he watched his brothers and sisters pass overhead, swooping and circling in a beautiful dance. "And when we wished to watch the other creatures of this world, we changed shape and walked as humans. Despite our new forms, some humans knew what we were. They recognized us."

"Warlocks and witches," I whispered.

Chang nodded. "Recognizing their great gift, we taught them magic."

"No," I cried, shaking my head in denial.

The dragon ignored my outburst and continued his story while watching the sky: "We taught them to control the weather, the seasons, life and death. We showed them how to extend their lives and how to heal nearly any injury. In the end, they were more like dragons than humans, but there was never enough power. We showed them how to stop time, steal souls, and scorch the sky, but it was never enough."

"Why?"

Chang paused and finally dropped his gaze to me. "Because they were always afraid that we knew more."

"So they killed you . . ."

"Yes," he hissed.

"I'm sorry."

I don't know whether Chang heard me. He'd lifted his head back toward the sky, his eyes following a brilliant blue-and-green dragon as it streaked across the heavens. "It has been more than a century since I saw another of my kind. Will you kill me now, warlock?"

"No!" I shouted. Digging my heels into the earth, I pushed back to my feet. Of course, standing didn't really make me feel better since the dragon towered over me. "Why the hell would I even think that? I don't give a damn what you are and you know it. My only concern is stopping this lunatic. Are you helping him?"

"No."

"Then why would I kill you? Not that I could. We both know I couldn't hurt you, Chang, so the question isn't fucking funny."

"I am a dragon."

"Yeah, and I'm a freaking warlock and a member of the goddamn Towers! You gonna kill me now?" At this point, anger was starting to overwhelm the fear I felt. Or maybe I was just shouting at the dragon because I was scared out of my mind. It wasn't the wisest course, but the past few days had succeeded in pushing me to my breaking point and I was a little beyond rational thought.

"Maybe."

"Damn it, Chang! I've had enough games!"

Magic crackled in the air and there was a low rumble of something like thunder even though there wasn't a cloud in the sky. One of the dragons roared as it passed overhead, as though it sensed the sudden surge in magic.

Trixie was right. I was losing control of the magic; my anger and frustration was overpowering my control.

Taking a couple steps closer to Chang, I held my hands out and open toward him. "I'm a warlock, Chang, but you know I wouldn't hurt you," I said in a low voice. "We've known each other for too long. You've helped me out of too many bad scrapes. I think we're as close to being friends as the two of us are capable of being." I closed my eyes and drew in a deep breath, savoring the smell of lavender hanging on the air. I'm sorry about your people and the Towers. I'm sorry—"

A hand landed on my shoulder and my eyes jumped open to find Chang, the human version of Chang, standing beside me in the little kitchenette in the warehouse below the earth. Worry drew deep lines in his wrinkled face and I couldn't remember him ever having that expression when he looked at me. "The fate of my people is not your fault."

"So you don't hate the Towers?"

A small smile pushed away some of the concern in

his eyes. "No, I hate them and would like to see them gone after their betrayal, but taking that hatred out on you will not bring back my lost people." The old man eased back into his chair as if his body was suddenly plagued with aches and pains, but there was a mischievousness glinting in his brown eyes. "But that's not to say that I didn't think of using you a time or two in hopes of causing the Towers problems. Of course, you've managed that on your own over the years. You didn't need any nudging from me."

"Are you helping this person working the Death Magic?"

Chang frowned at me and I knew I'd insulted him. "No."

"Do you know who this is?"

"No. I don't know him personally."

I clenched my teeth. He was evading my question with that little addition. Getting the truth out of Chang was sometimes like nailing Jell-O to the wall. The bastard hoarded information like he hoarded his other treasures and only willingly gave something away when he thought he could get something more valuable in return.

"Do you think this person is also a dragon?"

"No," he said quickly, the word jumping from his tongue sharp and clipped. I was afraid that he ruled out this person being a dragon because his actions were so tasteless and reprehensible. He simply didn't want to be related to this creature in any way.

"Then what in the world is doing this? It's not like

I can make a list of likely enemies. Everyone hates the fucking Towers."

"You can. There are not many races who are old enough to know about Death Magic and powerful enough to control it."

Closing my eyes, I rifled through the lists of creatures I had learned about while living in the Towers. When it came to magical powers, there weren't a lot of races that were a big threat. Most of the races that could use magic had only very specific and limited abilities. That's not to say those abilities couldn't be really fucking nasty, but there were limitations. Elves were great magic users, but they were limited specific nature-related abilities. Summer Court elves were into plant growth and weather magic, while Winter Court elves worked in glamour and illusions as well as weather magic. Dark elves were nasty, but even they weren't powerful enough for Death Magic.

In fact, warlocks and witches were the ones with the most scope and depth to their magic use. As far as I knew, our limitations were only a lack of knowledge and a lack of power to control the spell. The only other ones I had ever heard of who had that kind of magical range were dragons and . . . *fuck*.

My eyes popped open and I stumbled away from Chang. I paced as far as I could from him, but I think I was really just trying to get away from the idea in my head. Gideon had floated the notion days ago, but I knew that neither one of us actually thought it was possible. I couldn't accept it.

"No, Chang!" I snapped, turning around to point at the old man.

A smug smile rose on his lips. "Not liking the answer doesn't change it."

"No, they're dead."

"You thought all my people were dead."

"Fuck!" I shouted, half tempted to just sit down in the middle of the floor and stay there until the world crashed down around me. Unfortunately, that was looking a lot closer than it had just a few days ago. "What the hell am I supposed to do?"

"Kill him."

My head jerked up and glared at Chang. "Really? Kill a unicorn? You want a warlock to slaughter what is likely the *last unicorn*. I can't even begin to count all the things wrong with that statement."

"He is the last if he truly is a unicorn." Chang nodded and then continued, dashing the little hope that had burst forth that he could be wrong. "I would know if this person was a dragon. I can sense when there are others near. This is not a dragon. A warlock?"

I shook my head. "No. He may have looked human, but the feel of him was off. There was nothing human in him, and certainly nothing human in his magic."

"Was his hair like liquid starlight?"

I nodded, remembering thinking those exact words while the man was swinging.

"And in his eyes were the whole of the heavens?"

"Yeah."

Chang looked at me and the pity was obvious now. "Dragons are of fire and earth. Legends say that is why we like gold, silver, and gems so much—they are woven into our souls. I think we just like collecting things," he said with a wink. But he soon sobered from his bit of playfulness. "The unicorns were of the heavens. They are the purest form of magic, but only its lighter forms. They can control life and the mind. Their powers harness the purity of the soul and the movement of the planets. I've never heard of one using Death Magic—never would have thought it possible."

"That's why he struggled," I murmured, talking mostly to myself. "Because it's counter to his own instinctive magic."

"He's succeeded in mastering it."

But at what cost? The creature I glimpsed last night was not sane, not by a long shot. Had the Death Magic destroyed his mind? Or would outliving every single member of your race do that? Would watching all the unicorns get slaughtered by the Towers over too many long years drive you absolutely insane?

In the end, it didn't matter what drove the unicorn insane.

I stared at Chang across the open space of the kitchenette and there was a new distance between us that I had never felt before. For the first time, I felt like I was standing before him not as a tattoo artist but as a warlock, and he was sitting there not as a black-market dealer but as a dragon. Lines had been crossed today that were never meant to be crossed and I didn't think we'd ever be able to go back.

There was a part of me that wanted to ask him if he had any little magical relic or trinket that could help me—particularly if it meant that I could stop the unicorn without killing him—but I couldn't say the words. Chang shook his head as if he'd read my mind, and maybe he had. He was a dragon.

"I have nothing that would help you."

"Would you tell me if you actually did?"

Chang gave me a little smirk. "I would. There is no love lost between unicorns and dragons. This plan is a bad one for him. Too much death. And if the Towers realize they've missed a unicorn, they might start looking for dragons again."

A ghost of a smile returned to my lips for a moment. Chang was a very shrewd man . . . err . . . dragon. It was much easier to hide when someone wasn't actively looking for you.

"Do you think he's trying to free Lilith? He's gathering and perfecting Death Magic. It's the only reason I could think of for him doing this."

Chang's brow furrowed as he stared at me, his quick mind turning over my suggestion. "I think such a thing is possible with Death Magic, but I do not believe that is his goal. I find it hard to believe he would put trust in such a creature."

"He's insane," I said with a shrug.

"That may be true, but I still do not think he would take such steps to put power in the hands of another."

"Then what's the purpose?"

"I'm sorry," Chang said, shaking his head. "I cannot even begin to guess."

I nodded, accepting his answer. Chang had given me more information than I'd been able to discover on my own. I'd keep digging and hunting this bastard until it was finally over.

Getting up, Chang grabbed my untouched orange and carried it over to where I stood. The old man took my wrist and placed the orange into my open palm. "Two things," he started, the smirk gone from his expression. "First, I think you have a way to defeat this unicorn, but it means making a difficult choice." He paused and stared up into my eyes, as if he were trying to read something written on my soul, and then he lightly sniffed the air. "You're nearly there. I think you will make the right decision at the right time."

"How do you know?"

Chang chuckled and released my wrist. "I am a dragon. We know these things."

"And second?"

"Please, don't come back."

His words weren't a surprise, but that didn't stop the slash of pain that cut through my chest. I'd been visiting Chang for years for random magical items and words of advice. It hurt that I was no longer welcome in his underground domain. "Ever?"

The old man tilted his head slightly to the side in thought, his face scrunched up in a mass of wrinkles. "No. Just wait a long time."

"Should I ask what a long time is to a dragon?"

The old man chuckled. "You'll know."

Nodding, I could accept his wishes. I might not like them, but I could certainly understand them. I clutched the sanguinello in my left hand and extended my right hand to him, not really expecting him to take it. "I've appreciated all the help you've given me over the years and I promise I won't tell anyone your secret."

Chang hesitated, staring at my hand for a second before he finally shook it. "And I have appreciated the entertainment you have given me over the years. I am also disappointed that I never got the other two rivers from you."

A bark of unexpected laughter jumped from me, knocking my head back as I released his hand. Chang was always so damn practical. He'd had his heart set on getting the complete collection of water samples from the five rivers of the underworld. So far, he'd earned only three from me and I suspected that I was the only living person in this existence who possessed the other two.

"I guess I'll just have to use that as an excuse to gain entrance into your warehouse again."

Chang shook his head at me, a rueful expression on his face, as I turned and walked slowly back to the elevator. Being banned from Chang's hurt, but I liked to think that he was only keeping me out until the world was quiet again. Then he'd let me return. Of course, that was all assuming that I found a way to defeat an insane unicorn. My hopes were not high.

CHAPTER 9

I wished I could blame Chang. Or maybe Trixie, Serah, and everyone who had dropped chaos into my life. But in the end, I was to blame for not paying attention to my surroundings as I stepped back out on the street. My mind reeled from too much information and too few answers. Shuffling down the sidewalk with my hands shoved in my pockets, not watching my surroundings, I found my way back to my battered SUV. He was waiting for me. The white-haired lunatic leaned against the grille, smiling at me. I was in trouble. I just didn't realize how much, until pain exploded in the back of my head, sending me down into the darkness. *See, kids, it's important to pay attention to what the fuck you're doing.*

When I awoke, I was half frozen and my head was throbbing in time with my heart. I blinked, trying to open my eyes, but instantly wished I hadn't. Dirty light streamed in through some nearby windows, magnifying the pain in my head. I was surprised that I hadn't been bound, but then the unicorn had proven that he didn't need to bind me. He was more powerful than me and I didn't have a chance of escape unless he allowed it.

A groan rose from my lips as I pushed onto my forearms so I could look around the place. A warehouse. An abandoned warehouse. Why the hell did every asshole with an evil scheme have to hide out in an abandoned warehouse? Why couldn't I be kidnapped and taken to a nice B and B or a hotel that offered room service? No, it was always a warehouse filled with rusting equipment, broken wooden skids, and rats irritated at having their domain invaded by bleeding humans.

And did Low Town really have that many abandoned warehouses? The city council needed to do something about the job situation in this town.

"I told you I didn't hit him too hard," said an unknown woman in a petulant voice.

"You're right, Missy. I guess our young warlock has a harder head than I initially thought," responded her companion. This voice I recognized, sending a chill through me. It was the unicorn.

I didn't raise my eyes to them yet, but concentrated on looking around my surroundings as I slowly sat up. They were going to give me only a few more seconds to myself and I needed to know as much as I could about where I was if I was going to have any hope of escape. There was no benefit in attacking them. While I was sure that I could take out the human woman, there was no chance of defeating the unicorn, despite

Chang's words of encouragement. I needed more time. A plan to retreat to Simon's rooms in the Towers had started to form in my mind before I was attacked near my car. I had thought that I would do some more research, formulate a plan, but now my only focus was surviving the next few minutes.

With no brilliant ideas forthcoming, I planted my hands on the dirty concrete floor and raised my gaze to my kidnappers, preparing to get to my feet. But my heart stopped in my chest when my eyes fell on Trixie. The lovely elf was seated on the floor with her arms bound behind her around a pole. Blood matted her blonde hair on one side of her head. The worry I briefly glimpsed in her wide green eyes subsided the moment I met her gaze and then it was replaced by anger. Now that she was sure that I was alive, my dear girlfriend was pissed and ready to do some damage of her own.

The unicorn and the woman leaned against the pole on either side of Trixie, wide maniacal grins stretched across their faces as if they were waiting for me to start laughing at this wonderful surprise. Equal parts fear and rage swirled in my stomach and pumped through my veins.

It took some effort, but I managed to pull my eyes from Trixie and restart my heart as I stood. The world bobbed and swayed beneath me. The bitch had likely given me a concussion, but I didn't risk calling forth any magic to heal it. I didn't need to give these assholes any reason to attack me just yet. I'd survive a concussion. They weren't going to survive the shitstorm I was looking to drop on their heads now that I knew that it wasn't just me they were threatening.

"Who the fuck are you and what do you want?" I growled, rubbing my temple with the heel of my left hand.

"Oh my! Direct, isn't he?" the unicorn mocked with a high-pitched laugh. "I figured that old dragon would have told you."

"Just told me *what* you are," I muttered. No reason to deny it, since he already knew who, or rather, what, Chang was.

The unicorn gave a little push away from the pole and stepped forward so that he was standing between me and Trixie. "The name is Vincent, not that it really matters," he said with an elegant little bow and a smirk. With a flourish of his hand, he waved at the woman who remained at Trixie's side. "And this enchanting creature is Missy. She's the nymph who has been ridding your city of its human infestation, but then I'm sure you already guessed that."

Missy looked like your average, thirtysomething female—except for her eyes. Shoulder-length blonde hair framed a narrow oval face from which red eyes burned with the light of insanity. Dark energy hung around her like a second shadow. Kyle's potion had created a monster that I would never have expected. The power burned within her and her body wasn't able to contain it all. It oozed from her, burning away her soul with each passing day.

It was on the tip of my tongue to ask the woman why

she had felt the need to go down this self-destructive road of murder and pain, but I swallowed back the words. Hatred radiated from her like a nuclear plant in meltdown.

No, I kept my focus on Vincent. Nothing could stop him, but he was the one with the power to kill me in the blink of an eye. He was the one determined to turn Low Town into a ghost town in an effort to bring back . . . something. Chang had killed the suggestion of Lilith, leaving me struggling to figure out Vincent's master plan.

"So, what's the plan now, Vinnie? Hoping to wipe out all of Low Town?" I asked, dropping my hand back down to my side. At the same time, I shifted my left wrist, checking to see that my wand was still tucked securely up my sleeve. I wasn't yet sure what the hell I was going to do against the asshole, but for now I was content to just buy some time. The more time I had, the more opportunities there were to make something happen in my favor.

"I had thought about it," Vincent admitted, scratching his chin. "One town is as good as any other, but Low Town has two warlocks settled within her rotten bosom. I figured there had to be something special about this town if two warlocks were hiding here." He lowered his hand as a gruesome smile stretched across his thin lips and the same insane light flickered in his eyes. "I thought I would have to destroy every living thing within the wretched little burg just to complete my spell, but then I found something better."

"And what's that?"

Vincent waved his hand back at Trixie and cackled. "Why her, of course! She's just what I need to raise them." This time he lifted his hand to my left and I twisted around to gaze into the warehouse behind me.

I stumbled back a step in stunned horror at the sight of rows of pale white bodies . The closest wasn't more than twenty feet away from me. It was a naked woman wrapped in white fabric that shone like silk. Her long white hair looked like it had been recently brushed and spread in a fan beneath her. In the center of her forehead was a shining ruby about the size of my palm.

My gaze skipped over them all. They all looked like that. Perfectly groomed, wrapped in pristine white cloths with gems in the middle of their foreheads. Despite being dead for centuries, there was no hint of decay or rot. They could have all been sleeping. There had to have been at least fifty of them lined up there.

The vampires brought back to life were more than just a message to the Towers; they were an experiment in actually raising the dead. But it still didn't make any sense. How could killing Trixie give him the power to raise all of his people? Or maybe he didn't intend to raise them all with just her? Maybe he needed only one and then together they would fan out across the city, murdering people until all the unicorns were returned to the living.

I shook my head as I turned back to Vincent. He was smiling as he brushed his hair back to reveal the onyx stone winking in the middle of his forehead. The stories I'd heard while living in the Towers said that in human form the unicorn's horn was replaced by a priceless gem of remarkable size. Supposedly the only way to get the gem and the core of the unicorn's power was to kill it while it was in human form. But then, the gem wasn't nearly as valuable as the horn.

"I don't get it. What could killing Trixie get you? Killing an elf isn't going to raise all the dead."

"No, you idiot!" Vincent screamed, stomping his foot like a three-year-old preparing for a massive tantrum. "It's not her. It's what she's carrying."

I tried not to react, but I felt myself grow sick and pale at his words. He knew about our child. Trixie wasn't showing and we had told very few people, but somehow he knew.

The wicked grin returned to Vincent's face as soon as he realized that he had me.

"How did you know?" I demanded in a rough voice over the lump in my throat.

Vincent giggled with glee. "How could I not? I am a unicorn. We are the keepers of life and innocence, guardians of the pure. I would have been able to sense the growth of your child from across the globe. I have spent a lifetime preserving the remains of my people and when I sensed your child spring to life, I knew it was time to finally act."

"There's no point in this," I said in a low, even voice, while inwardly I was fighting the urge to rip this fucker's face off. "One child, one life, won't give you the years needed to bring back all of these unicorns."

Rushing back over to Trixie's side, Vincent knelt beside her and lightly patted her on the top of her head. She tried to jerk away from him, but her struggles only amused him. "You see, that's what I thought was the key to Death Magic, too," he admitted, sounding excited with the idea of talking a little shop with a fellow spell weaver. "And humans are all the same. You're lucky if you can squeeze about seventy years out of them before they're wrung dry."

Giving Trixie one last affectionate look, he pushed back to his feet and turned toward me. "But then I made the most brilliant accident while in Charlotte. I grabbed a child who had been destined to be one of you," he said with a sneer as he pointed at me. "The poor thing just didn't know it yet." He paused, giving me this faux sad face before loudly clapping his hands together. "But I saved her from that nasty fate. She did give one last burst of magic energy to save herself, created out of the stress of the situation. Surprised the heck out of both of us!"

"And because of her, you were able to raise all the vampires you murdered," I finished, grinding the words between my teeth as I spoke.

Vincent danced around in a little circle as he giggled with manic glee. "The power from that little girl alone raised all those blood suckers and I still had plenty left over!" When he stopped, he looked disappointed by the fact that I wasn't celebrating with him. "Don't you see? I figured it out! It wasn't just a matter of lifespan and years. Even a witch doesn't have that long of a life; a few centuries at best. But it's also about potential!

A witch will pull in and use magic in multiple ways throughout her lifetime. It's the potential to change and affect lives; the potential to change the world around her in so many ways. That's the real power of Death Magic. You harness the years *and* the potential!"

And in my child, Vincent saw an enormous lifespan and amazing potential because the child would have the ability to tap magic through its elvish heritage and my warlock genes. In the end, it was enough to bring back the unicorns from the dead.

My stomach twisted as I watched Vincent celebrate his breakthrough, my mind blank as to what I could do to get out of this mess. No, that was wrong. I needed to get Trixie out of this mess and permanently away from this bastard. But knowing that I was up against an insane unicorn with way too much power at his fingertips, I was left struggling for an edge.

"To tell you the truth," Vincent continued with a heavy sigh, "I wasn't sure what I was going to do to generate enough energy. I thought I might blow up a few grade schools, but that wasn't going to be enough. But you solved my problem! And I even get the wonderful pleasure of killing the child of a warlock while he watches."

"And what about her?" I jerked my head toward the murderous woman, still unsure of how she fit into the picture with Vincent. If he'd found all he needed with Trixie and my child, then why would he ever need to work with a human? I'd always assumed that he'd need the help killing innocents to raise the necessary power. "You don't need her."

"My sweet little Missy?" Vincent cooed. He stepped over to the mad woman and pinched her cheek. "No, I guess I don't need her, but then you don't really *need* a pet. She amuses me and has such a brilliant talent for killing." The unicorn gave me a little shrug as if embarrassed by his sentimental weakness. "And if I should ever need a little Death Magic to raise another army of zombies, Missy would be so happy kill some poor souls for me."

"I'm happy to kill for Vinnie," she purred.

"I'm sure you are," I muttered, inwardly wishing that they'd just kill each other, but that wasn't going to happen. Not for this happy couple. "What—"

Shots rang out, echoing through the massive warehouse and cutting off my question. I dropped to the ground, seeking some kind of cover when there was none near me. Lying flat on the dirty concrete, I chanced a look around to find Serah coming in from a side entrance with Gideon hot on her heels. The cavalry had arrived at last.

"Watch out! He's a unicorn!" I shouted as I pushed off the ground and scurried over to Trixie. I never saw the warlock react to my words, but then Gideon was a master at hiding his emotions. He just kept his eyes his adversary, while Serah kept the other bitch busy.

Just a couple feet away from Trixie, a massive force slammed into my chest, knocking me away from her. My shoulder hit the concrete first and my right arm went numb for a second from the impact. Gritting my teeth, I pushed back to my feet, flexing my fingers against the pain as I quickly checked to make sure that my arm hadn't been knocked out of its socket. My shoulder hurt like hell and my skull felt like it had been cracked, but my brains weren't leaking out so I'd push on.

A quick assessment of the magic in the air revealed that Gideon was attempting to put a binding spell on Vincent to keep the fucker from killing one of us with magic. I was willing to be a whole lot less subtle. I already owed magic two years for killing; what did it matter if I tacked on a third? It took frighteningly little time to mentally call up a spell that would rip Vincent's heart from his chest.

The reluctance I'd felt just a short time ago at Chang's about killing the last unicorn? Gone. Evaporated in an instant when I saw Trixie held captive. Vincent was insane and he was killing innocent people to raise the dead. He'd threatened Trixie. Threatened my child. He was going to die.

With a rush of twisted magical energy, I threw it at the unicorn, ready to send him screaming into the next life, but it never reached him.

Vincent's high-pitched laugh rose above the gunshots and the screaming. With a light wave of his hand, he pushed away the spell I'd created as if it were a butterfly fluttering about his head. "Did you really think you could get to me so easily?" he chuckled. "Your magic is useless."

It looked like he was right, but there had to be a way. The Towers had destroyed nearly every dragon and unicorn on the planet. I didn't have a freaking clue how they managed to do it, but I was willing to bet that they'd done it with magic, since they didn't do a damn thing without it.

My gaze darted briefly to Serah as she fired at Missy. The killer was bleeding from several gunshot wounds but they weren't slowing her down. Serah popped out a spent magazine as she ran, leaving it to clatter against the concrete floor and reaching for a fresh one from her coat pocket. The TAPSS investigator turned and fired again.

As Gideon aimed a new and lethal spell at Vincent, I magically jerked some rusted rebar free from a partially crumbling pillar. The steel rod whistled through the air as it cut across the warehouse, chasing behind Missy until it finally caught her. With a twist of my wrist, the rebar wrapped around the woman, pinning her arms against her sides and trapping her legs together so that she dropped to her knees with an enraged scream.

"Keep your gun on her!" I shouted at Serah while I turned my attention back to Vincent. The unicorn needed to go down, if only for a few moments. Anything so I could get Trixie out of danger.

Taking my lead from Gideon, I tried to match a second binding spell to the one he was attempting, hoping that power from both of us might work.

But still, Vincent waved it off with a yawn. "Here. Allow me to give you a lesson."

I didn't have time to even flinch at those words. The

magical energy crushed me to the ground. It wasn't the same as when he'd used Death Magic, but rather it tasted sweet like spun sugar and caramel apples. Yet, it was tainted and twisted, leaving you sure that the caramel also contained poison. Pain clamped down on my muscles and my scream was echoed by Gideon's. Out of the corner of my eye, I saw the warlock hit the ground a second before me.

I blinked and found myself staring at Trixie. Her mouth was open, but I couldn't hear her shouting over the roar in my ears. Or maybe that was my own screaming. The blood in my veins was on fire, pouring through my body so that it ignited each organ. The elf strained against the ropes that held her arms behind her. She was getting free, but I was afraid that she'd come to me if she did. I didn't want her to save me. I wanted her out of here. I wanted her safe.

The pain suddenly eased. My gaze darted to Vincent to find that blood had blossomed on his shoulder. With Missy somewhat secure, Serah got one shot off at the unicorn, but now she had his attention. The TAPSS investigator dropped her gun to her side and took a wary step back toward her captive. Missy snarled as she struggled to get free. Blood soaked her long-sleeved cotton shirt from her gunshot wounds, but she didn't seem to notice. The rebar was keeping her trapped and all she wanted to do was to tear into Serah. But she didn't need to. Vincent was about to do that.

"Vincent!" I shouted, my voice hoarse from screaming.

"Later," the unicorn muttered, making a little shoving motion in my direction so that I stumbled back to the ground as the wave of magic hit me.

Gideon caught on that we needed to be more direct in our approach. He punched Vincent with a nasty spell that was meant to boil the creature's flesh off his bones. A small shriek cut through the air as Vincent wasn't able to immediately unwind the spell. Large red blisters broke out across his hands and face before popping, making it look like his skin was starting to ooze away.

With a snarl, Vincent made a single slashing motion at Gideon and the warlock went down with a gasp. He landed on his side facing me and I could see that the front of his shirt had been shredded and was becoming dark red with his blood. Gideon didn't move for several seconds despite the fact that Vincent was closing in on him.

"Vincent!" I screamed, trying to draw the unicorn away from my companion, but he paused only long enough to toss a spell behind his shoulder. I cringed, waiting for it to hit, but it never did. Trixie screamed, her body twisting against her bonds as she attempted to get away.

Swearing vehemently, I quickly unraveled the spell attacking the elf as I pushed to my feet. Her screams stopped a second later and she nodded her thanks to me. With Vincent's attention trained on Gideon, Serah rushed over to start cutting through Trixie's ropes.

For a breath, the world slowed down and everything became startlingly clear. Gideon and I couldn't

beat Vincent. The Towers might have crushed the unicorns and driven them to extinction, but it couldn't be
done with one warlock and another who'd never finished his apprenticeship. Vincent had centuries of experience and access to power that I couldn't tap on my
best day. At my peak, I couldn't use the same powers
that Vincent had punched through me . I needed an
edge, something to level the playing field, or we were
all dead.

Pulling my wand out of my left sleeve, I pushed the
tip into the palm of my left hand as I looked over at
Serah. "Stay there with Trixie and don't move until I
tell you," I said in a calm voice.

"Gage," Trixie rasped, fear filling her wide green
eyes.

I wanted to apologize to her. To reassure her that
everything would be okay. But as I hovered on the
precipice in that second, I knew the road I stood on
would take me farther away from the woman I loved.
There would be no going back. There was only this
road or death. I gave her a small smile. I was choosing
life for her and my child.

Using my wand like a knife, I cut the demon's
symbol into my palm. As I finished the last line, I whispered the words of the spell I used to unlock the doorway. And the whole world changed in the blink of an
eye.

I roared as a torrent of energy flooded into my
frame, lifting me up until my toes barely scraped the
ground. My arms were flung out to my sides as the

energy filled every fiber of my being. Pain was erased and I felt alive!

No, it was better than that. I felt powerful. It wasn't the same power that I tapped into every time I cast a spell. It wasn't the energy cast by every living creature on the planet. This was darker magic, drawing from the well of energy in the Underworld. This was the power of the demons. True death magic.

As I slowly settled back down onto my feet, a darkness fully cloaked me, wrapping its way around my soul. I could feel a low chuckle echo up through my body before thumping against my brain. *Zyrus.* The demon was no longer outside, terrorizing anyone who came close. No, the demon was now inside of me and reveling in its newfound freedom. It could now feel things in ways it never could before when set loose upon this world. Dark, malicious emotions twined with mine, blending and merging so that it was difficult to determine where I ended and the demon began. The next laugh I heard rumbled up my own throat.

Vincent froze a couple feet from Gideon and stared at me. There was a mix of horror and hatred in his lean face, twisting his features so that his inner insanity and ugliness were visible to the naked eye. A grin stretched my mouth wide and the demon's twisted joy washed through me and became my own. Together, we had the power to take down the unicorn, and Vincent knew it.

His eyes darted back to Gideon as the warlock moved slowly, trying to push into a sitting position.

The unicorn lunged at him. I wasn't sure if he was trying to attack him or simply trying to use him as a shield, but we weren't going to allow it. Dropping my wand on the ground, I reached out both hands and threw out a chunk of the energy boiling within me, throwing Vincent toward the wall farthest from Gideon. A pain-filled cry rose from the unicorn as he crashed against it and fell to his knees.

I walked deeper into the warehouse, sparing a quick glance at Gideon, who was now watching me in stunned horror. The air crackled and snapped with magical energy. Overhead lights popped out but were quickly replaced by glowing red orbs hovering in the air. Zyrus stirred within me as I neared the injured warlock, sensing an easy target.

He caused you trouble, my master.

"He's not our target," I snarled, forcing the demon to focus on the unicorn that was rising to his feet.

He will harm us. We will have to kill him later.

"Later." I clamped down on my control of the demon and closed the distance between myself and Vincent, which helped Zyrus to forget about Gideon. The demon he'd glimpsed something from the future regarding Gideon, but I couldn't worry about that now. I had enough trouble in my present to deal with. The future could wait.

The unicorn was ready for me, instantly pummeling me with some threads of Death Magic he'd found a way to save. It either wasn't as strong as what he'd used on Gideon and me, or the presence of Zyrus was making a significant difference, because the spell caused only a slight cramping before dissipating completely.

"Now it's my turn," I murmured, unleashing a series of spells that rolled off my fingertips like fat drops of rain. There was no need for remembering complicated words or symbols. With Zyrus I was tapped into the raw energy of the Underworld and I could twist it into doing my every whim. The power had become just an extension of who I was, like another hand or leg. Or maybe it was just a bit of my soul. It didn't matter. I didn't need to think about it and I didn't want to.

Vincent's maniacal laughter was replaced by his screams, which helped to ease some of the anger that had lit a fire in my brain. The horrible tension in my shoulders and the throbbing in my head slipped away with Vincent's pain and blood.

"Gage!" Gideon shouted in my ear. His hand clamped down on my shoulder and he jerked me around so that I was half turned away from Vincent. I blinked, feeling slightly dazed. I'd lost track of time, as if my body had stepped outside the stream of seconds as they ticked by. I shook my head to clear it and Zyrus roared inside me at the interruption. I was confused. Why had the warlock stopped me? Why was he touching me? Why was he alive . . .

"Gage, you've got to stop this. There's no reason to torture him," Gideon argued. He was partially bent over as he stood and his face was deathly pale from blood loss. I could sense the pain that wracked his body, and it pleased Zyrus. "Just end it now," he whispered through broken lips.

"No reason?" The words tumbled from me, but they echoed through my brain as well. Who had said them? Was that me? Zyrus? "That son of a bitch has killed dozens to raise the dead. He tried to kill us. He was planning to kill my girlfriend and our child. Wouldn't you let him suffer if it was your family being threatened?"

"No. I don't believe in torture," Gideon said firmly. He straightened a little, meeting my gaze. Something he saw there made him flinch and his frown deepened, but I didn't care.

"Lies," I snarled. Knocking his hand off my shoulder, I gave him a hard shove so that he was thrown to the ground several feet away from me. "You're a warlock. A member of the Towers. You all torture. You thrive on fear. I was there. I know. You're like them."

"That's not true, Gage. Think. Take a deep breath and think. I've protected you. I have just as much to lose as you. I would do anything to protect Ellen and my daughter."

An image of Ellen smiling up at me at the Christmas party, the warm sympathy filling her brown eyes, danced through my brain. She wouldn't like me hurting her husband. She wouldn't like me fighting with the man who had protected me from the Towers. It was like a punch to the gut. For a moment, I could feel my mind ripping free of Zyrus.

A loud, harsh gasp filled the silence of the warehouse and I stumbled back a step. It was like coming up for air after being submerged for far too long. I mentally clawed for some handhold, anything to keep from letting Zyrus take over again, but I knew it was a fight I couldn't win for long.

"Watch out!" Serah screamed.

I twisted around to Vincent in time to see him pulling together a new spell. In that instant, I lost my fight against Zyrus and the demon surged back into the driver's seat of my body and mind. Chunks of broken glass, wood, and steel jumped from the warehouse floor and flew through the air. Pure, raw energy grabbed Vincent and pressed him, spread-eagled, against the wall, so that the flying flotsam could spear him through the arms and legs.

Vincent laughed, a low, choking sound. "It's fitting. A warlock destroys the last unicorn this world will ever see. And to do it, he had to be possessed by a demon. How will history remember this event? Who will be painted as the monster?"

A slow grin spread across my faces and I stepped close to him. "No one will remember." I reached out my right hand toward the rows of pristine unicorns and their bodies ignited one after another. Vincent's screams were more deafening than when I'd tortured him. He struggled, fighting to pull free of his bonds both physical and magical, but it was for nothing. I stared at him, drinking in the pain deeply etched into his pale face as he watched the black smoke billowing through a broken out skylight. The last remains of his people were reduced to ash.

His screams became heavy sobs as he hung his head. The last hope of the unicorns was gone in a cloud of greasy black smoke.

"No one will remember you," I said softly, my voice almost a caress. "No one will remember your fight to save your people. No one will even know you ever existed."

Vincent raised his eyes to my face and I knew I'd never forget the hatred that blazed there. I was glad.

Lightning quick, I pulled a large shard of glass from where it was pinning his wrist and plunged it straight through his heart. The unicorn gasped and stiffened in pain, and the mad light disappeared from his eyes.

As I turned away, I became aware of Missy's hysterical screaming. Pulling the shard of glass from Vincent's chest, I walked toward her, leaving a trail of unicorn blood behind me as it dripped from the glass. Standing before her, Zyrus stirred, overjoyed to see her bouncing between mindless rage and abject despair at the death of her companion. Her eyes were wide, and spittle and blood dripped from her lips. She tried to rise and attack me, but she couldn't get to her feet while still wrapped in the steel rebar.

"How could you! He was beautiful! He was perfect!" she screamed at me until her voice started to become hoarse.

In the distance, I thought I could hear Trixie shouting for me. Or maybe it was Gideon. But I couldn't focus on it. Missy was a Christmas gift just waiting to be unwrapped. Clenching the glass shard in my hand,

I grabbed a chunk of her hair and wrenched her head back, holding it at an awkward angle. She could no longer move, but it didn't stop her enraged screaming. That was good.

With the glass in my hand, I slashed across her stomach, letting blood pour forth from the massive wound. Her angry curses instantly turned to pain-filled screams that echoed off the walls of the warehouse. With a chuckle, I plunged the glass into her heart. The screams stopped with a gasp. I released her hair, letting her fall to the ground in a heap as life drained quickly out of her body.

Backpedaling from Missy, I clung to the relief and joy that Zyrus felt because there was something sick churning in my stomach. I could hear Trixie weeping softly and it was like little daggers driving straight into my heart. Unfortunately, Zyrus heard the sound as well. The temporary pleasure it got from slaughtering the last unicorn was shoved aside by a hunger for yet another kill. A pregnant elf.

I tried to clamp down on the demon, but the longer it was roaming free within me, the more destruction it caused, the stronger it became so that it was nearly impossible to hold my position. Stealing a glance at Trixie, I was nearly ripped to shreds by fear when I saw that she was slowly approaching me.

"No," I rasped, falling backward to my ass just so that I couldn't walk toward her. "Get out of here."

"Gage . . ."

"Gideon, get her out of here!" I roared with more

force as I vainly struggled to think of a way to get Zyrus out of me. If she came too close, if she touched me, I was going to kill her and I wouldn't be able to stop myself. The demon was pooling all of its energy toward that one mindless goal.

She wants to leave you. She will leave you and take your child.

"She needs to leave me," I groaned. I clutched my head with both my hands, wishing I could rip my skull open just so I could pull Zyrus out of my brain. Pain lanced through me as the demon screamed and slashed holes into my soul. "It's not safe. She needs to leave." I kept repeating the words while squeezing my eyes shut, hoping that if I heard the mantra over and over again I would get control over Zyrus.

You can't let her leave us.

"Gage?" Trixie's voice sounded closer. Touchably close.

"Gideon!" I screamed in desperation, my voice cracking. The warlock was the only thing that could protect her from me.

A breeze brushed against me as the warlock rushed in, intercepting Trixie. "You can't. Leave this place."

"He needs help," Trixie argued, panic entering her lovely voice.

"He's going to kill you if you don't leave," Gideon snapped.

I sensed movement near me and I wanted to cry. I'd forgotten about Serah. A gentle hand touched mine and my control over Zyrus snapped like a rubber band.

We lunged for her, mouth open and fingers curled as if they were tipped with talons, ready to shred flesh until there was nothing left but a bloody puddle. A low rush of energy shoved Serah out of my reach and a scream exploded from my throat.

Using the demon's momentary shock and disappointment, I tangled up some dark energy with my fingers and slammed my hands down on the cold concrete. At the same time, I whispered the same words I'd used while carving the demon's symbol into my hand. Chunks of concrete exploded up into the air around me as magic blasted down into the foundation. In a flash of bright white light, the demon's symbol was carved into the concrete. With the last breath I could draw, I shouted the binding spell.

Zyrus gathered its energy and launched us at Trixie and Gideon, but my body crashed against an invisible barrier marked by the edge of the symbol in the concrete floor. The demon's rage consumed me until I felt my own consciousness floating back away from Trixie's horrified looks and Gideon's sadness. My body slammed into the barrier again and again in the demon's desperate bid to be free, but the binding spell held.

You've betrayed me!

"No, you are attempting to betray me," I said in a low, broken voice. My throat was raw from the screaming, and I no longer cared that my companions could hear me speaking to the demon I'd summoned. "Our target was the unicorn. That was all."

I want the elf.

"You can't have her. And neither can I."

"Gage, please, let me help you," Trixie said softly, tears streaking down her too pale face. Blood stained her tangled blonde hair and there was more blood on her wrists where she'd struggled against the ropes. She'd been hurt because of me and I wanted to cry. This was my fault.

I slowly collapsed in the middle of the symbol, my legs folded in front of me. I couldn't remember ever feeling so tired in my life. My body ached. Pain reached down to my soul as Zyrus continued to throw a temper tantrum within me.

Let her help you.

Zyrus taunted, but we were one and I knew its hope was to have Trixie step inside the binding spell so that it could attack. I was too tired to keep holding it back. Zyrus would win and Trixie would be dead.

"You called me Master," I murmured, ignoring Gideon's stunned expression. "You will obey me."

Zyrus cursed me, causing more pain to tear through my head, but I forced an ugly laugh when I wanted to scream. "You need me." When the demon stilled and grew thoughtful, I closed my eyes and said silently, *We need each other.*

The demon sensed the promise in those words and I felt its smile. Its struggles for control ceased completely and Zyrus redirected the energy that it had toward healing all my aches and pains.

Turning my left hand over so that the palm was up, I

looked at Gideon, who was watching me warily. "Heal the cuts," I said, because I knew the demon would never willingly erase his doorway into my body.

The warlock slowly released Trixie, making sure that she didn't rush toward me before he approached us. Zyrus stirred restlessly within me, but it didn't act as if it was plotting an attack. It was fighting its own instincts demanding that it kill the warlock. Without crossing the barrier created by the symbol in the floor, Gideon reached out his wand and used the same healing spell he'd taught me just days ago. The cuts slowly disappeared, not even leaving behind a scar.

Zyrus gave a final snarl through my head before the demon was pulled from me and into the symbol upon which I sat. With the symbol no longer etched into my hand, the demon's powers were sucked into the concrete floor. It was still close, watching everyone and everything, but it could no longer reach out and harm anyone.

I slumped, leaning heavily to the side on my right forearm. Never had I felt so drained in my life. It was like my very life force had been used up by the demon. And maybe it had.

"Is it gone?" Gideon asked cautiously.

I nodded, patting the concrete with my right hand. "Trapped outside of me."

And still no one approached me. No one held me, offering comfort or support. They stayed back, afraid.

"What the hell was that all about?" Serah demanded loudly as she walked toward Gideon and

Trixie, still giving me a wide berth. "Your eyes were glowing red."

"A bad spell," I lied.

"Bullshit," Gideon snapped, drawing my gaze up to his face. He was pissed. "What the fuck do you think you were doing? You—"

"You would have done the same!" I growled at him. Anger helped put some energy back into my frame so that I could push to my feet. I swayed slightly. While the pain was gone, I was still exhausted to my core. Zyrus rumbled beneath me, but it could only look on and cheer my rage. I ignored the demon. It had caused enough trouble for one day. "If that had been Ellen tied up, you would have done—"

"No. Never!"

"Then you're a coward and she'd be dead. We'd all be dead." I stepped closer to the warlock, getting up in his face so that he couldn't look away from me. "We had nothing. Vincent was toying with us. I wasn't going to let that thing kill Trixie and my child because you're afraid."

Gideon glowered at me, looking at if he'd like nothing more than to break my nose with his fist, but he held back. It was probably best because I wasn't holding on to my own emotions too well My mind had become a little frayed at the edges and I couldn't risk looking too deeply at things. I wasn't ready to start thinking about the fact that I'd killed the last unicorn and destroyed the bodies of the others. I didn't want to think about the fact that I'd very nearly killed my own girlfriend and our child because I'd let a demon control me. The disgust and self-loathing would have snapped what little hold I had on my sanity.

"The Towers will find out," Gideon said. The warlock blinked and I saw a brief shimmer of tears in his cold eyes. My bravado wavered. What I'd thought was anger in his voice was actually gut-wrenching fear for me; fear and disappointment.

"Tell them. I'm not afraid of the Towers anymore."

Gideon nodded. He blinked again and the tears disappeared. His expression was cold and empty. "I'd once said that we would end this."

I recalled the moment vividly in my mind. He'd been holding the dead body of a young girl in his arms; an apprentice witch who had tried to escape the Towers and got caught in the crossfire of a magic fight. I hadn't thought of Alice in weeks. Another victim of the Towers.

"And that's exactly what I'm going to do."

Gideon turned away and clamped a firm hand on Serah's elbow. He nearly dragged her out of the building with him, not uttering another word. I felt the tiny tugs of a smile at the corners of my mouth. The woman had been in over her head for the first moment, but it hadn't slowed her down. She also didn't exhibit an ounce of fear for Gideon as she argued with him every step of the way. Not only did she not understand what had happened, but she wasn't willing to abandon me. It was touching and misguided. I needed to do something about her.

It was with some reluctance that I looked back at Trixie. She stood several feet away, her arms wrapped tightly around herself. Her tears had dried on her face and the love I was so accustomed to seeing in her eyes had been replaced by fear and a horribly deep sadness.

"You summoned a demon," she whispered as if she had to say the words aloud so that she could finally grasp what had happened.

"I couldn't let Vincent kill you."

"Maybe you should have." She shook her head and bit down on her lower lip. "You say it's gone, trapped, but I can still feel it on you. It's what I've been feeling for days now. You've tainted yourself."

"And I'd do it again to keep you safe."

"No!" she shouted, her calm shattering at last. "You can't do this to yourself. Not for me. I'll stay. I'll stay and we'll be a family together here in Low Town. Just promise me that you'll never summon the demon again."

I wish I could say that her offer tempted me. It hung in the air between us like a golden apple on a low branch. I would have the only thing I had ever wanted in this world — the woman I had loved for years. All I had to do was say yes.

"Go home to your people, Trixie. I'll come for you and our child when I've made this world safe for us. We'll be a family then."

Trixie nodded and turned away without another word. There were no more tears, but then we'd shed too many for ourselves lately. We'd run out at last. I watched her slowly walk between the smoldering remains of the unicorns, her thin body partially obscured by tendrils of smoke and floating ash, until she stepped outside and out of my life.

No matter how much I loved her and wanted her to stay, she had to leave. It would not be safe to be together until the Towers had been taken down. I would end this.

On a roar of pain ripped from soul, I summoned up a burst of energy and directed it at the symbol carved into the floor, pulverizing the concrete to tiny pebbles so that the portal was closed forever. Stepping outside, I reduced the warehouse to ash. It was a beginning.

EPILOGUE

Serah found me two weeks later, sitting on the wooden stairs behind Asylum, my elbows resting on my knees as I stared blindly out at the thickening darkness. Bronx had just shown up for his shift and I'd left our new tattoo artist in his capable hands. I'd hired the guy the week before as well as another artist who was coming in afternoons four days a week. My own schedule was empty, but then I was bowing out, preferring to rent out the space rather than ink. My heart wasn't in it anymore. I had other things demanding my attention.

"Hey Houdini." Serah greeted me with a tense smile that did nothing to erase the worry in her eyes. "How's tricks?"

"Just a bunch of white rabbits and playing cards," I murmured as a reluctant smile tugged at one corner of my mouth. Something in me flinched to see her again. When she stepped into the darkness, memories of the warehouse flashed through my brain. But then the horror never completely faded from my mind. The blood of the dead was never completely washed from my hands.

But as I pushed through the horror, I found that a small part of me was relieved to see her. While I had no love for TAPSS, the investigator had proven herself to be a dedicated force for good. I respected her brains and tenacity—I just hoped they didn't get her killed.

"What are you doing back here?" she asked, taking a quick glance around the empty parking lot and the adjoining alley.

"Am I under investigation, Officer?" I mocked.

Serah glared at me, tucking her hands into the pockets of her puffy winter coat. The pale blue under the harsh glare of the security light was an almost cheery spot in the night.

"I'm not with TAPSS anymore."

"Why?"

"Harvey canned me two weeks ago."

"I'm sorry."

Serah shrugged and gave me a little smile. "I knew it would happen. He warned me and I ignored him. It's the price I had to pay."

"Stubborn ass," I murmured, managing a faint smile.

"Yeah, well, I've got something better. I'm starting a private investigation firm. I figure I'll have more luck helping people that way rather than wasting another minute with the police or TAPSS." She stared at me a moment before shaking her head. "It's freaking cold and you seem to have forgotten your coat."

I didn't know if it was so much that I'd forgotten my coat as it was that I simply didn't care. My thoughts were muddled tonight, but I had good reason. "I came out here to think."

"Want to talk about it?"

The first genuine smile I'd had in two weeks lifted my mouth. "No, but thanks. I'll be fine."

"I heard that Trixie left. I'm sorry."

A soft grunt escaped me and I nodded, my gaze dropped down to my hands without really seeing them. Trixie was gone, but I could still feel her. I blinked and my eyes focused on her name tattooed on my inner left wrist. I'd completed it two days after she left, when I'd found one of her hairs in my brush. By adding it to the potion I'd placed in the ink, I could now feel her at all times. She was sad but safe.

Serah pulled a knit hat out of her pocket and pulled it down over the top of my head to my ears. "Looking at you makes me cold," she complained.

"I've been meaning to ask, how did you and Gideon find me?" I asked after an extended silence. I'd been pondering that since Gideon wouldn't have been able to use whatever usual tracking spell he preferred to keep an eye on me. Vincent had blanketed that warehouse in cloaking magic to stay hidden from the Towers.

"Oh, that," she said, her grin growing. "I'd stopped by Asylum to tell you that we'd figured out the tattooed lunatic was the ex-wife of the man who'd been murdered at the last site. Turns out he divorced her because she couldn't have kids."

"And after discovering that he'd remarried and had the family she couldn't have caused her to go screaming over the deep end," I finished.

"Something like that."

"Anyway . . ." I prompted.

She gave a small shrug, shoving her hands back into her pockets. "About the time I showed up and was looking in your window that warlock popped in. He thought you were in some kind of trouble. When we couldn't find you here, he did some kind of spell and we poofed over to corner of Main and Pershing. After some looking around, we spotted blood on the sidewalk. I guess it was yours because Gideon managed to use that to track you to that warehouse."

And the rest was history, so to speak. I'd heard snatches of the story on the news over the past several days, but I hadn't really paid much attention. I'd been focused on my own plans.

"Was there a reason for your stopping by today?" I asked when Serah didn't move on to a new topic.

"Well, I was just thinking that you said you'd wipe my memory once this whole thing was over. You know, protect your secret." She looked expectantly at me, but I said nothing. "It's been two weeks," she nudged.

"Do you want to forget?"

"No!" she said quickly, jerking back a half step. "I want to remember."

"Then you will."

"Are you sure? You're not going to wipe my memory?"

I smiled at her as I pushed to my feet so I could descend the three stairs to the ground. "Good night, Serah. Good work. Sleep well. I'll most likely wipe your memory in the morning."

She gave me a little bow and laughed, catching my little joke that her memories were in fact safe from me. "As you wish."

Straightening, she paused on her way back into the parlor, looking over her shoulder at me. The smile was gone and the worry had returned to her gaze. I had no more comforting words. I could only hope that she didn't come to regret remembering exactly what I was. That kind of knowledge always seemed to carry with it a high price.

I waited another ten minutes before following her into the parlor. My muscles were stiff and my feet were nearly numb from sitting outside for so long. The warmth of the shop helped me thaw, filling my body with biting pins and needles as blood flowed into my extremities again.

Locking the back door, I stopped and closed my eyes, drinking in the sounds coming from the front of the shop. Bronx's deep voice rumbled as he told a story, punctuated by a burst of laughter from the new guy. All this was underscored by the steady buzz of a tattooing gun as it steadily carved through the flesh of a client. Six months ago, the buzzing noise was the most comforting sound in the world to me. It was the sound of normalcy. It was the sound of my ordered life. It was the sound of control.

But now it was a reminder of what was and could never be again.

In the middle of the room, I pulled up the trapdoor that covered the basement stairs. Descending to the lower level, I pulled the door closed after me so that I was swallowed up by the absolute darkness. But I didn't need any light. I'd descended these stairs hundreds of times.

At the foot of the stairs, I reached out and grabbed the beaded pull chain on my first try. The small dirt-floor room was flooded with dim yellow light. Across the room near my work bench, Lilith stood with her arms folded over her stomach as she glared at me. I wasn't surprised. The shadowy figure had been haunting me since the showdown at the warehouse. At what she hoped were my vulnerable moments, a transparent vision of the Queen of the Underworld would appear in expectation of scaring me out of my current course of action.

"It doesn't have to be this way, Gage," she whispered to me. I was no longer sure if I was actually hearing her voice or if the words were merely floating across my brain.

"I don't see how I have any other choice in the matter," I replied, walking past her to the one cabinet with a large padlock on the front. From the far wall with the spray-painted demon symbol, I could feel Zyrus stirring. The demon had been giving me a wide berth recently while I was in the basement at the parlor, but then we'd been spending a great deal of time together in my rooms at the Towers.

Of course, the Towers were less than pleased with Gideon's news that I was dealing with demons. But for now, they held back, watching and concocting a plan to deal with me. For now, they steered clear of me while I was in Simon's rooms as well as in Low Town. There hadn't even been a whispered sighting of a warlock or witch in Low Town since the unicorn's death. The Towers were afraid, though they'd never admit that one lone warlock had a chance at defeating them. But then, they hadn't a clue as to what I planned.

Without bothering to pull the key out of my pocket, I unlocked the padlock with a wave of my hand and pulled it free of the cabinet. As I opened the double doors, I whispered the reveal spell and a pair of bottles appeared in the very front of the top shelf. There was a slight tremble in my fingers as I picked up the bottle labeled "Styx."

"Don't do this, Gage," Lilith snarled, but I noticed that her image was already fading. "I don't need you. I will find another. Come into my domain, and I'll destroy what's left of your soul."

The demon's laugh tumbled through my head and I smiled at the misty remains of the dark queen. "You're just one stop on my journey to getting the life I want."

Placing the bottle on the workbench, I pulled my long-sleeved shirt over my head and stood bare-chested in the cold, letting the heavy silence sink into me. I glanced down at the tattoo I'd had Bronx complete for me a week ago. It was the demon's symbol drawn over my heart. The ink had included a mixture of angel feather and water from Acheron, the Underworld river of pain. The unique potion acted as a buffer between Zyrus and myself, allowing me to have better control over the demon and its powers while not falling to the rush of its emotions quite so easily.

"Are you ready?"

Defeat Lilith and free the Underworld from her grasp, and we will lead an army to destroy the Towers.

It was a fair trade and I had nothing left to lose. Picking up the bottle, I pulled the cork out and held the glass vial aloft in a toast. "For Trixie and my child."

I drank down the Styx, the very water that was supposed to have made Achilles invulnerable, and I waited for darkness to claim me. When my two years in the Underworld were complete, I'd have all the powers of the demons with me. I would reduce the Towers to nothing but fire and blood.

I'd make this world safe for my love. Or I would make it burn.

ACKNOWLEDGMENTS

There was a time when I didn't know if this book would ever see the light of day. But when I sat at the computer, I knew that Gage had one more story that he had to tell the world. One last warning. One last lesson.

I want to give a big thanks to the Harper Voyager crew who has seen me through nine books. Pam and Jessie, you're always there to cheer on my books and I will always be grateful. A big thanks to Diana for taking a chance on a dreamer addicted to the written word. We worked on eight books together and I've learned so much from you. And a big thanks to Kelly for being there to safely escort Gage into the waiting arms of readers one last time.

Last but far from least, thank you to all readers who have taken a chance on a guy determined to find his way through a strange world while protecting those he loves.